#31. MIDNA COVERED IN WOUNDS

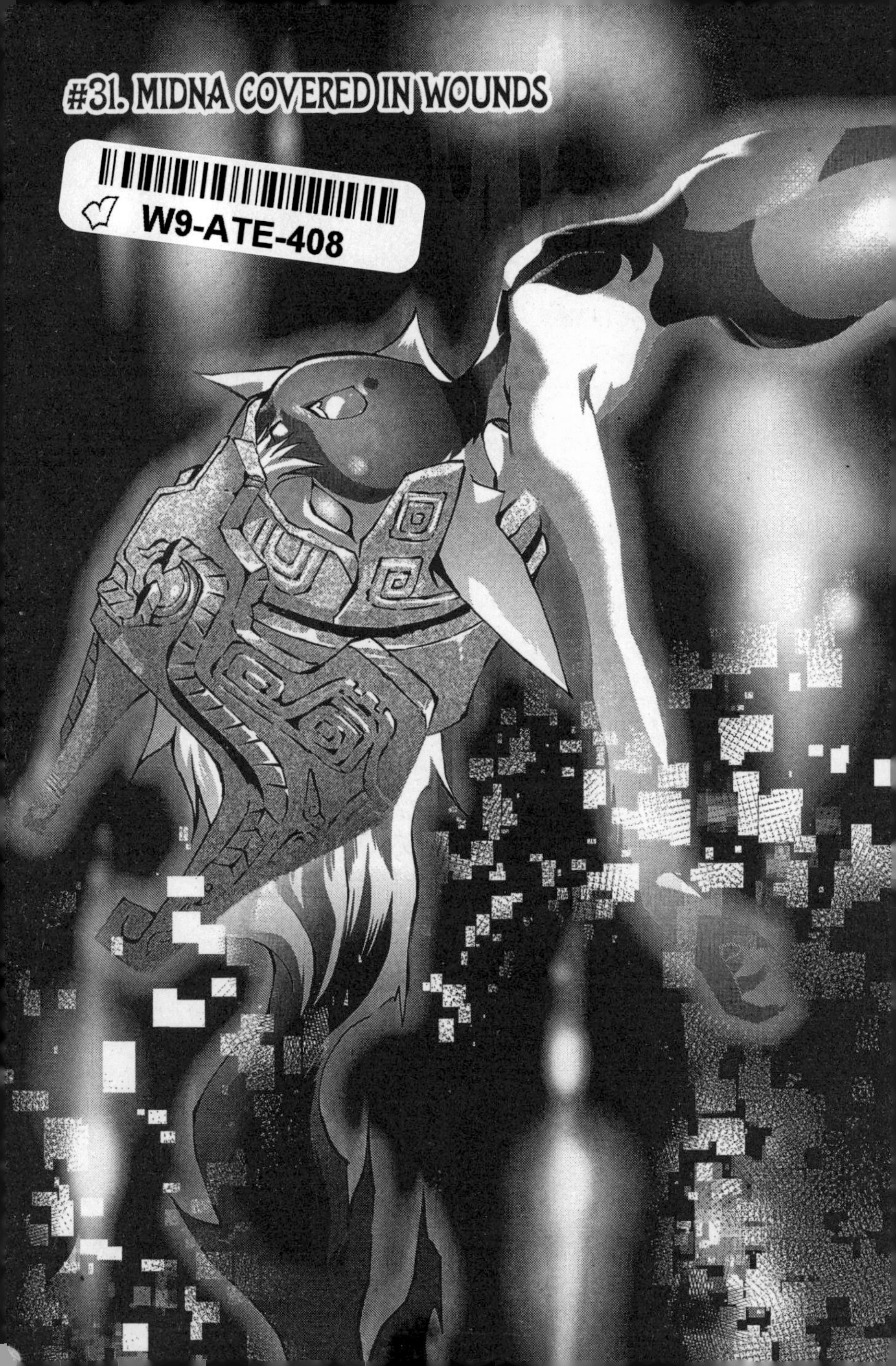

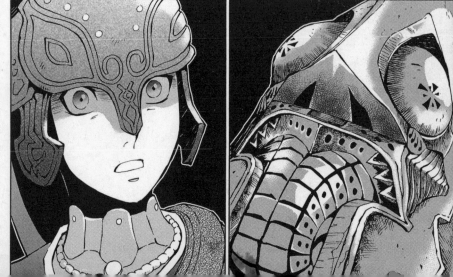

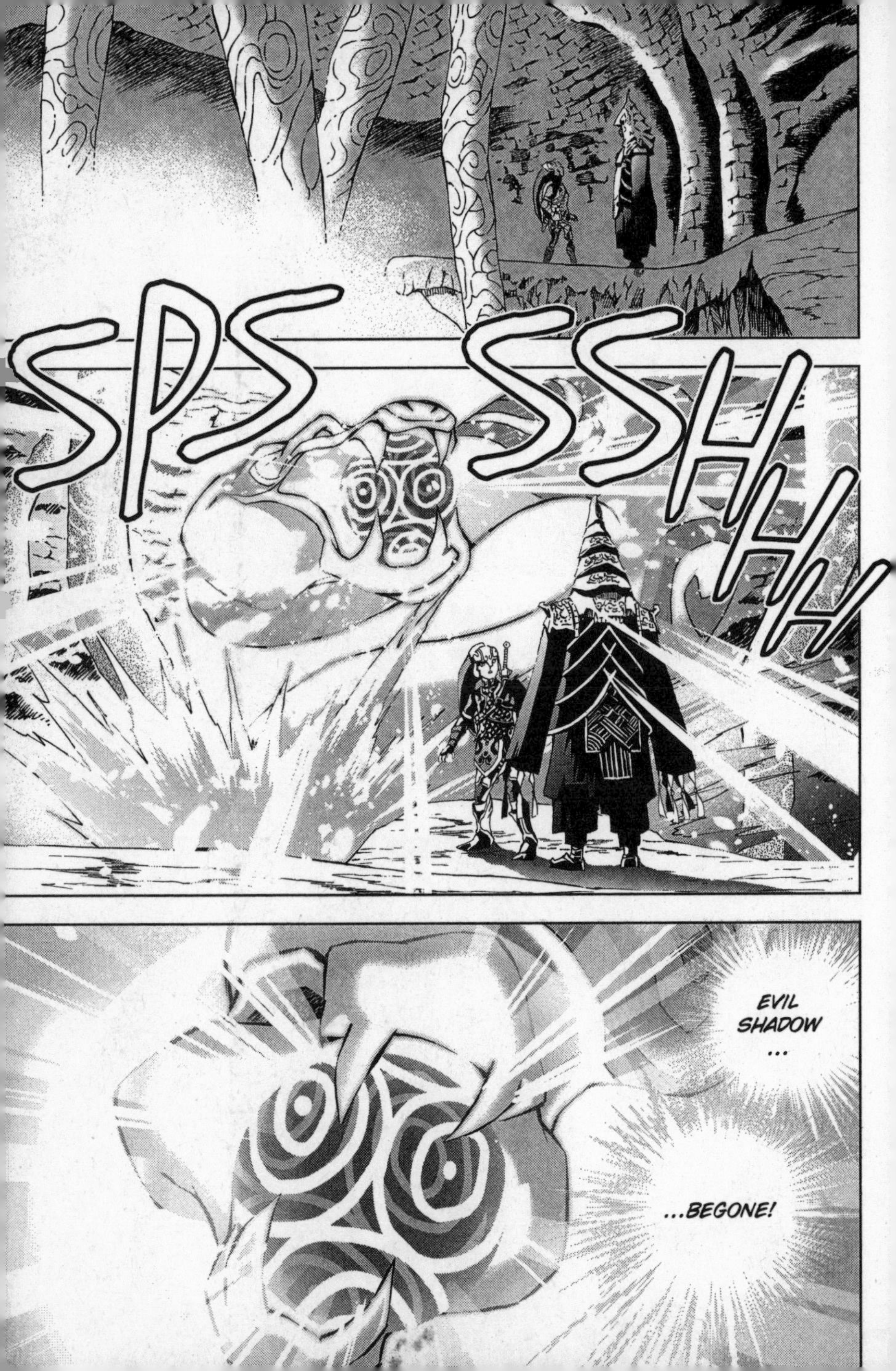
SPS SSHHH
EVIL SHADOW...
...BEGONE!

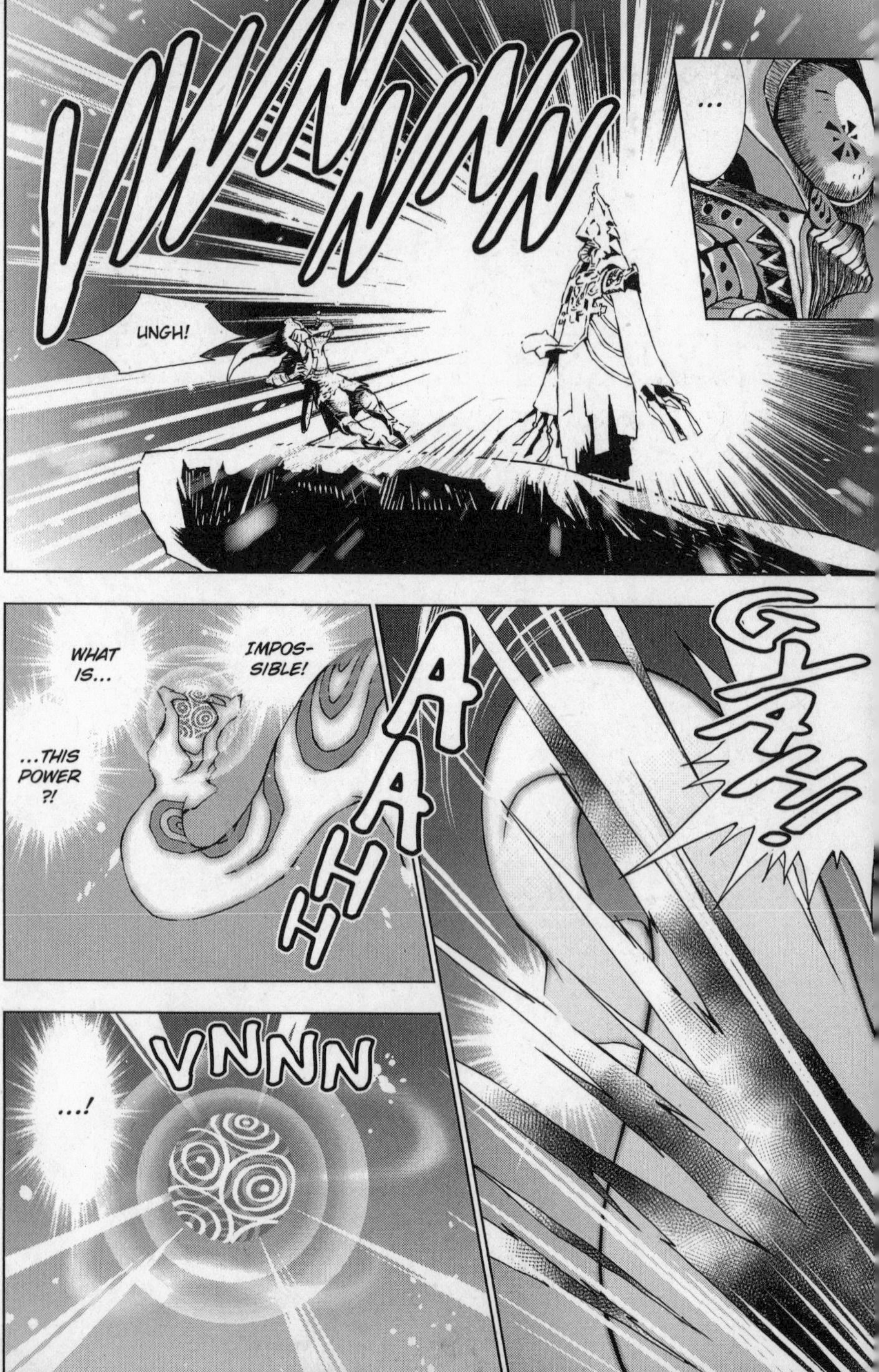
…
UNGH!
GYAH!!
AAHHH
IMPOS-SIBLE!
WHAT IS…
…THIS POWER ?!
VNNN
…!

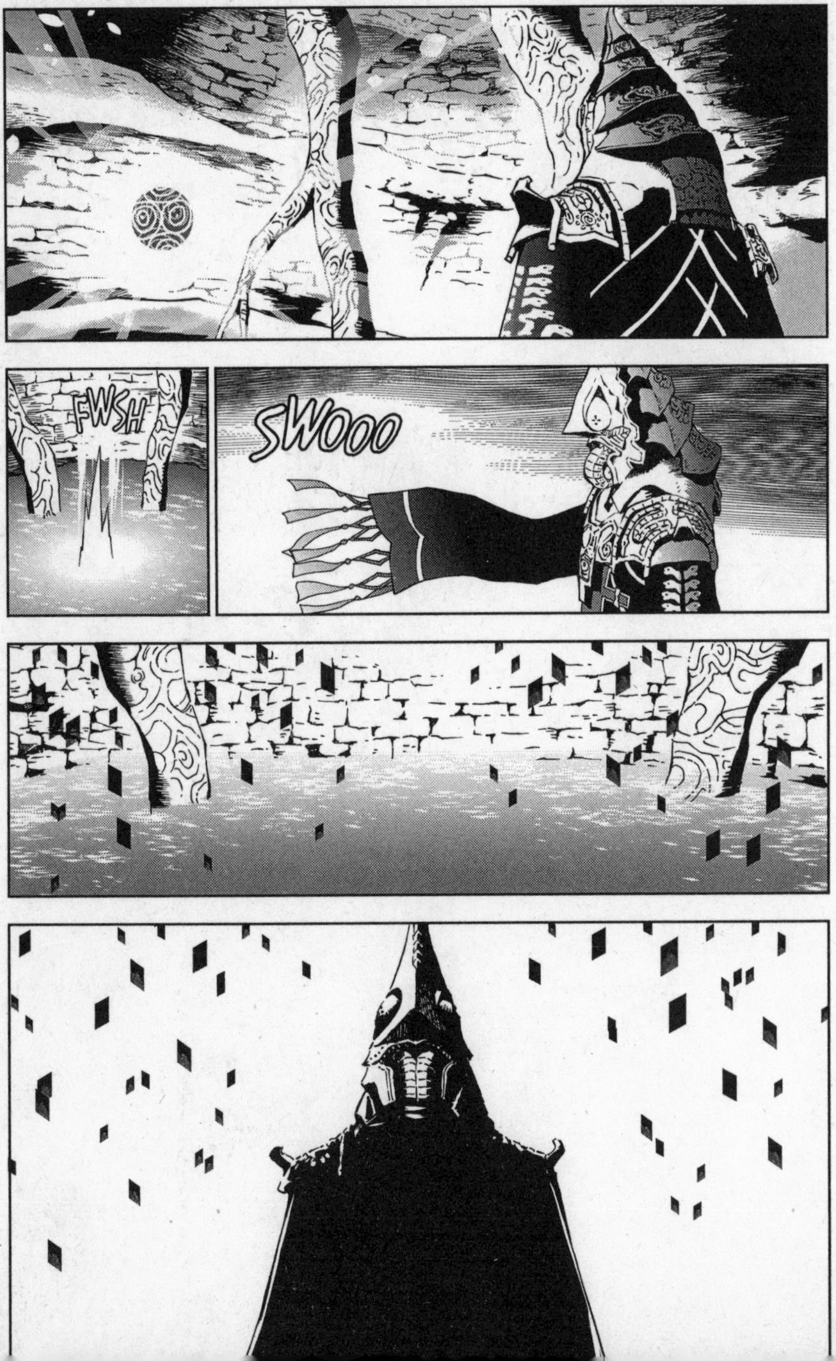
SWOOO
FWSH

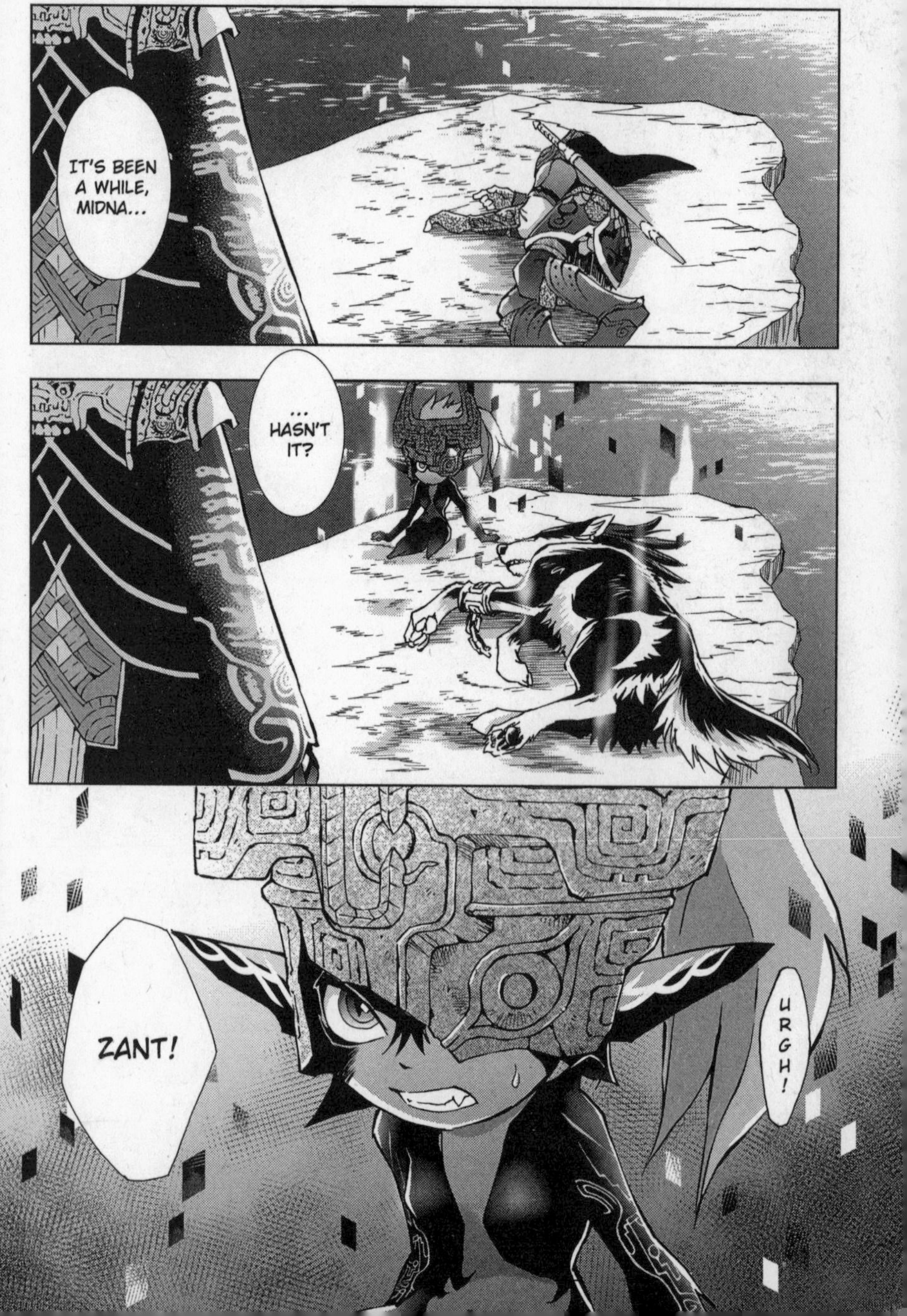
IT'S BEEN A WHILE, MIDNA...
... HASN'T IT?
URGH!
ZANT!

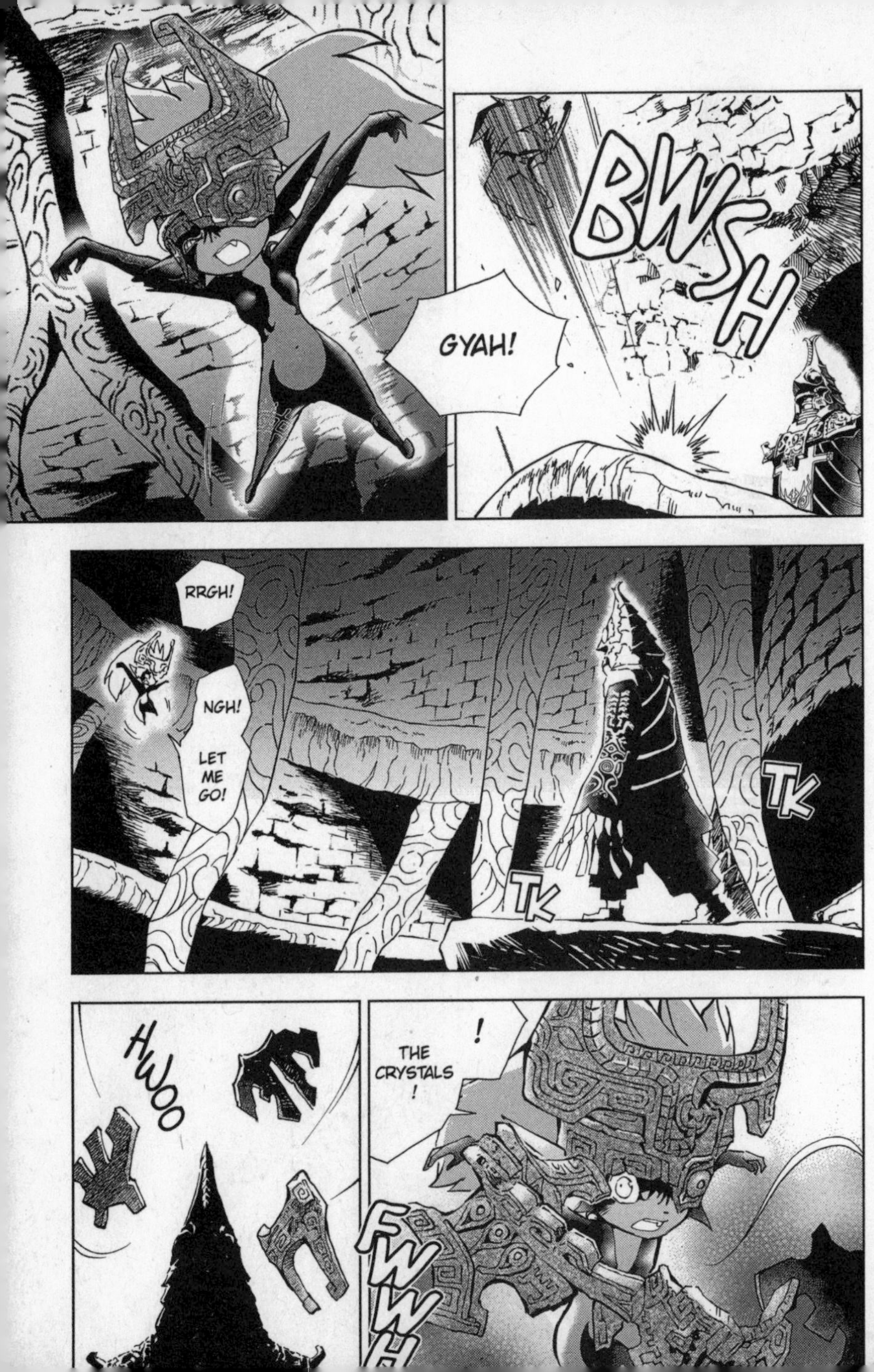
BWSH
GYAH!
RRGH!
NGH!
LET ME GO!
TK
TK
!
THE CRYSTALS !
FWWH
HWOO

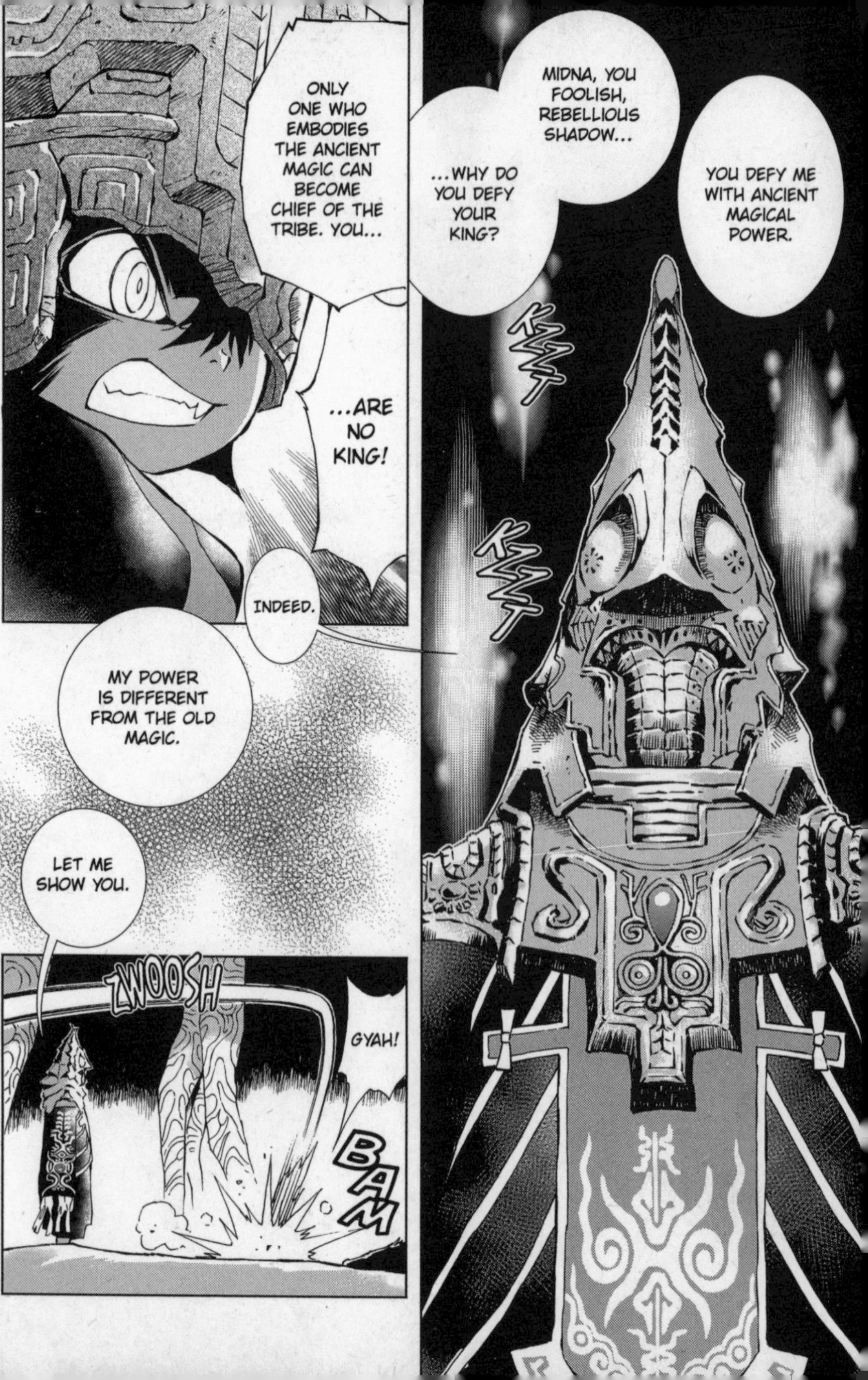
MIDNA, YOU FOOLISH, REBELLIOUS SHADOW...
YOU DEFY ME WITH ANCIENT MAGICAL POWER.
...WHY DO YOU DEFY YOUR KING?
KZZT
KZZT
ONLY ONE WHO EMBODIES THE ANCIENT MAGIC CAN BECOME CHIEF OF THE TRIBE. YOU...
...ARE NO KING!
INDEED.
MY POWER IS DIFFERENT FROM THE OLD MAGIC.
LET ME SHOW YOU.
ZWOOSH
GYAH!
BAM

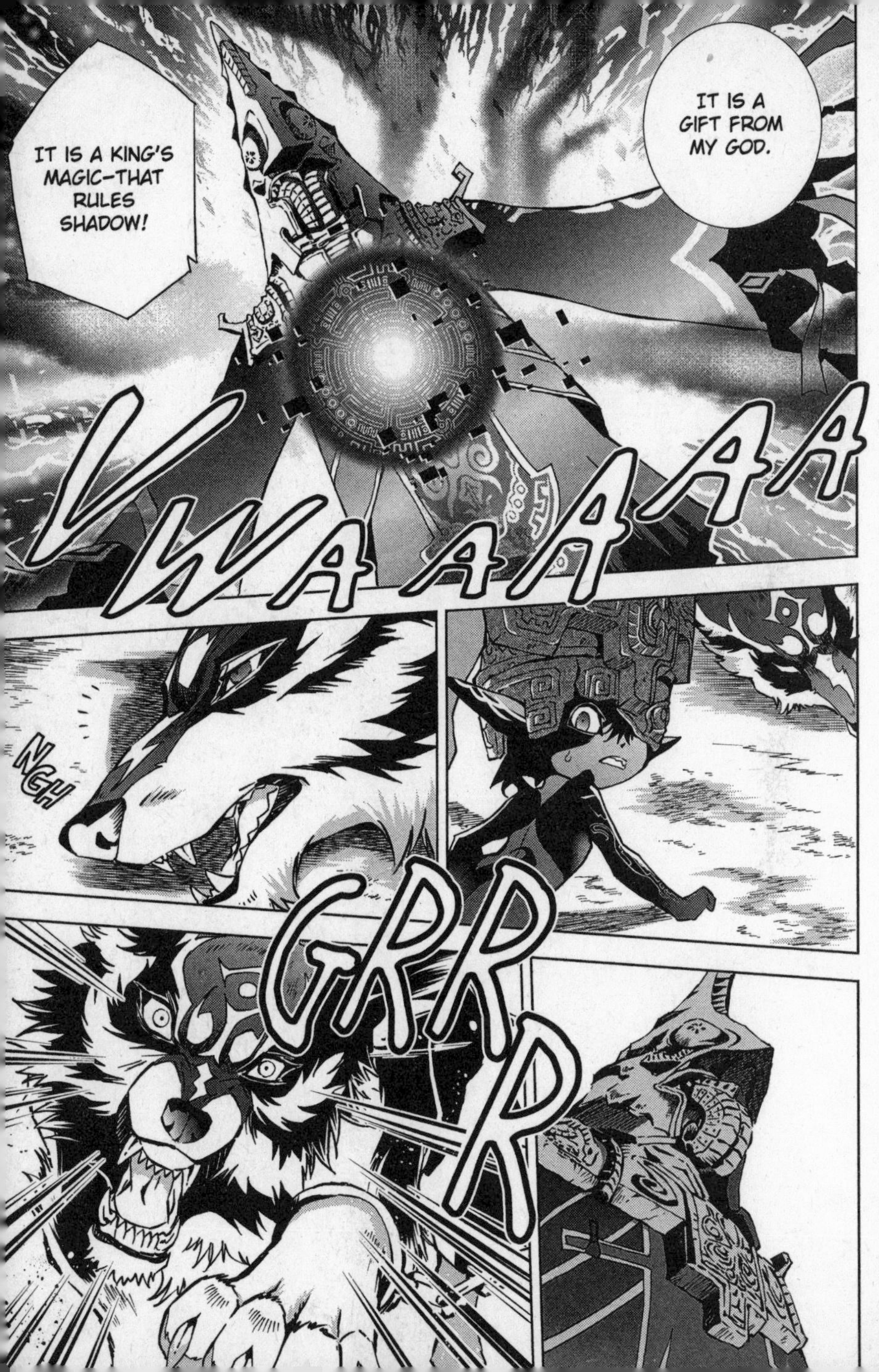
IT IS A GIFT FROM MY GOD.
IT IS A KING'S MAGIC—THAT RULES SHADOW!
VWAAAAA
NGH
GRRR

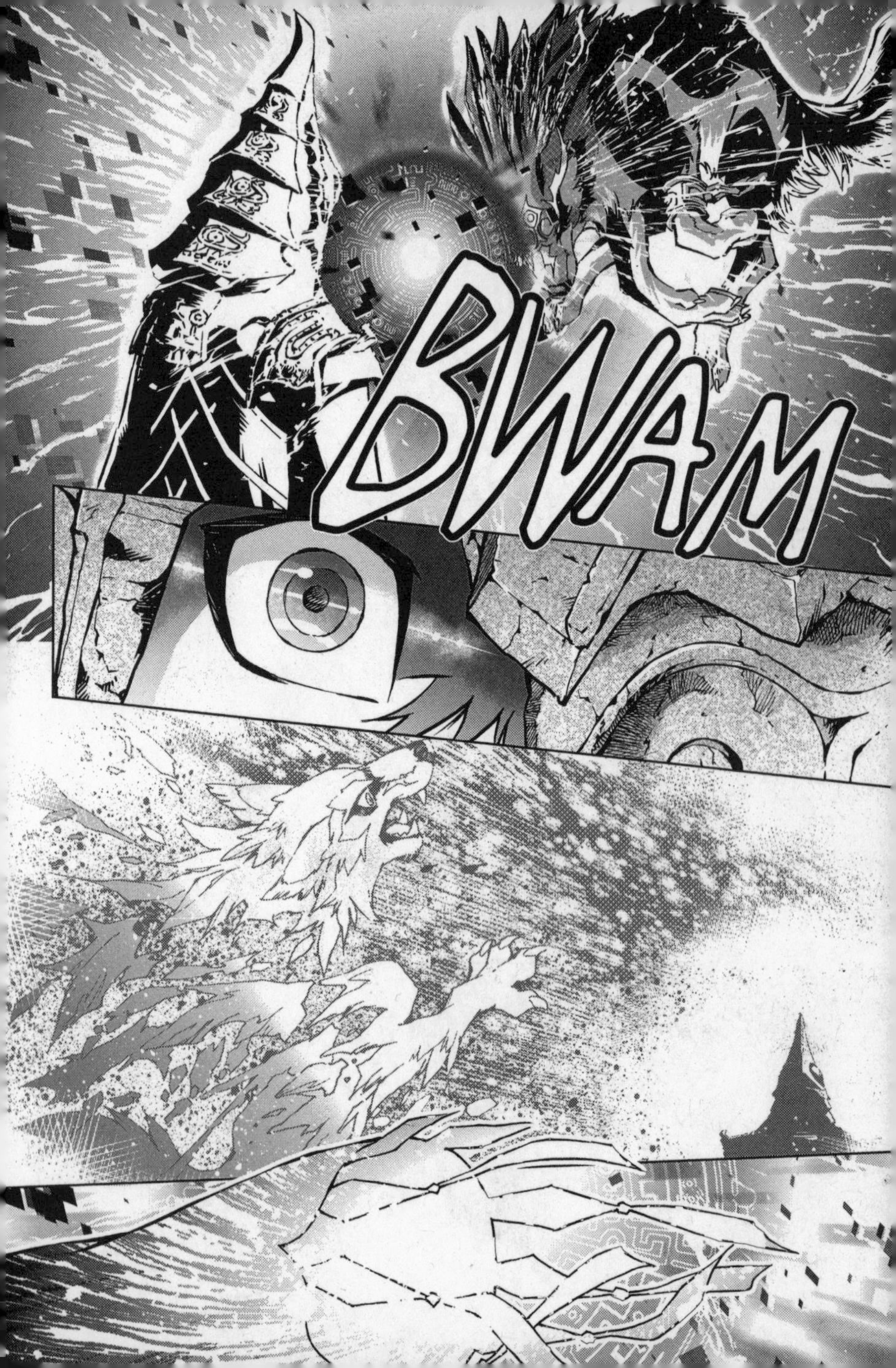
BWAM

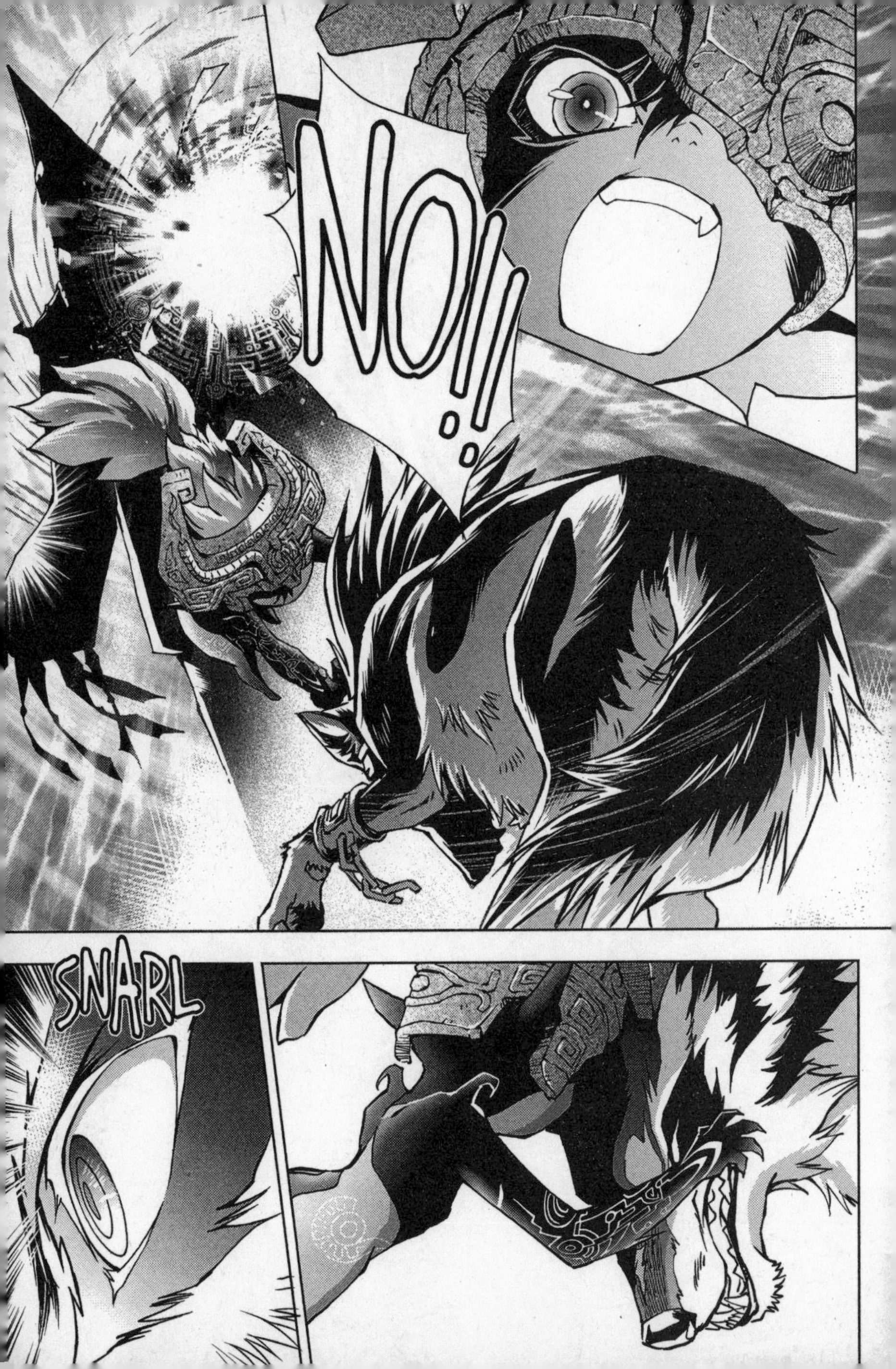
NO!!!
SNARL

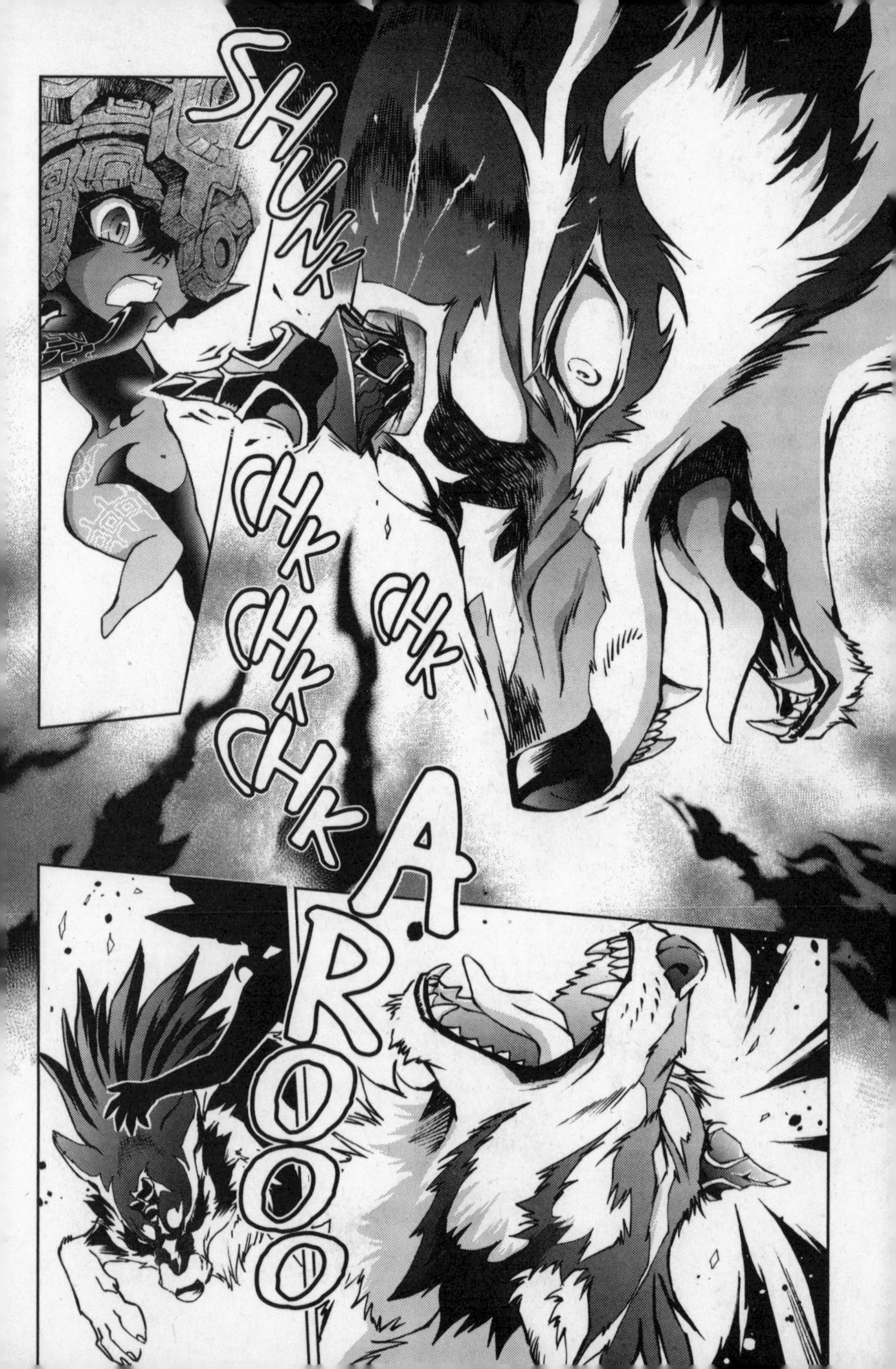
SHUNK
CHK
CHK CHK CHK
AROOOO

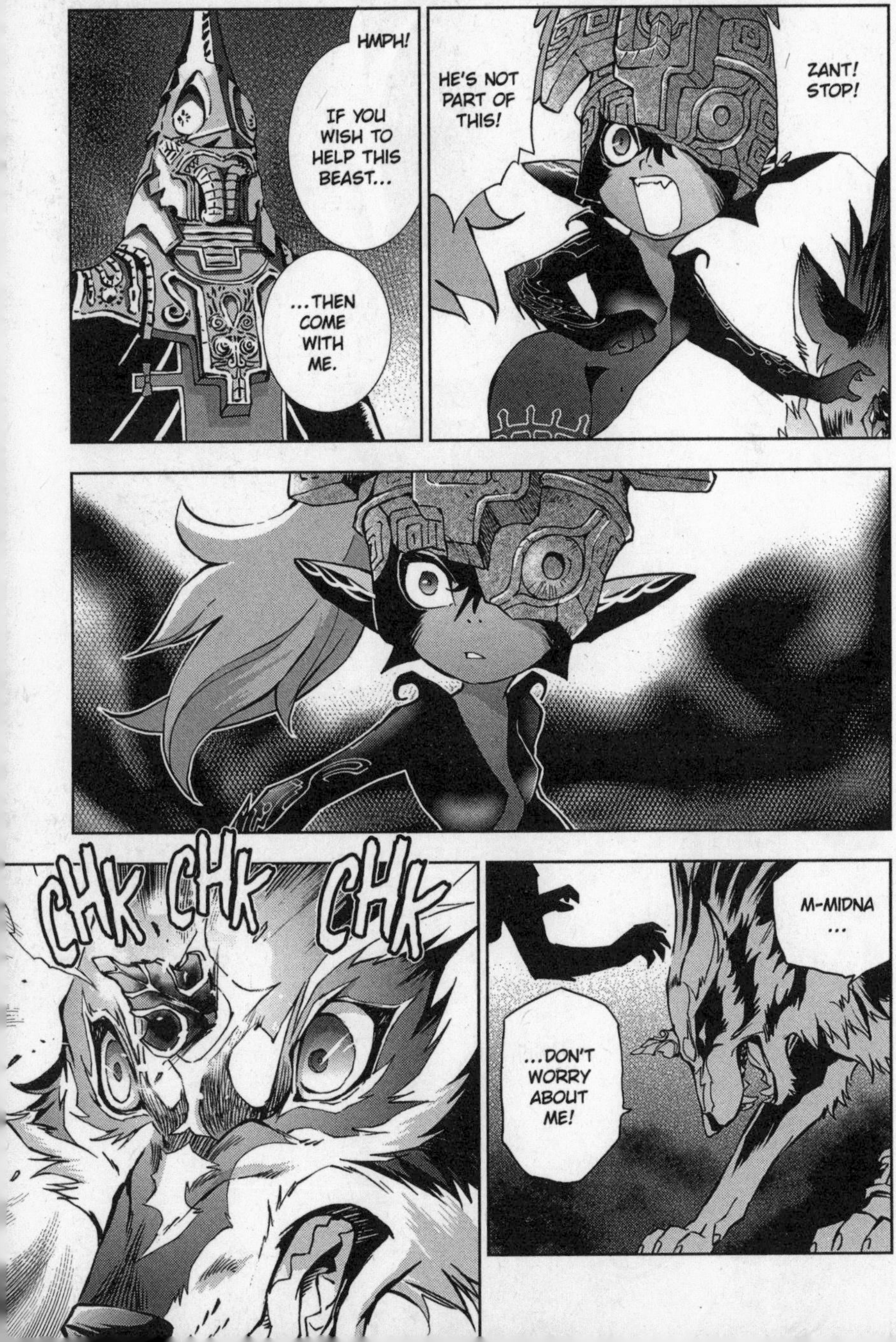
ZANT! STOP!
HE'S NOT PART OF THIS!
HMPH!
IF YOU WISH TO HELP THIS BEAST...
...THEN COME WITH ME.
M-MIDNA ...
...DON'T WORRY ABOUT ME!
CHK CHK CHK

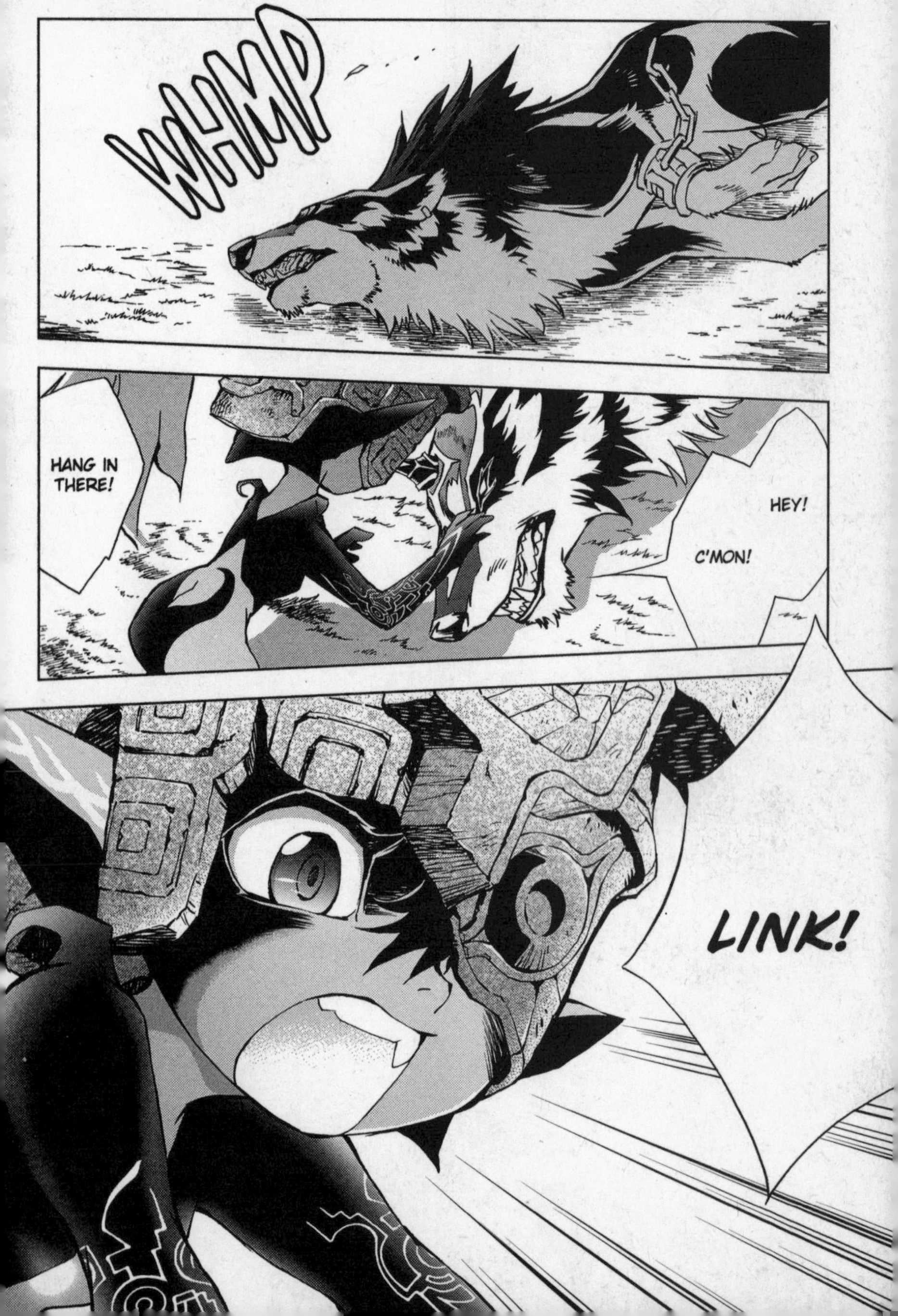
WHMP
HEY!
C'MON!
HANG IN THERE!
LINK!

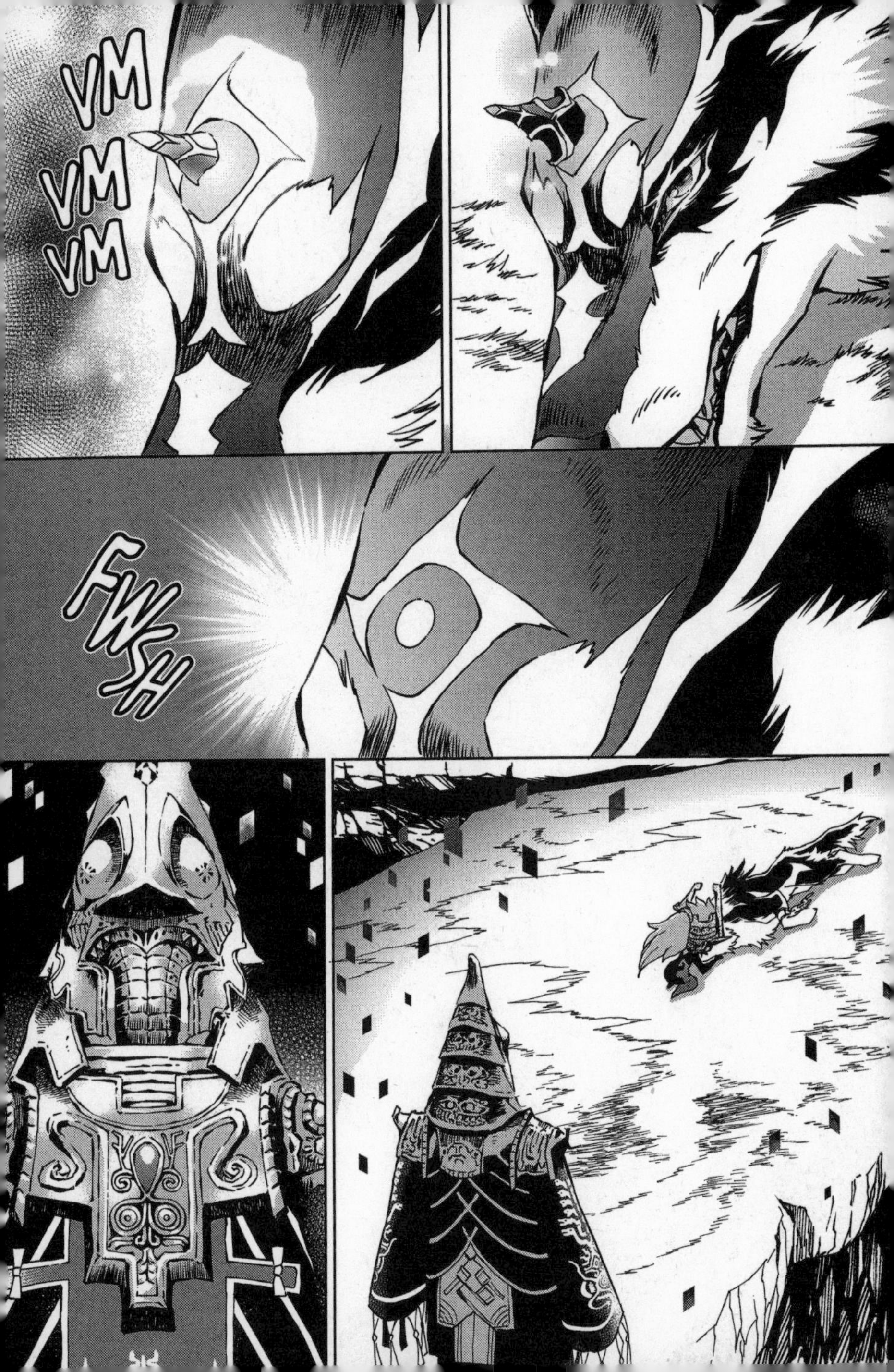
VM
VM
VM
VM
FWSH

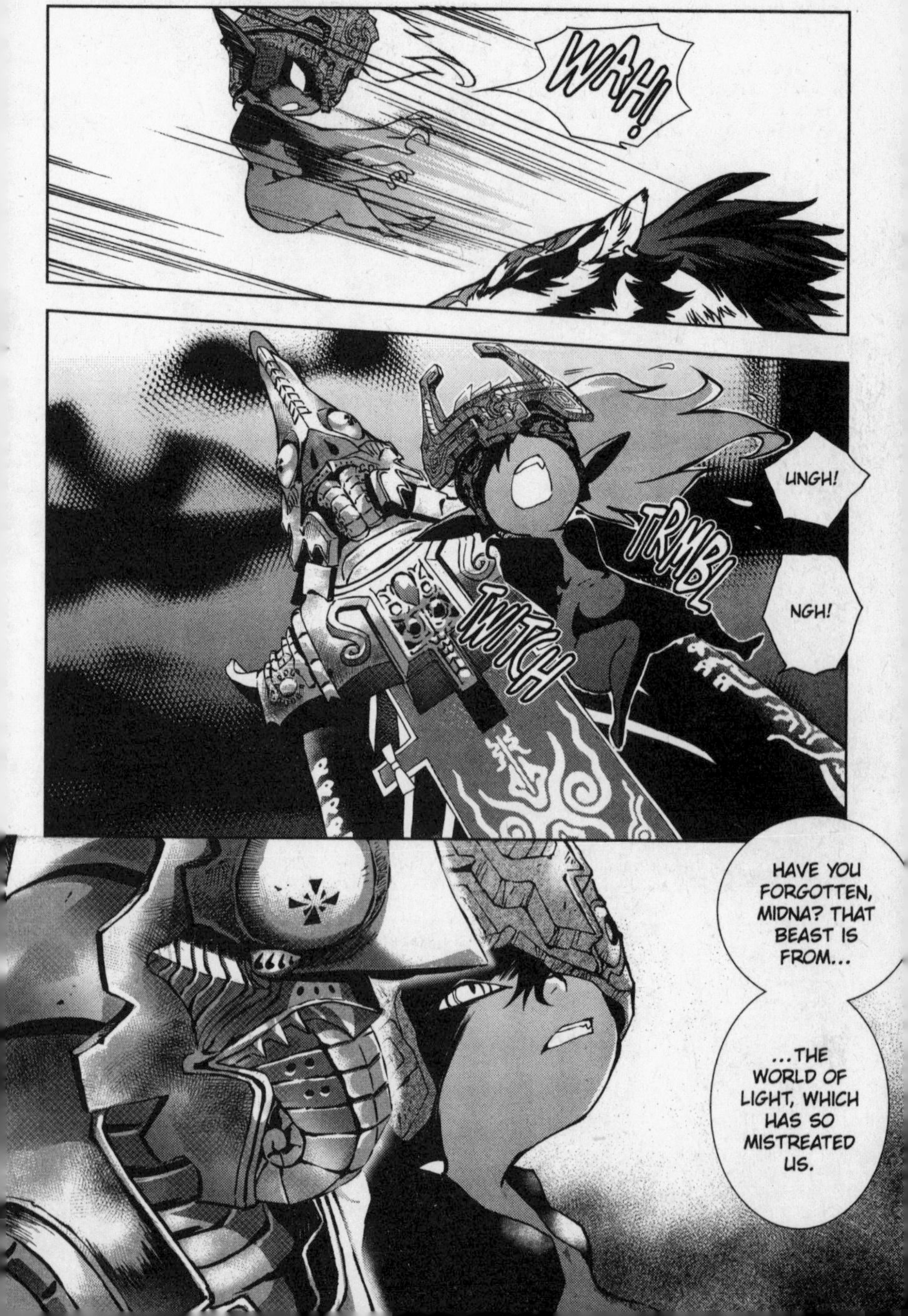
WAH!
UNGH!
TRMBL
NGH!
TWITCH
HAVE YOU FORGOTTEN, MIDNA? THAT BEAST IS FROM...
...THE WORLD OF LIGHT, WHICH HAS SO MISTREATED US.

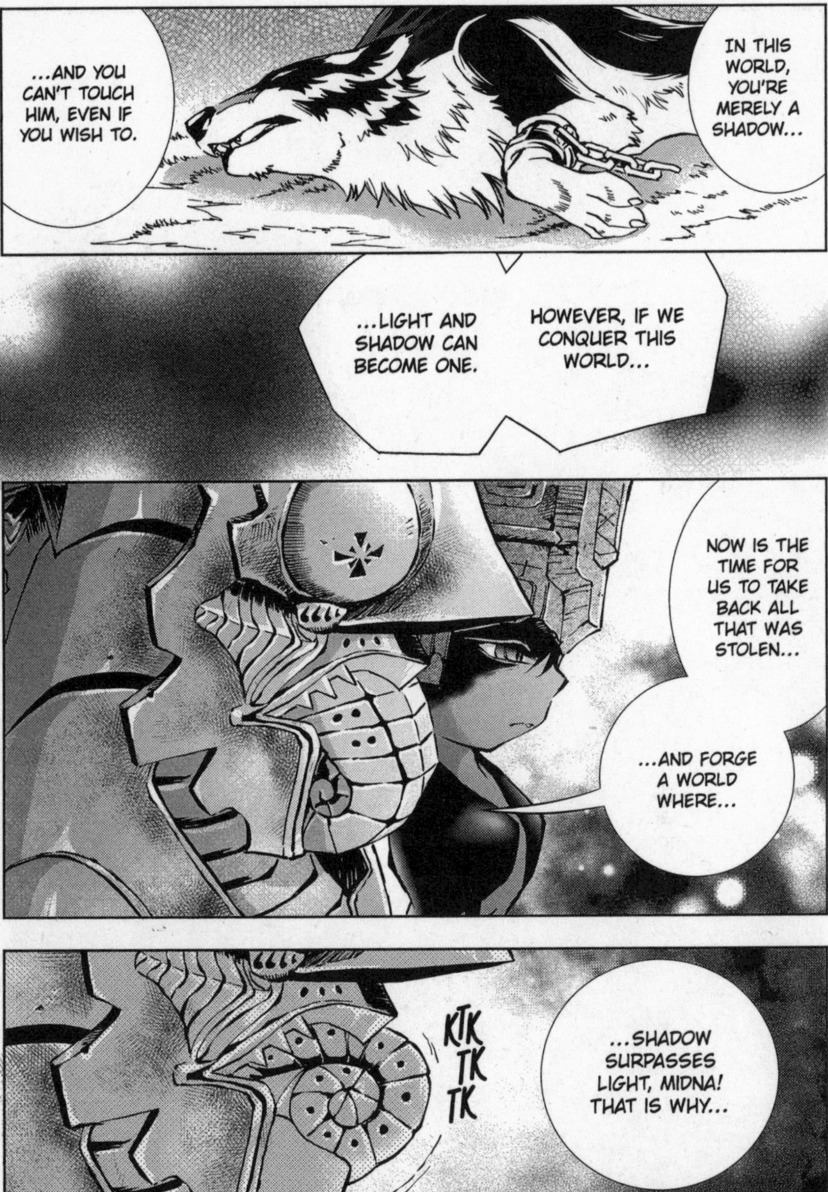
IN THIS WORLD, YOU'RE MERELY A SHADOW...
...AND YOU CAN'T TOUCH HIM, EVEN IF YOU WISH TO.
HOWEVER, IF WE CONQUER THIS WORLD...
...LIGHT AND SHADOW CAN BECOME ONE.
NOW IS THE TIME FOR US TO TAKE BACK ALL THAT WAS STOLEN...
...AND FORGE A WORLD WHERE...
...SHADOW SURPASSES LIGHT, MIDNA! THAT IS WHY...
KTK TK TK

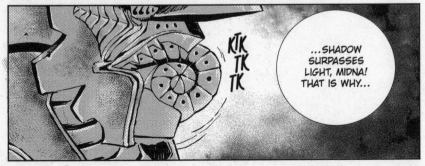

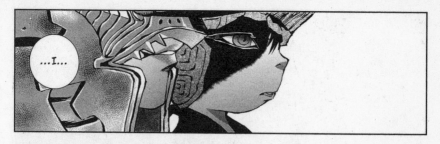

...I...

...
WANT
...

...YOU.

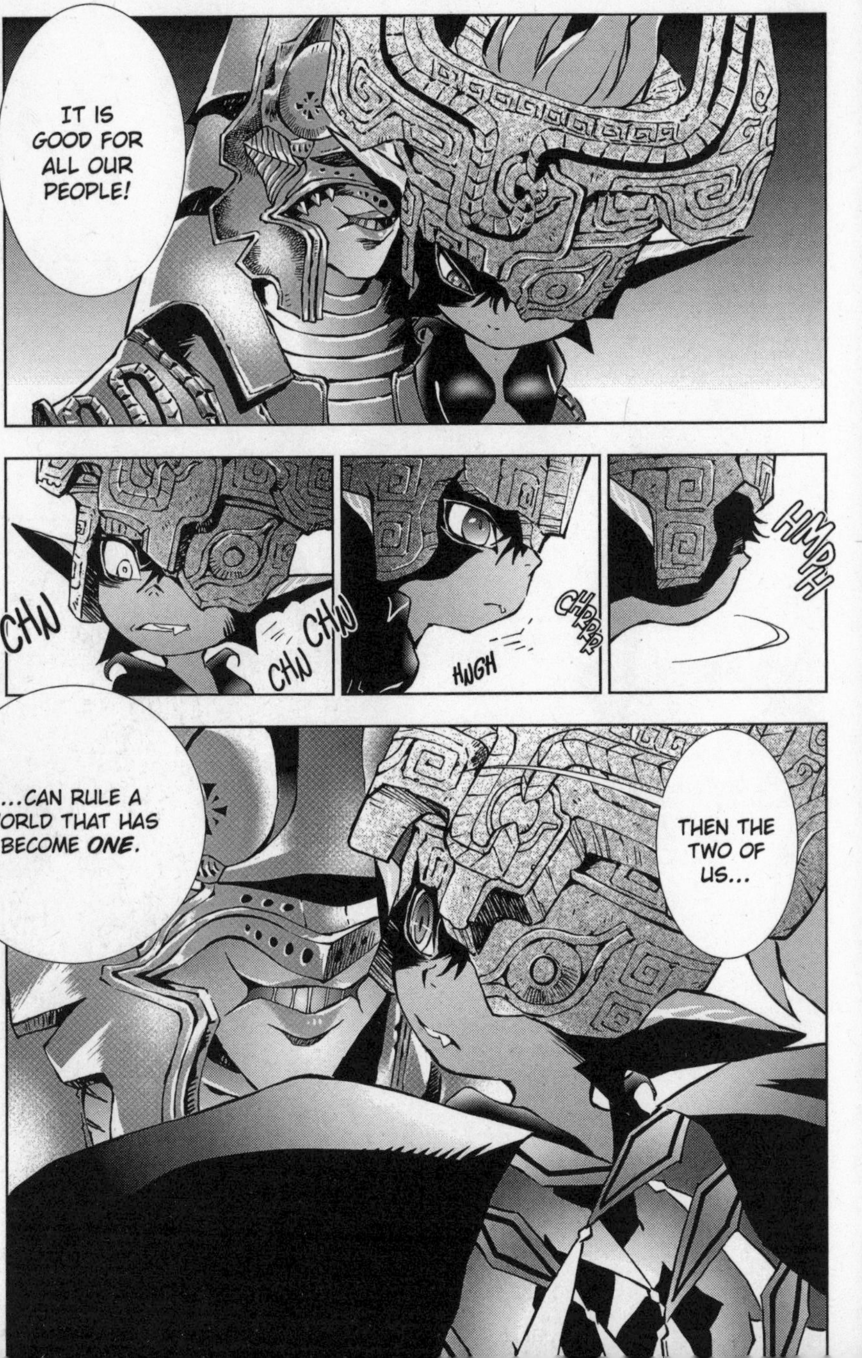
IT IS GOOD FOR ALL OUR PEOPLE!
HMPH
CHRRR
HNGH
CHN CHN
CHN
THEN THE TWO OF US...
...CAN RULE A WORLD THAT HAS BECOME *ONE*.

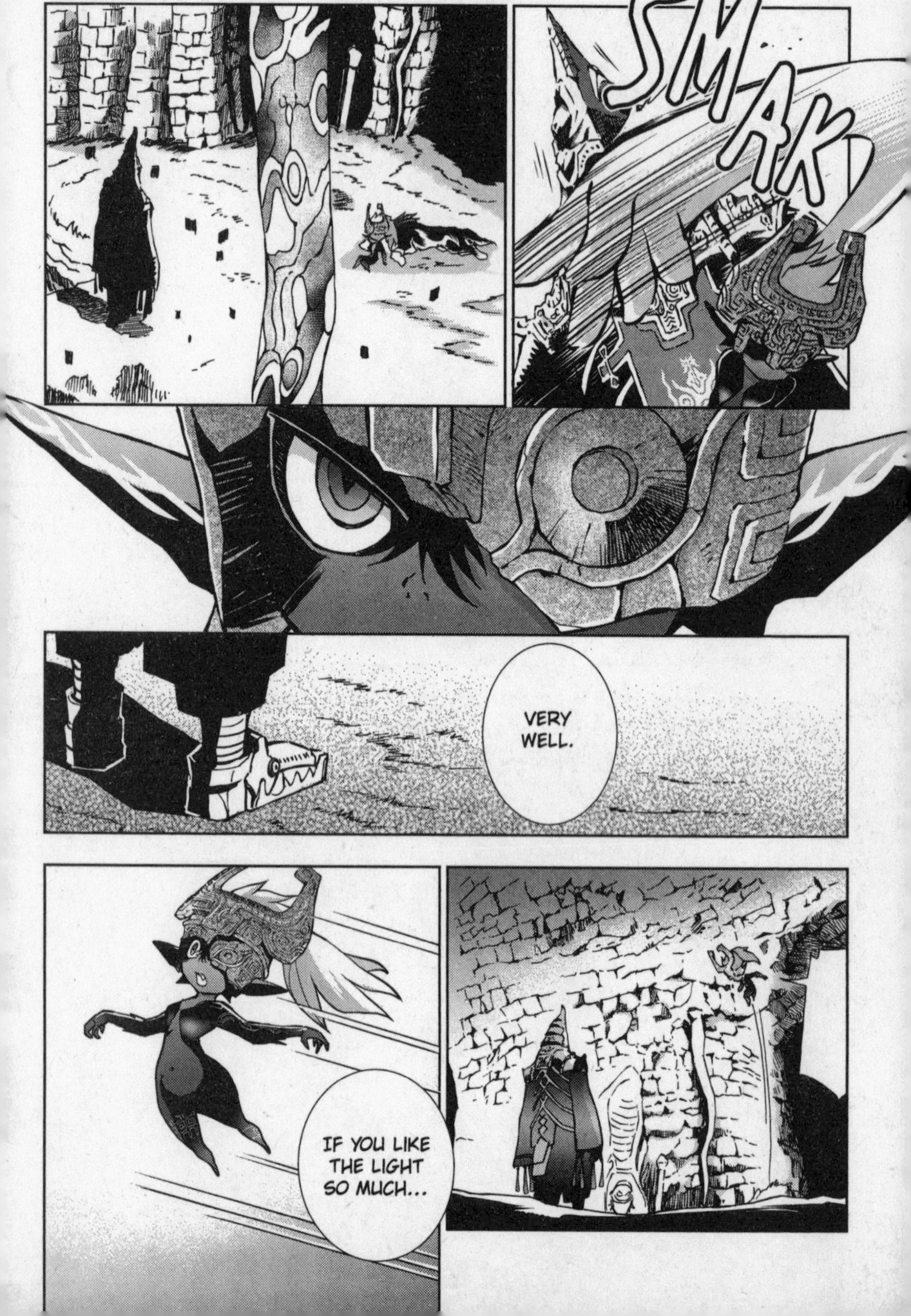
SMAK
VERY WELL.
IF YOU LIKE THE LIGHT SO MUCH...

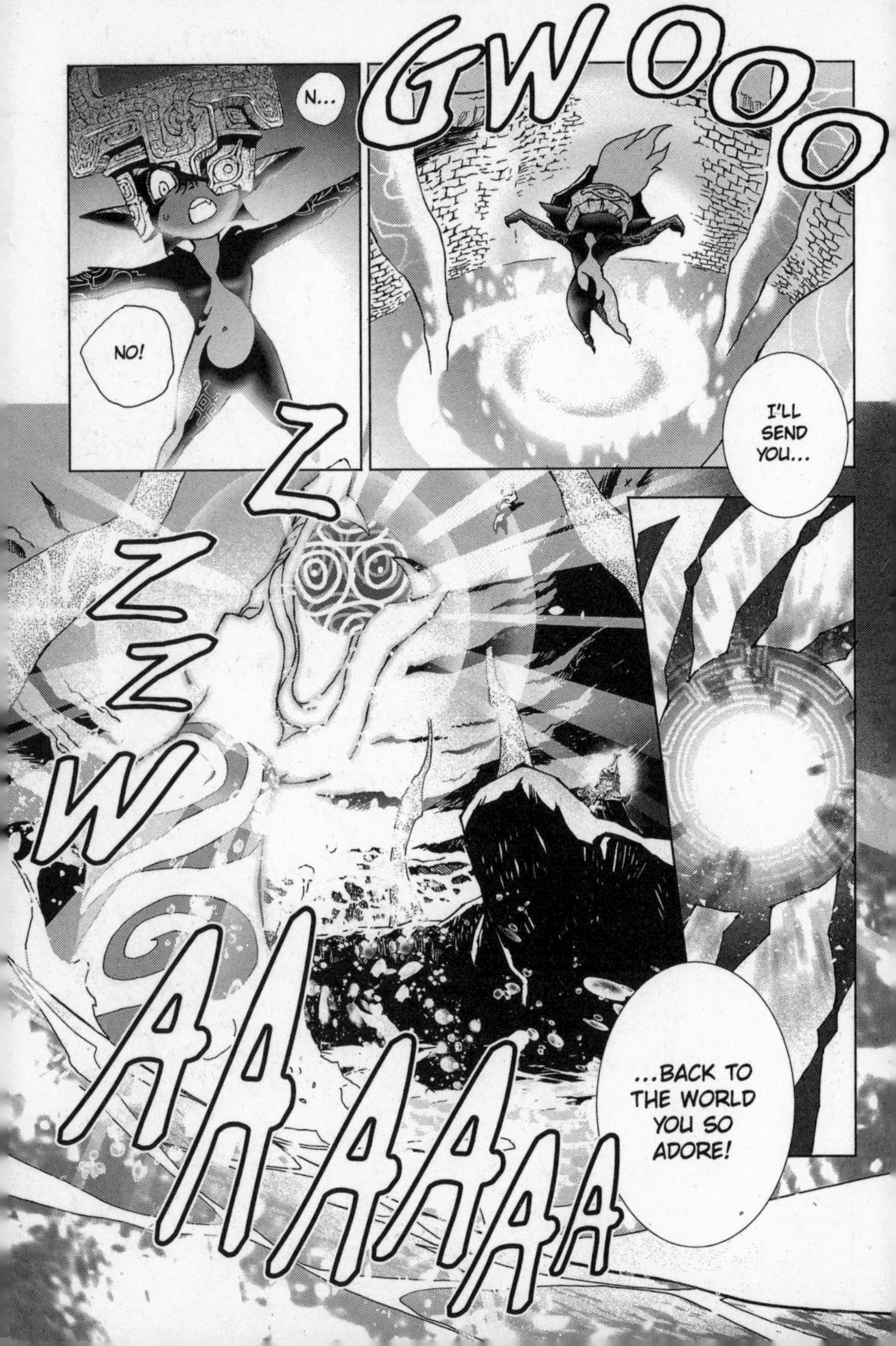
GWOOO
I'LL SEND YOU...
N...
NO!
ZZZWGAAAAAA
...BACK TO THE WORLD YOU SO ADORE!

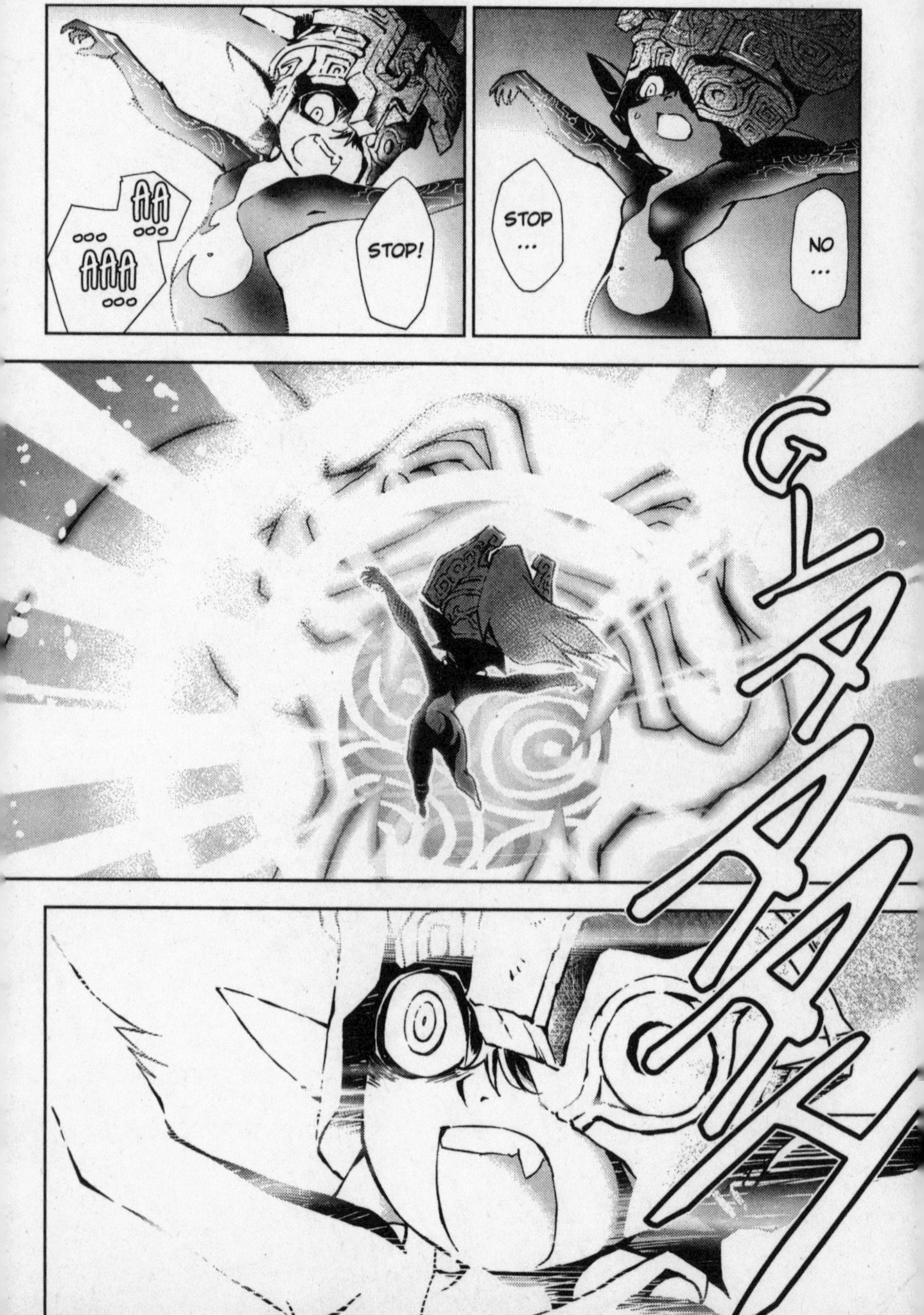

NO ...
STOP ...
STOP!
AA ooo ooo AAA ooo
GYAAASH

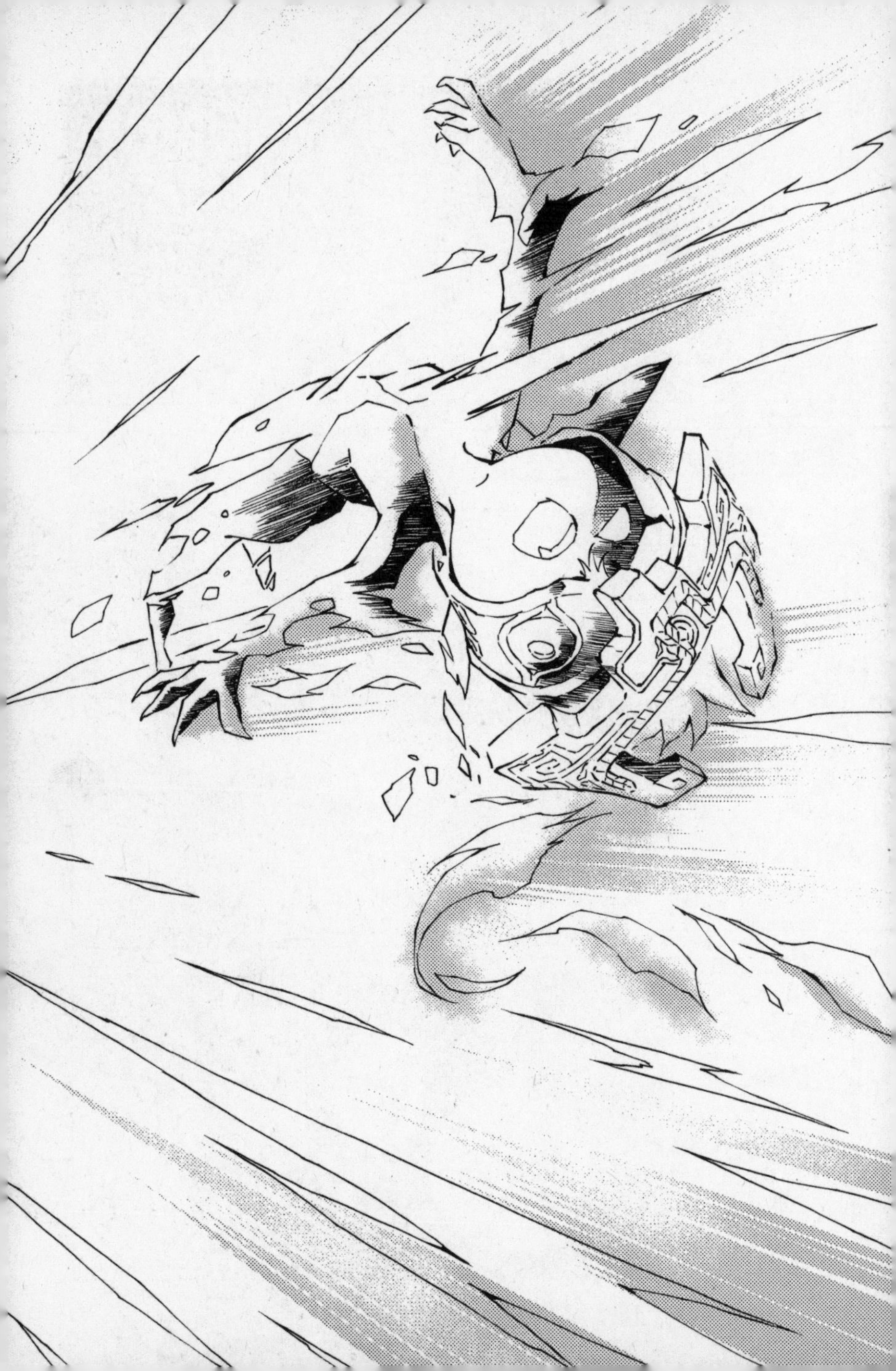

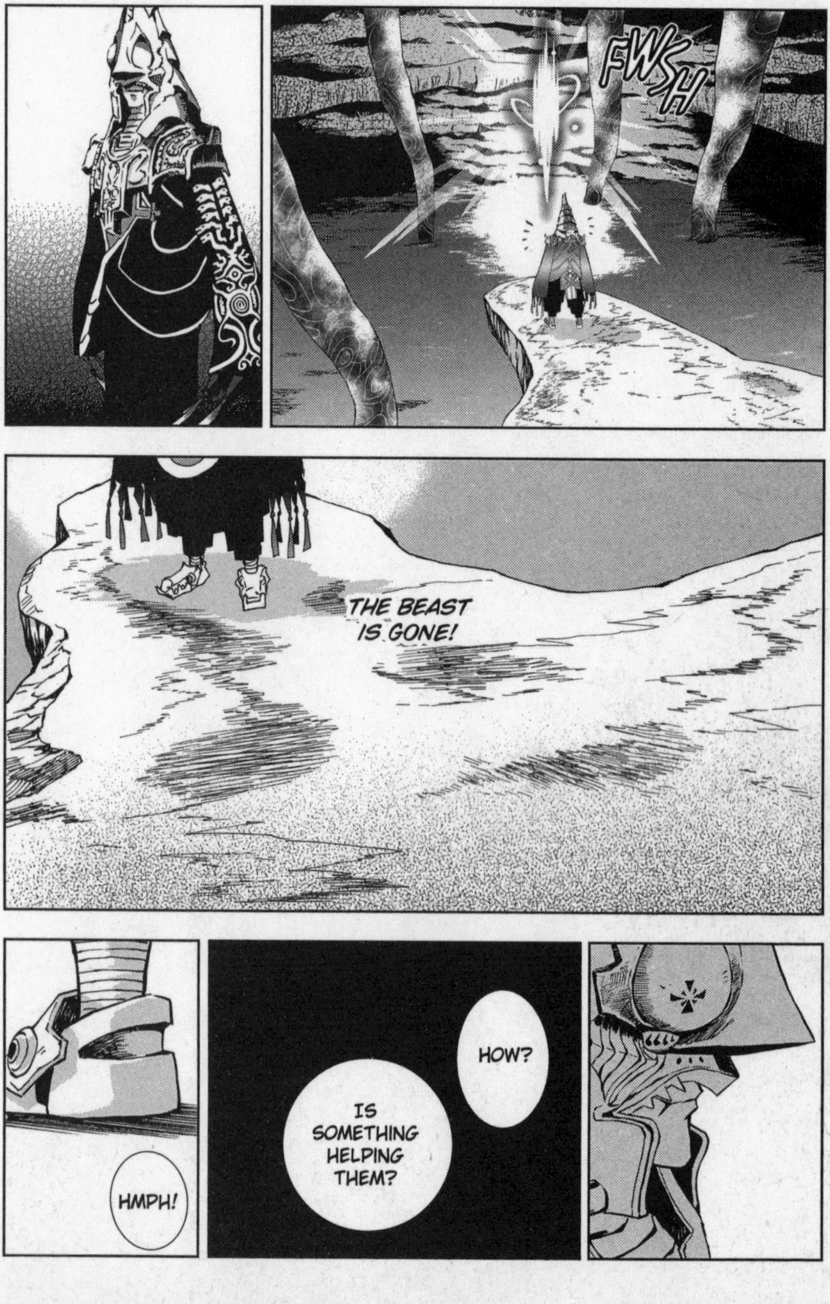
FWSH
THE BEAST IS GONE!
HOW?
IS SOMETHING HELPING THEM?
HMPH!

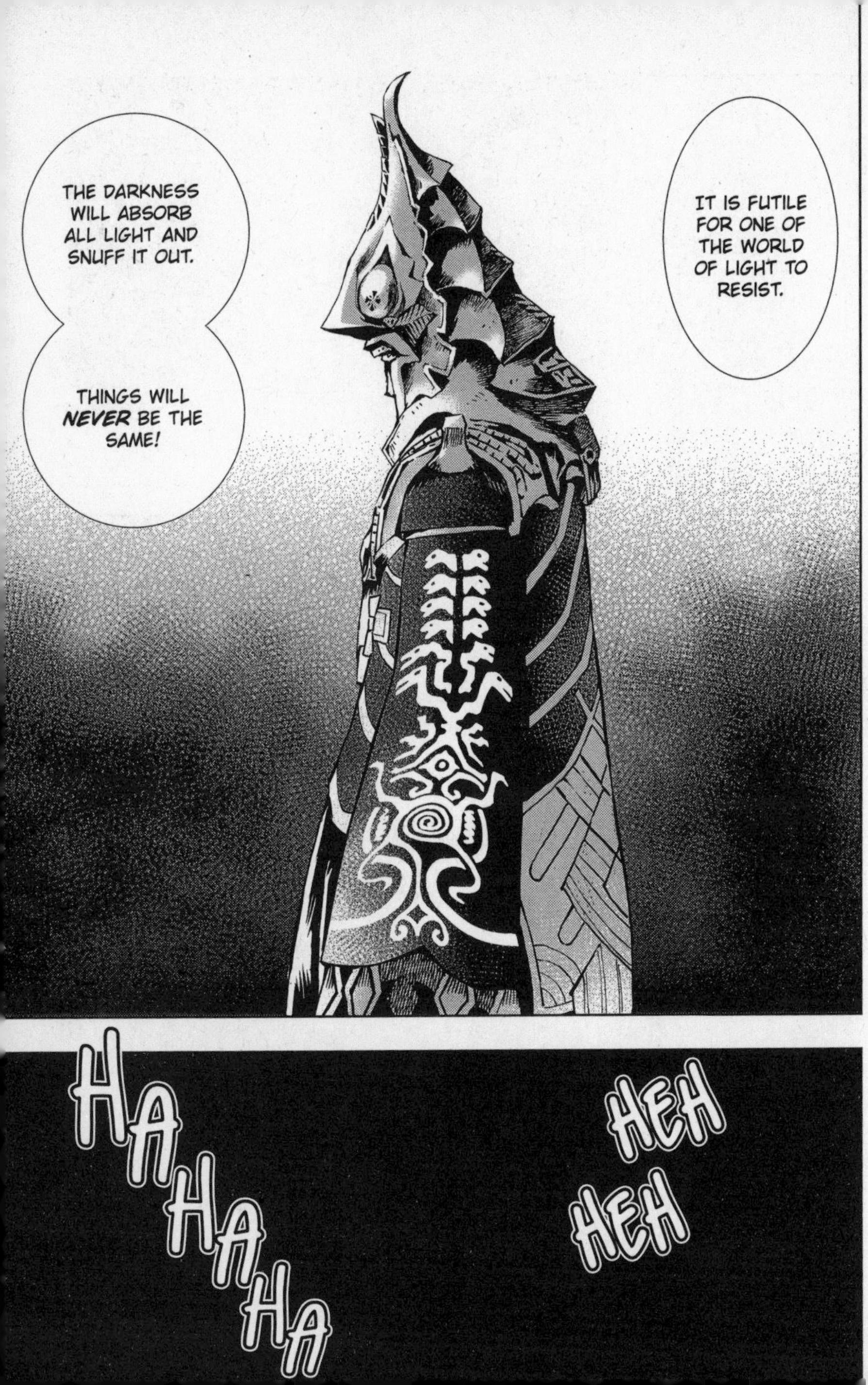
IT IS FUTILE FOR ONE OF THE WORLD OF LIGHT TO RESIST.
THE DARKNESS WILL ABSORB ALL LIGHT AND SNUFF IT OUT.
THINGS WILL ***NEVER*** BE THE SAME!
HEH HEH
HAHAHAHA

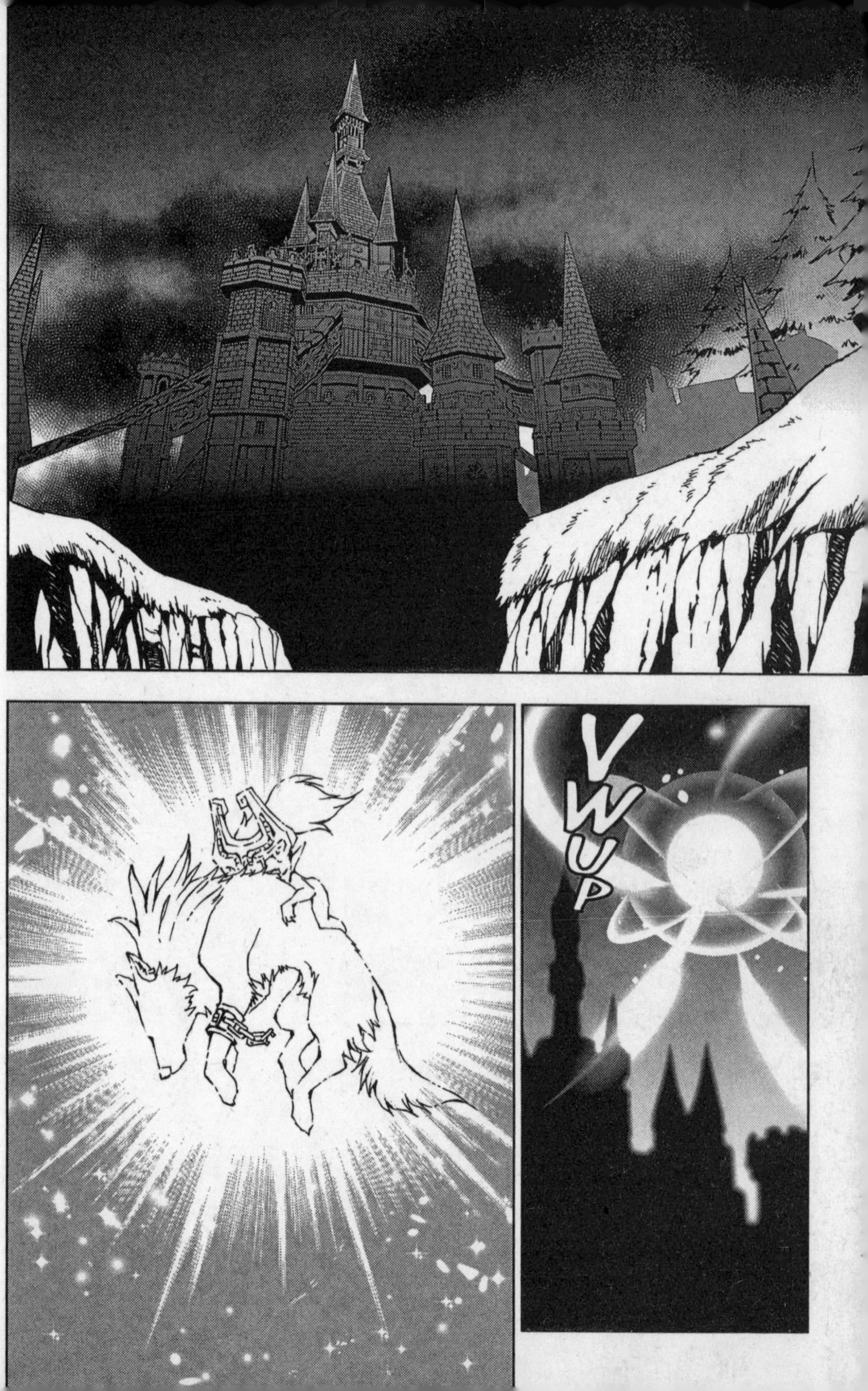
VWUP

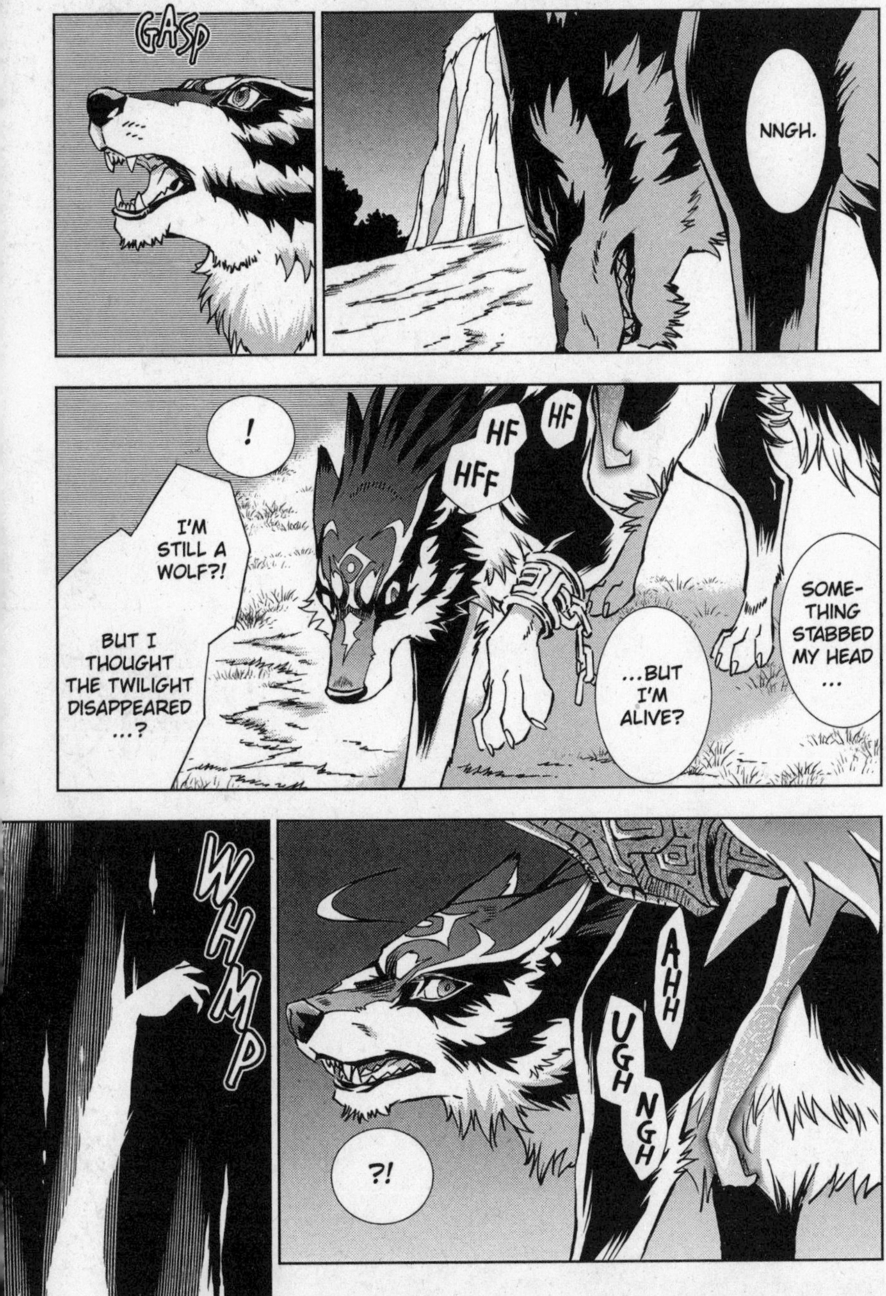
NNGH.
GASP
HF
HF
HFF
SOME-THING STABBED MY HEAD...
...BUT I'M ALIVE?
!
I'M STILL A WOLF?!
BUT I THOUGHT THE TWILIGHT DISAPPEARED...?
AHH
UGH
NGH
?!
WHMP

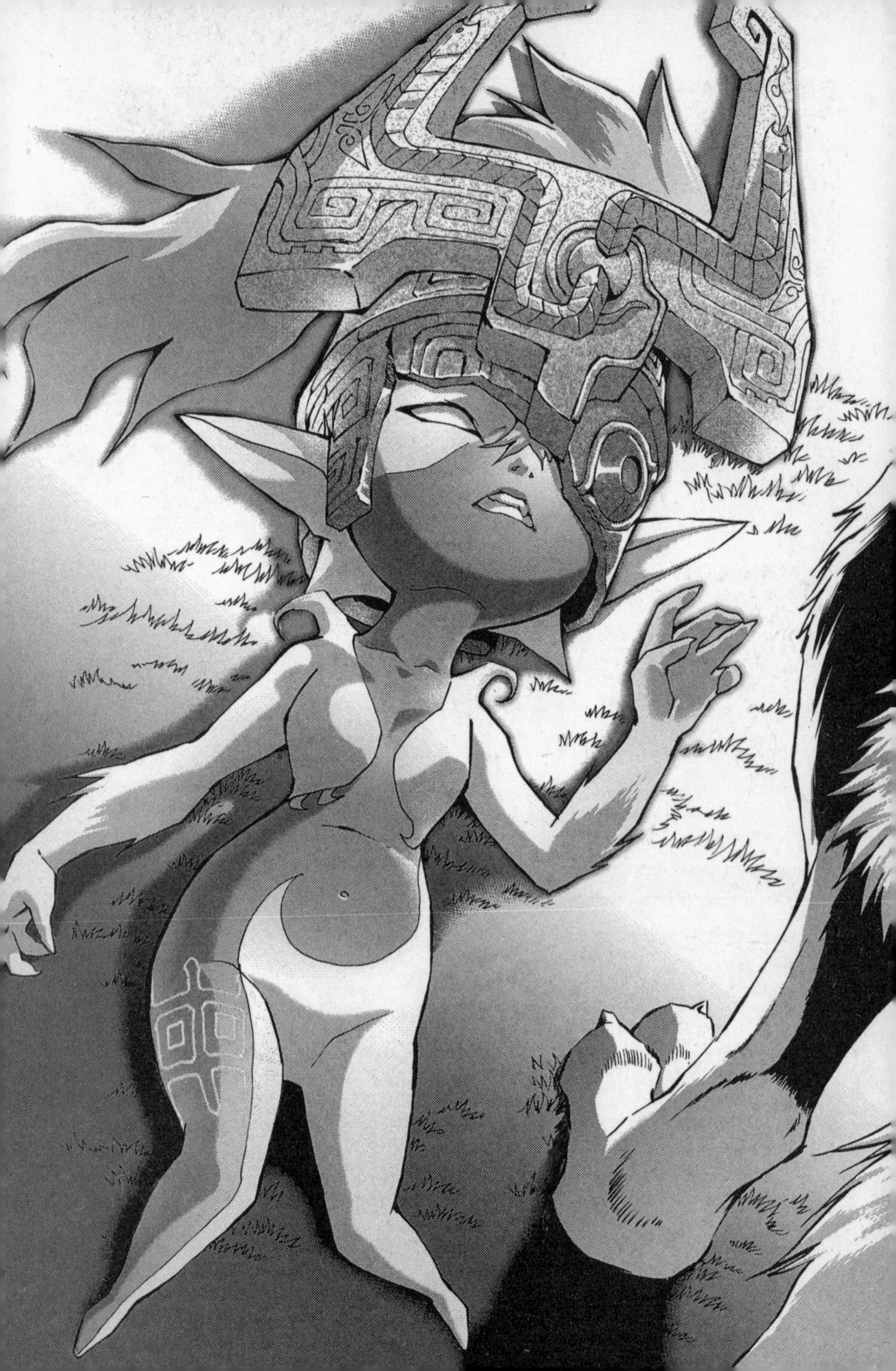

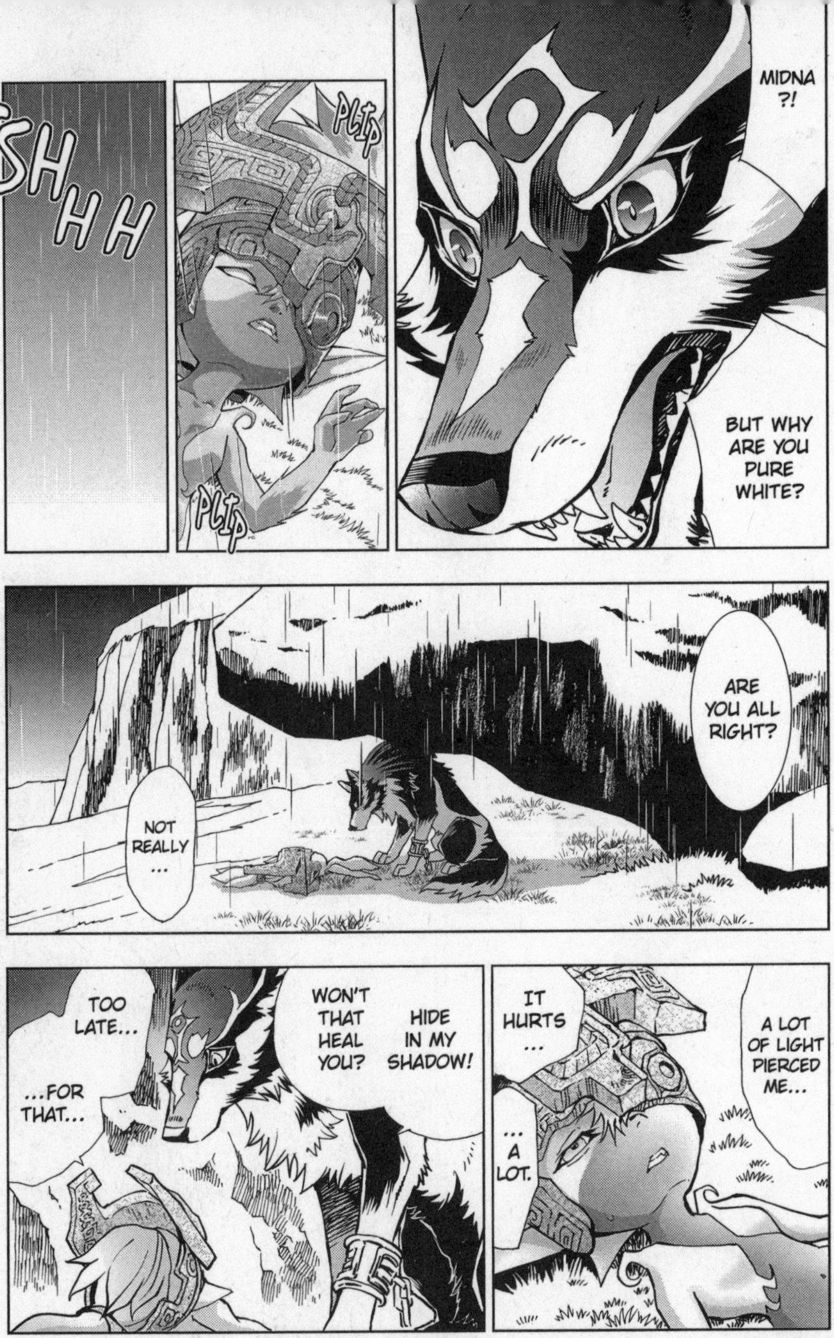
MIDNA ?!
BUT WHY ARE YOU PURE WHITE?
PLIP
PLIP
TSHHHH
ARE YOU ALL RIGHT?
NOT REALLY ...
A LOT OF LIGHT PIERCED ME...
IT HURTS ...
... A LOT.
HIDE IN MY SHADOW!
WON'T THAT HEAL YOU?
TOO LATE...
...FOR THAT...

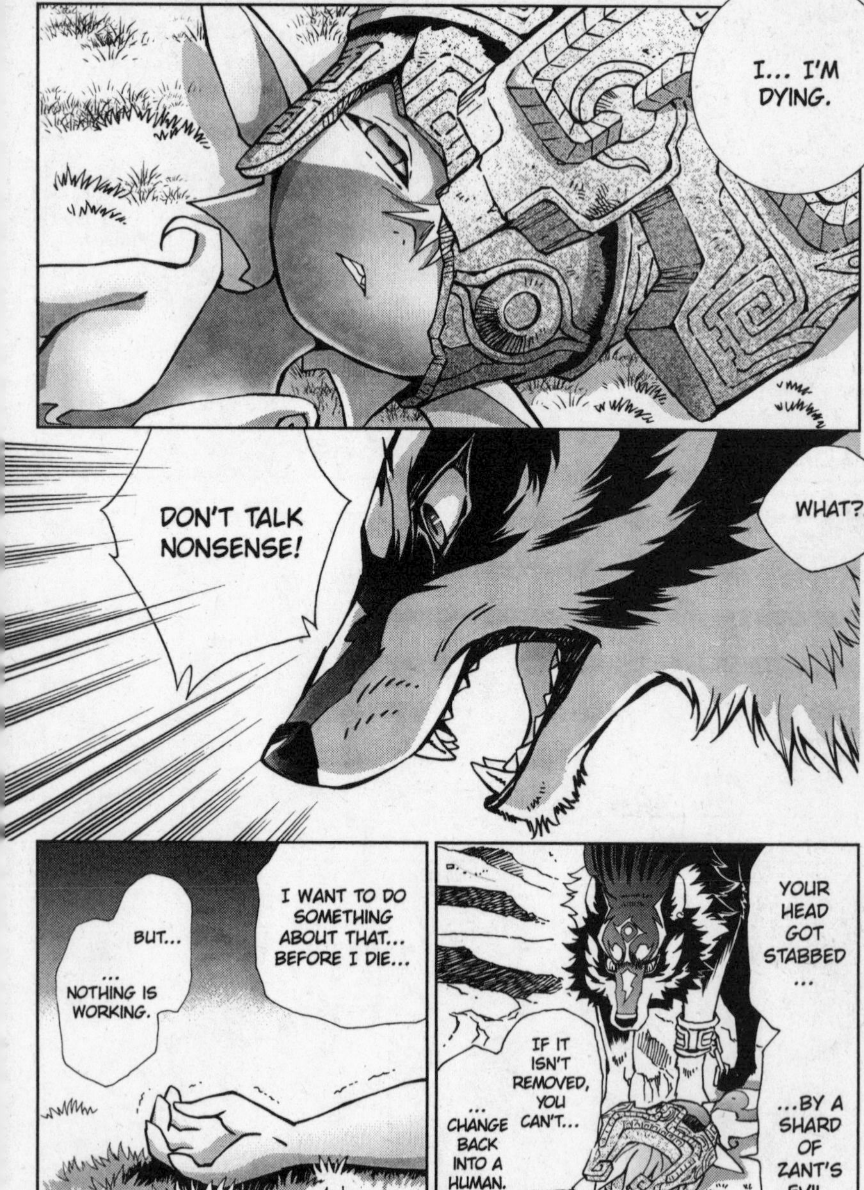
I... I'M DYING.
WHAT?!
DON'T TALK NONSENSE!
YOUR HEAD GOT STABBED...
...BY A SHARD OF ZANT'S EVIL.
IF IT ISN'T REMOVED, YOU CAN'T...
...CHANGE BACK INTO A HUMAN.
I WANT TO DO SOMETHING ABOUT THAT... BEFORE I DIE...
BUT...
...NOTHING IS WORKING.

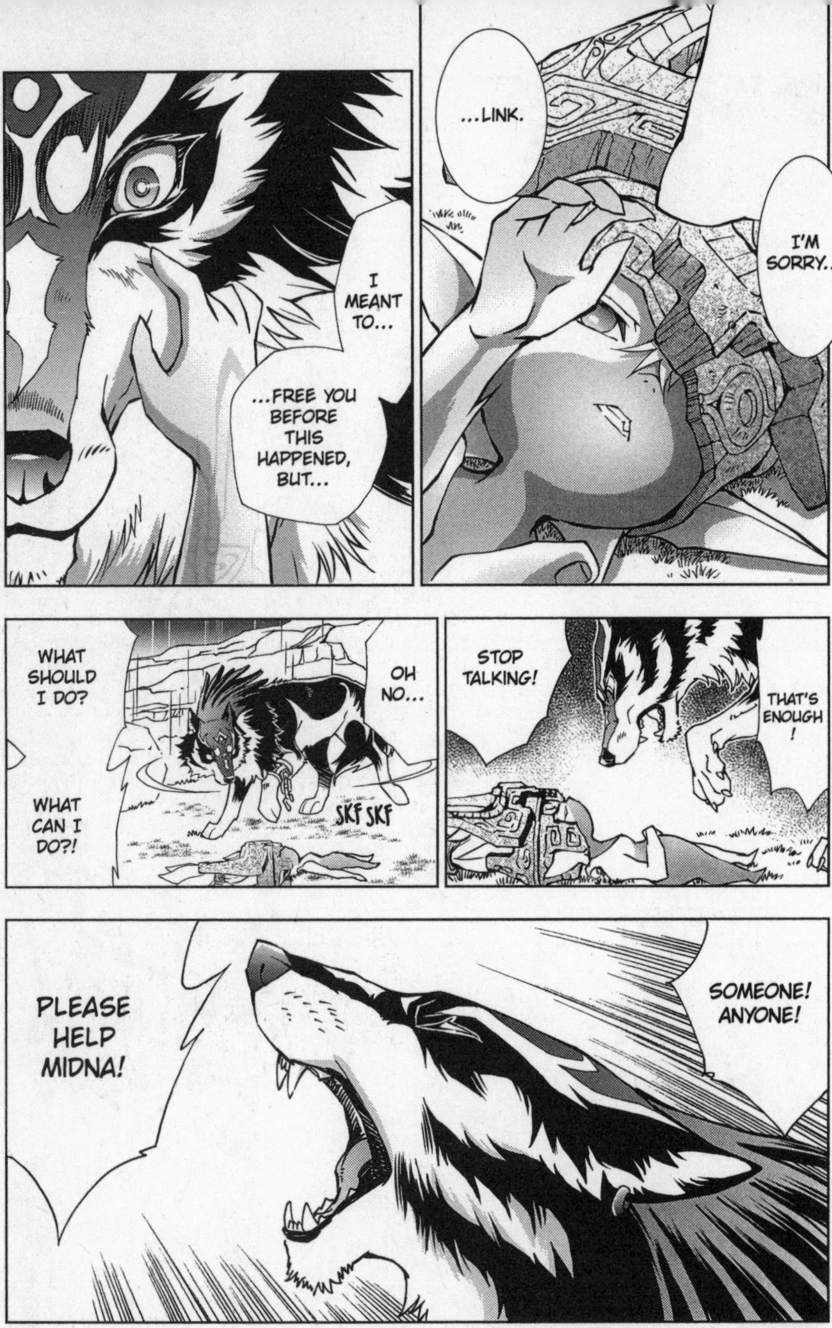
...LINK.
I'M SORRY...
I MEANT TO...
...FREE YOU BEFORE THIS HAPPENED, BUT...
THAT'S ENOUGH!
STOP TALKING!
OH NO...
WHAT SHOULD I DO?
WHAT CAN I DO?!
SKF SKF
SOMEONE! ANYONE!
PLEASE HELP MIDNA!

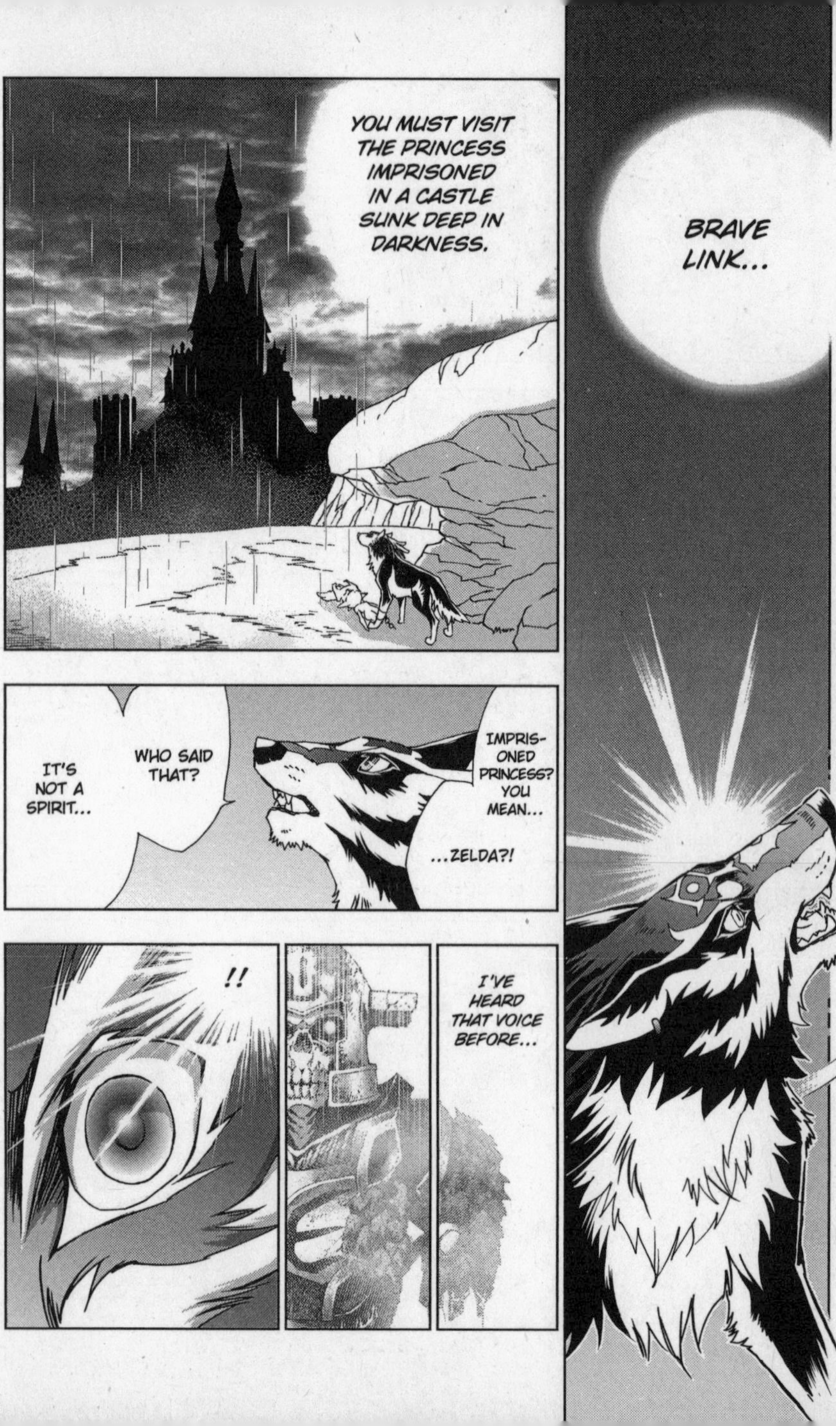
BRAVE LINK...
YOU MUST VISIT THE PRINCESS IMPRISONED IN A CASTLE SUNK DEEP IN DARKNESS.
IMPRISONED PRINCESS? YOU MEAN...
...ZELDA?!
WHO SAID THAT?
IT'S NOT A SPIRIT...
I'VE HEARD THAT VOICE BEFORE...
!!

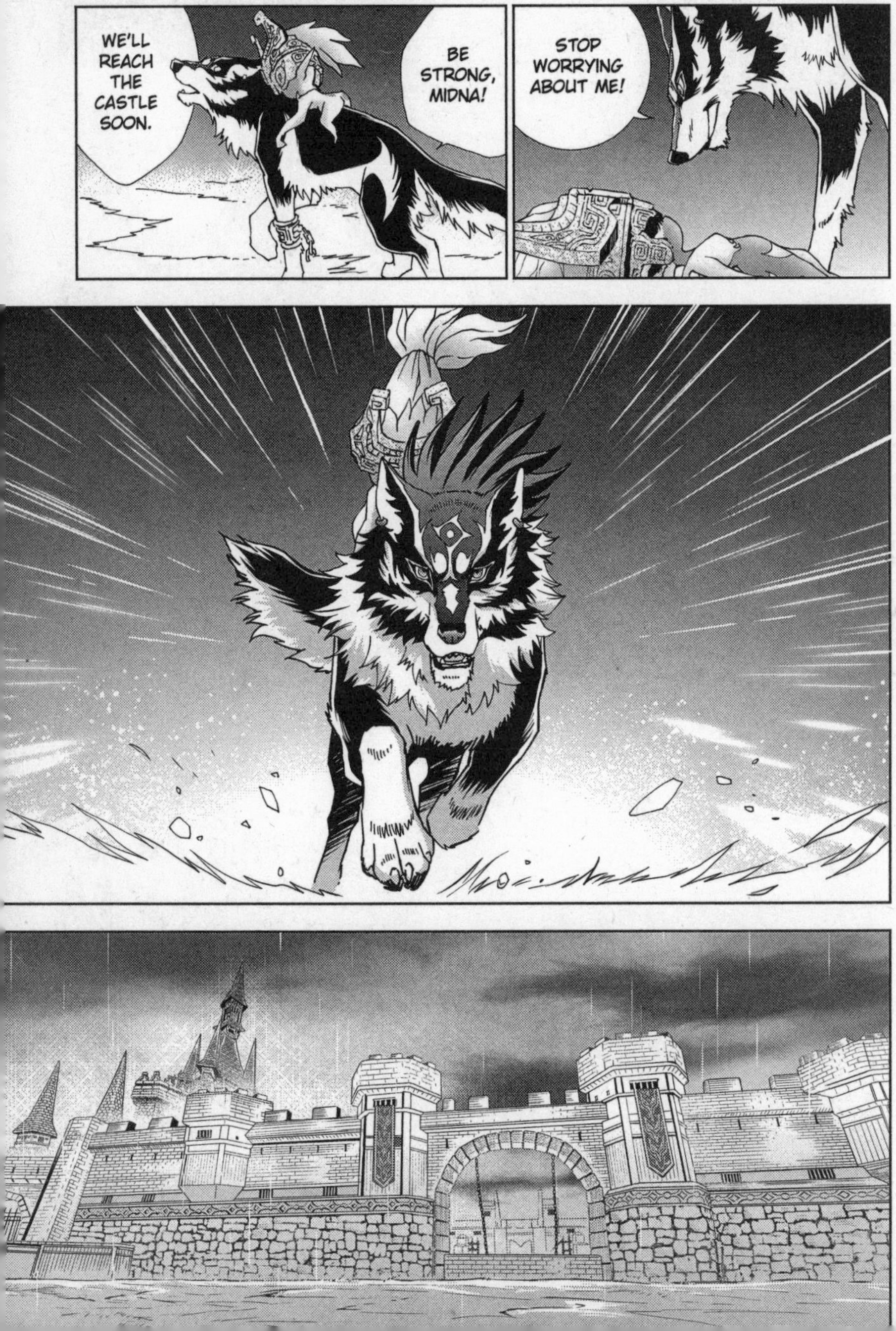
WE'LL REACH THE CASTLE SOON.
BE STRONG, MIDNA!
STOP WORRYING ABOUT ME!

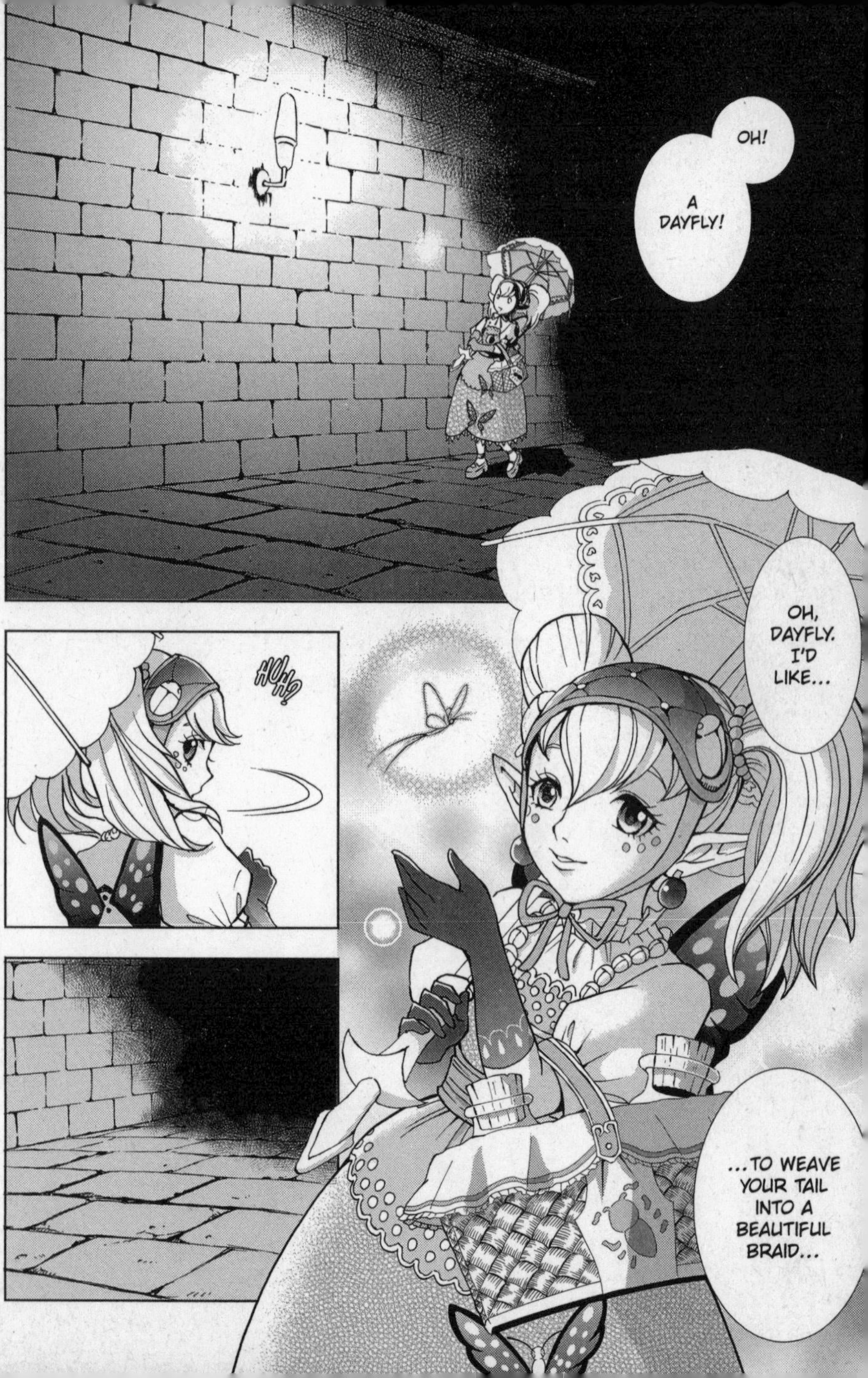
OH!
A DAYFLY!
HUH?
OH, DAYFLY. I'D LIKE...
...TO WEAVE YOUR TAIL INTO A BEAUTIFUL BRAID...

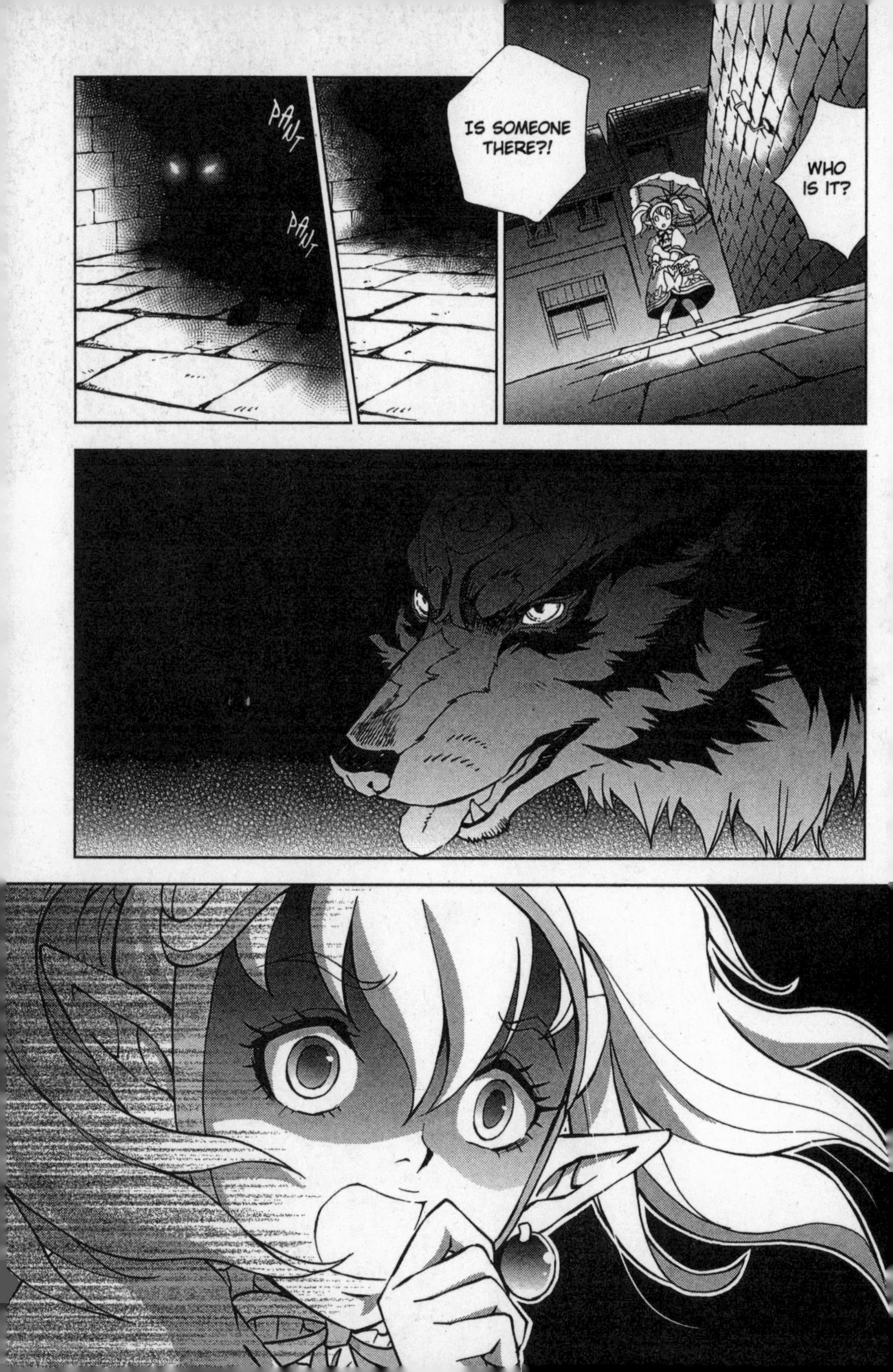
IS SOMEONE THERE?!
WHO IS IT?
PANT
PANT

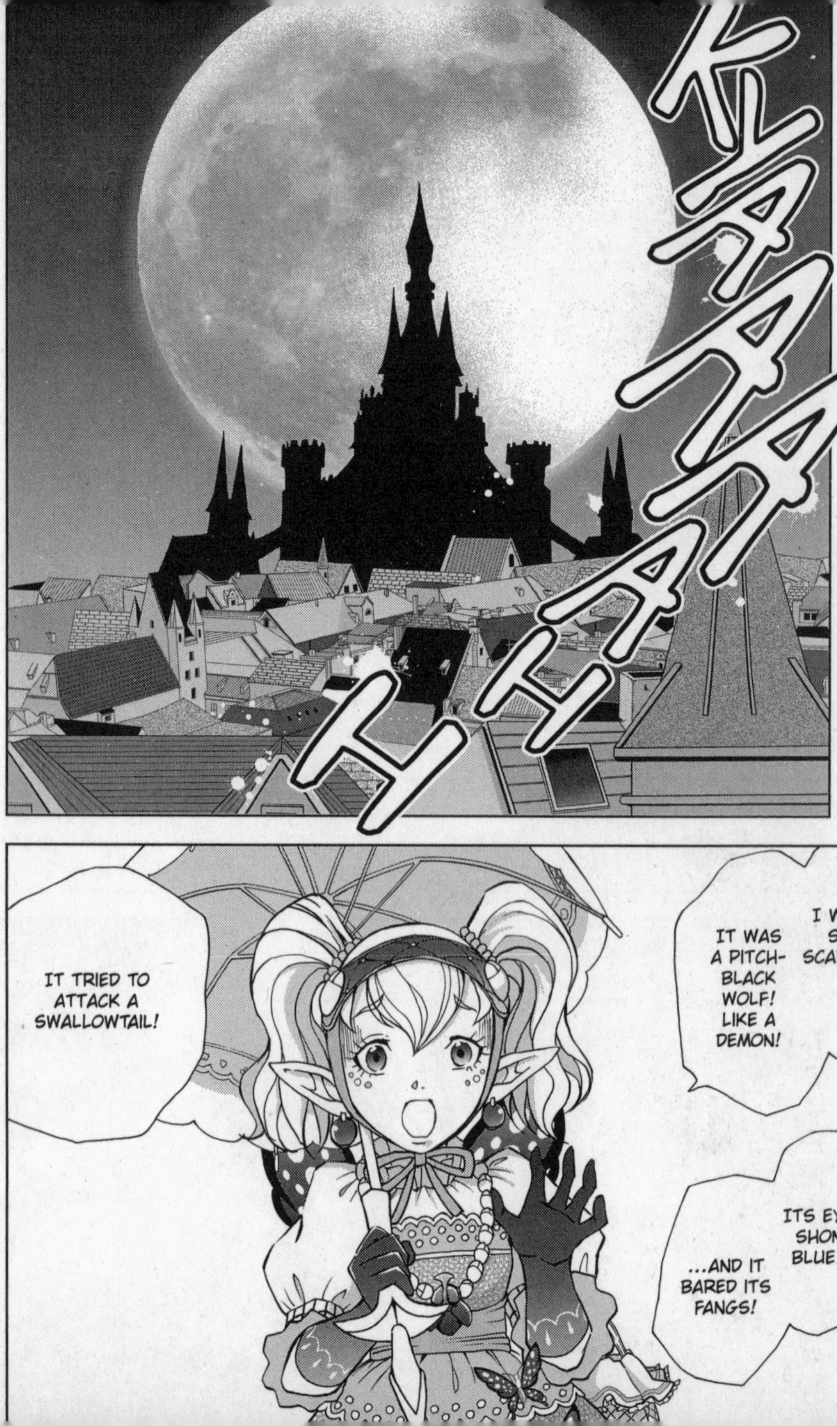
KYAAAAAHH
I WAS SO SCARED!
IT WAS A PITCH-BLACK WOLF! LIKE A DEMON!
IT TRIED TO ATTACK A SWALLOWTAIL!
ITS EYES SHONE BLUE...
...AND IT BARED ITS FANGS!

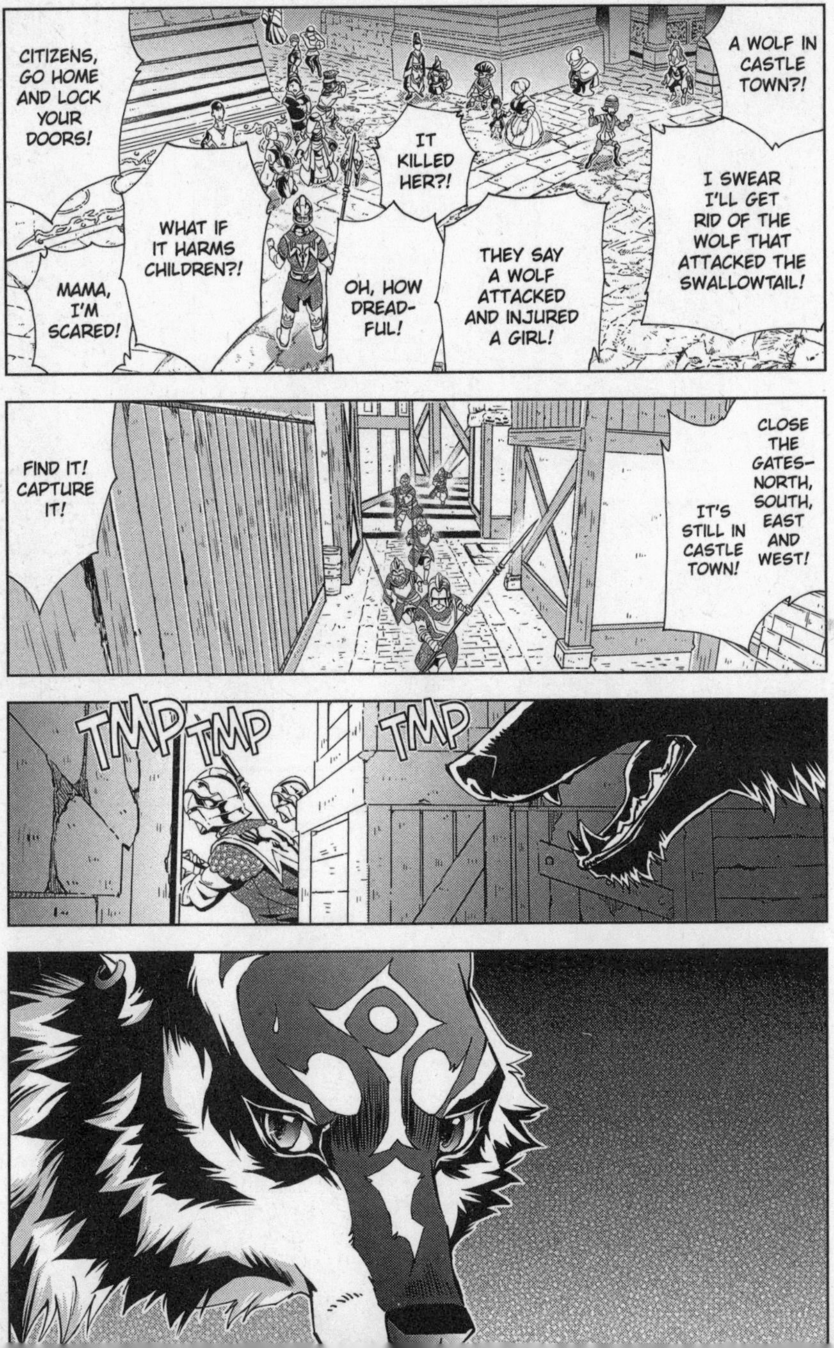
A WOLF IN CASTLE TOWN?!
I SWEAR I'LL GET RID OF THE WOLF THAT ATTACKED THE SWALLOWTAIL!
IT KILLED HER?!
THEY SAY A WOLF ATTACKED AND INJURED A GIRL!
OH, HOW DREAD-FUL!
CITIZENS, GO HOME AND LOCK YOUR DOORS!
WHAT IF IT HARMS CHILDREN?!
MAMA, I'M SCARED!
CLOSE THE GATES-NORTH, SOUTH, EAST AND WEST!
IT'S STILL IN CASTLE TOWN!
FIND IT! CAPTURE IT!
TMP
TMP
TMP

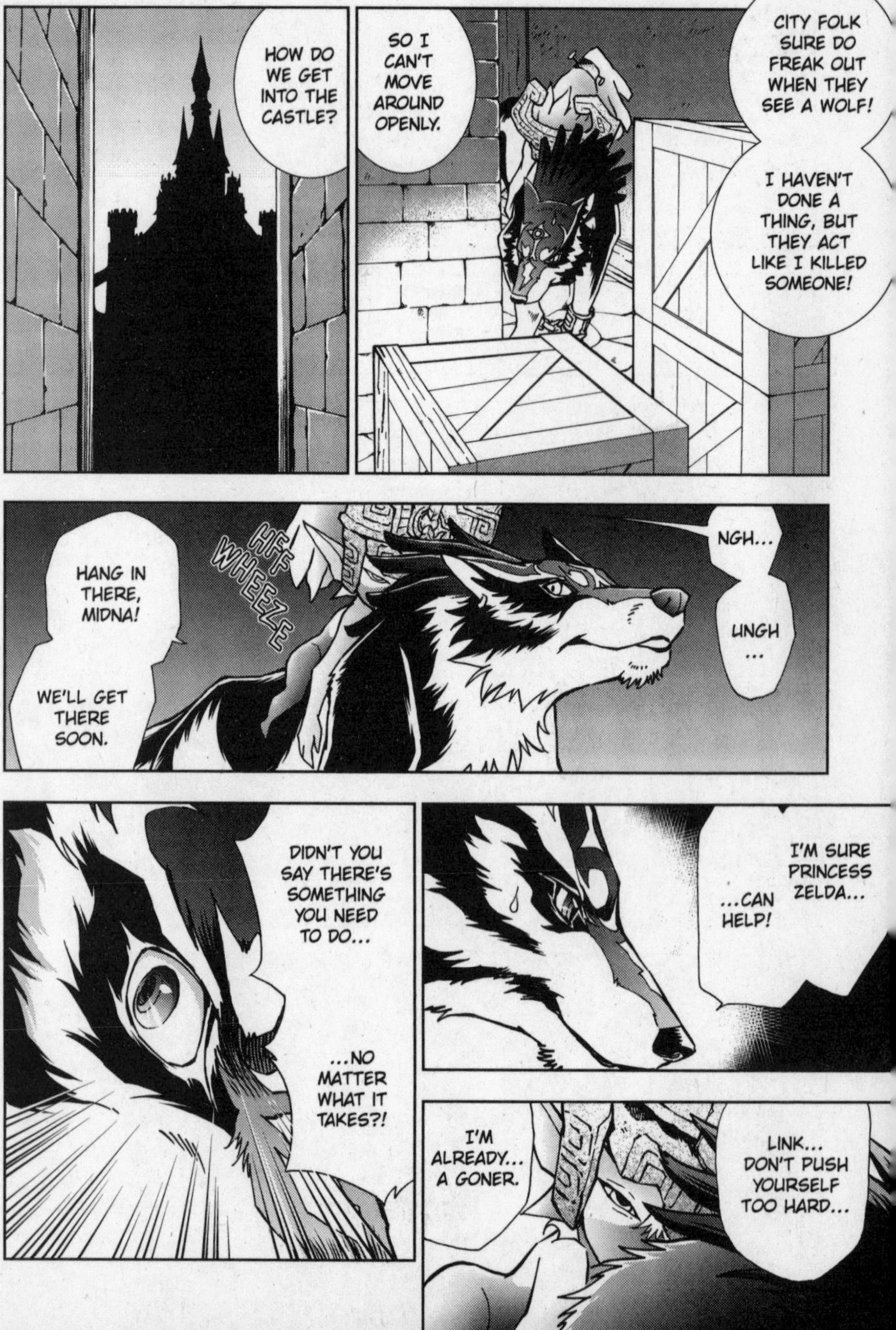
CITY FOLK SURE DO FREAK OUT WHEN THEY SEE A WOLF!
I HAVEN'T DONE A THING, BUT THEY ACT LIKE I KILLED SOMEONE!
SO I CAN'T MOVE AROUND OPENLY.
HOW DO WE GET INTO THE CASTLE?
NGH...
UNGH ...
HFF WHEEZE
HANG IN THERE, MIDNA!
WE'LL GET THERE SOON.
I'M SURE PRINCESS ZELDA...
...CAN HELP!
LINK... DON'T PUSH YOURSELF TOO HARD...
I'M ALREADY... A GONER.
DIDN'T YOU SAY THERE'S SOMETHING YOU NEED TO DO...
...NO MATTER WHAT IT TAKES?!

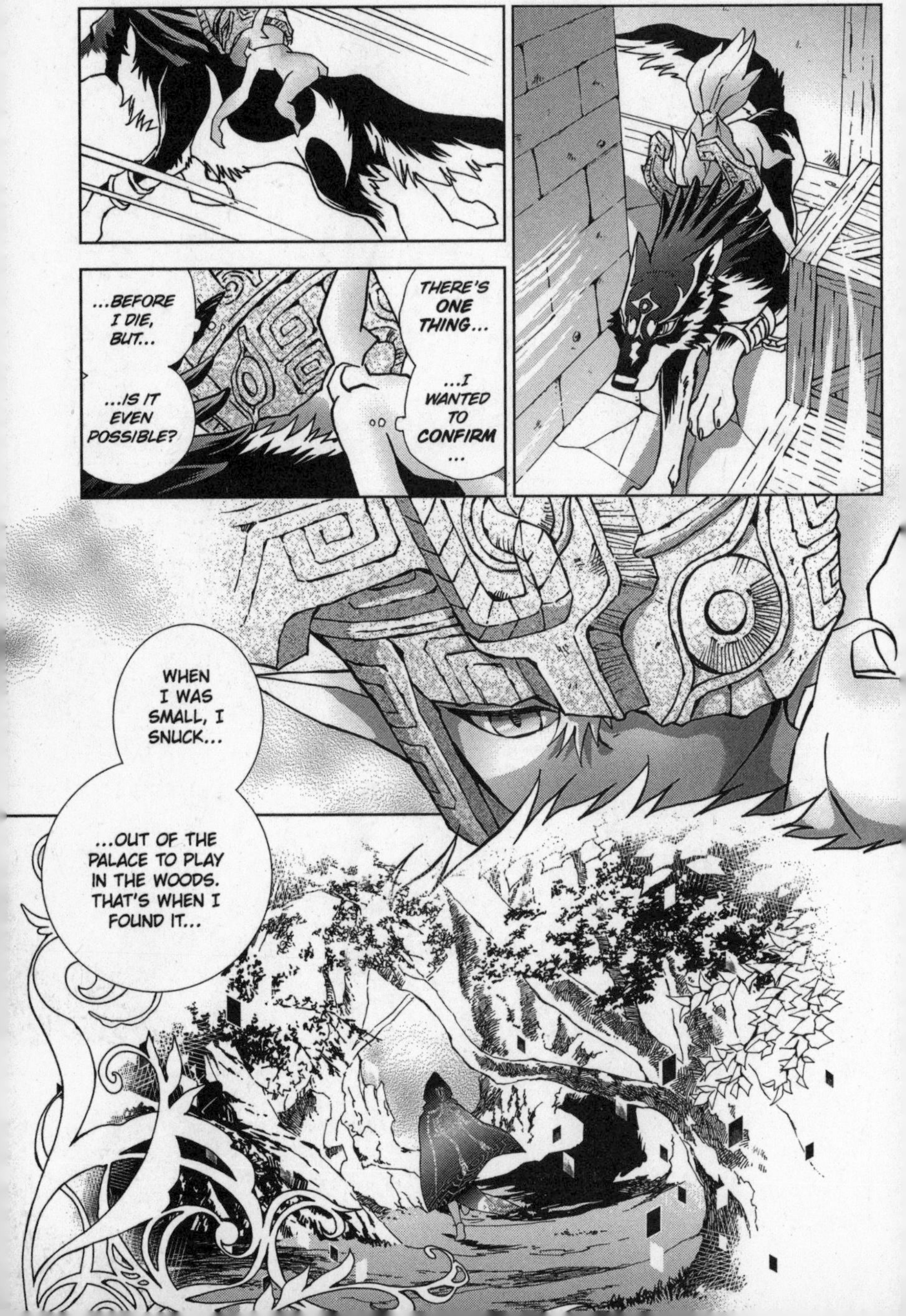
THERE'S ONE THING...
...I WANTED TO CONFIRM...
...BEFORE I DIE, BUT...
...IS IT EVEN POSSIBLE?
WHEN I WAS SMALL, I SNUCK...
...OUT OF THE PALACE TO PLAY IN THE WOODS. THAT'S WHEN I FOUND IT...

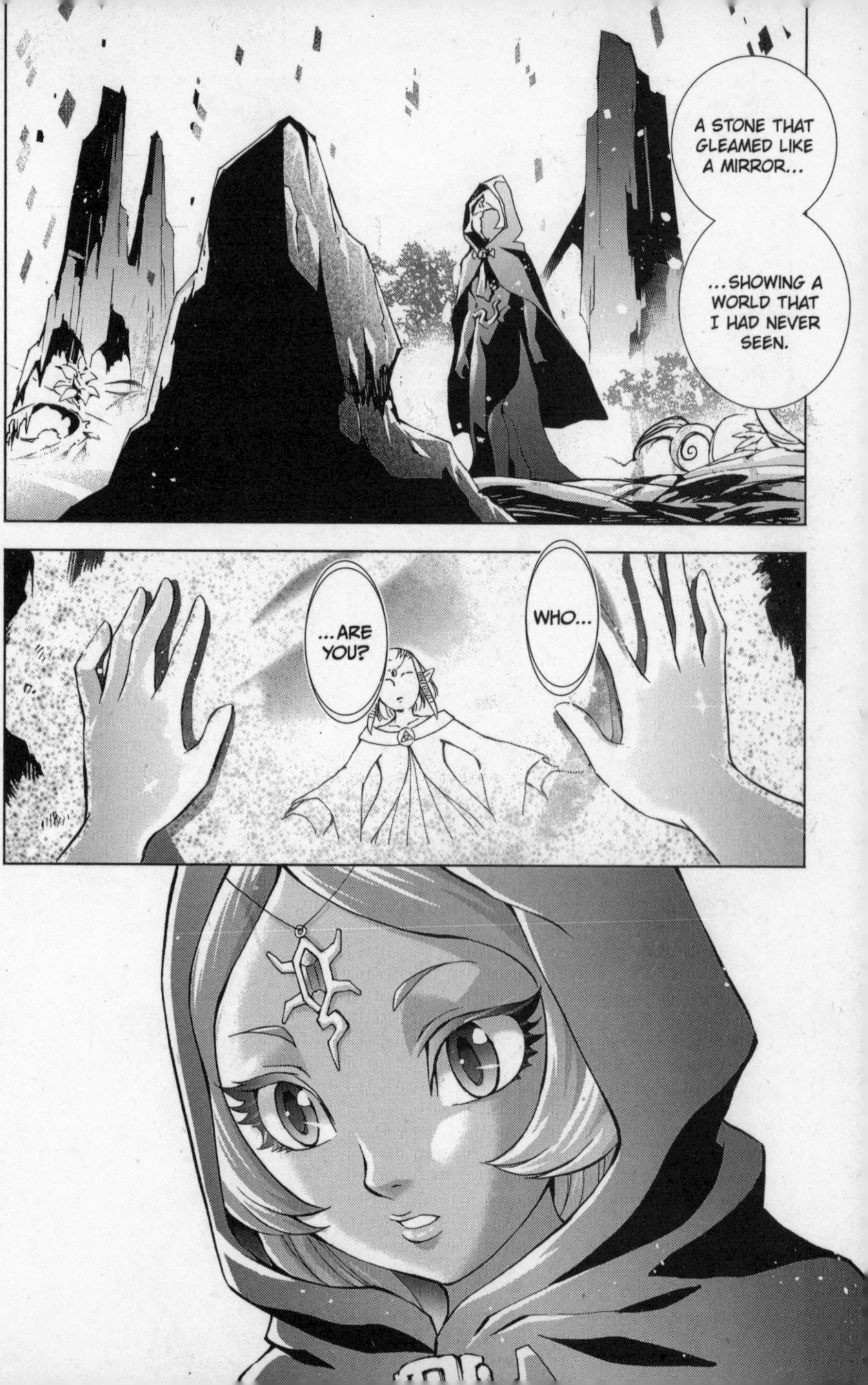
A STONE THAT GLEAMED LIKE A MIRROR...
...SHOWING A WORLD THAT I HAD NEVER SEEN.
WHO...
...ARE YOU?

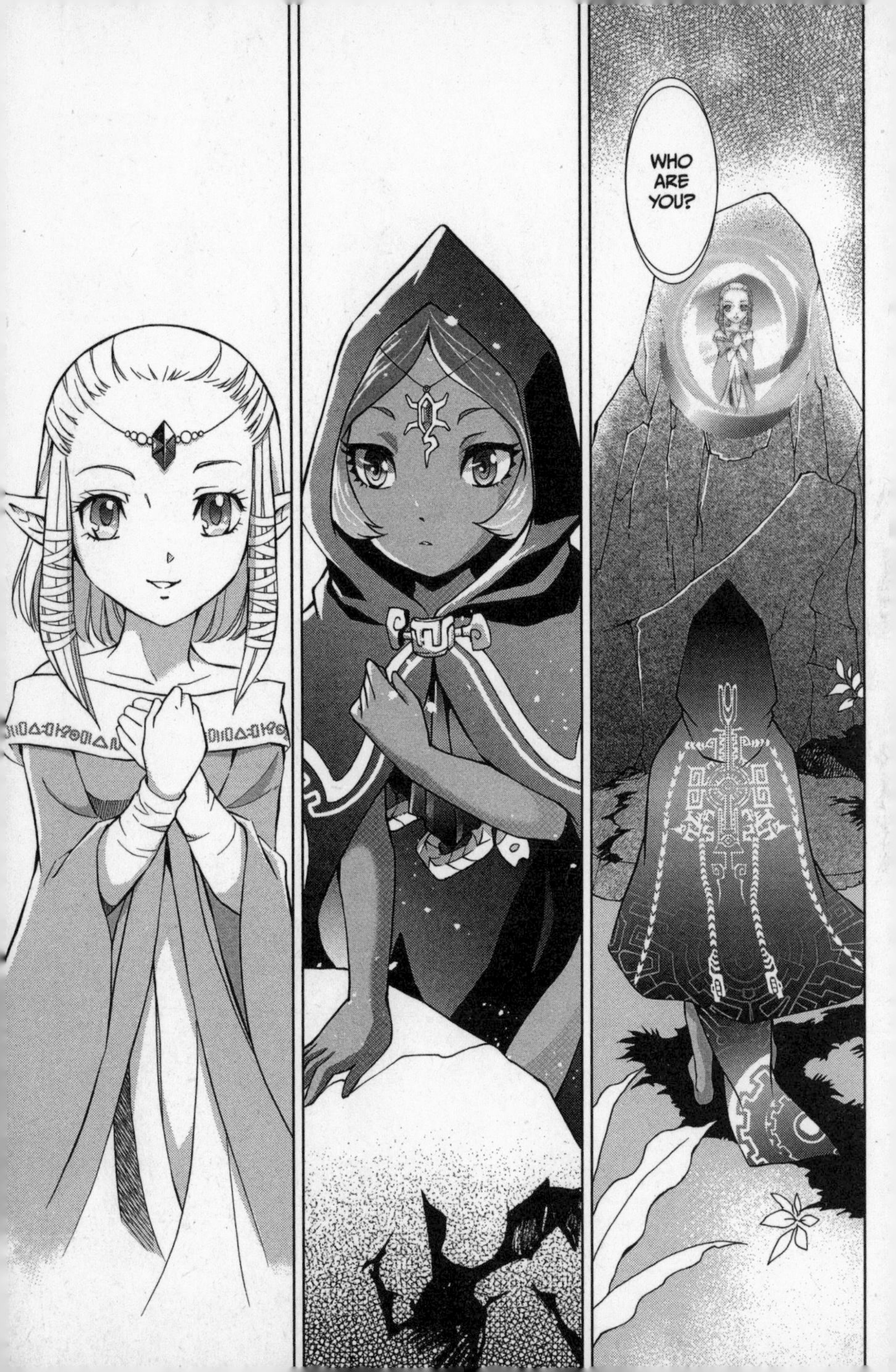
WHO ARE YOU?

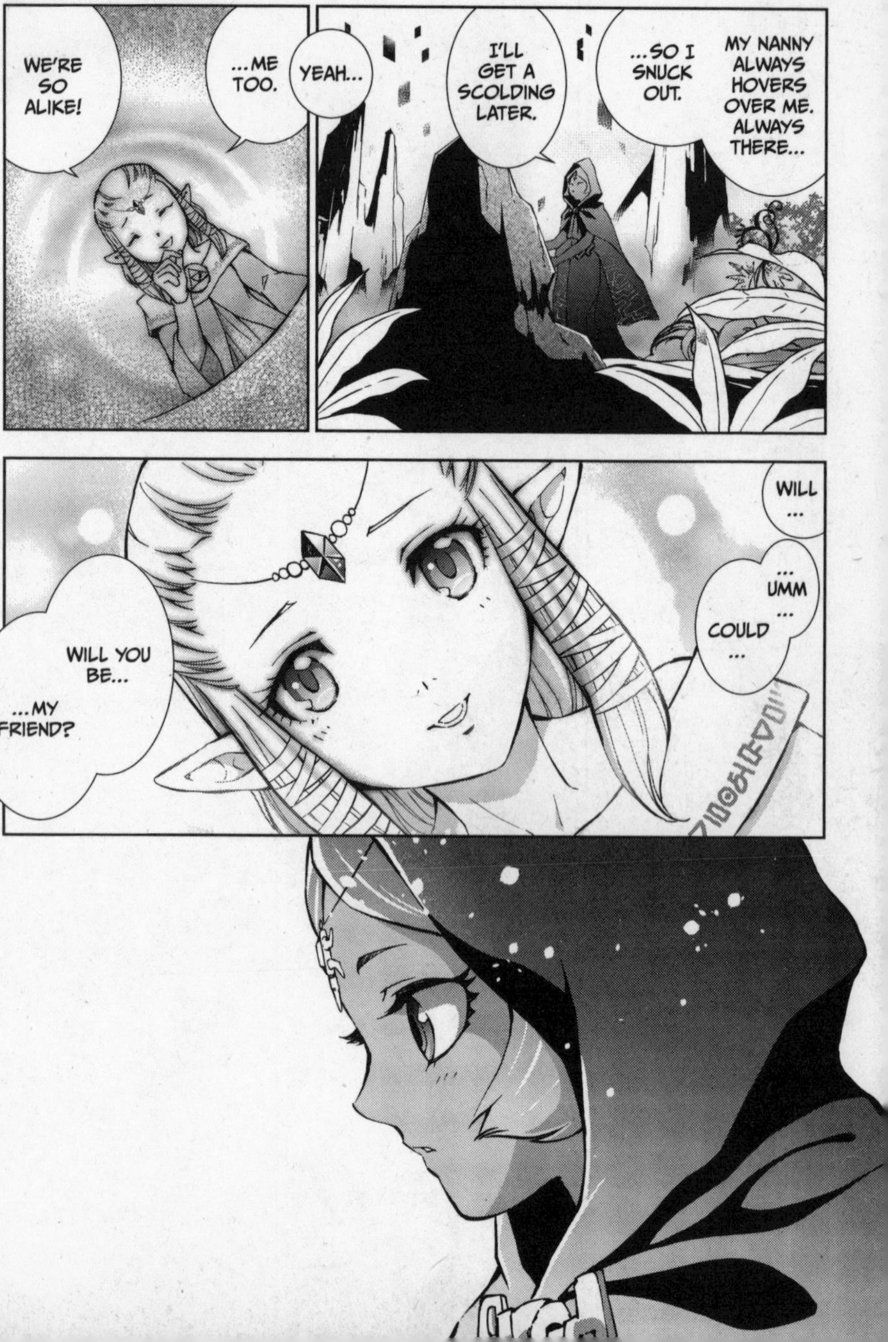
MY NANNY ALWAYS HOVERS OVER ME. ALWAYS THERE...
...SO I SNUCK OUT.
I'LL GET A SCOLDING LATER.
YEAH...
...ME TOO.
WE'RE SO ALIKE!
WILL ...
... UMM ...
COULD ...
WILL YOU BE...
...MY FRIEND?

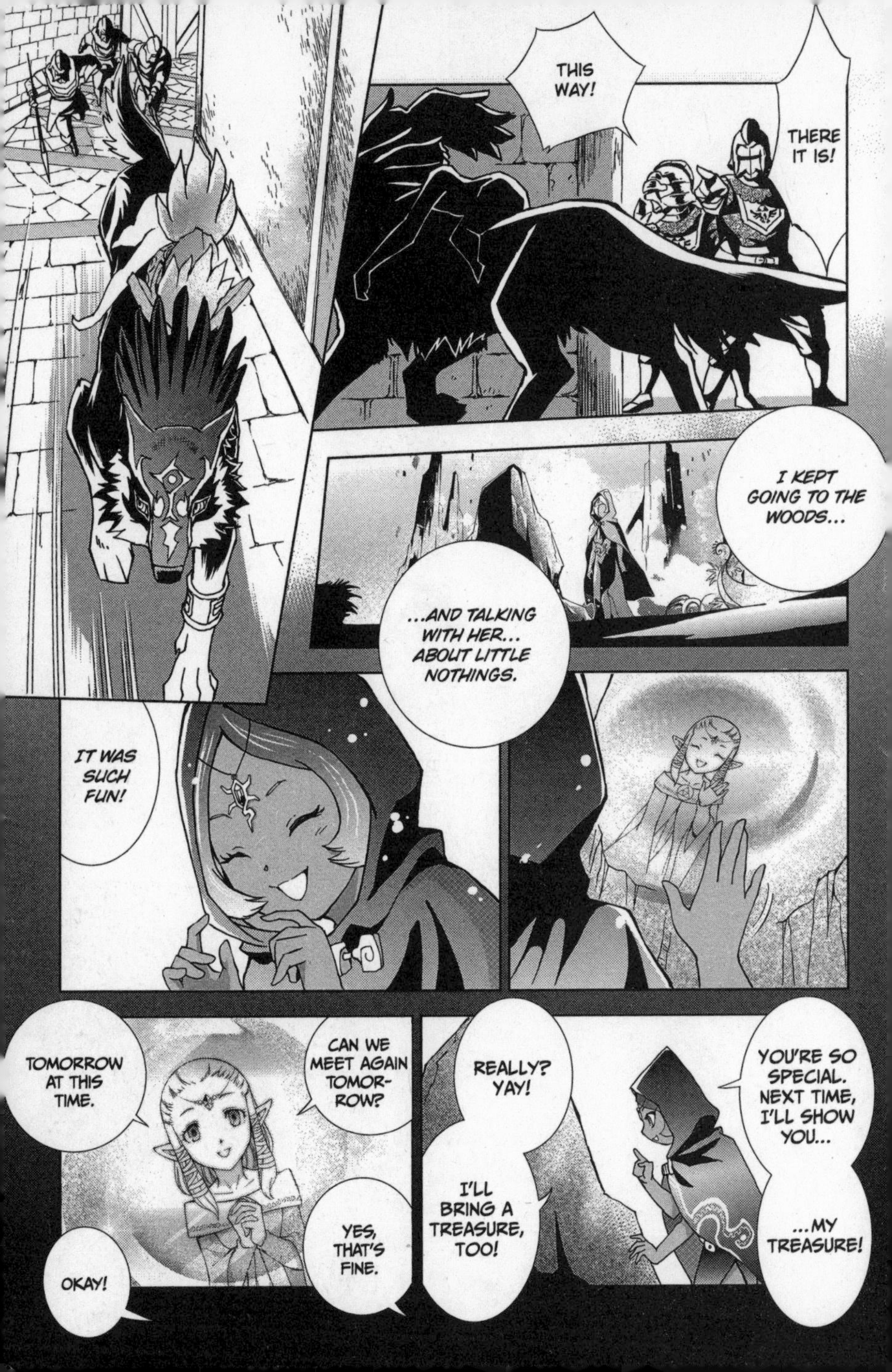
THIS WAY!
THERE IT IS!
I KEPT GOING TO THE WOODS...
...AND TALKING WITH HER... ABOUT LITTLE NOTHINGS.
IT WAS SUCH FUN!
YOU'RE SO SPECIAL. NEXT TIME, I'LL SHOW YOU...
REALLY? YAY!
...MY TREASURE!
I'LL BRING A TREASURE, TOO!
CAN WE MEET AGAIN TOMOR-ROW?
TOMORROW AT THIS TIME.
YES, THAT'S FINE.
OKAY!

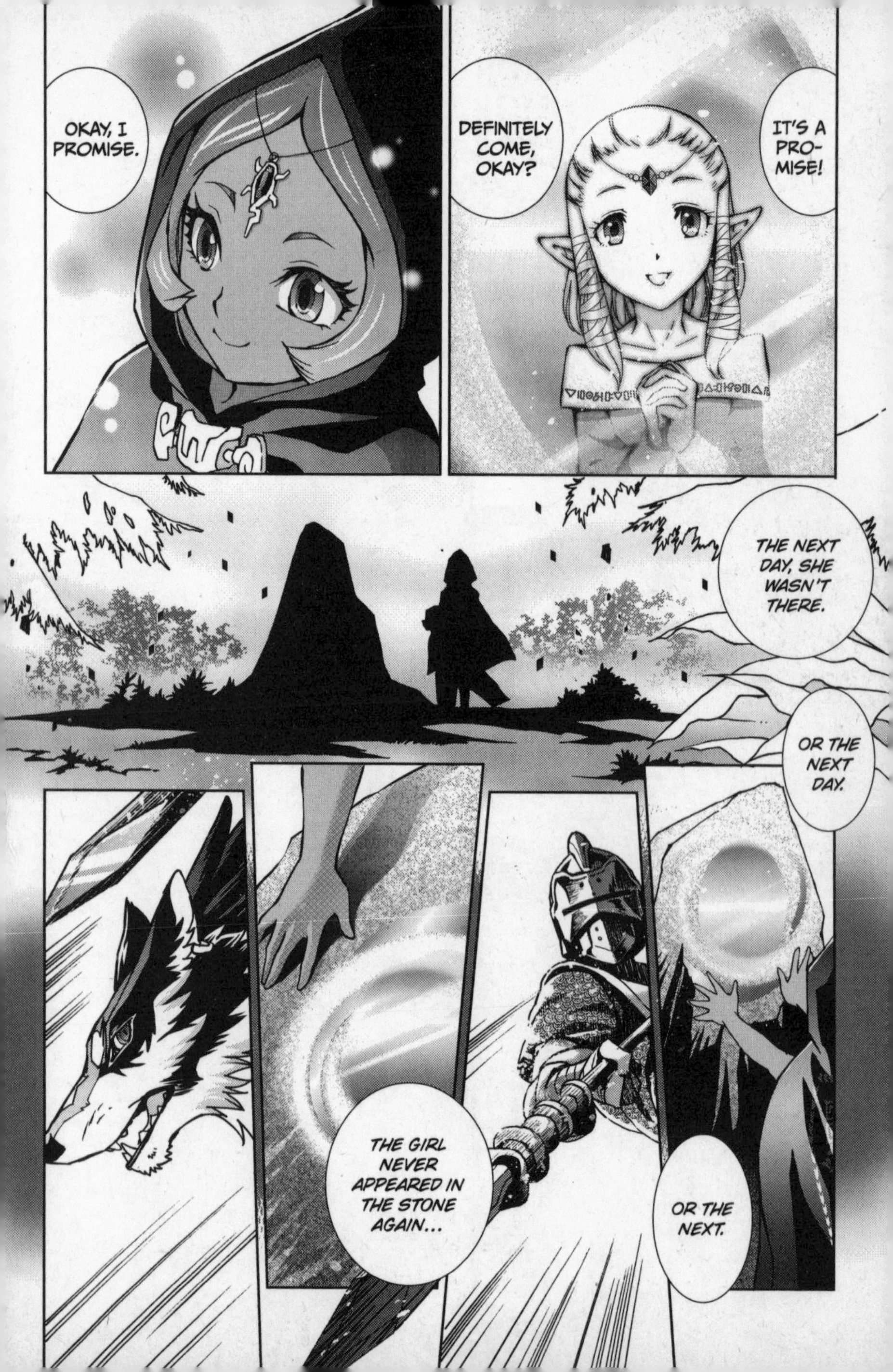
IT'S A PROMISE!
DEFINITELY COME, OKAY?
OKAY, I PROMISE.
THE NEXT DAY, SHE WASN'T THERE.
OR THE NEXT DAY.
OR THE NEXT.
THE GIRL NEVER APPEARED IN THE STONE AGAIN...

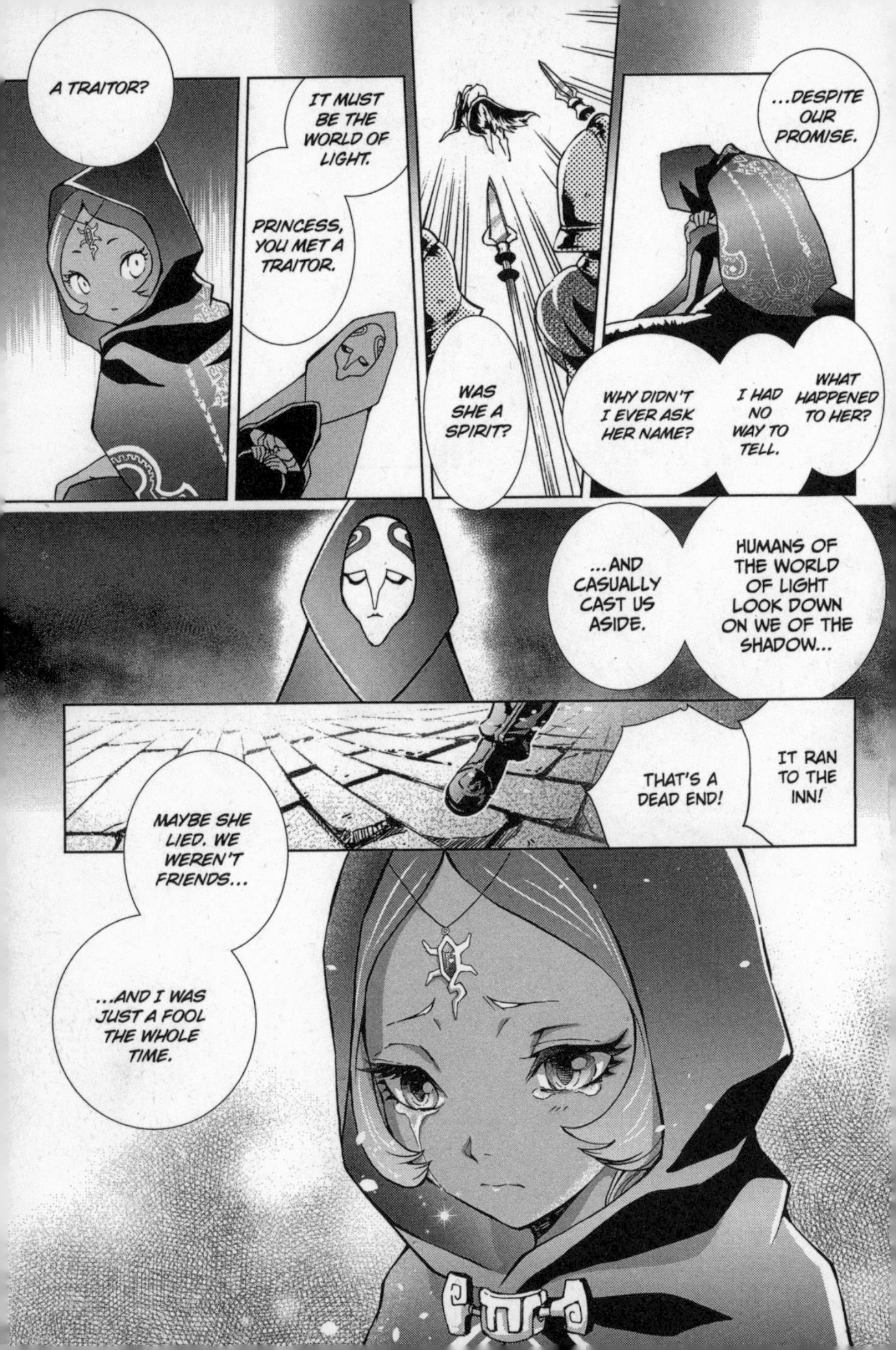
...DESPITE OUR PROMISE.
WHAT HAPPENED TO HER?
I HAD NO WAY TO TELL.
WHY DIDN'T I EVER ASK HER NAME?
WAS SHE A SPIRIT?
IT MUST BE THE WORLD OF LIGHT.
PRINCESS, YOU MET A TRAITOR.
A TRAITOR?
HUMANS OF THE WORLD OF LIGHT LOOK DOWN ON WE OF THE SHADOW...
...AND CASUALLY CAST US ASIDE.
IT RAN TO THE INN!
THAT'S A DEAD END!
MAYBE SHE LIED. WE WEREN'T FRIENDS...
...AND I WAS JUST A FOOL THE WHOLE TIME.

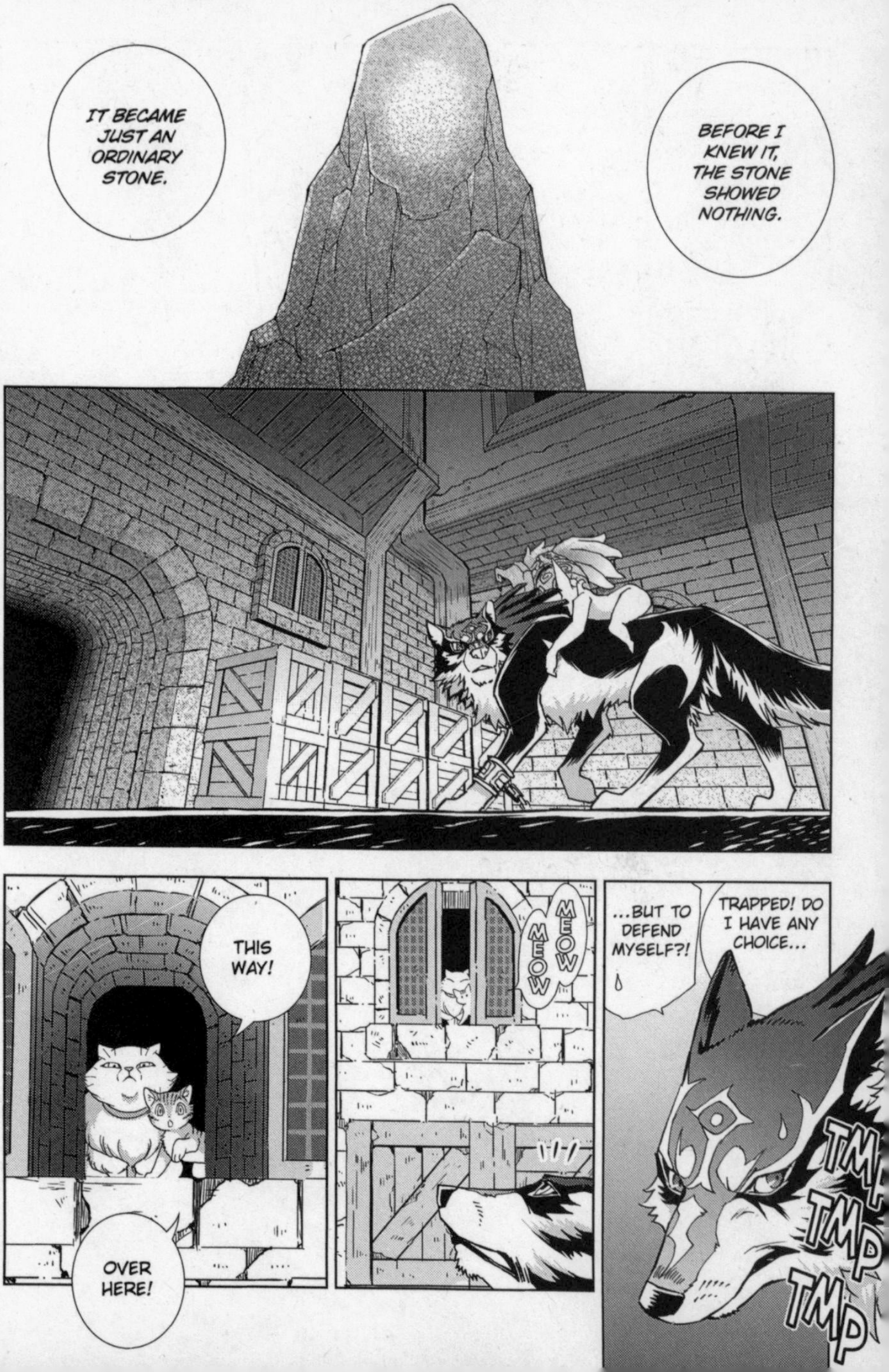
BEFORE I KNEW IT, THE STONE SHOWED NOTHING.
IT BECAME JUST AN ORDINARY STONE.
TRAPPED! DO I HAVE ANY CHOICE...
...BUT TO DEFEND MYSELF?!
TMP TMP TMP
MEOW MEOW
THIS WAY!
OVER HERE!

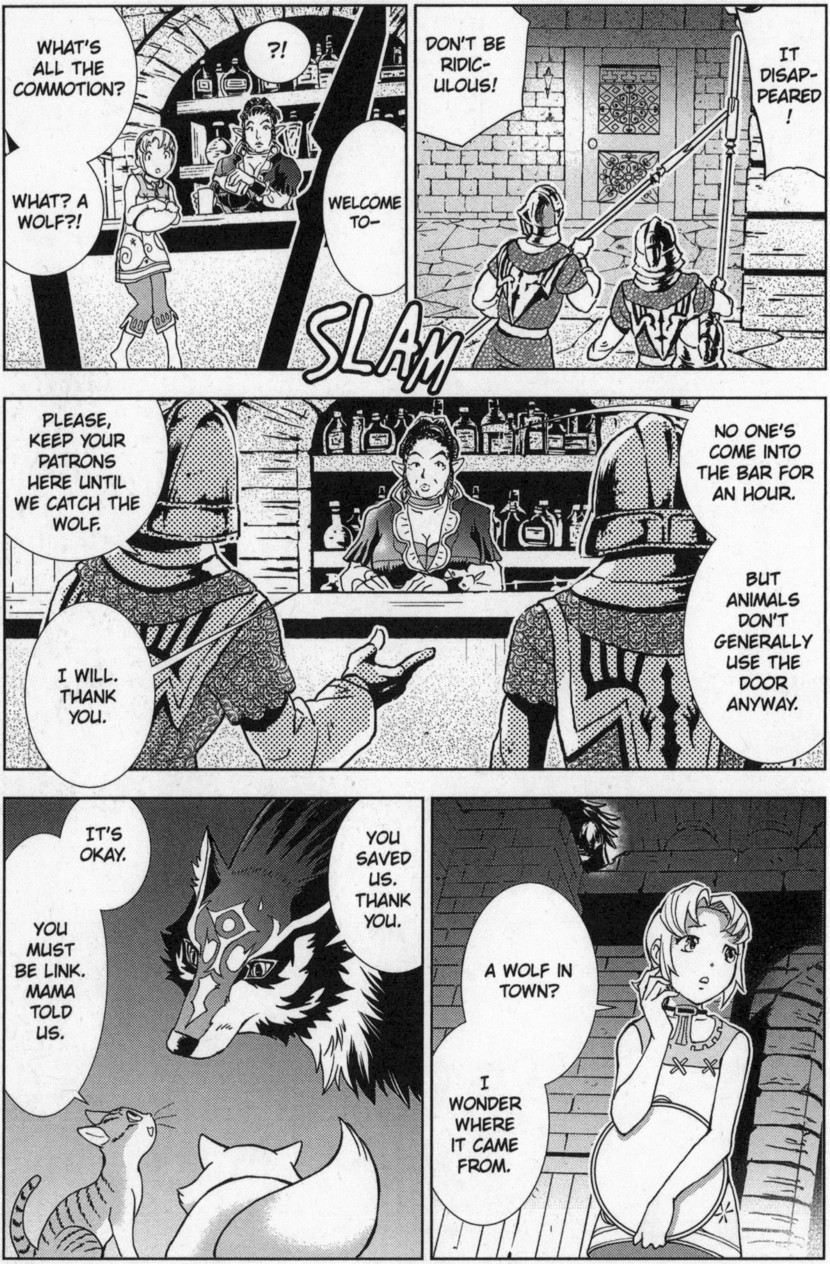
IT DISAPPEARED!
DON'T BE RIDICULOUS!
SLAM
?!
WHAT'S ALL THE COMMOTION?
WELCOME TO—
WHAT? A WOLF?!
NO ONE'S COME INTO THE BAR FOR AN HOUR.
BUT ANIMALS DON'T GENERALLY USE THE DOOR ANYWAY.
PLEASE, KEEP YOUR PATRONS HERE UNTIL WE CATCH THE WOLF.
I WILL. THANK YOU.
A WOLF IN TOWN?
I WONDER WHERE IT CAME FROM.
YOU SAVED US. THANK YOU.
IT'S OKAY.
YOU MUST BE LINK. MAMA TOLD US.

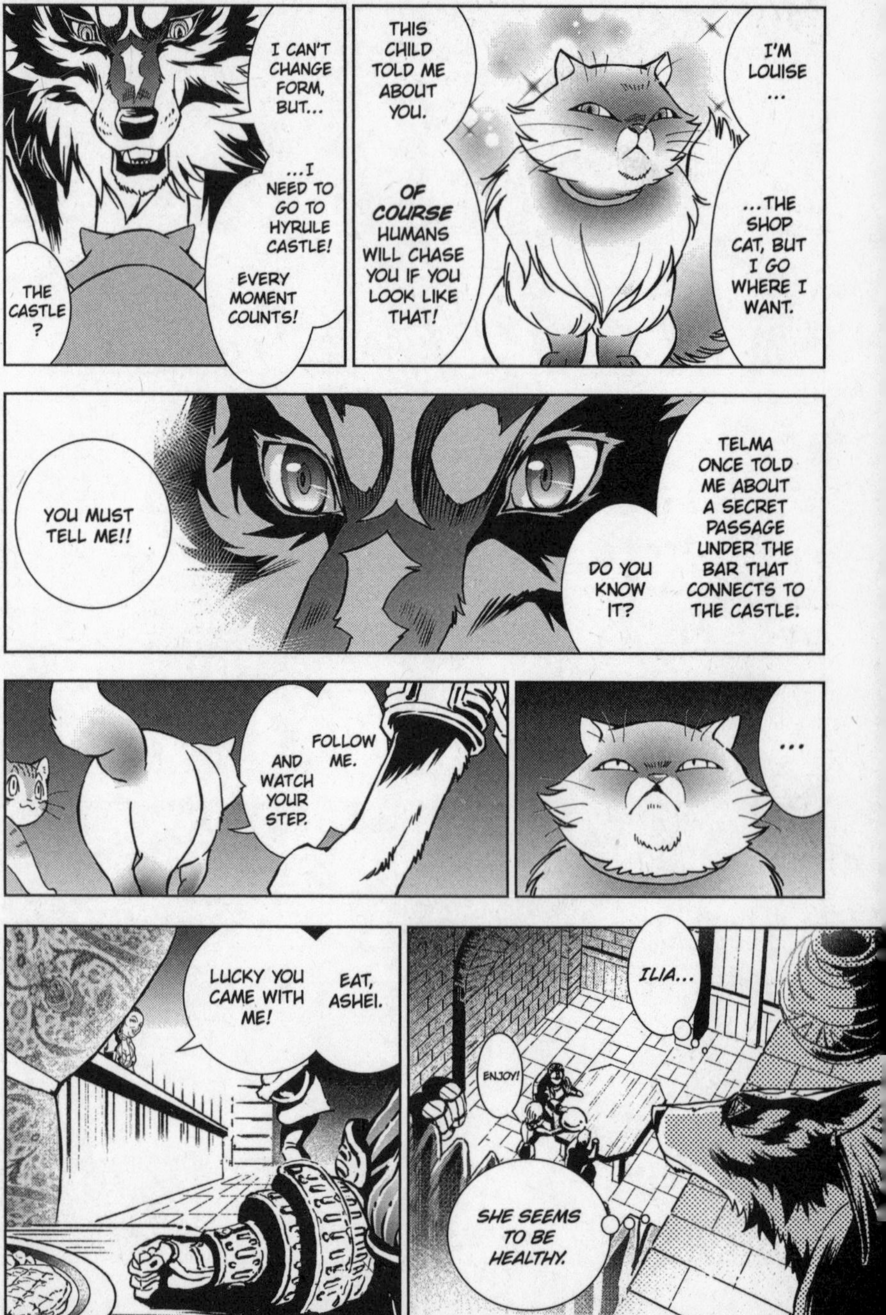
I'M LOUISE ...
...THE SHOP CAT, BUT I GO WHERE I WANT.
THIS CHILD TOLD ME ABOUT YOU.
OF COURSE HUMANS WILL CHASE YOU IF YOU LOOK LIKE THAT!
I CAN'T CHANGE FORM, BUT...
...I NEED TO GO TO HYRULE CASTLE!
EVERY MOMENT COUNTS!
THE CASTLE?
TELMA ONCE TOLD ME ABOUT A SECRET PASSAGE UNDER THE BAR THAT CONNECTS TO THE CASTLE.
DO YOU KNOW IT?
YOU MUST TELL ME!!
...
FOLLOW ME.
AND WATCH YOUR STEP.
ILIA...
ENJOY!
SHE SEEMS TO BE HEALTHY.
EAT, ASHEI.
LUCKY YOU CAME WITH ME!

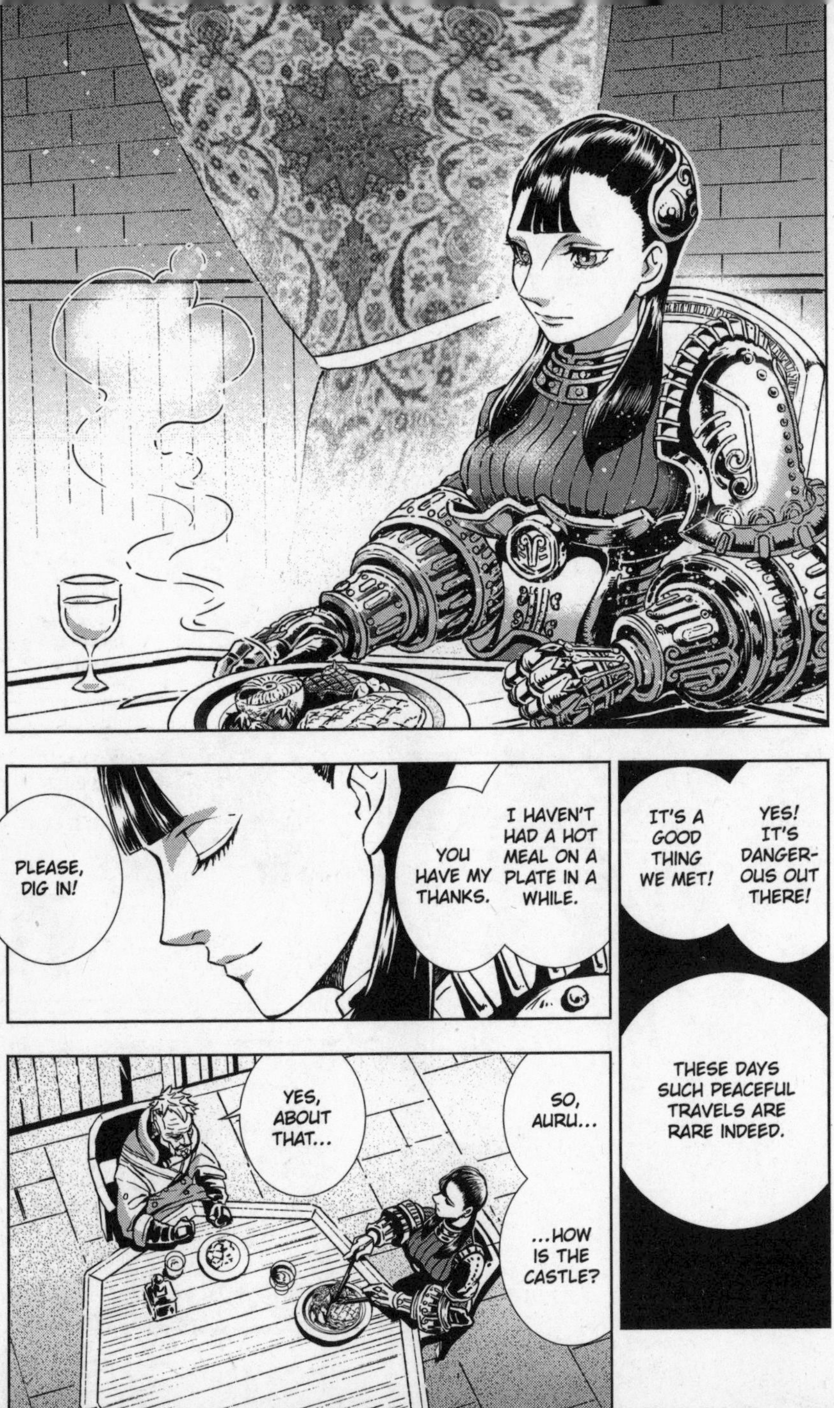
YES! IT'S DANGER-OUS OUT THERE!
IT'S A GOOD THING WE MET!
THESE DAYS SUCH PEACEFUL TRAVELS ARE RARE INDEED.
I HAVEN'T HAD A HOT MEAL ON A PLATE IN A WHILE.
YOU HAVE MY THANKS.
PLEASE, DIG IN!
SO, AURU...
...HOW IS THE CASTLE?
YES, ABOUT THAT...

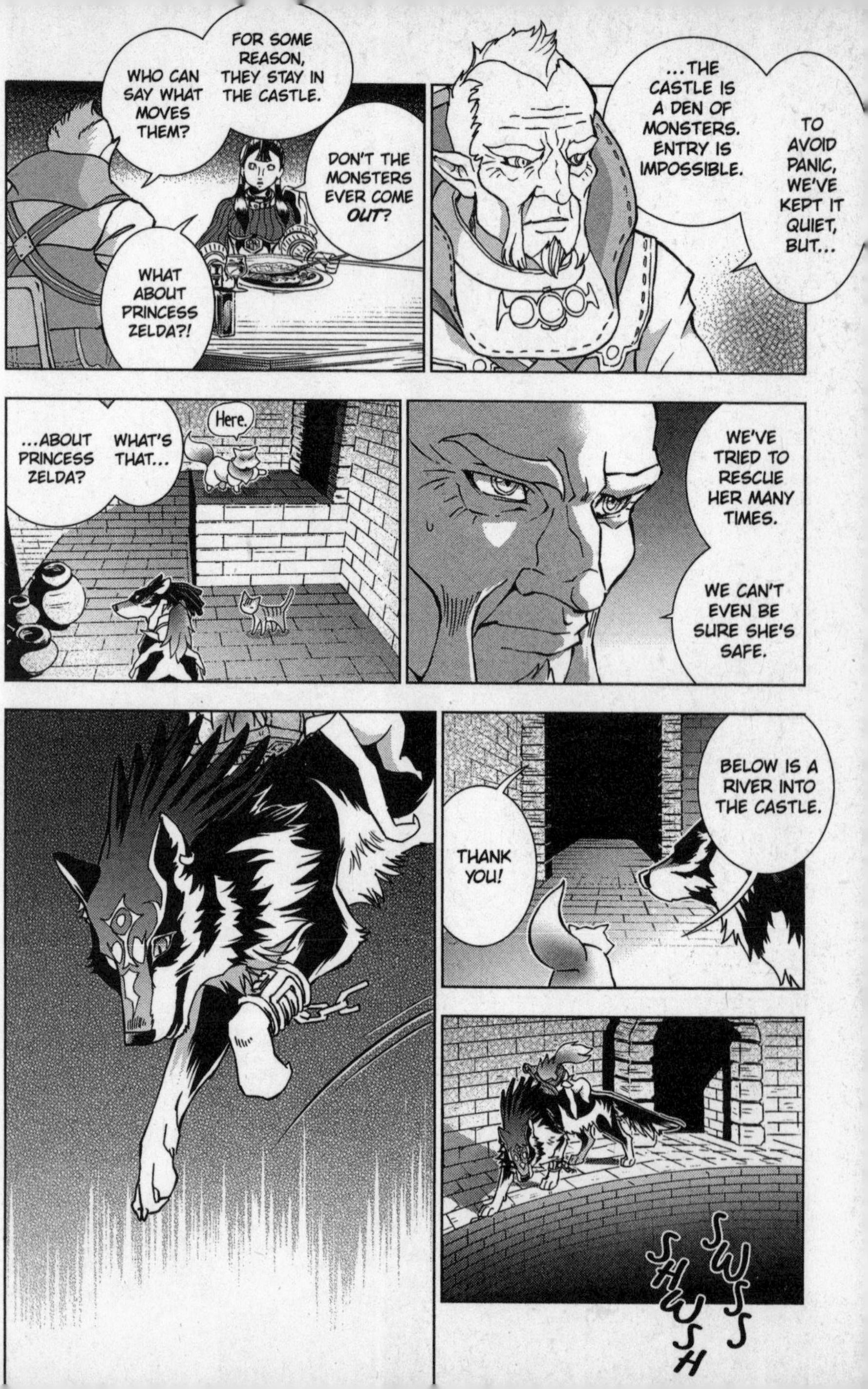
...THE CASTLE IS A DEN OF MONSTERS. ENTRY IS IMPOSSIBLE.
TO AVOID PANIC, WE'VE KEPT IT QUIET, BUT...
FOR SOME REASON, THEY STAY IN THE CASTLE.
WHO CAN SAY WHAT MOVES THEM?
DON'T THE MONSTERS EVER COME OUT?
WHAT ABOUT PRINCESS ZELDA?!
WE'VE TRIED TO RESCUE HER MANY TIMES.
WE CAN'T EVEN BE SURE SHE'S SAFE.
Here.
WHAT'S THAT...
...ABOUT PRINCESS ZELDA?
BELOW IS A RIVER INTO THE CASTLE.
THANK YOU!
SWSS
SHWSH

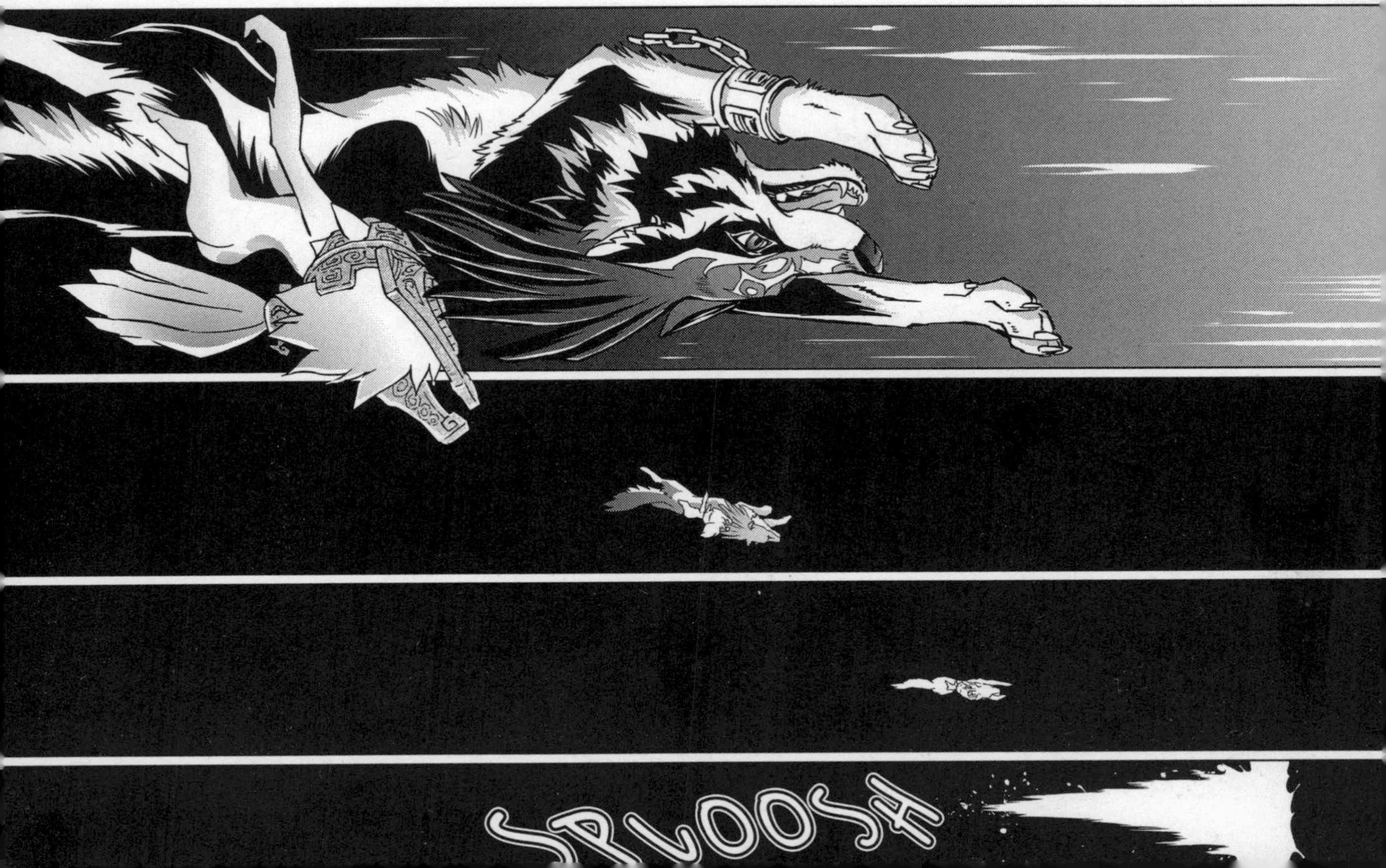
SPLOOSH

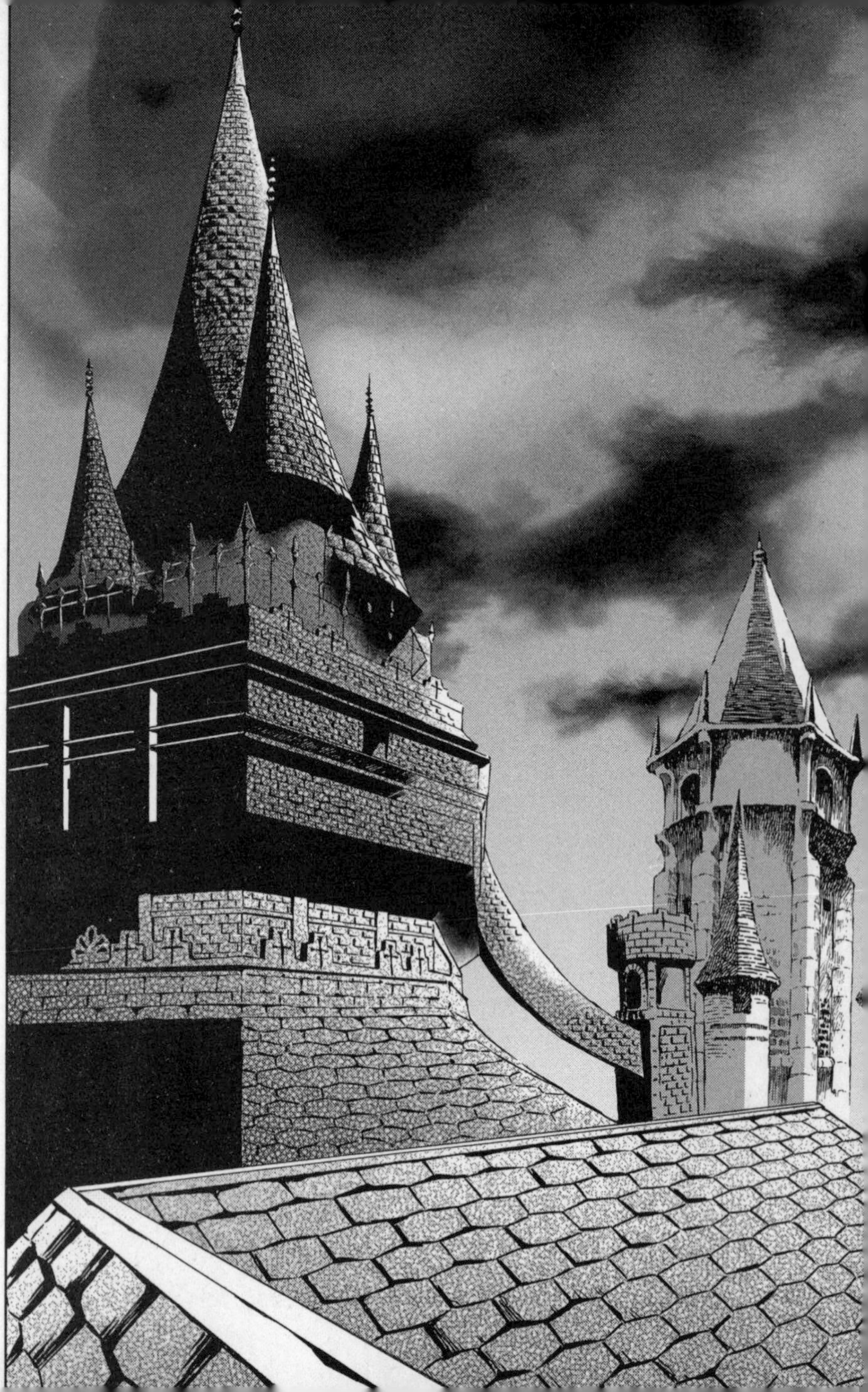

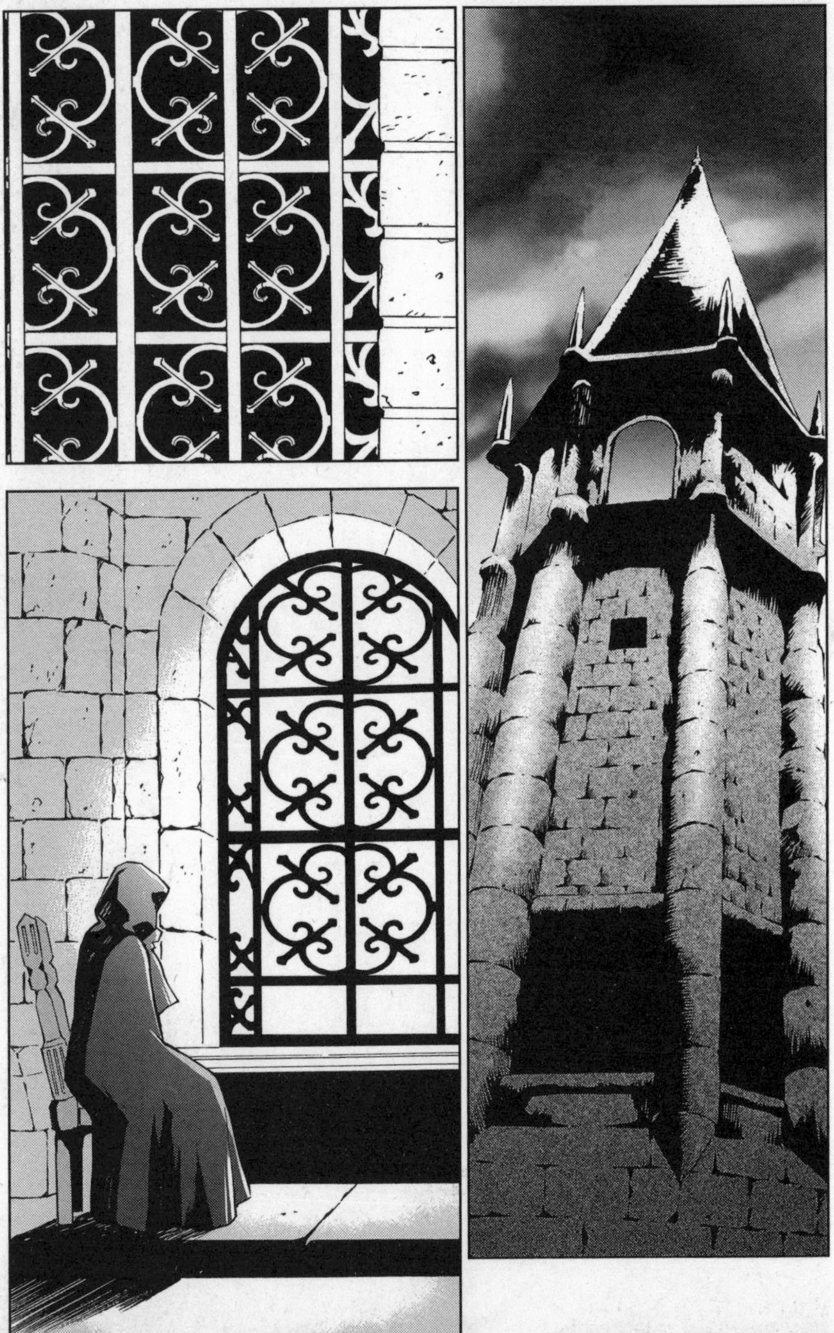

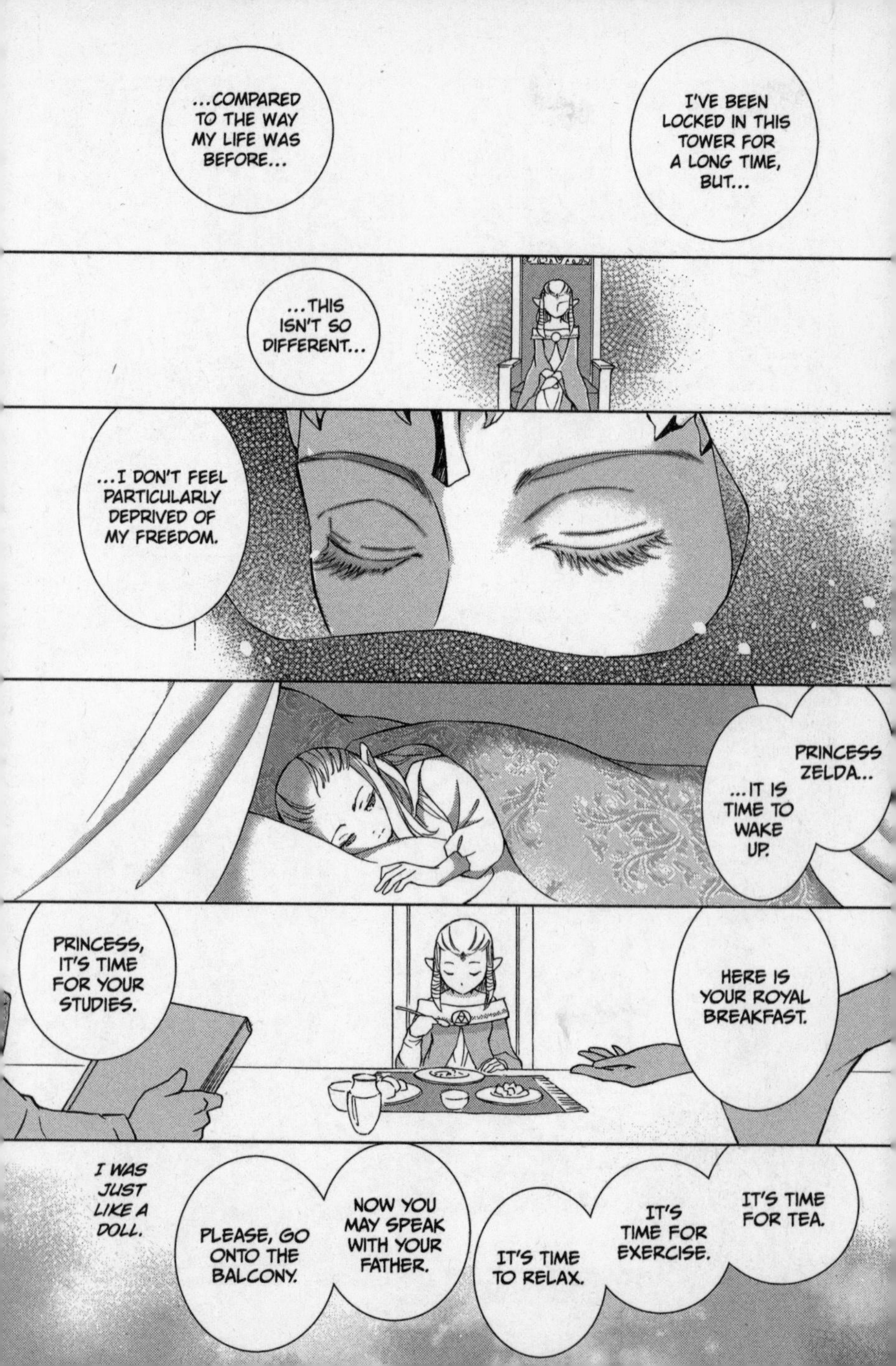
I'VE BEEN LOCKED IN THIS TOWER FOR A LONG TIME, BUT...
...COMPARED TO THE WAY MY LIFE WAS BEFORE...
...THIS ISN'T SO DIFFERENT...
...I DON'T FEEL PARTICULARLY DEPRIVED OF MY FREEDOM.
PRINCESS ZELDA...
...IT IS TIME TO WAKE UP.
HERE IS YOUR ROYAL BREAKFAST.
PRINCESS, IT'S TIME FOR YOUR STUDIES.
IT'S TIME FOR TEA.
IT'S TIME FOR EXERCISE.
IT'S TIME TO RELAX.
NOW YOU MAY SPEAK WITH YOUR FATHER.
PLEASE, GO ONTO THE BALCONY.
I WAS JUST LIKE A DOLL.

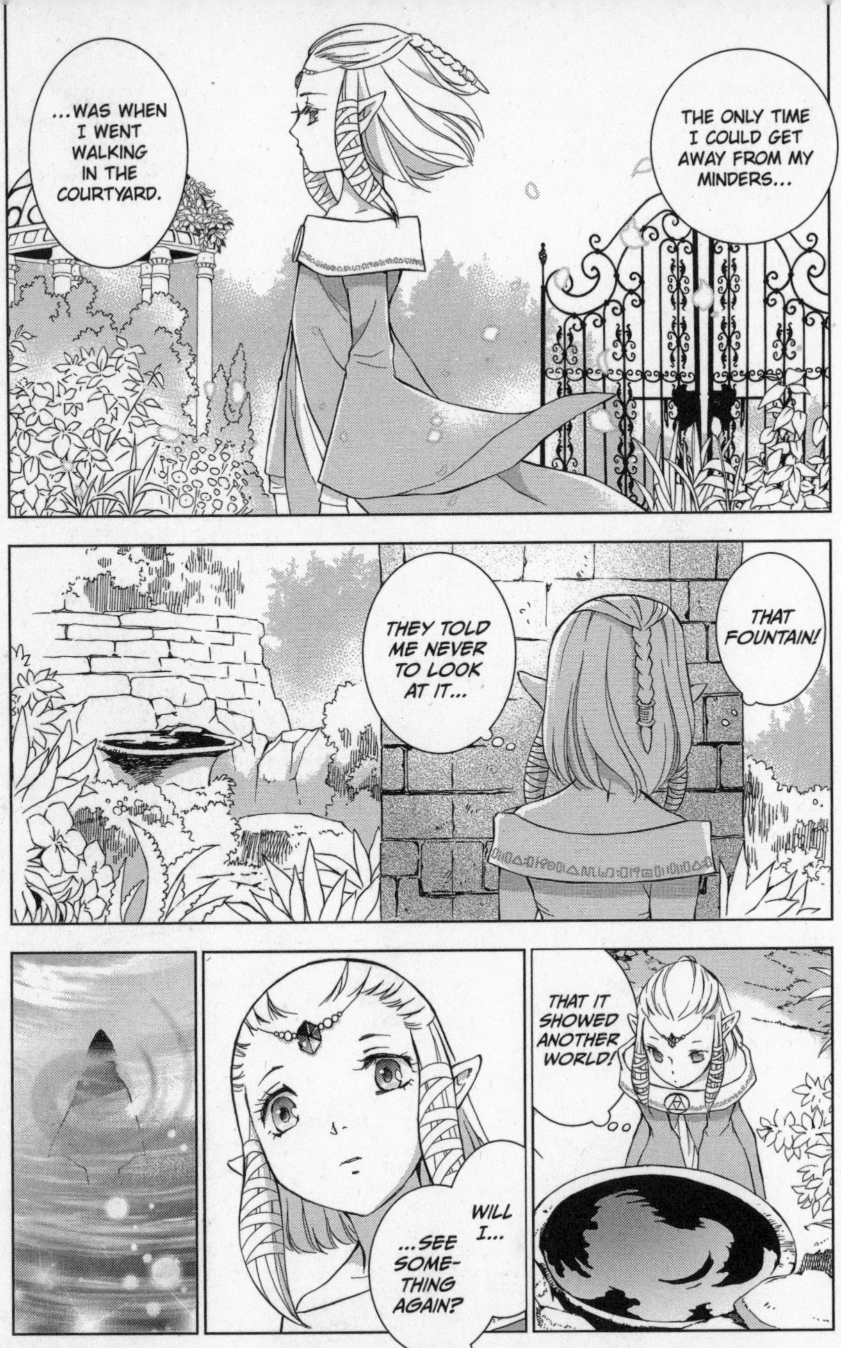
THE ONLY TIME I COULD GET AWAY FROM MY MINDERS...
...WAS WHEN I WENT WALKING IN THE COURTYARD.
THAT FOUNTAIN!
THEY TOLD ME NEVER TO LOOK AT IT...
THAT IT SHOWED ANOTHER WORLD!
WILL I...
...SEE SOME-THING AGAIN?

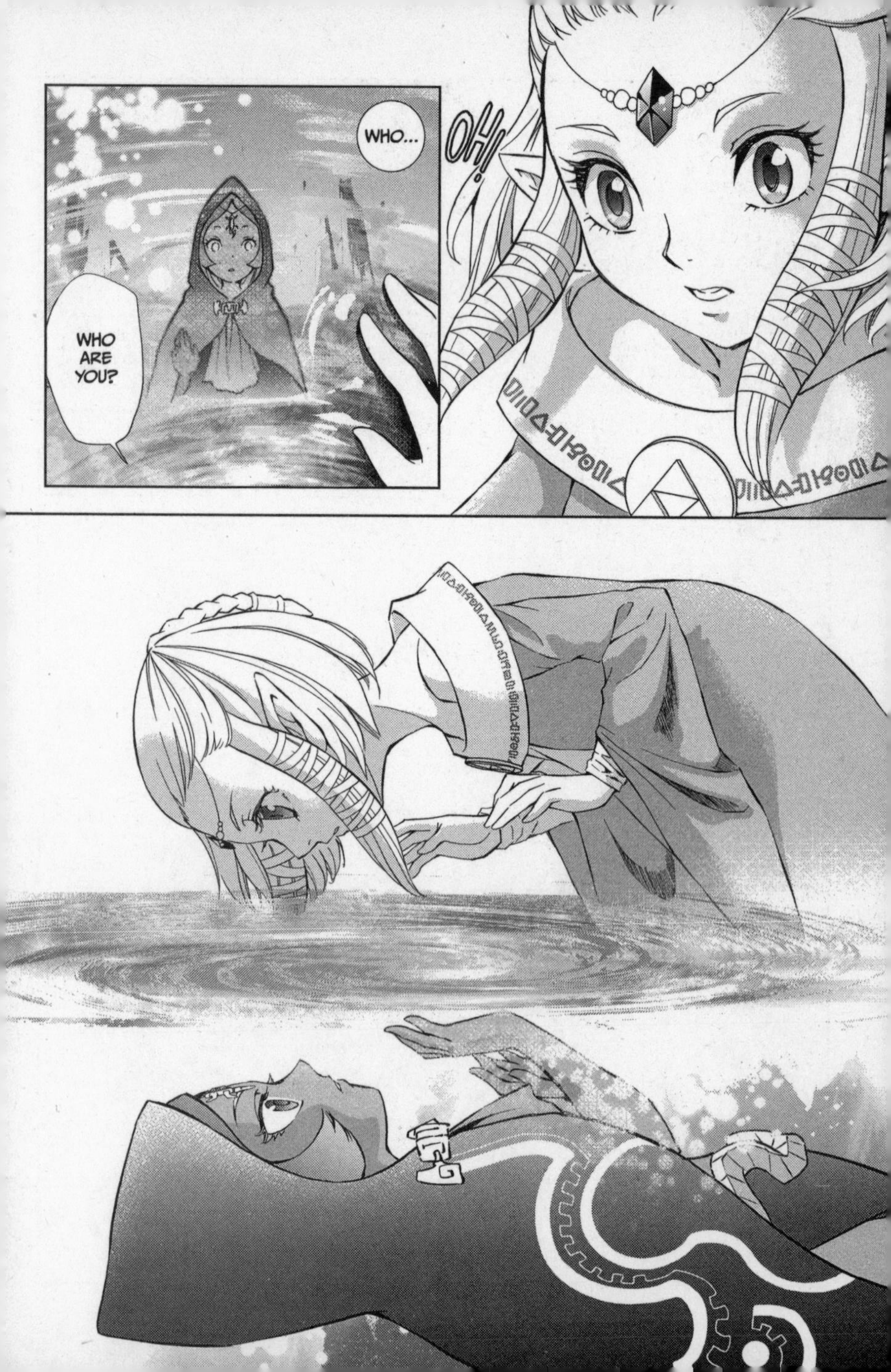
OH!
WHO...
WHO ARE YOU?

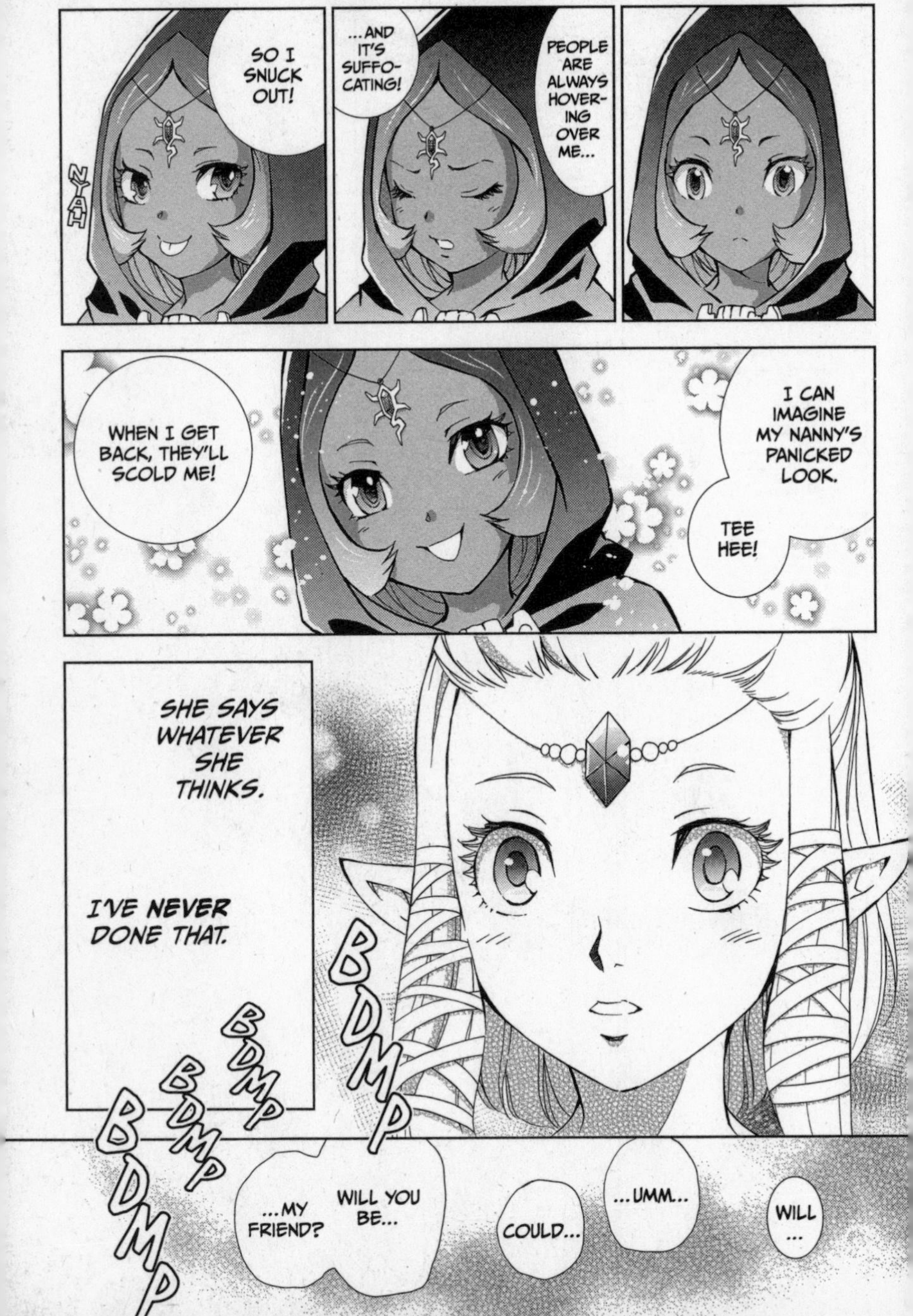
PEOPLE ARE ALWAYS HOVERING OVER ME...
...AND IT'S SUFFOCATING!
SO I SNUCK OUT!
NYAH
I CAN IMAGINE MY NANNY'S PANICKED LOOK.
TEE HEE!
WHEN I GET BACK, THEY'LL SCOLD ME!
SHE SAYS WHATEVER SHE THINKS.
I'VE NEVER DONE THAT.
BDMP
BDMP
BDMP
BDMP
WILL ...
...UMM...
COULD...
WILL YOU BE...
...MY FRIEND?

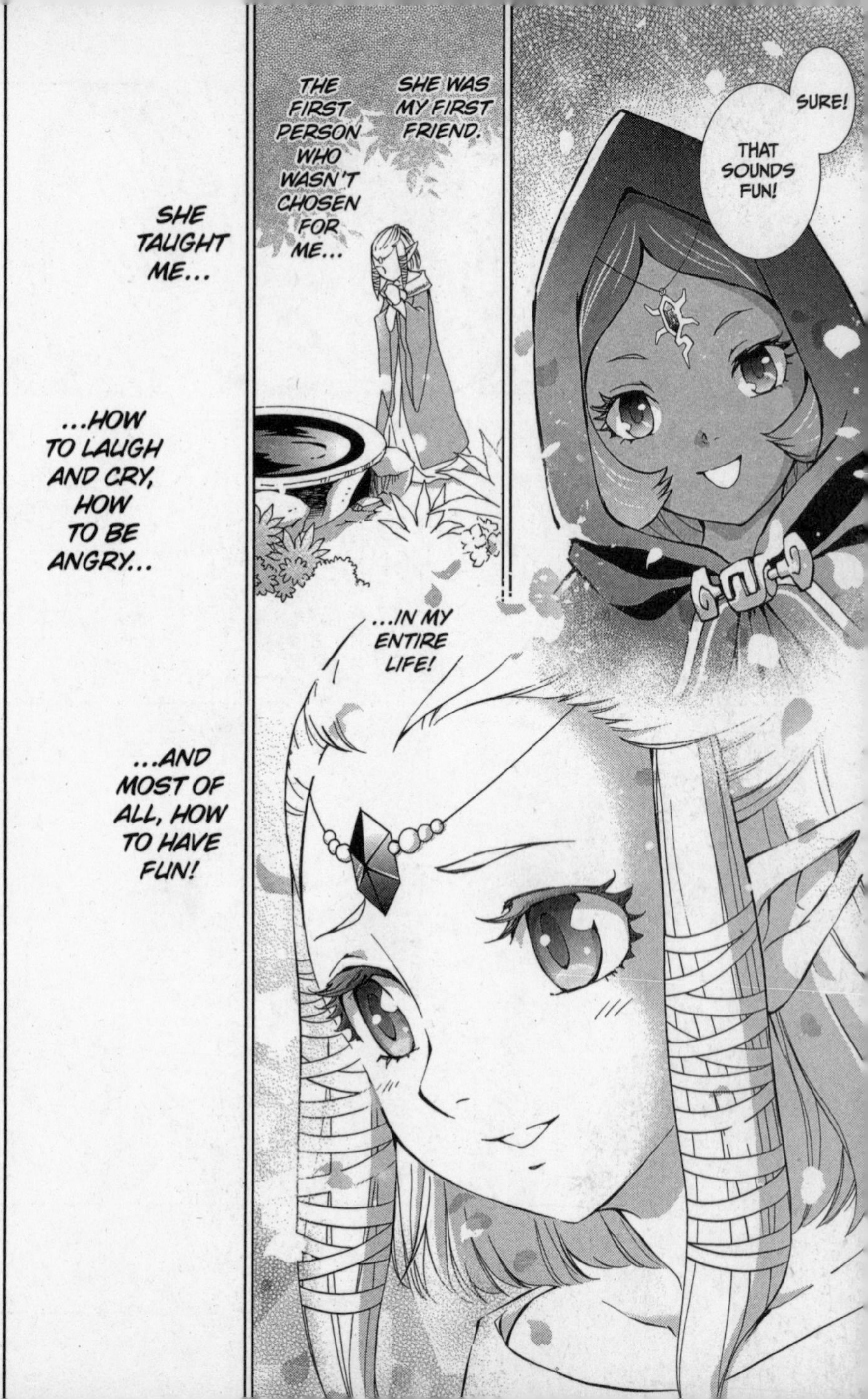
SURE!
THAT SOUNDS FUN!
SHE WAS MY FIRST FRIEND.
THE FIRST PERSON WHO WASN'T CHOSEN FOR ME...
...IN MY ENTIRE LIFE!
SHE TAUGHT ME...
...HOW TO LAUGH AND CRY, HOW TO BE ANGRY...
...AND MOST OF ALL, HOW TO HAVE FUN!

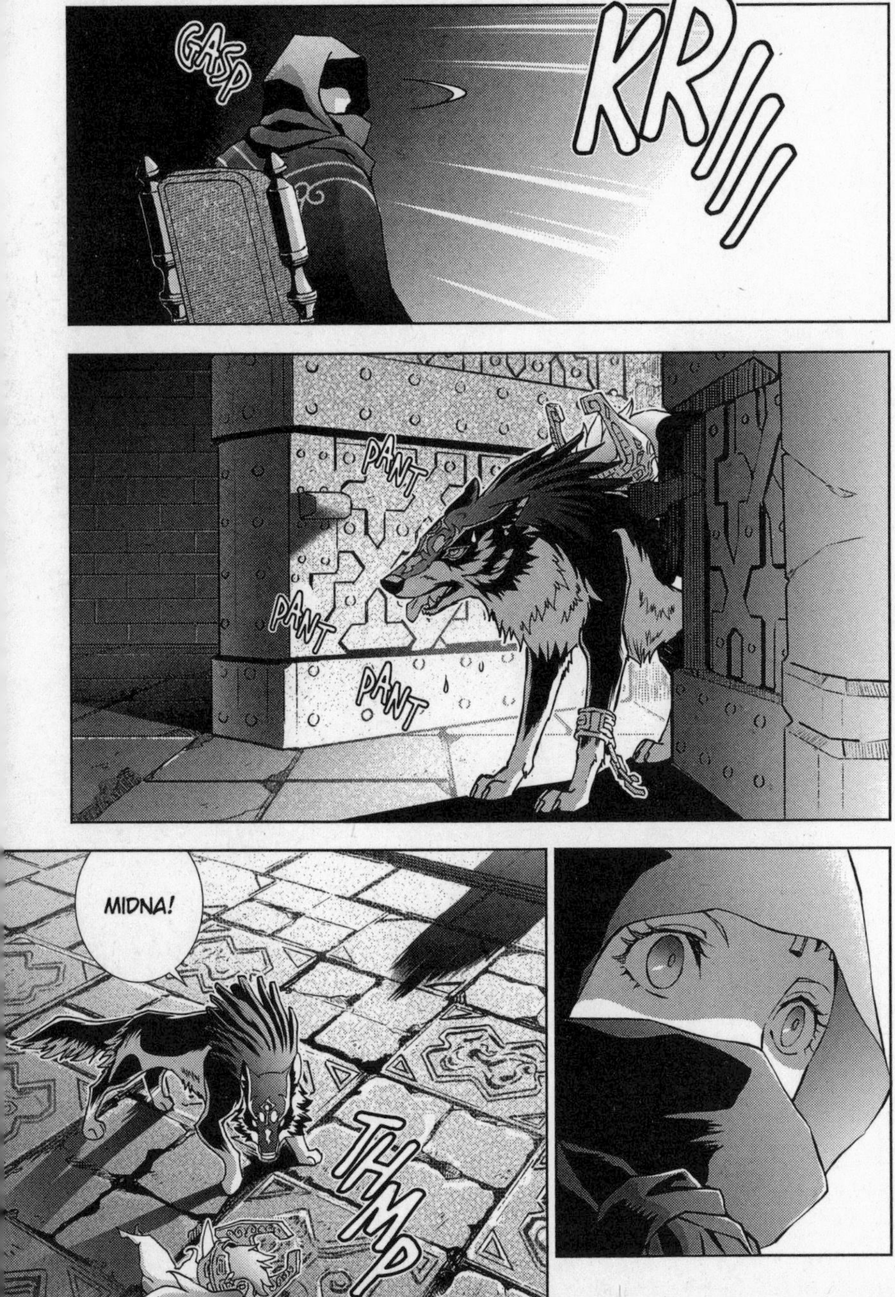
KRIIII
GASP
PANT
PANT
PANT
MIDNA!
THMP

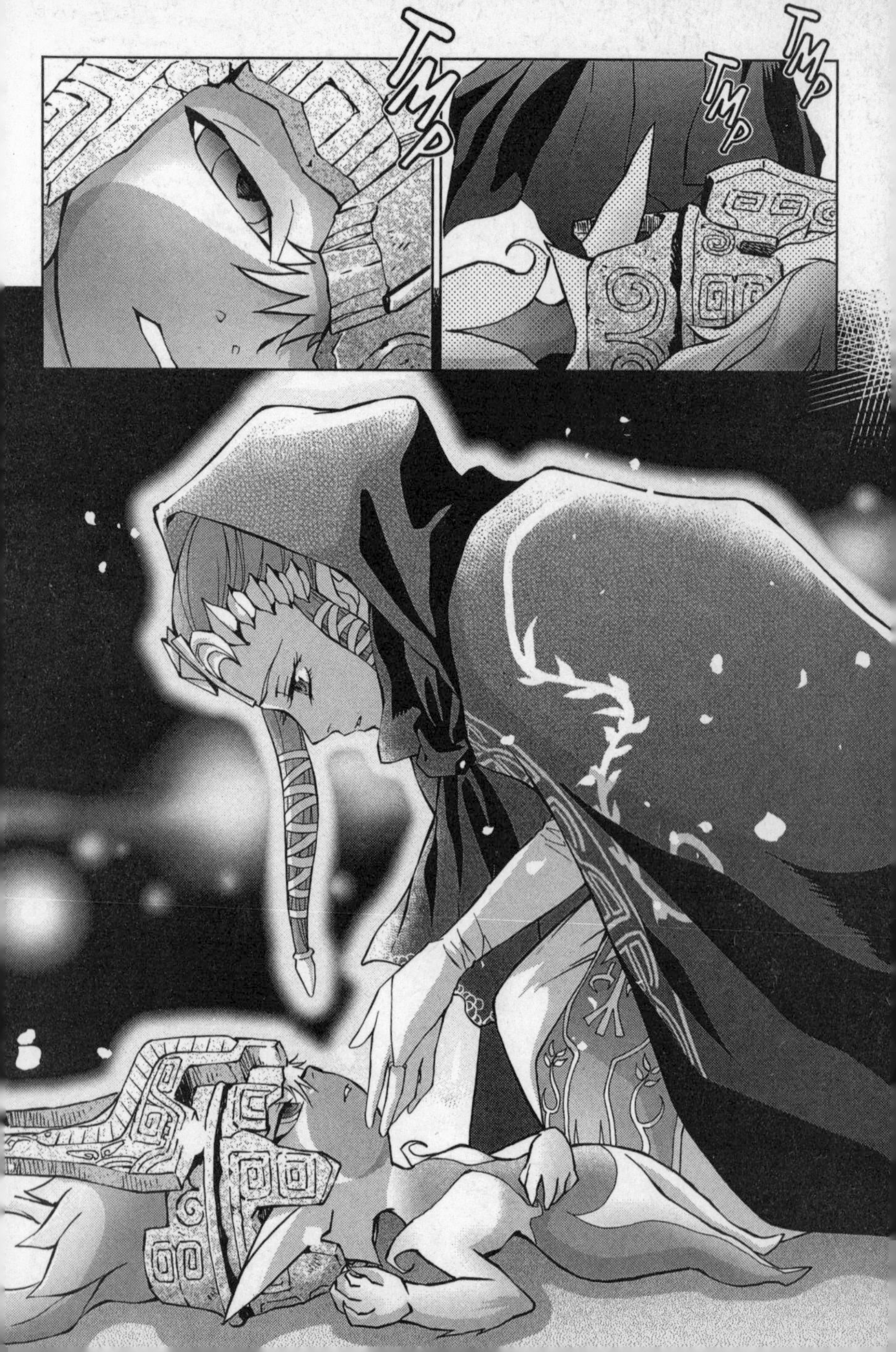
TMP
TMP
TMP

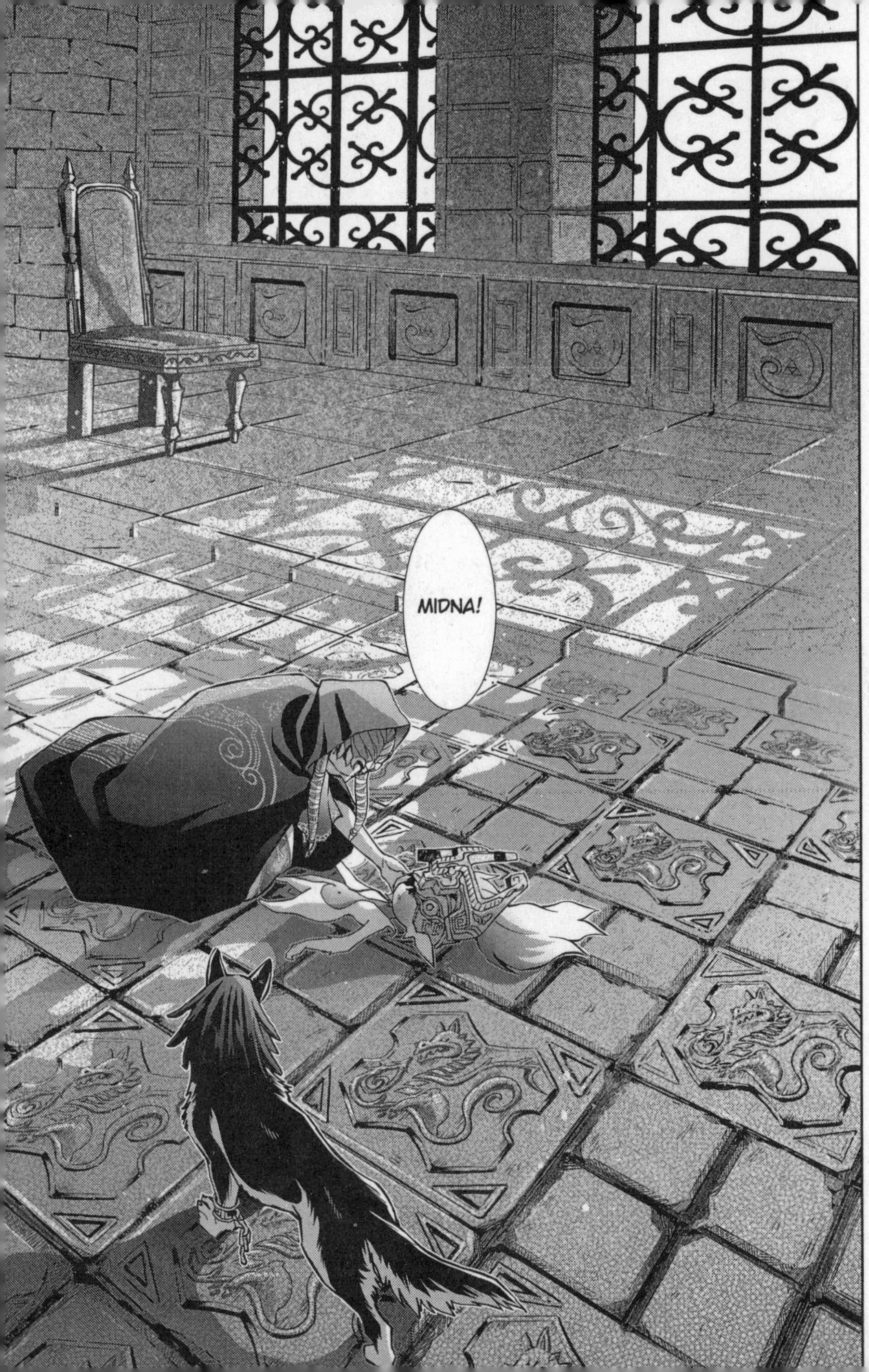
MIDNA!

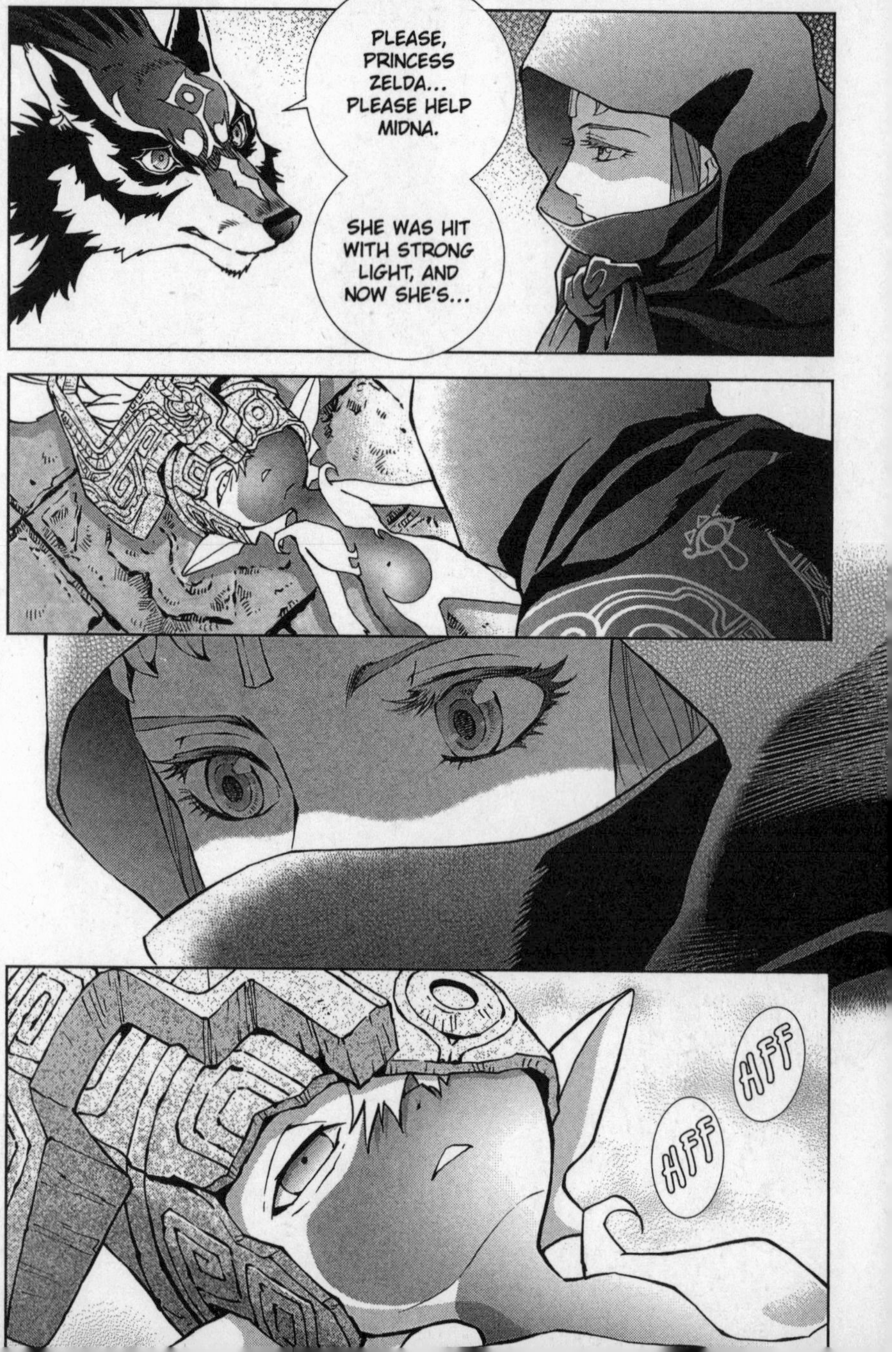
PLEASE, PRINCESS ZELDA... PLEASE HELP MIDNA.
SHE WAS HIT WITH STRONG LIGHT, AND NOW SHE'S...
HFF
HFF

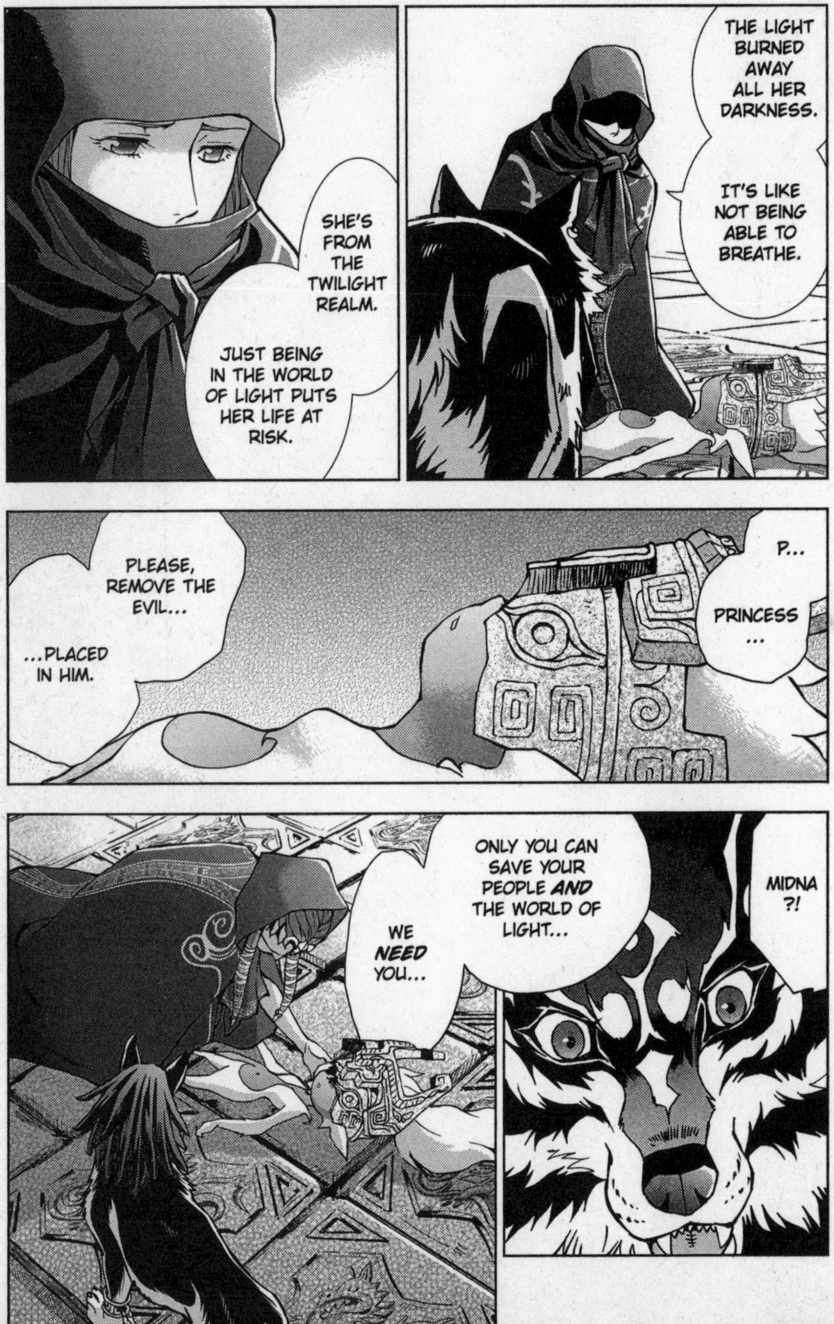
THE LIGHT BURNED AWAY ALL HER DARKNESS.
IT'S LIKE NOT BEING ABLE TO BREATHE.
SHE'S FROM THE TWILIGHT REALM.
JUST BEING IN THE WORLD OF LIGHT PUTS HER LIFE AT RISK.
P...
PRINCESS...
PLEASE, REMOVE THE EVIL...
...PLACED IN HIM.
MIDNA ?!
ONLY YOU CAN SAVE YOUR PEOPLE *AND* THE WORLD OF LIGHT...
WE *NEED* YOU...

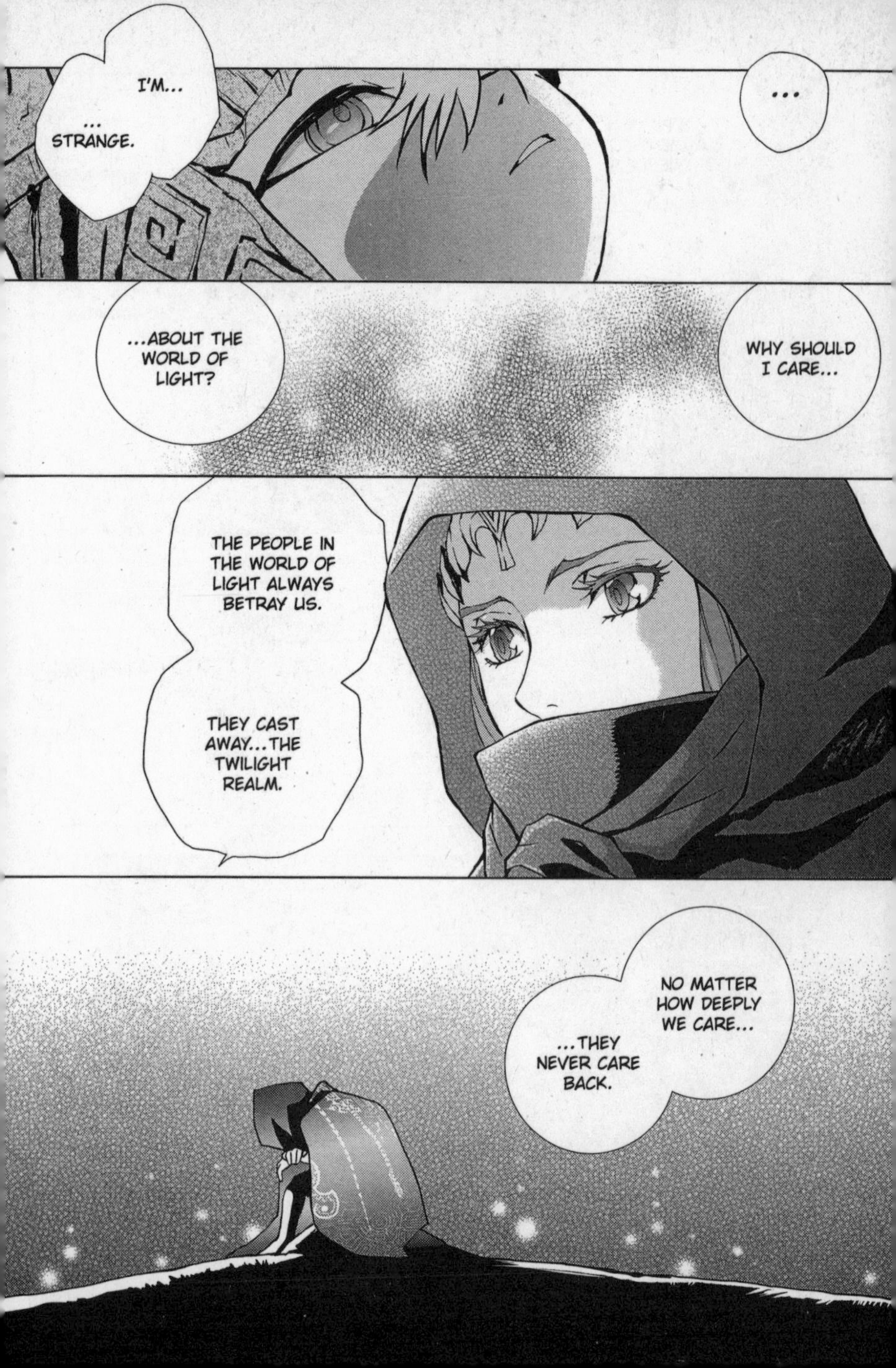
...
I'M...
...STRANGE.
WHY SHOULD I CARE...
...ABOUT THE WORLD OF LIGHT?
THE PEOPLE IN THE WORLD OF LIGHT ALWAYS BETRAY US.
THEY CAST AWAY...THE TWILIGHT REALM.
NO MATTER HOW DEEPLY WE CARE...
...THEY NEVER CARE BACK.

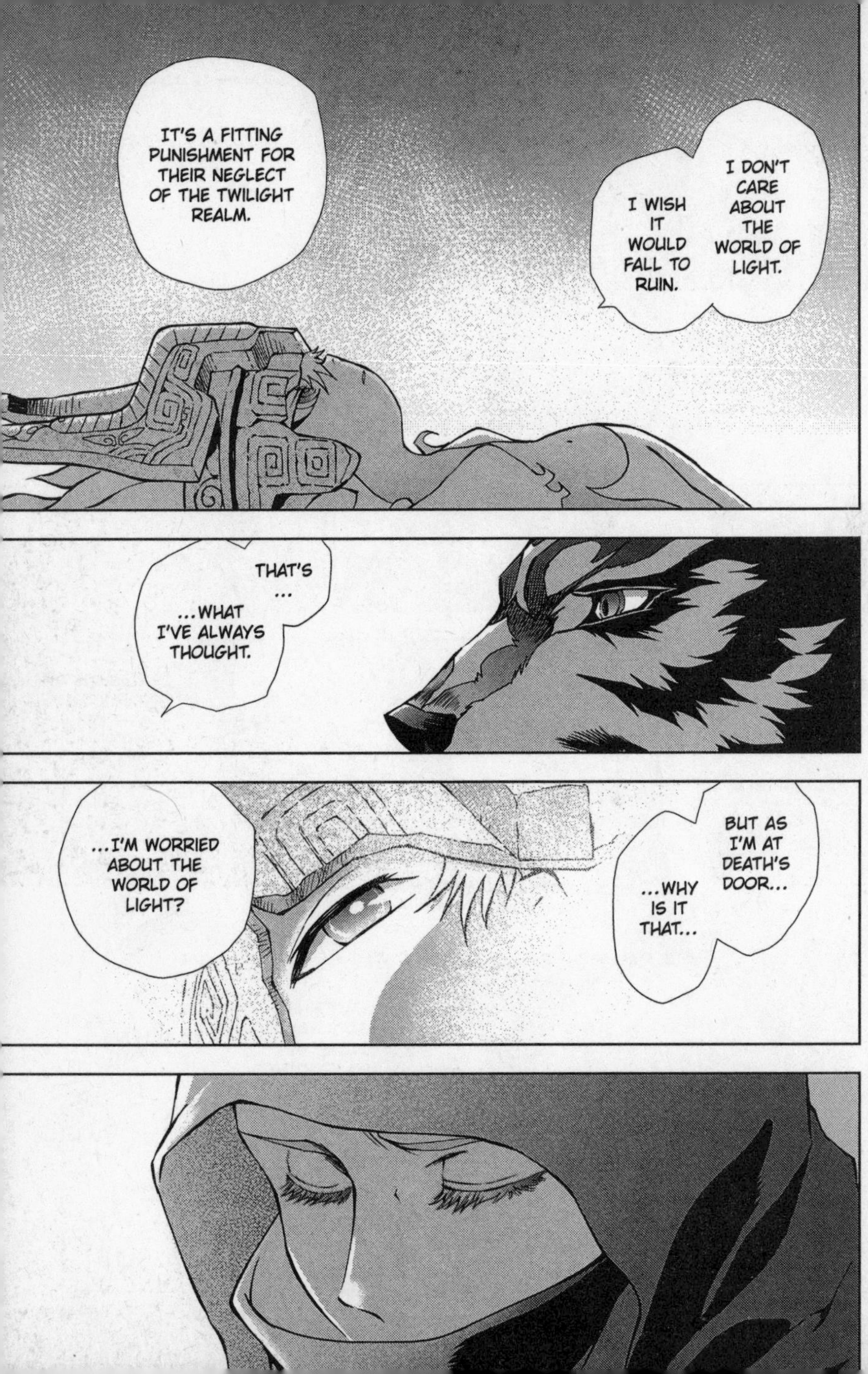
I DON'T CARE ABOUT THE WORLD OF LIGHT.
I WISH IT WOULD FALL TO RUIN.
IT'S A FITTING PUNISHMENT FOR THEIR NEGLECT OF THE TWILIGHT REALM.
THAT'S ...
...WHAT I'VE ALWAYS THOUGHT.
BUT AS I'M AT DEATH'S DOOR...
...WHY IS IT THAT...
...I'M WORRIED ABOUT THE WORLD OF LIGHT?

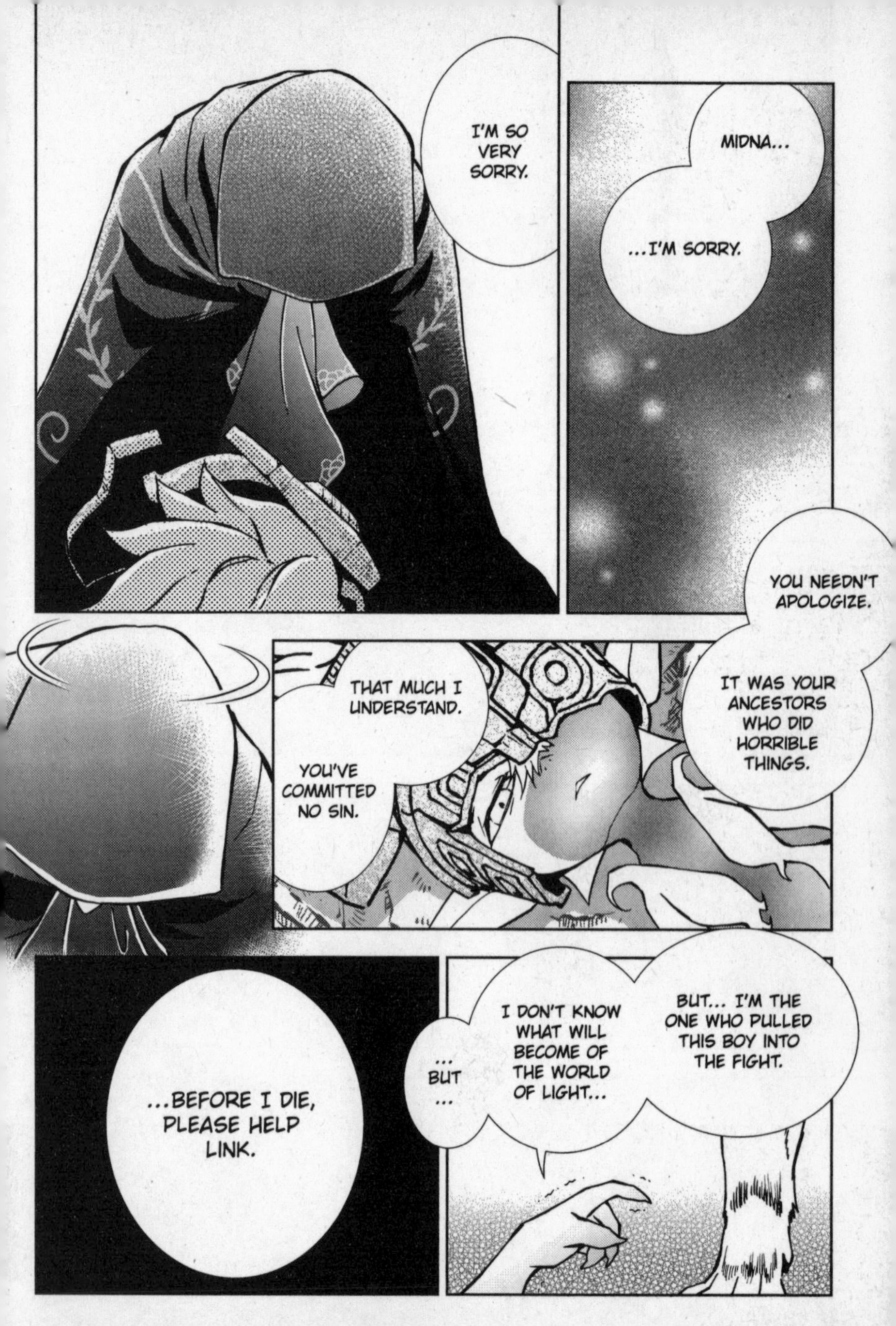
MIDNA...
...I'M SORRY.
I'M SO VERY SORRY.
YOU NEEDN'T APOLOGIZE.
IT WAS YOUR ANCESTORS WHO DID HORRIBLE THINGS.
THAT MUCH I UNDERSTAND.
YOU'VE COMMITTED NO SIN.
BUT... I'M THE ONE WHO PULLED THIS BOY INTO THE FIGHT.
I DON'T KNOW WHAT WILL BECOME OF THE WORLD OF LIGHT...
...BUT...
...BEFORE I DIE, PLEASE HELP LINK.

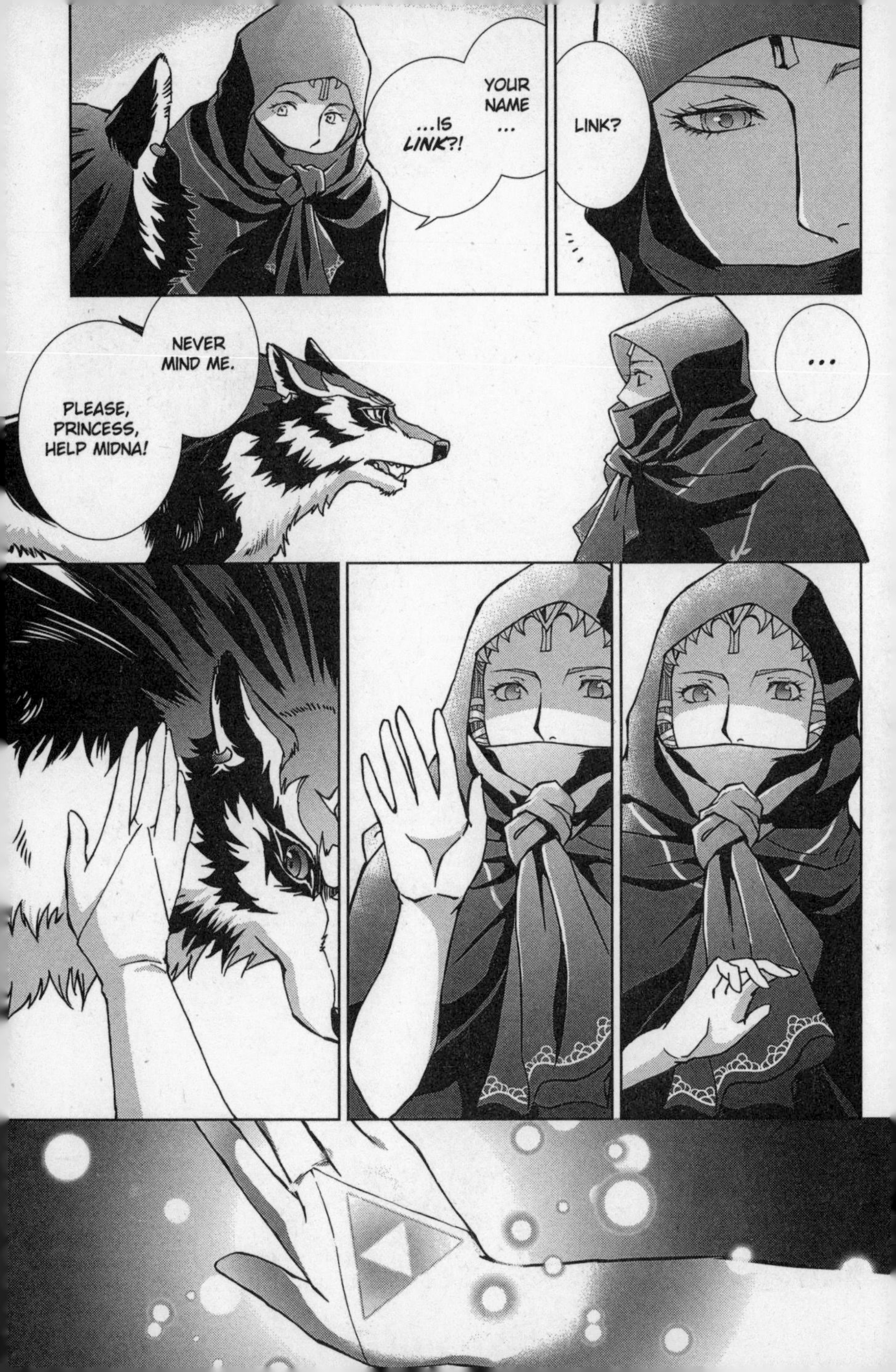
LINK?
YOUR NAME ...
...IS LINK?!
...
NEVER MIND ME.
PLEASE, PRINCESS, HELP MIDNA!

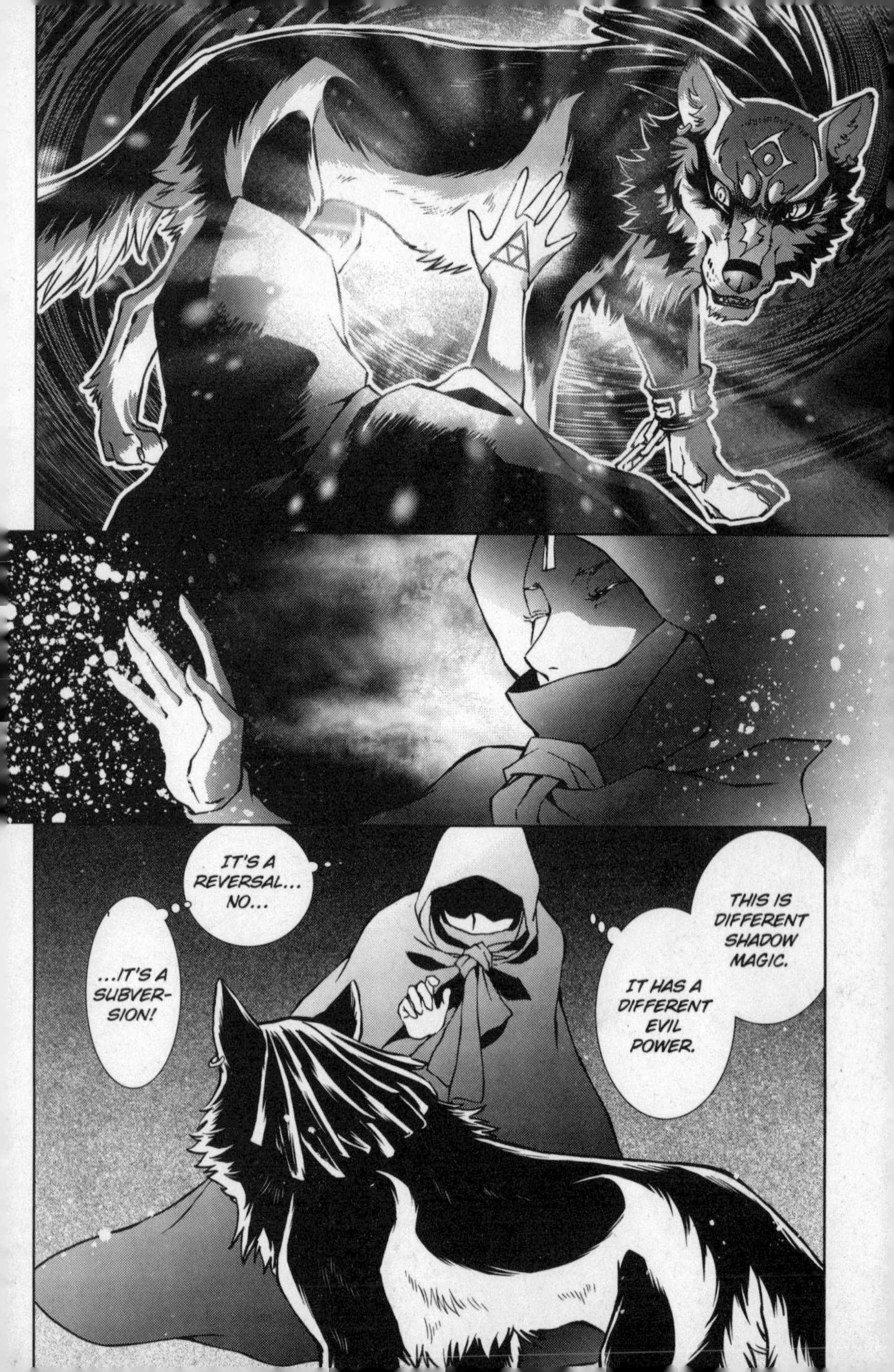
THIS IS DIFFERENT SHADOW MAGIC.
IT HAS A DIFFERENT EVIL POWER.
IT'S A REVERSAL... NO...
...IT'S A SUBVERSION!

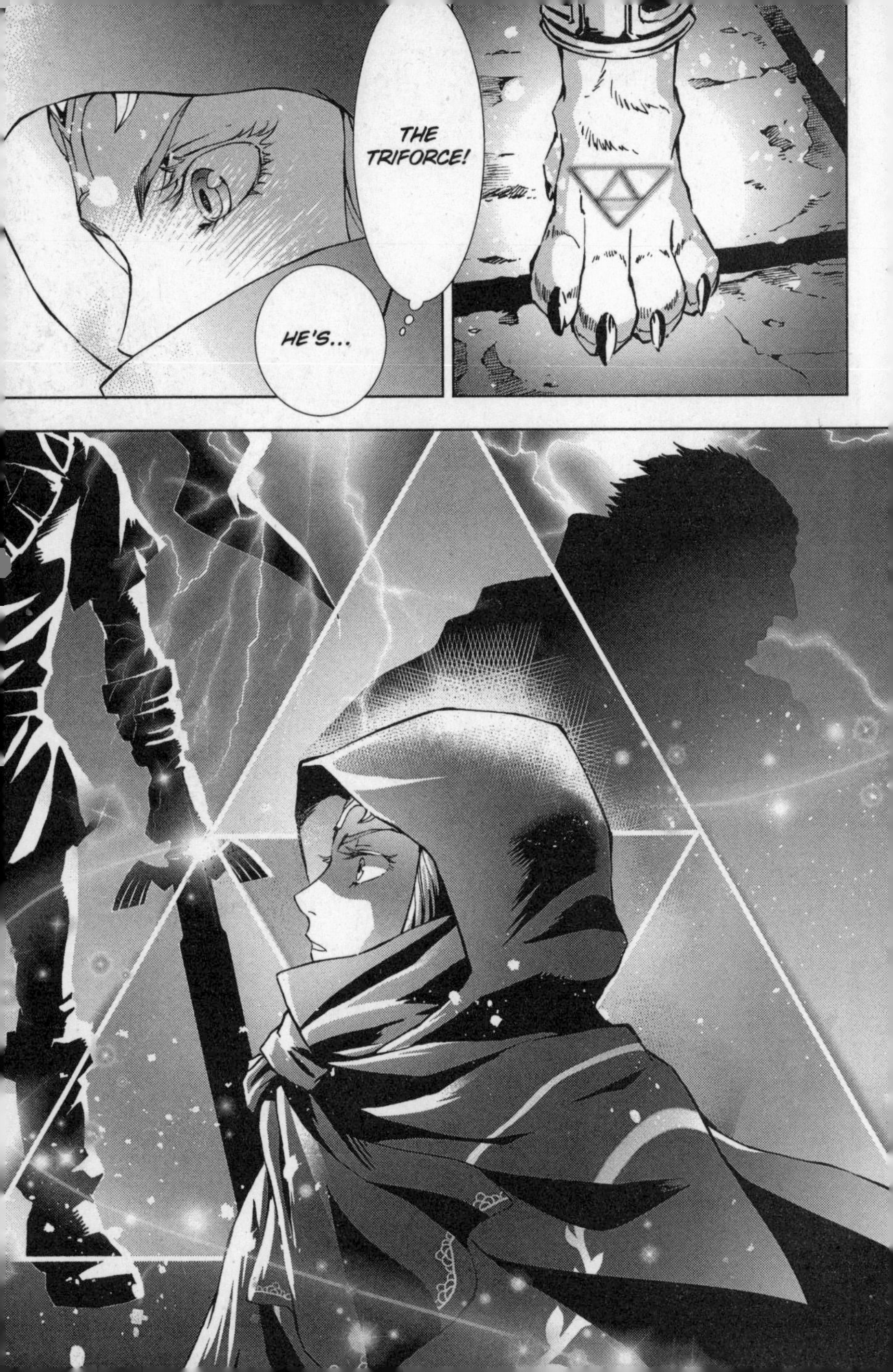
THE TRIFORCE!
HE'S...

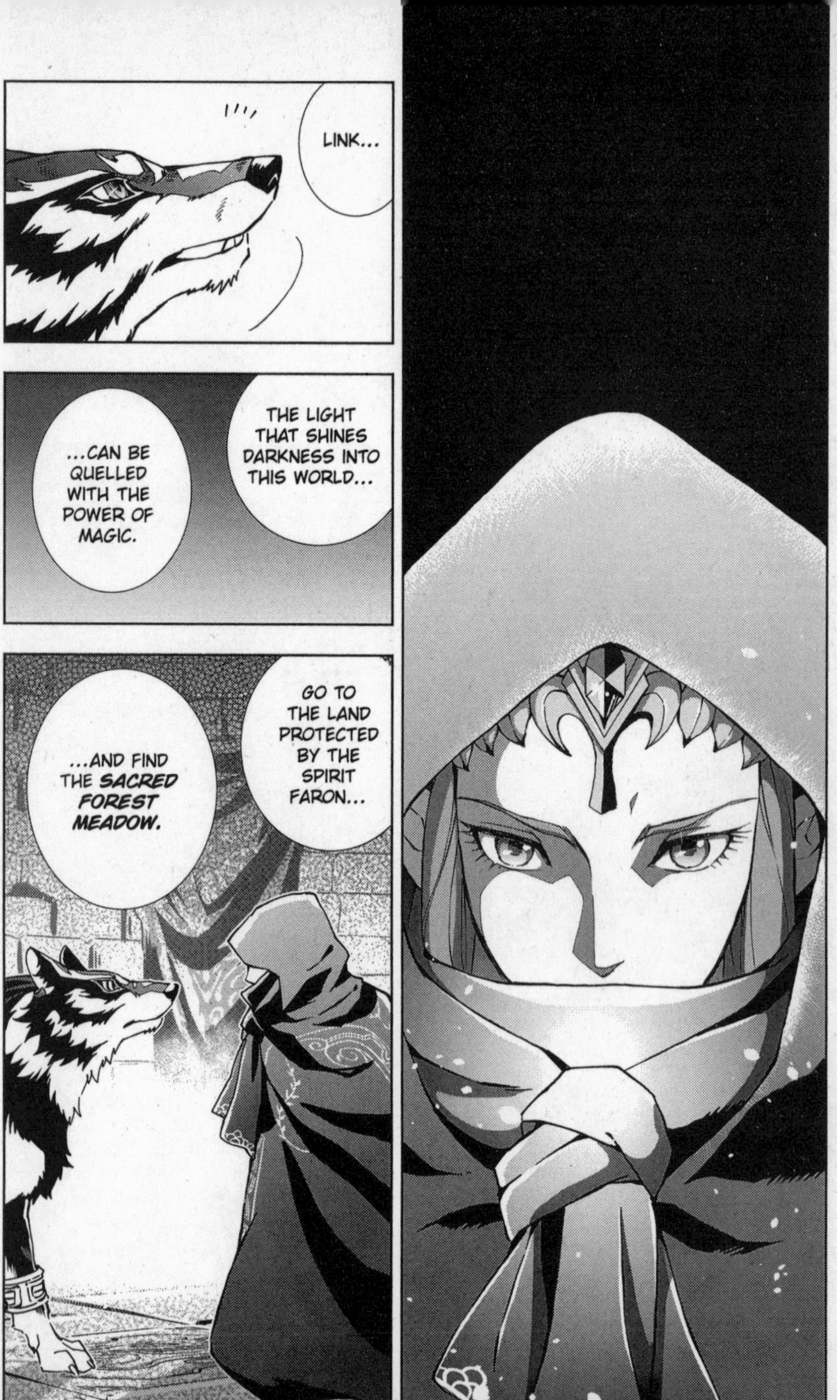

LINK...
THE LIGHT THAT SHINES DARKNESS INTO THIS WORLD...
...CAN BE QUELLED WITH THE POWER OF MAGIC.
GO TO THE LAND PROTECTED BY THE SPIRIT FARON...
...AND FIND THE *SACRED FOREST MEADOW.*

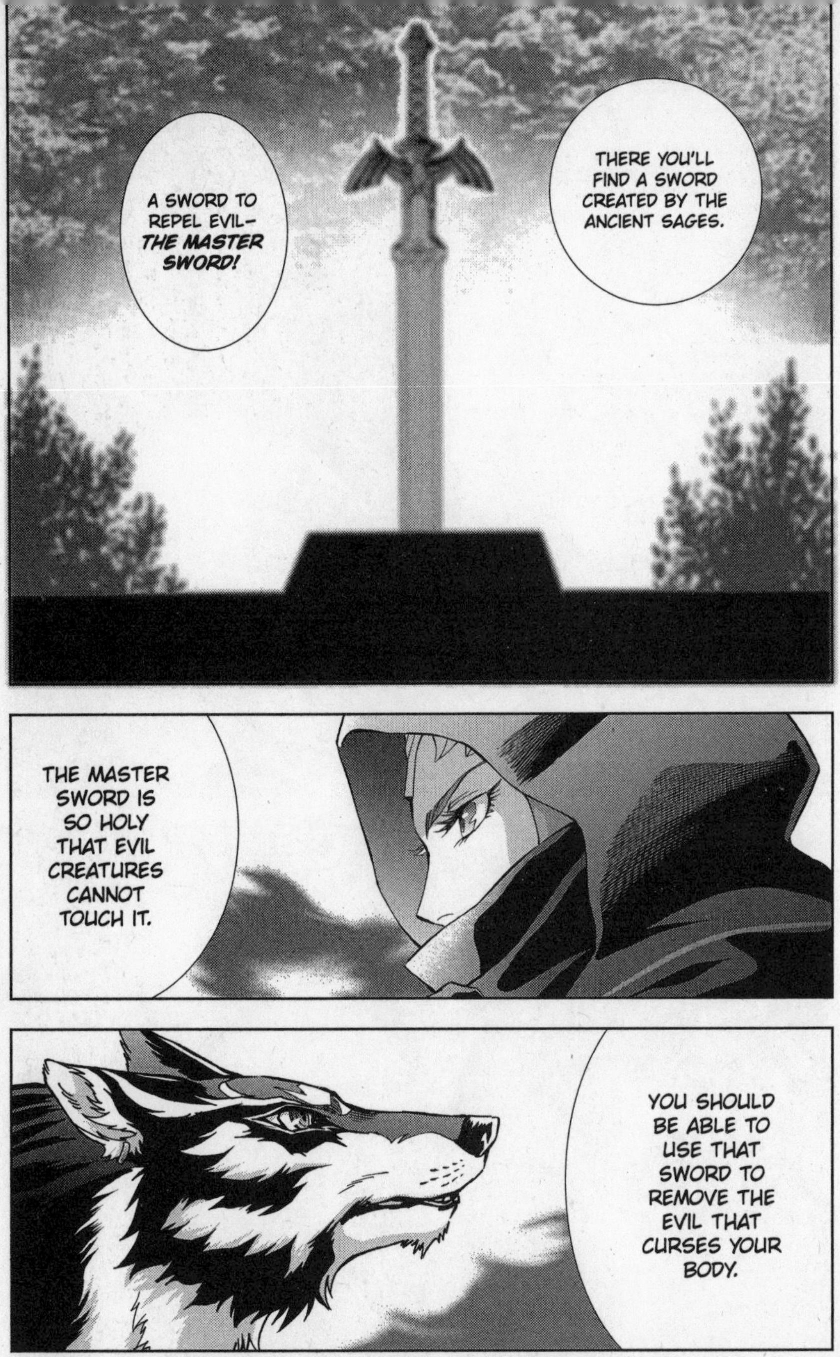
THERE YOU'LL FIND A SWORD CREATED BY THE ANCIENT SAGES.
A SWORD TO REPEL EVIL— *THE MASTER SWORD!*
THE MASTER SWORD IS SO HOLY THAT EVIL CREATURES CANNOT TOUCH IT.
YOU SHOULD BE ABLE TO USE THAT SWORD TO REMOVE THE EVIL THAT CURSES YOUR BODY.

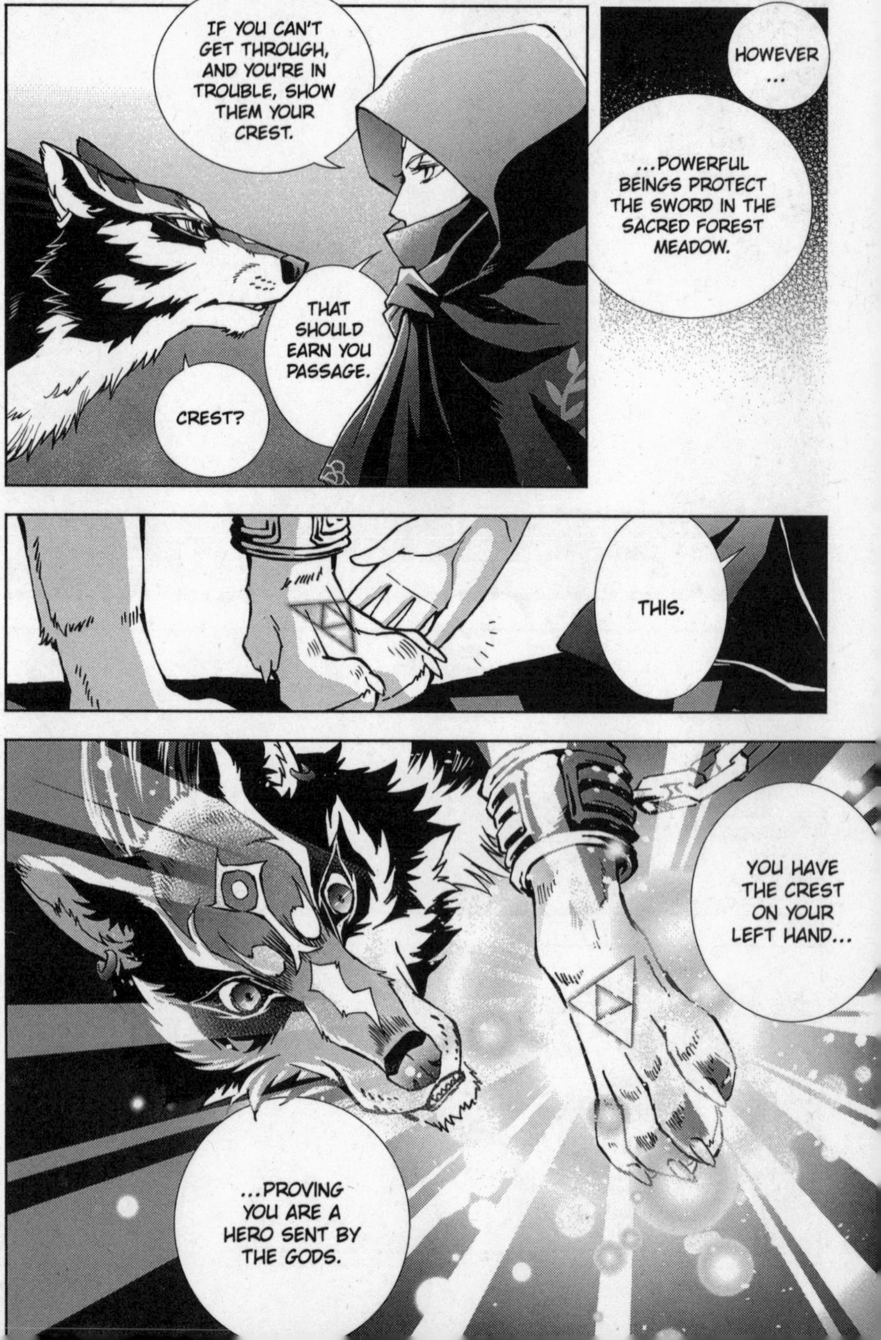
HOWEVER...
...POWERFUL BEINGS PROTECT THE SWORD IN THE SACRED FOREST MEADOW.
IF YOU CAN'T GET THROUGH, AND YOU'RE IN TROUBLE, SHOW THEM YOUR CREST.
THAT SHOULD EARN YOU PASSAGE.
CREST?
THIS.
YOU HAVE THE CREST ON YOUR LEFT HAND...
...PROVING YOU ARE A HERO SENT BY THE GODS.

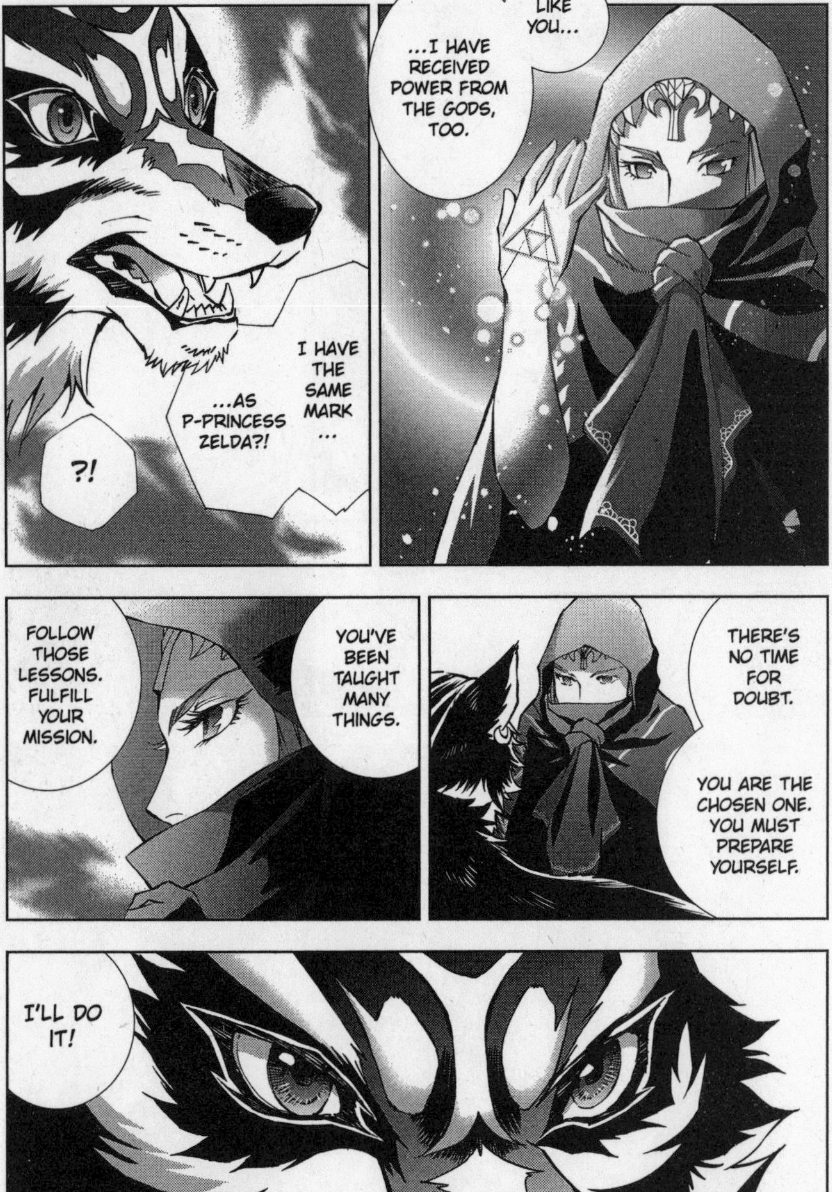
LIKE YOU...
...I HAVE RECEIVED POWER FROM THE GODS, TOO.
I HAVE THE SAME MARK ...
...AS P-PRINCESS ZELDA?!
?!
THERE'S NO TIME FOR DOUBT.
YOU ARE THE CHOSEN ONE. YOU MUST PREPARE YOURSELF.
YOU'VE BEEN TAUGHT MANY THINGS.
FOLLOW THOSE LESSONS. FULFILL YOUR MISSION.
I'LL DO IT!

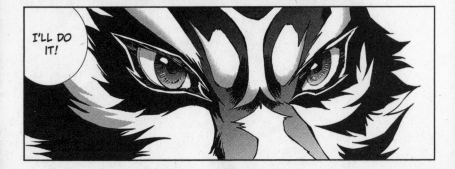

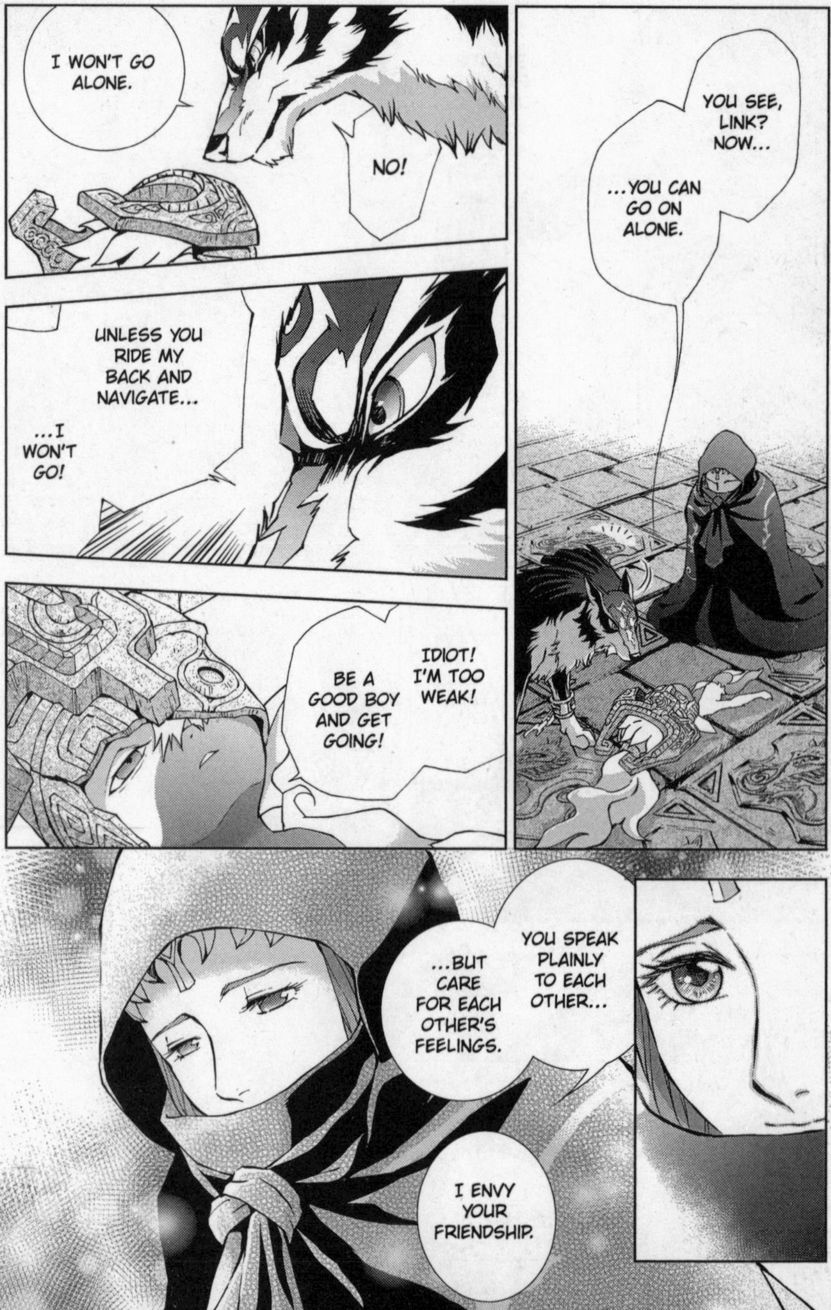
YOU SEE, LINK? NOW...
...YOU CAN GO ON ALONE.
NO!
I WON'T GO ALONE.
UNLESS YOU RIDE MY BACK AND NAVIGATE...
...I WON'T GO!
IDIOT! I'M TOO WEAK!
BE A GOOD BOY AND GET GOING!
YOU SPEAK PLAINLY TO EACH OTHER...
...BUT CARE FOR EACH OTHER'S FEELINGS.
I ENVY YOUR FRIENDSHIP.

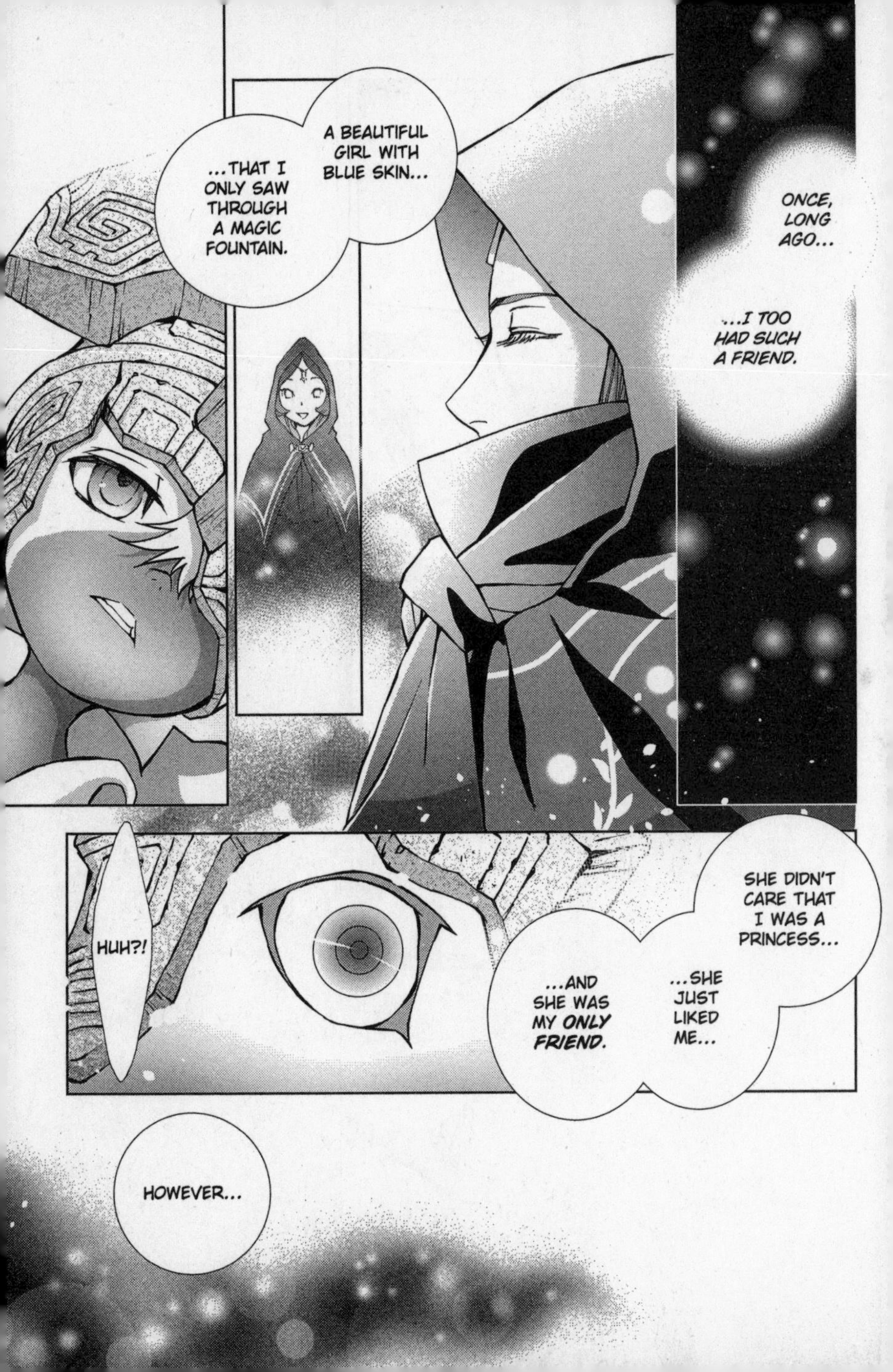
ONCE, LONG AGO...
...I TOO HAD SUCH A FRIEND.
A BEAUTIFUL GIRL WITH BLUE SKIN...
...THAT I ONLY SAW THROUGH A MAGIC FOUNTAIN.
SHE DIDN'T CARE THAT I WAS A PRINCESS...
...SHE JUST LIKED ME...
...AND SHE WAS MY *ONLY FRIEND*.
HUH?!
HOWEVER...

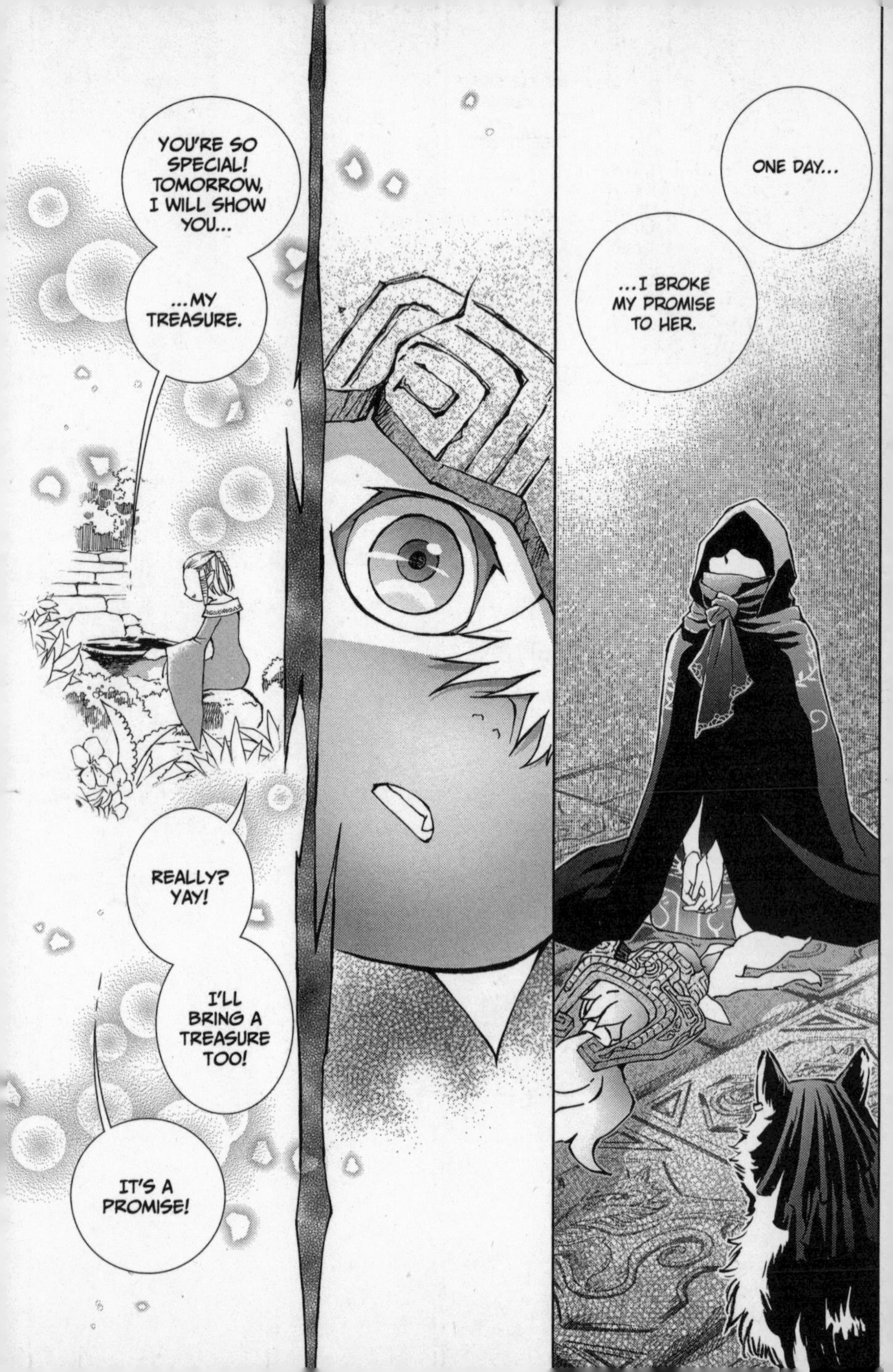
ONE DAY...
...I BROKE MY PROMISE TO HER.
YOU'RE SO SPECIAL! TOMORROW, I WILL SHOW YOU...
...MY TREASURE.
REALLY? YAY!
I'LL BRING A TREASURE TOO!
IT'S A PROMISE!

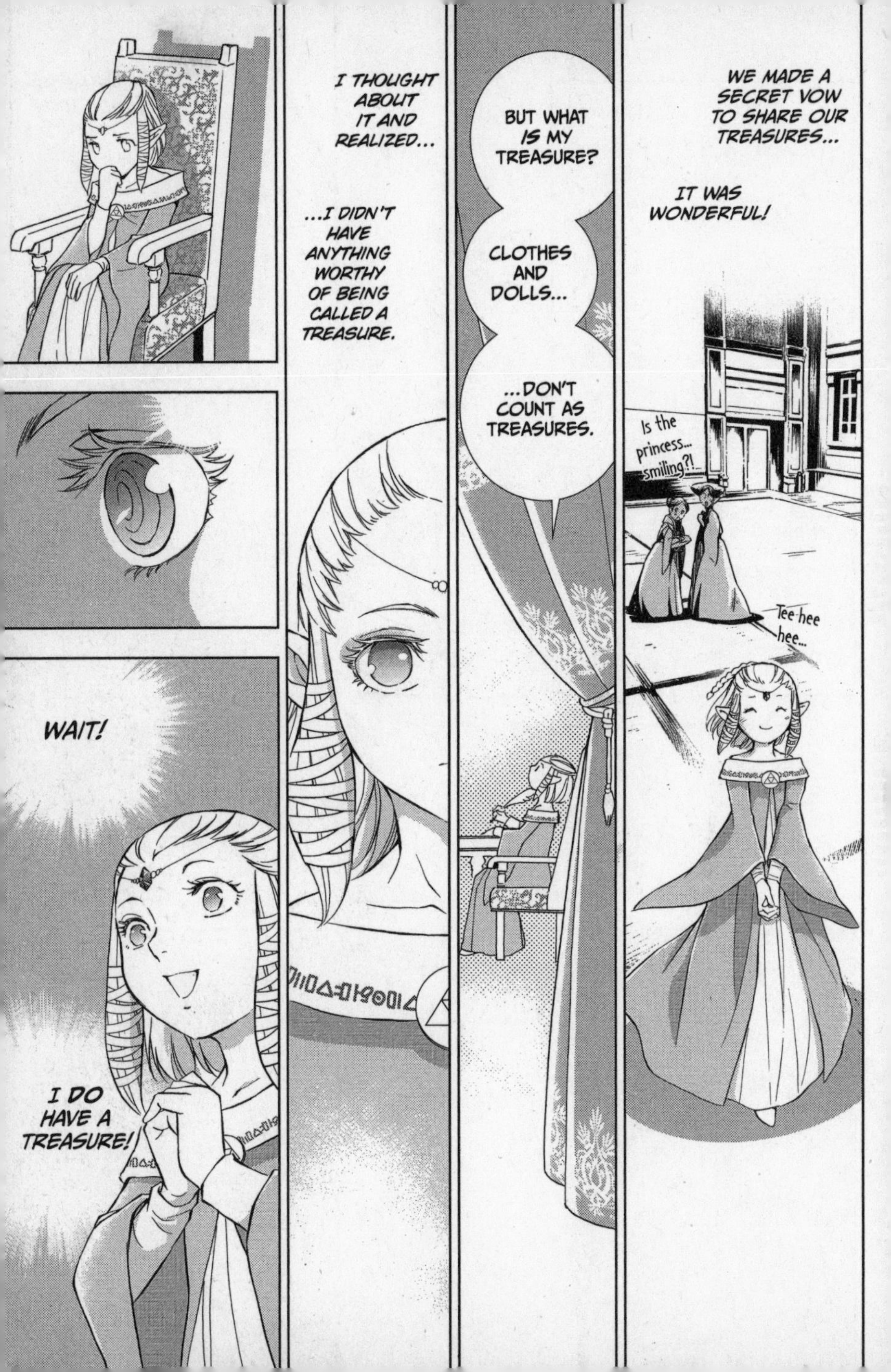
WE MADE A SECRET VOW TO SHARE OUR TREASURES...
IT WAS WONDERFUL!
Is the princess... smiling?!
Tee hee hee...
BUT WHAT IS MY TREASURE?
CLOTHES AND DOLLS...
...DON'T COUNT AS TREASURES.
I THOUGHT ABOUT IT AND REALIZED...
...I DIDN'T HAVE ANYTHING WORTHY OF BEING CALLED A TREASURE.
WAIT!
I DO HAVE A TREASURE!

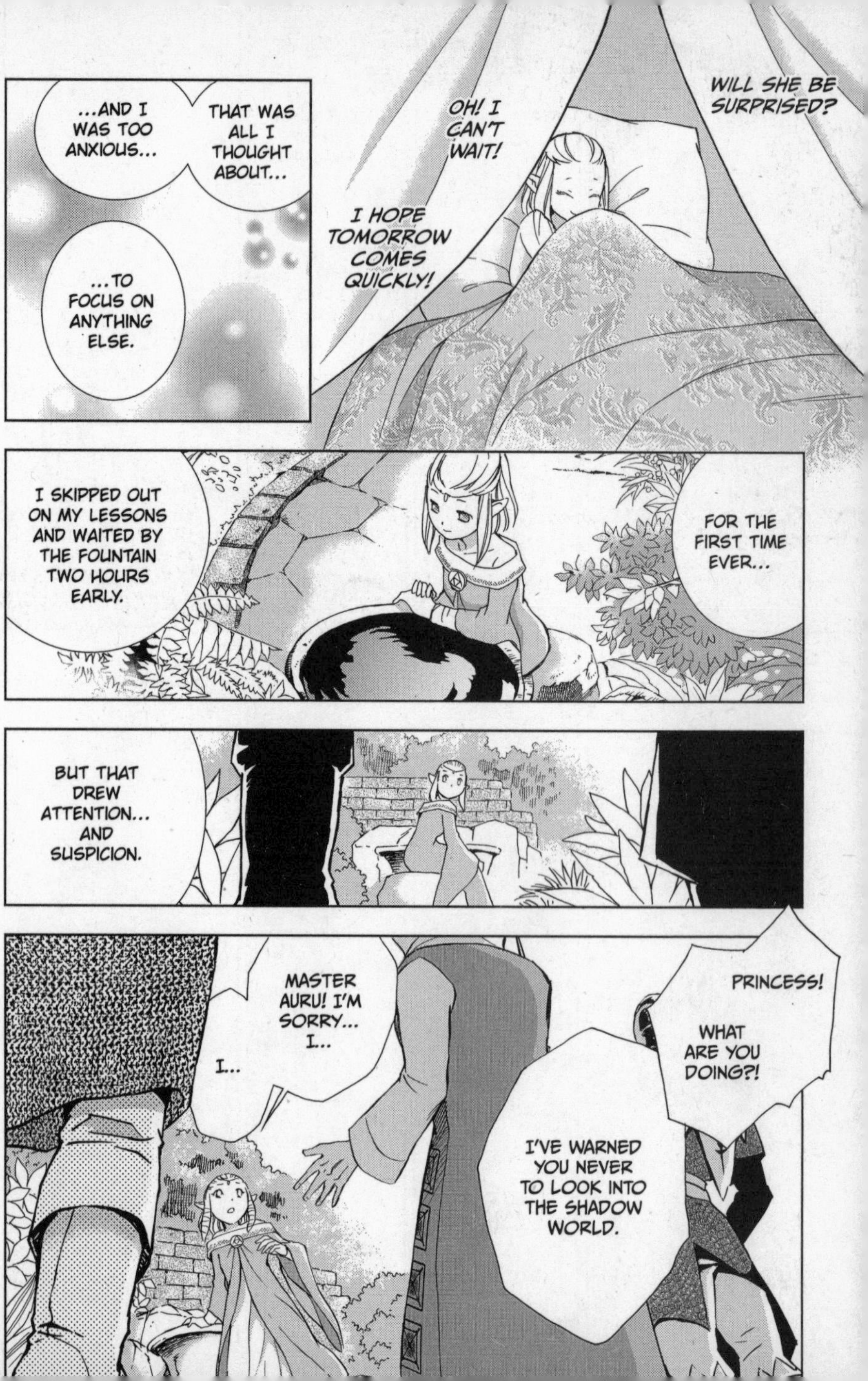

WILL SHE BE SURPRISED?
OH! I CAN'T WAIT!
I HOPE TOMORROW COMES QUICKLY!
THAT WAS ALL I THOUGHT ABOUT...
...AND I WAS TOO ANXIOUS...
...TO FOCUS ON ANYTHING ELSE.
FOR THE FIRST TIME EVER...
I SKIPPED OUT ON MY LESSONS AND WAITED BY THE FOUNTAIN TWO HOURS EARLY.
BUT THAT DREW ATTENTION... AND SUSPICION.
PRINCESS!
WHAT ARE YOU DOING?!
I'VE WARNED YOU NEVER TO LOOK INTO THE SHADOW WORLD.
MASTER AURU! I'M SORRY... I...
I...

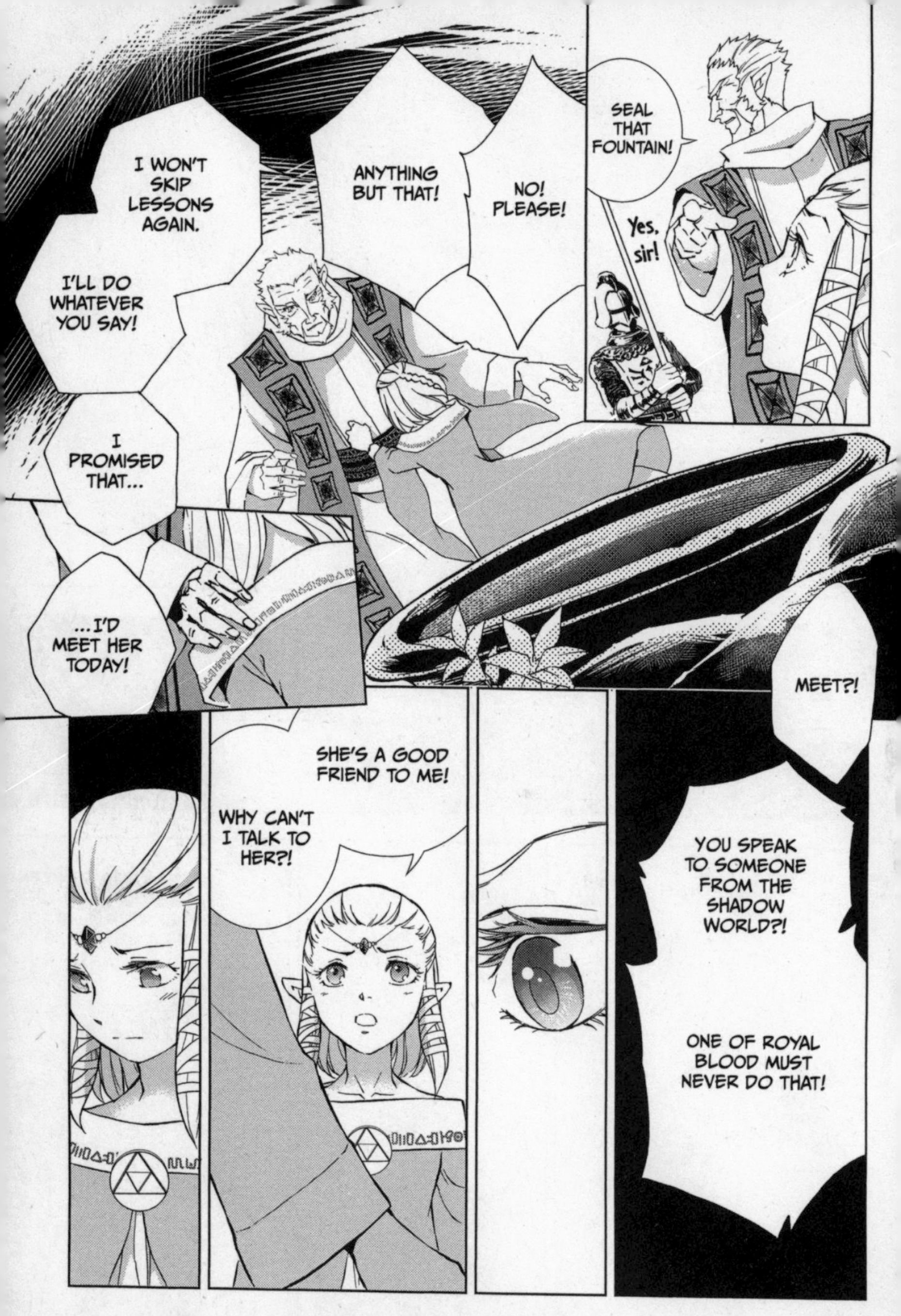
SEAL THAT FOUNTAIN!
Yes, sir!
NO! PLEASE!
ANYTHING BUT THAT!
I WON'T SKIP LESSONS AGAIN.
I'LL DO WHATEVER YOU SAY!
I PROMISED THAT...
...I'D MEET HER TODAY!
MEET?!
YOU SPEAK TO SOMEONE FROM THE SHADOW WORLD?!
ONE OF ROYAL BLOOD MUST NEVER DO THAT!
SHE'S A GOOD FRIEND TO ME!
WHY CAN'T I TALK TO HER?!

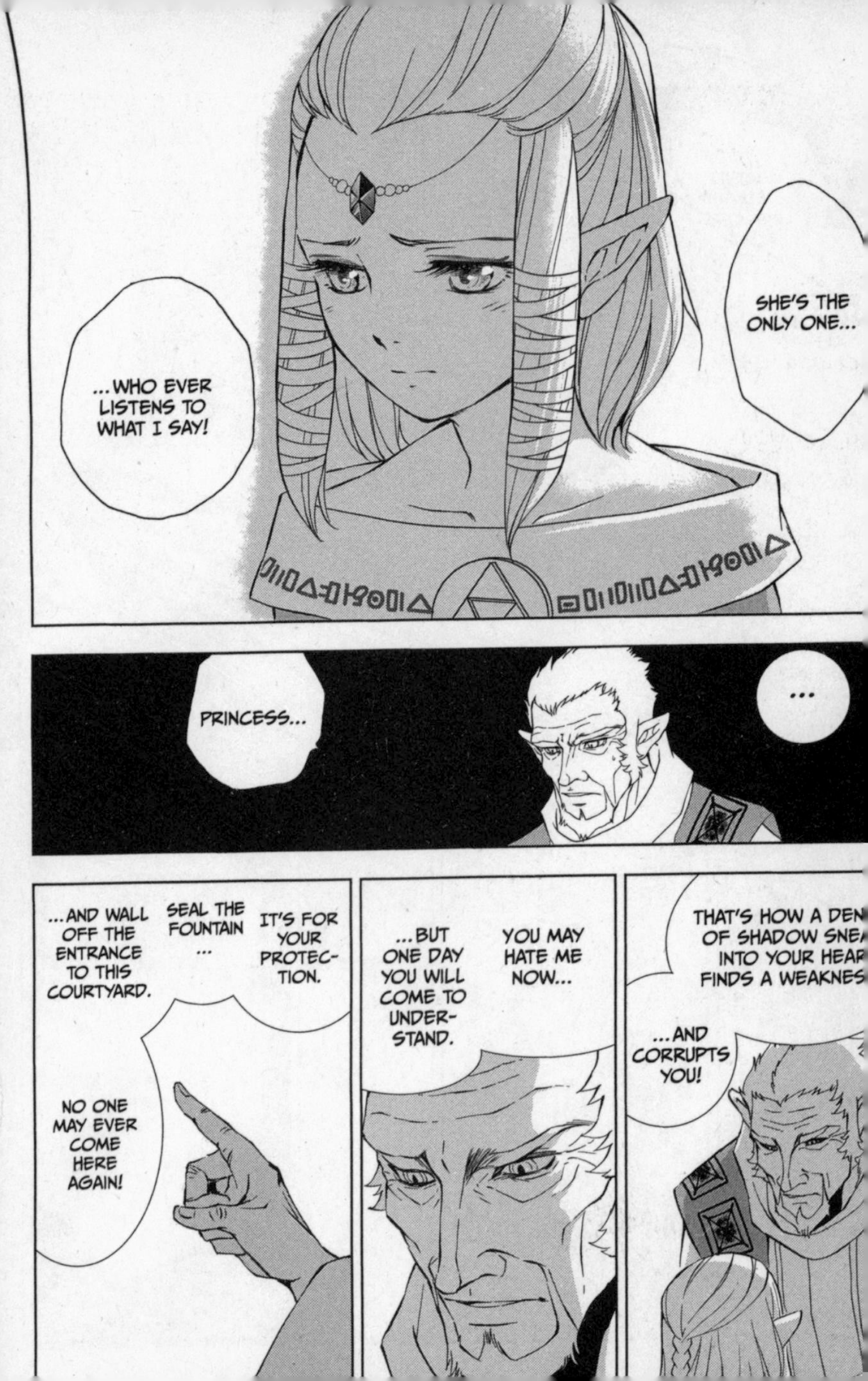
SHE'S THE ONLY ONE...
...WHO EVER LISTENS TO WHAT I SAY!
...
PRINCESS...
THAT'S HOW A DEN OF SHADOW SNE INTO YOUR HEA FINDS A WEAKNES
...AND CORRUPTS YOU!
YOU MAY HATE ME NOW...
...BUT ONE DAY YOU WILL COME TO UNDER-STAND.
IT'S FOR YOUR PROTEC-TION.
SEAL THE FOUNTAIN ...
...AND WALL OFF THE ENTRANCE TO THIS COURTYARD.
NO ONE MAY EVER COME HERE AGAIN!

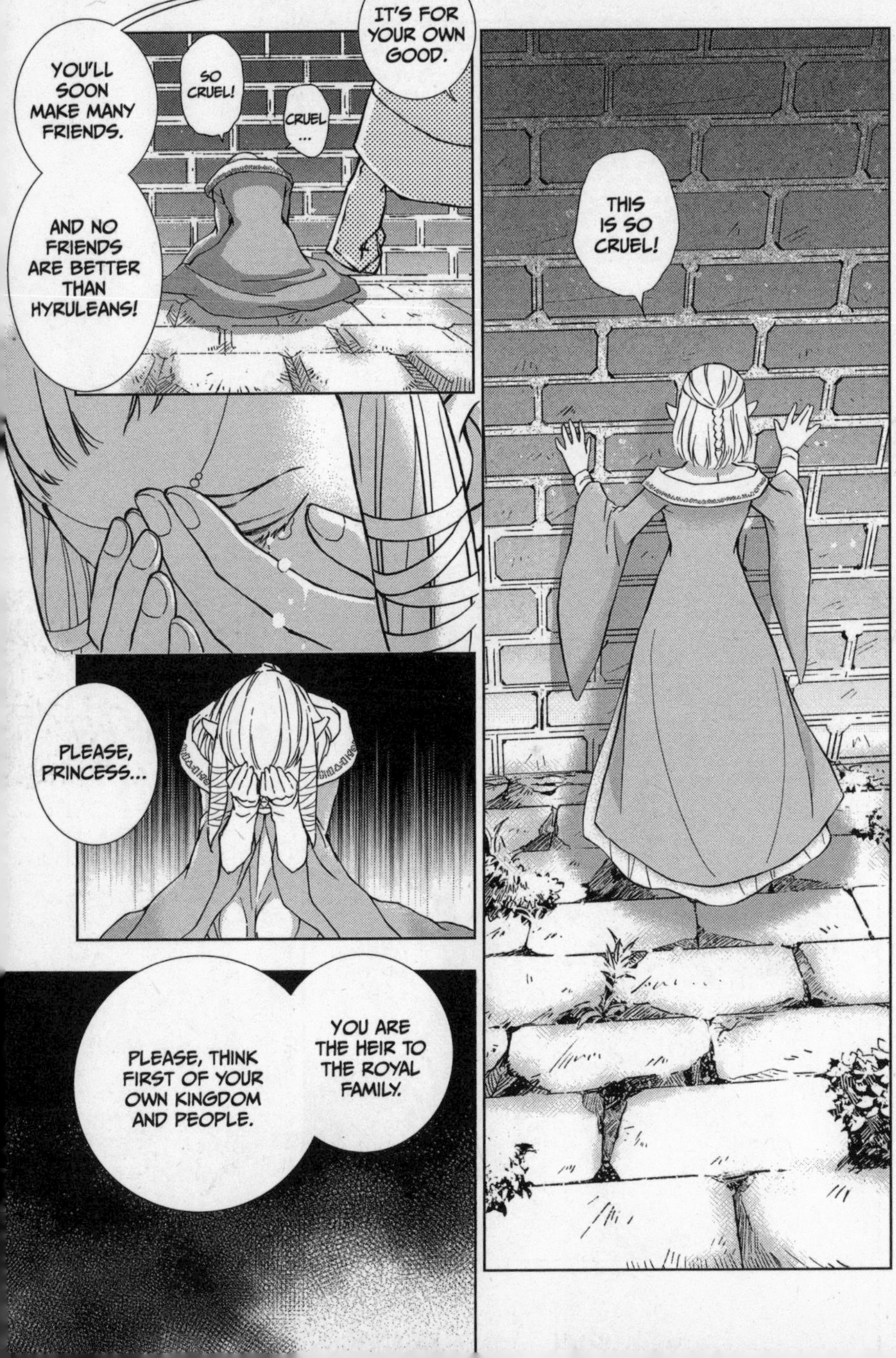
THIS IS SO CRUEL!
SO CRUEL!
CRUEL...
IT'S FOR YOUR OWN GOOD.
YOU'LL SOON MAKE MANY FRIENDS.
AND NO FRIENDS ARE BETTER THAN HYRULEANS!
PLEASE, PRINCESS...
YOU ARE THE HEIR TO THE ROYAL FAMILY.
PLEASE, THINK FIRST OF YOUR OWN KINGDOM AND PEOPLE.

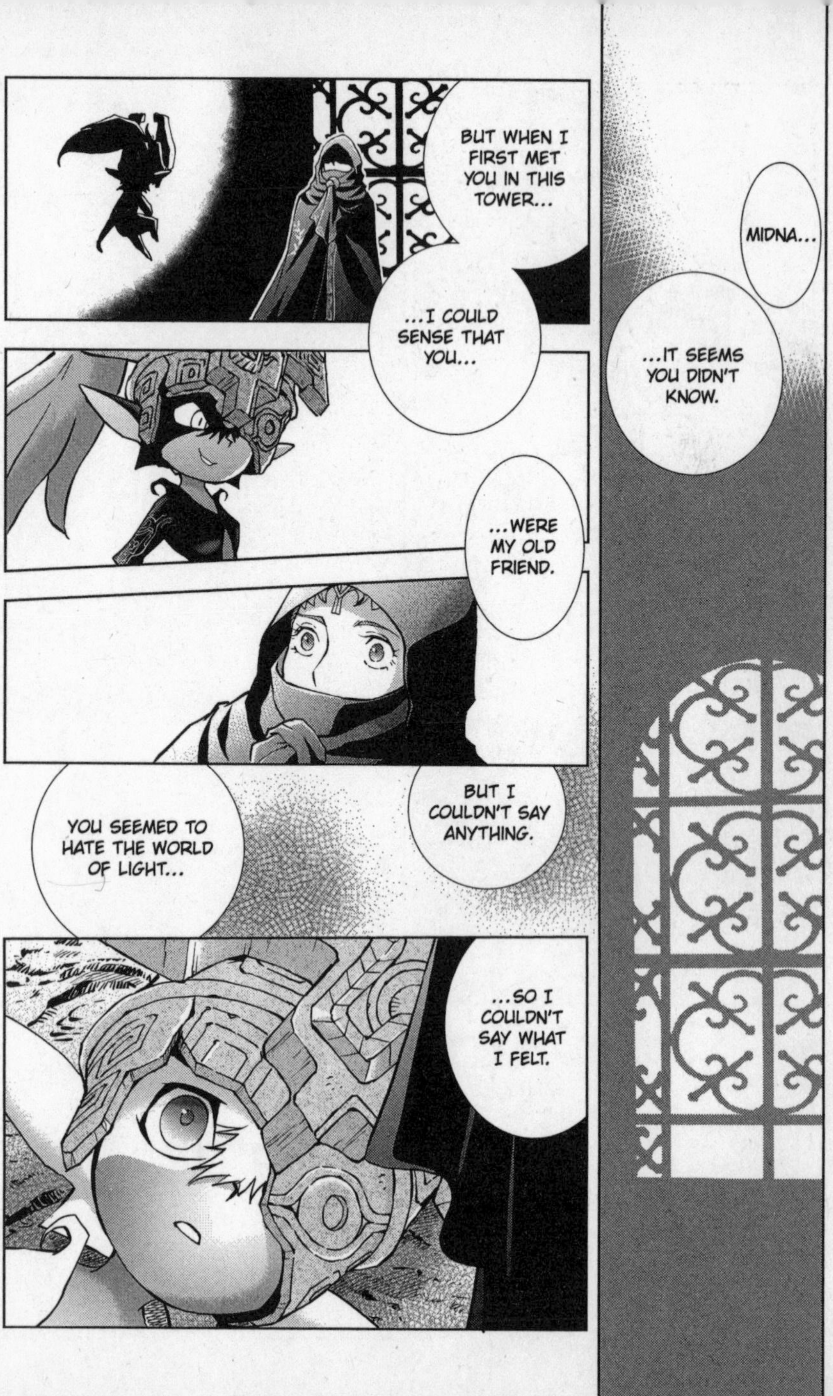
MIDNA...
...IT SEEMS YOU DIDN'T KNOW.
BUT WHEN I FIRST MET YOU IN THIS TOWER...
...I COULD SENSE THAT YOU...
...WERE MY OLD FRIEND.
BUT I COULDN'T SAY ANYTHING.
YOU SEEMED TO HATE THE WORLD OF LIGHT...
...SO I COULDN'T SAY WHAT I FELT.

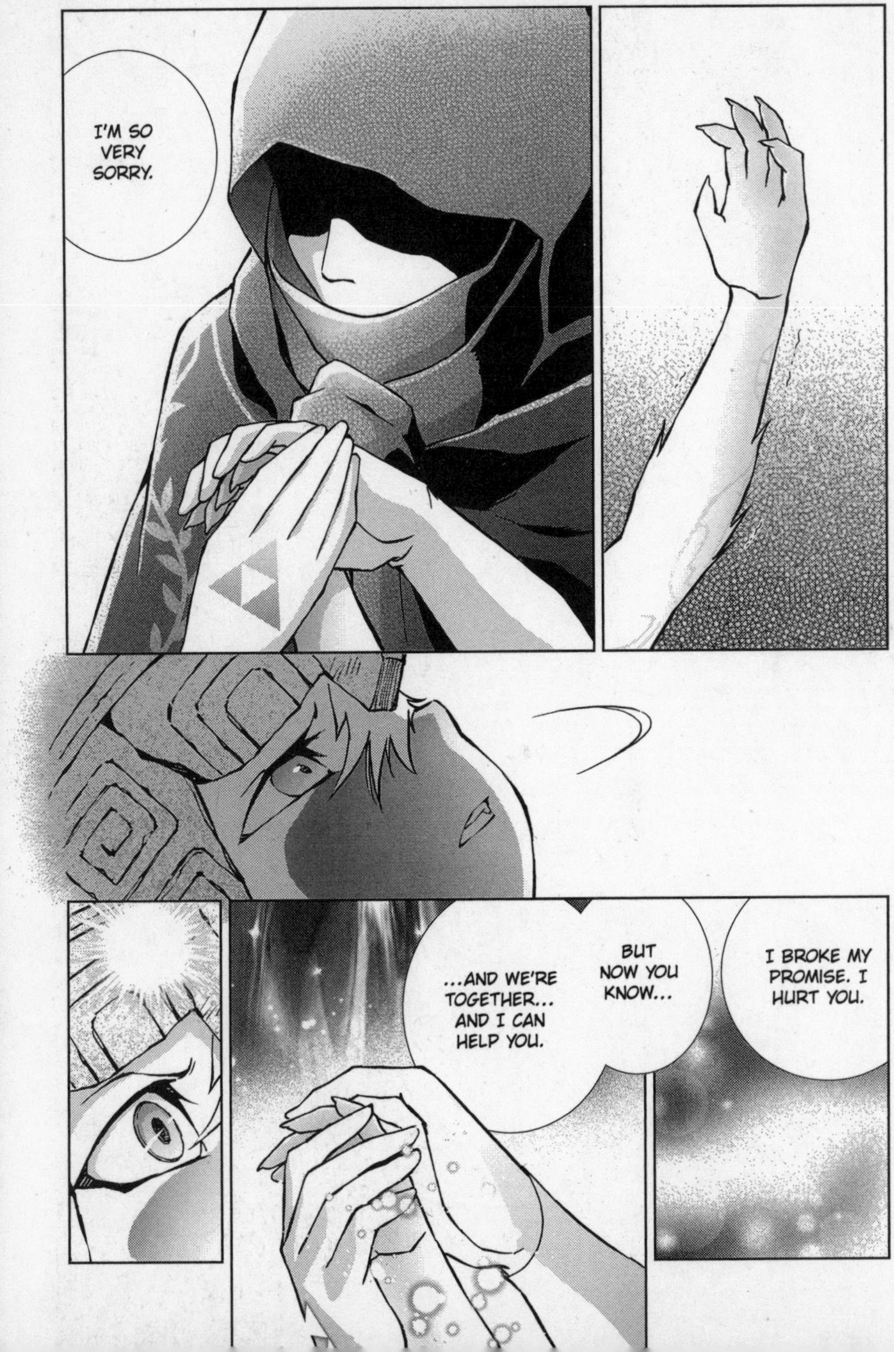
I'M SO VERY SORRY.
I BROKE MY PROMISE. I HURT YOU.
BUT NOW YOU KNOW...
...AND WE'RE TOGETHER... AND I CAN HELP YOU.

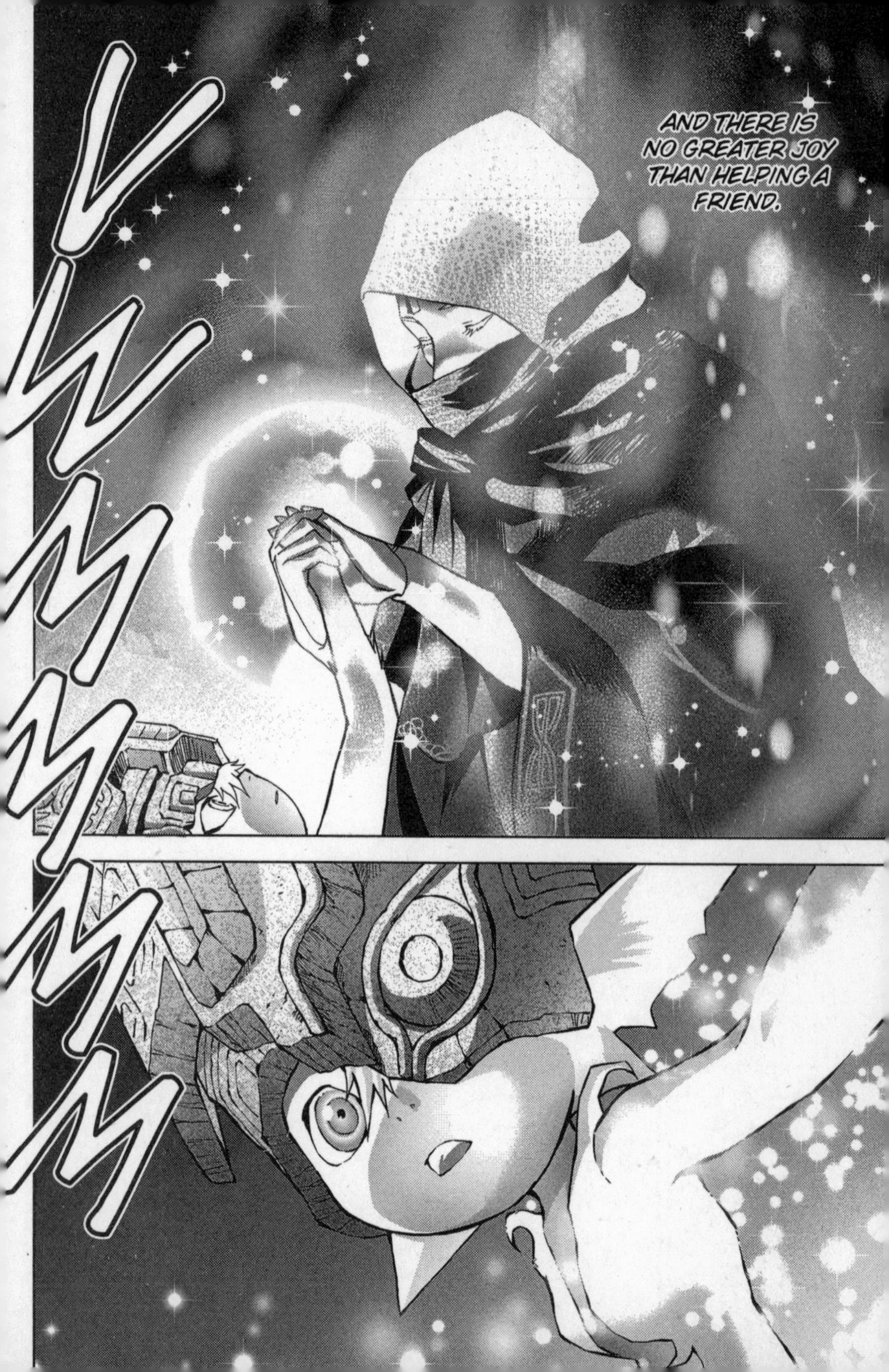
AND THERE IS NO GREATER JOY THAN HELPING A FRIEND.
VWMMMMM

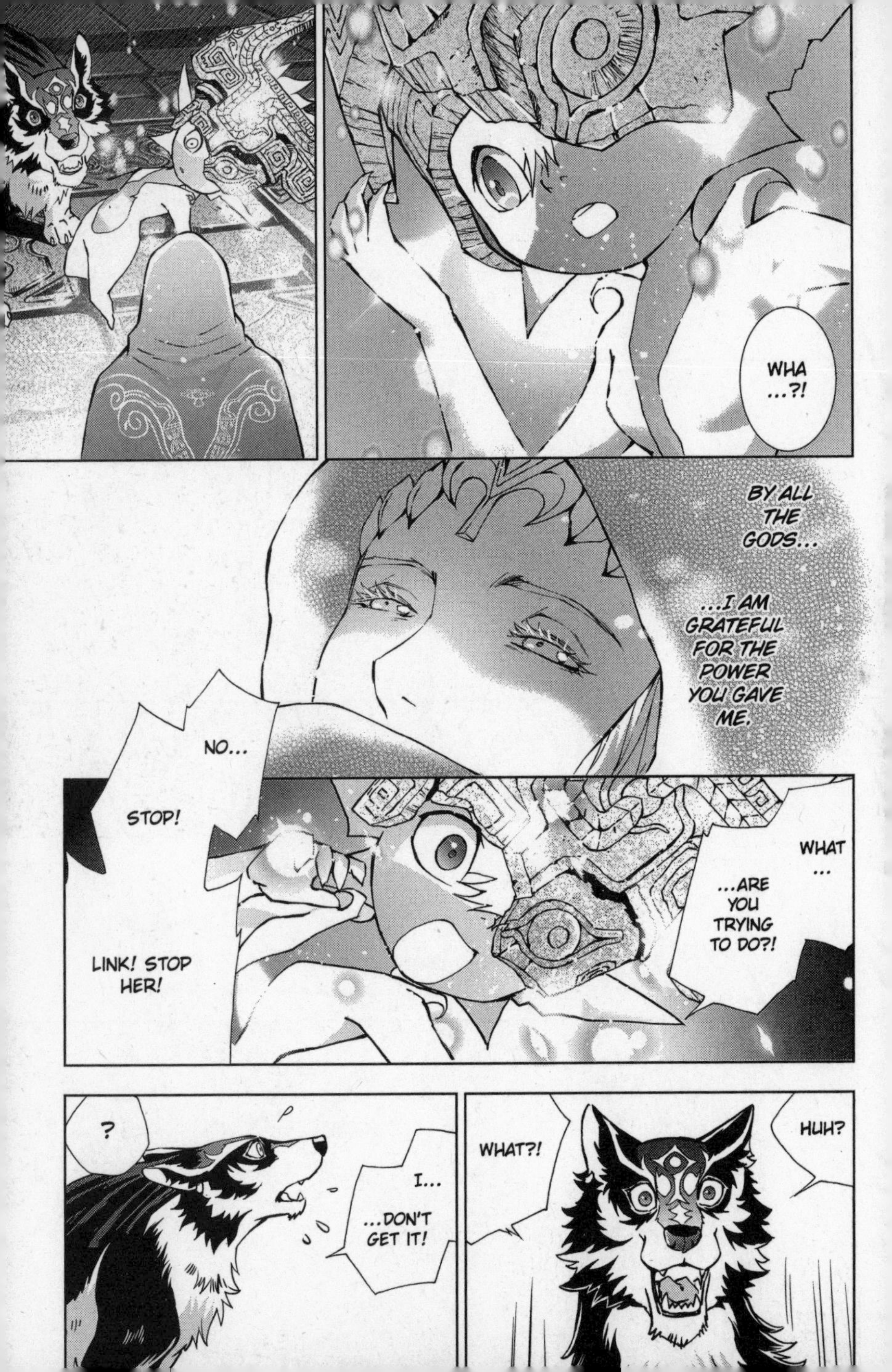
WHA ...?!
BY ALL THE GODS...
...I AM GRATEFUL FOR THE POWER YOU GAVE ME.
WHAT ...
...ARE YOU TRYING TO DO?!
NO...
STOP!
LINK! STOP HER!
HUH?
WHAT?!
?
I...
...DON'T GET IT!

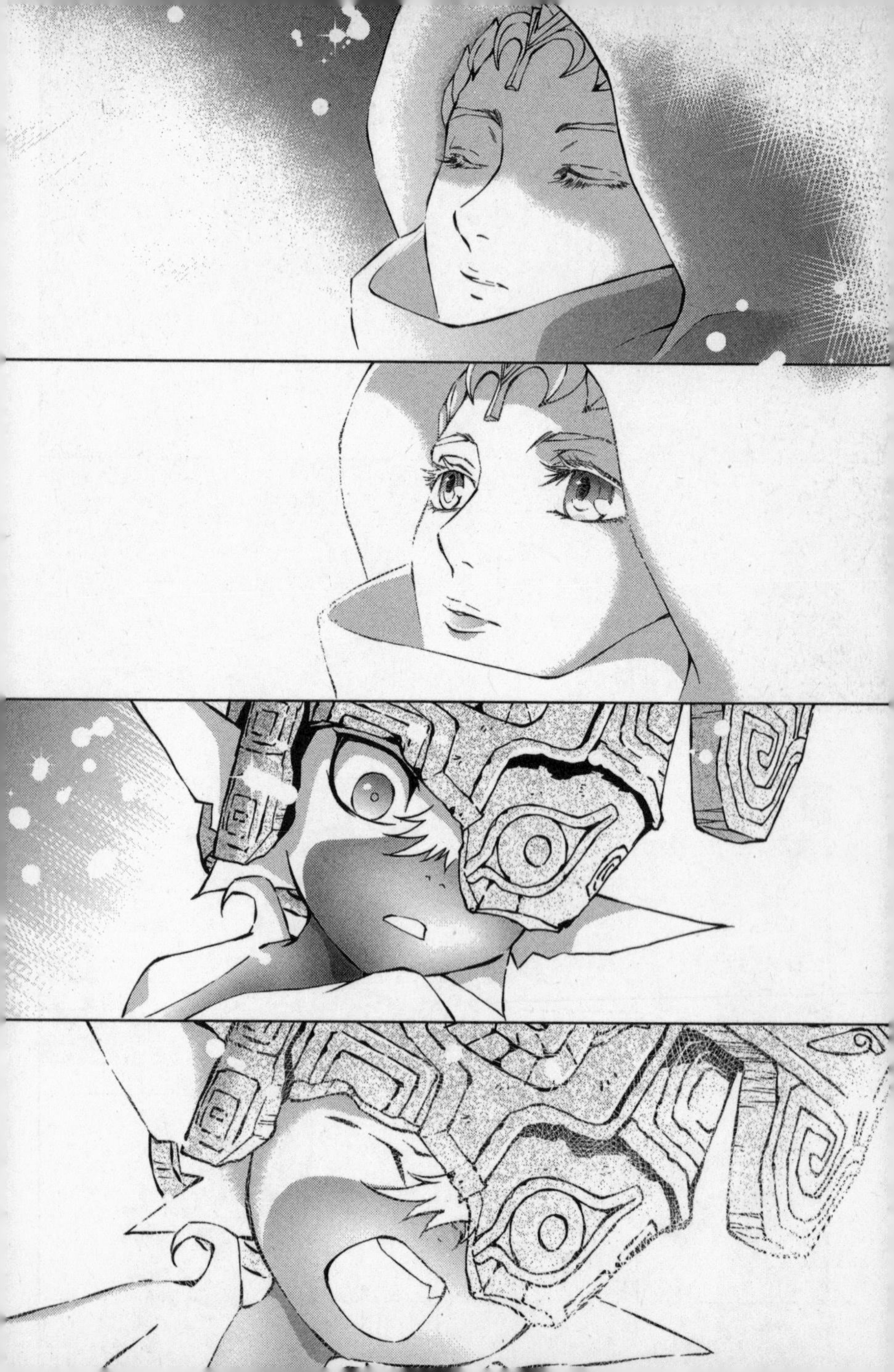

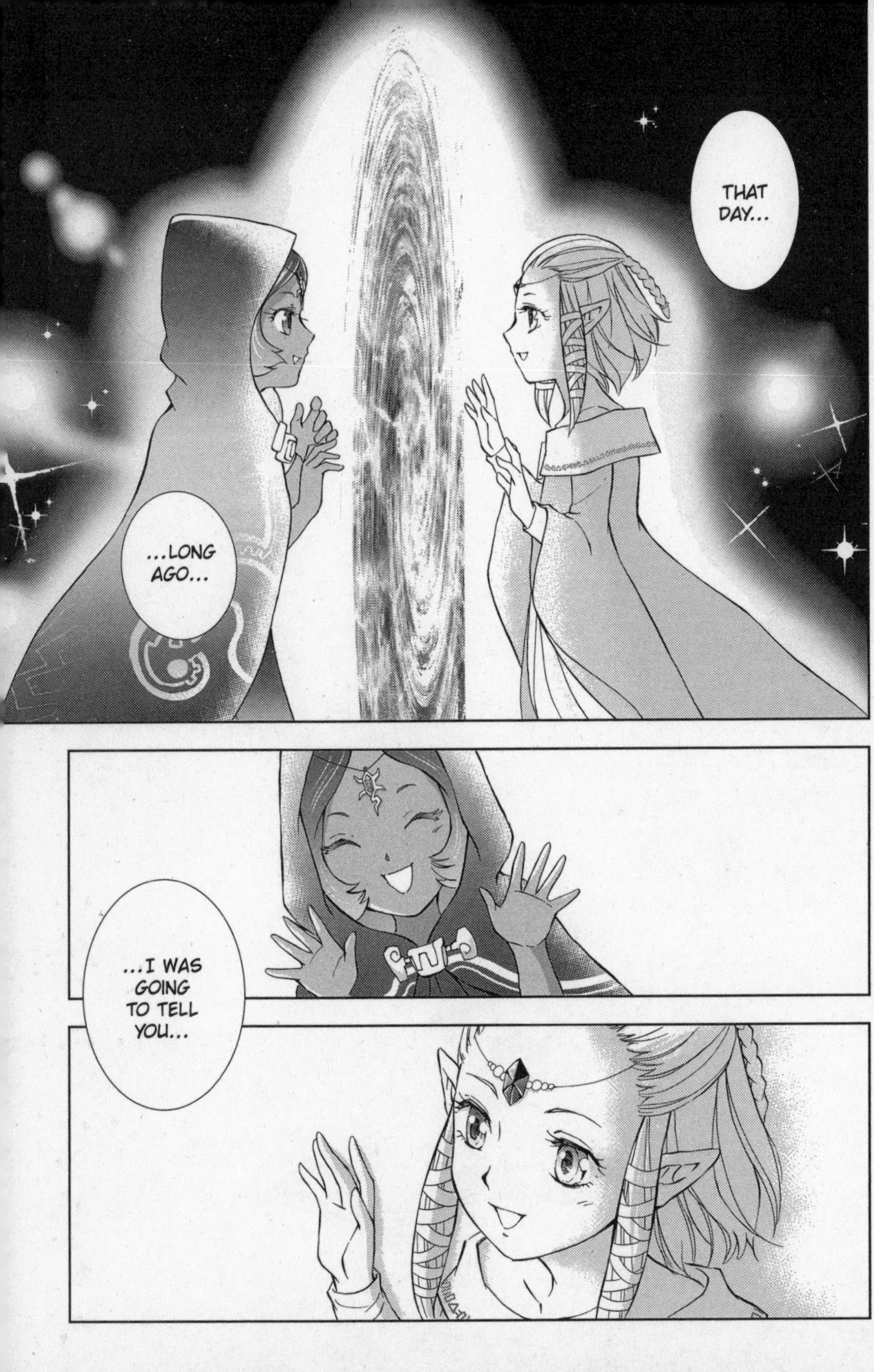
THAT DAY...
...LONG AGO...
...I WAS GOING TO TELL YOU...

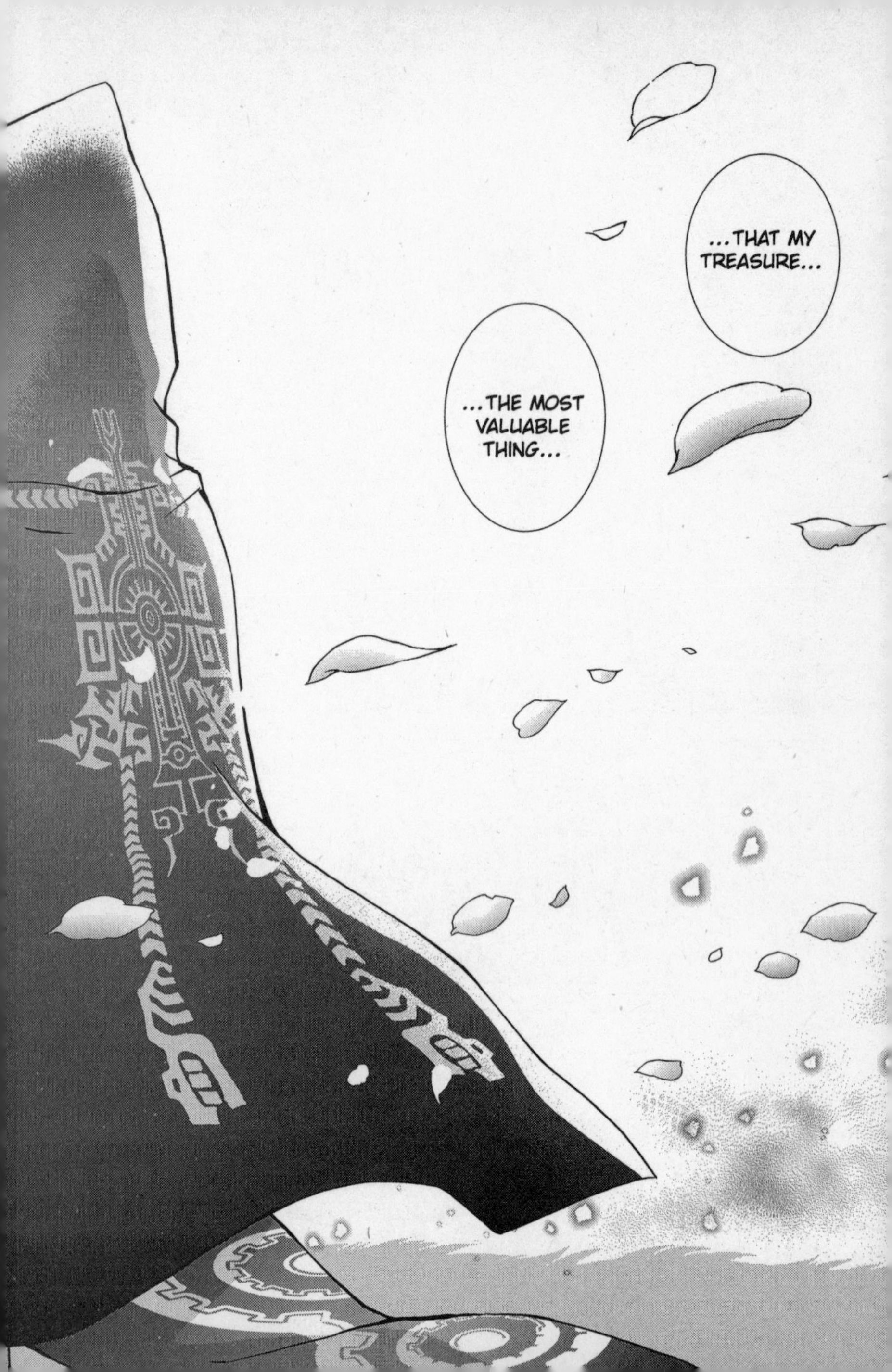
...THAT MY TREASURE...
...THE MOST VALUABLE THING...

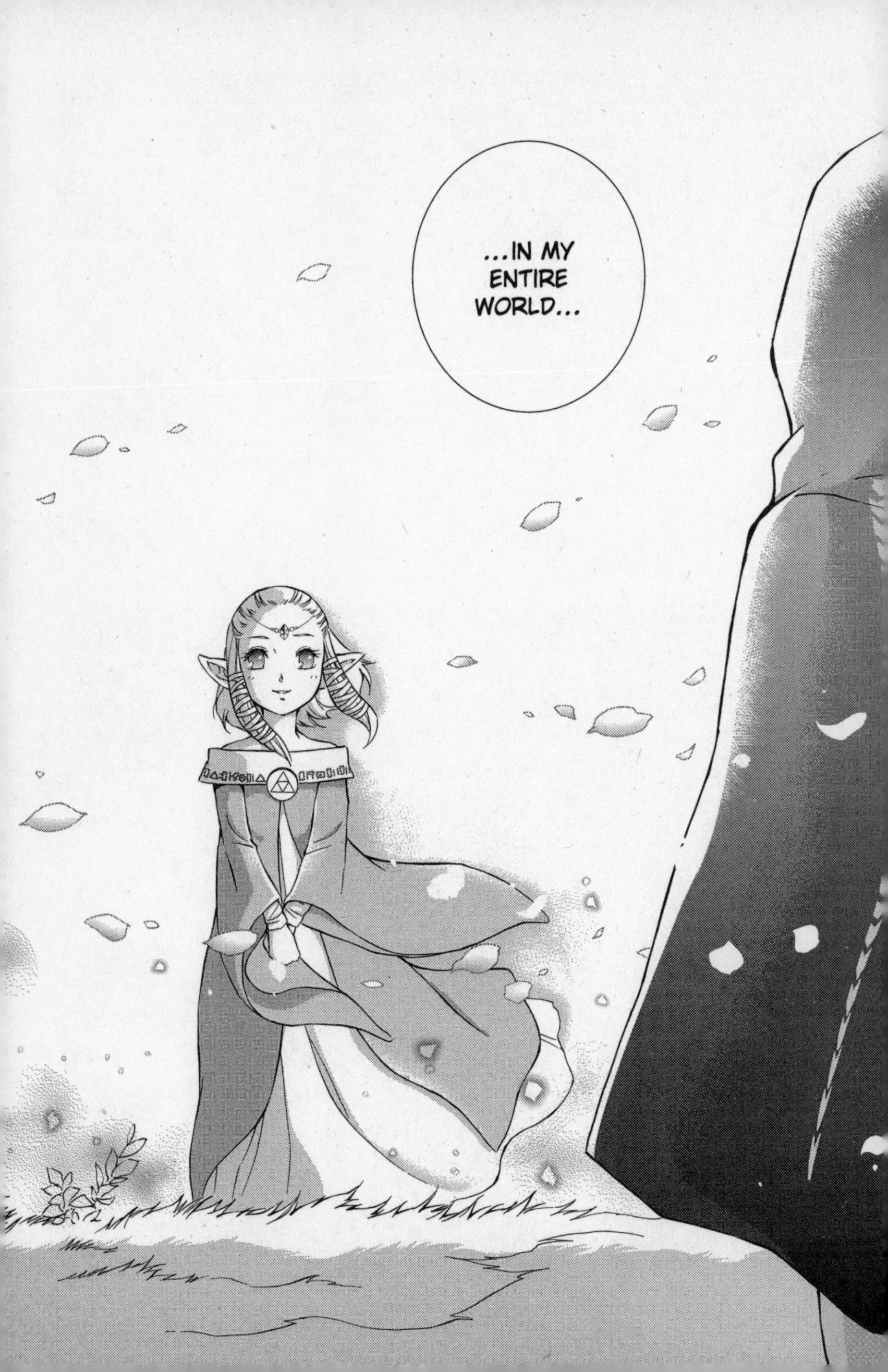
...IN MY
ENTIRE
WORLD...

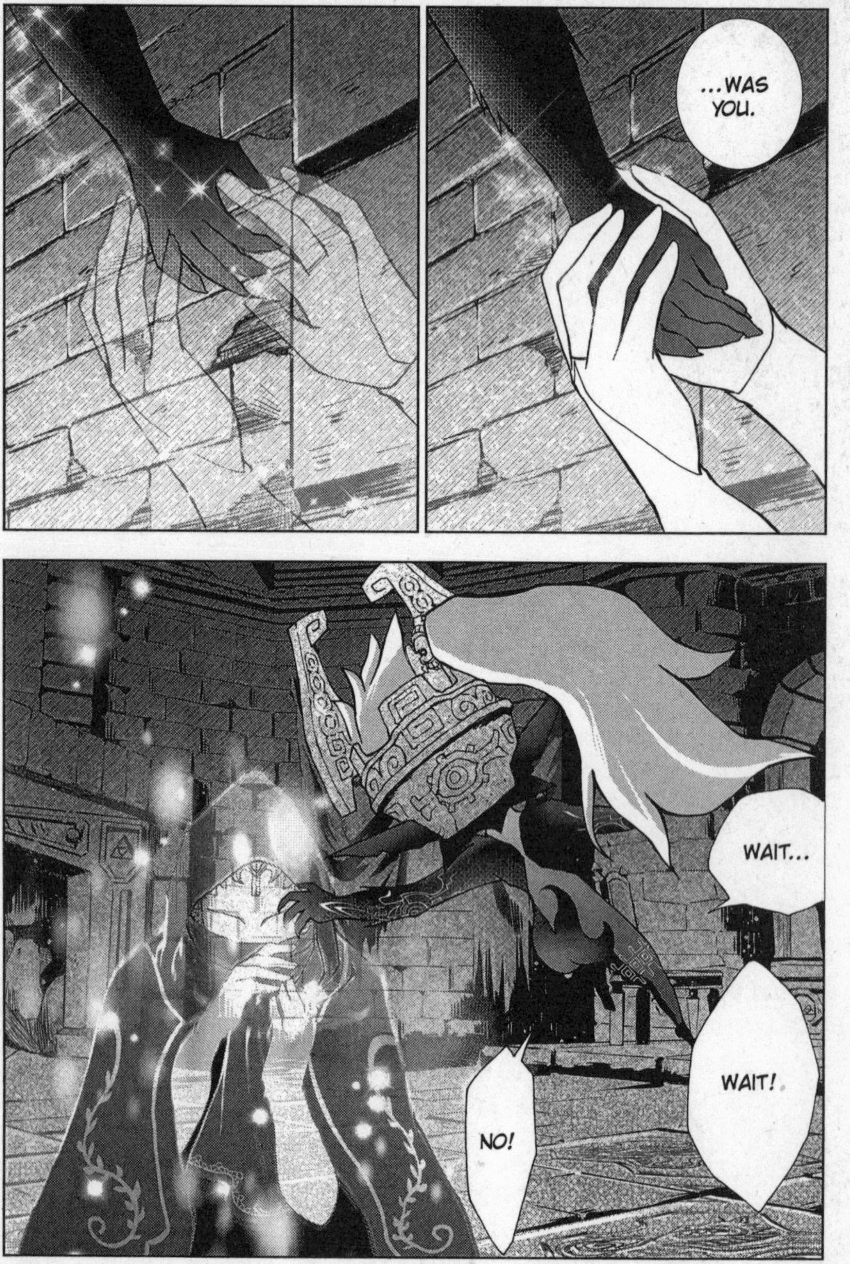
...WAS YOU.
WAIT...
WAIT!
NO!

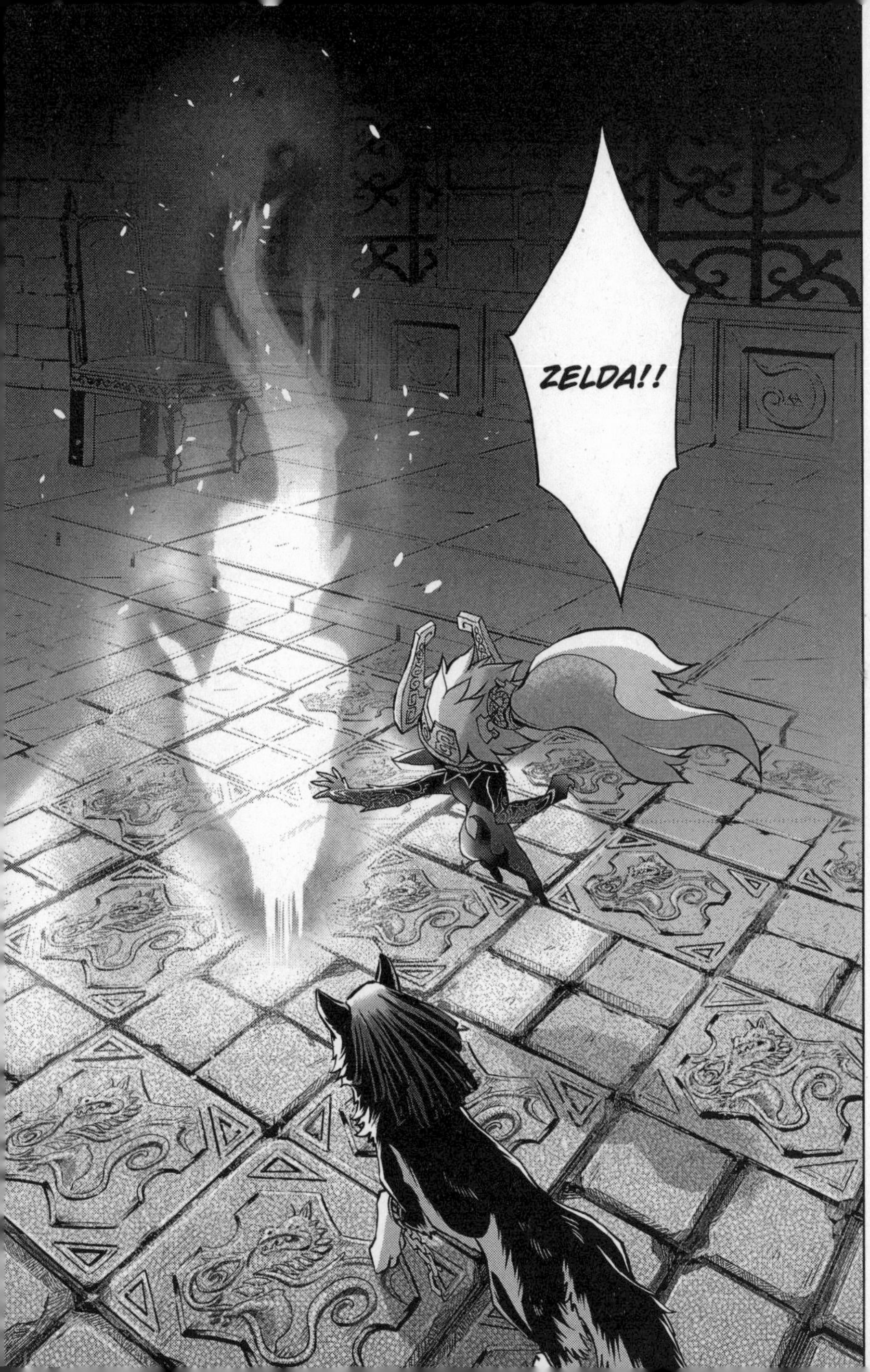
ZELDA!!

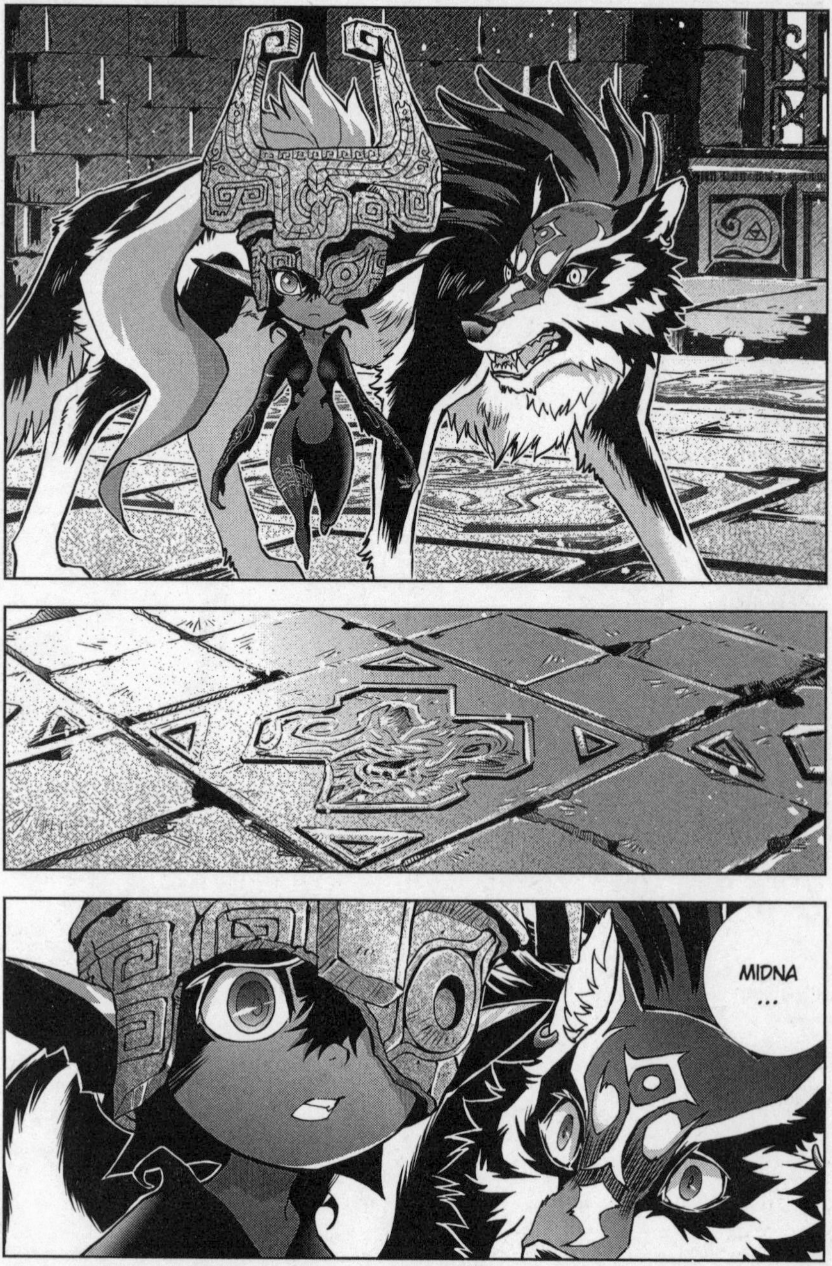
MIDNA
...

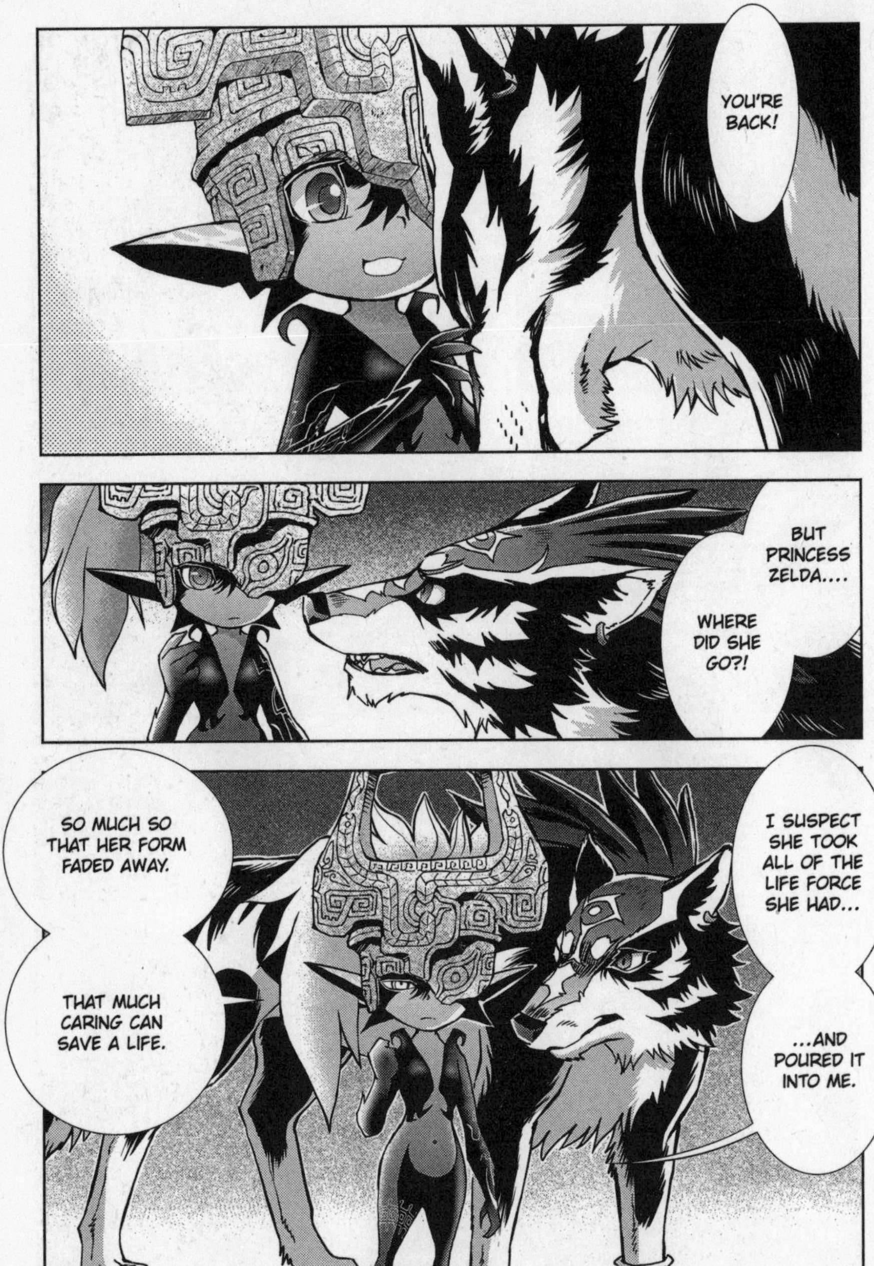
YOU'RE BACK!
BUT PRINCESS ZELDA....
WHERE DID SHE GO?!
I SUSPECT SHE TOOK ALL OF THE LIFE FORCE SHE HAD...
...AND POURED IT INTO ME.
SO MUCH SO THAT HER FORM FADED AWAY.
THAT MUCH CARING CAN SAVE A LIFE.

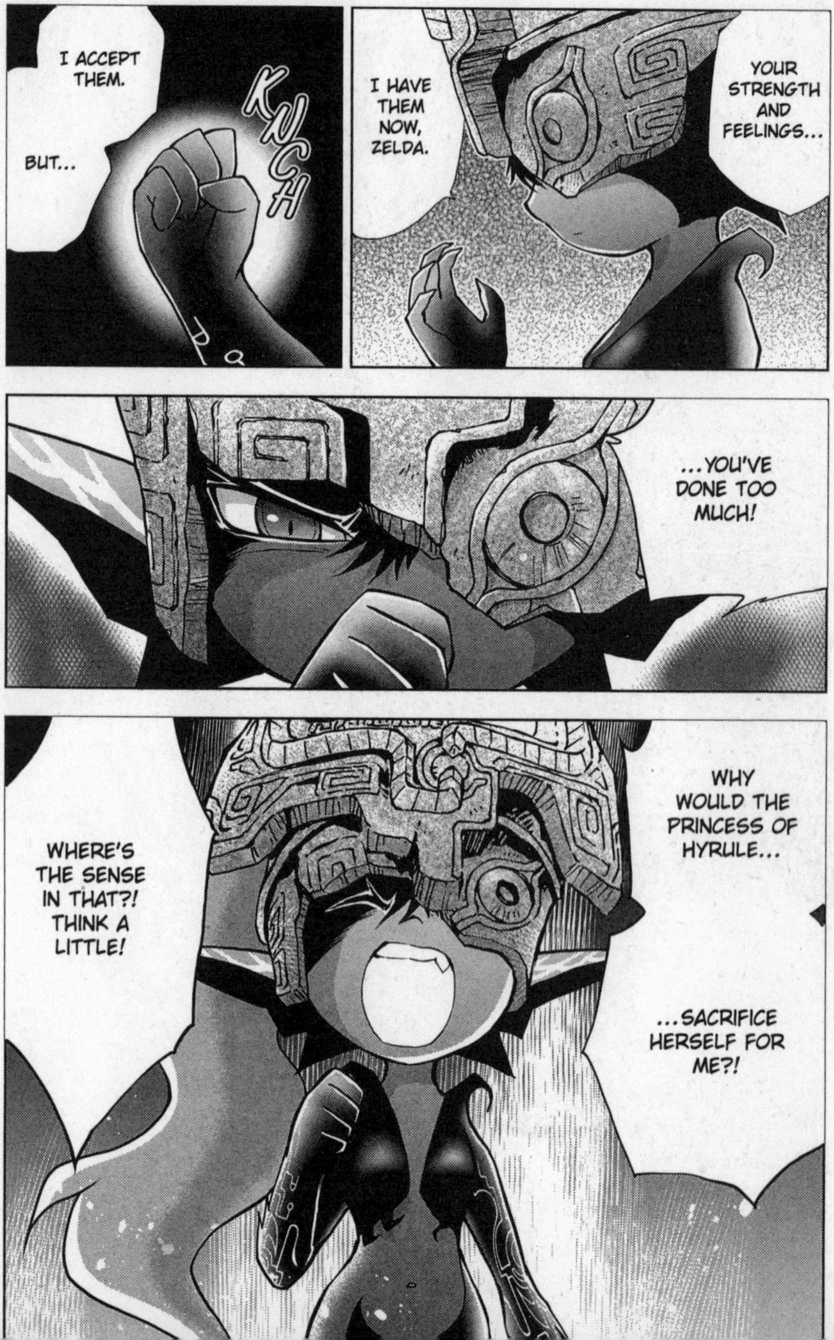
YOUR STRENGTH AND FEELINGS...
I HAVE THEM NOW, ZELDA.
I ACCEPT THEM.
BUT...
...YOU'VE DONE TOO MUCH!
WHY WOULD THE PRINCESS OF HYRULE...
...SACRIFICE HERSELF FOR ME?!
WHERE'S THE SENSE IN THAT?! THINK A LITTLE!

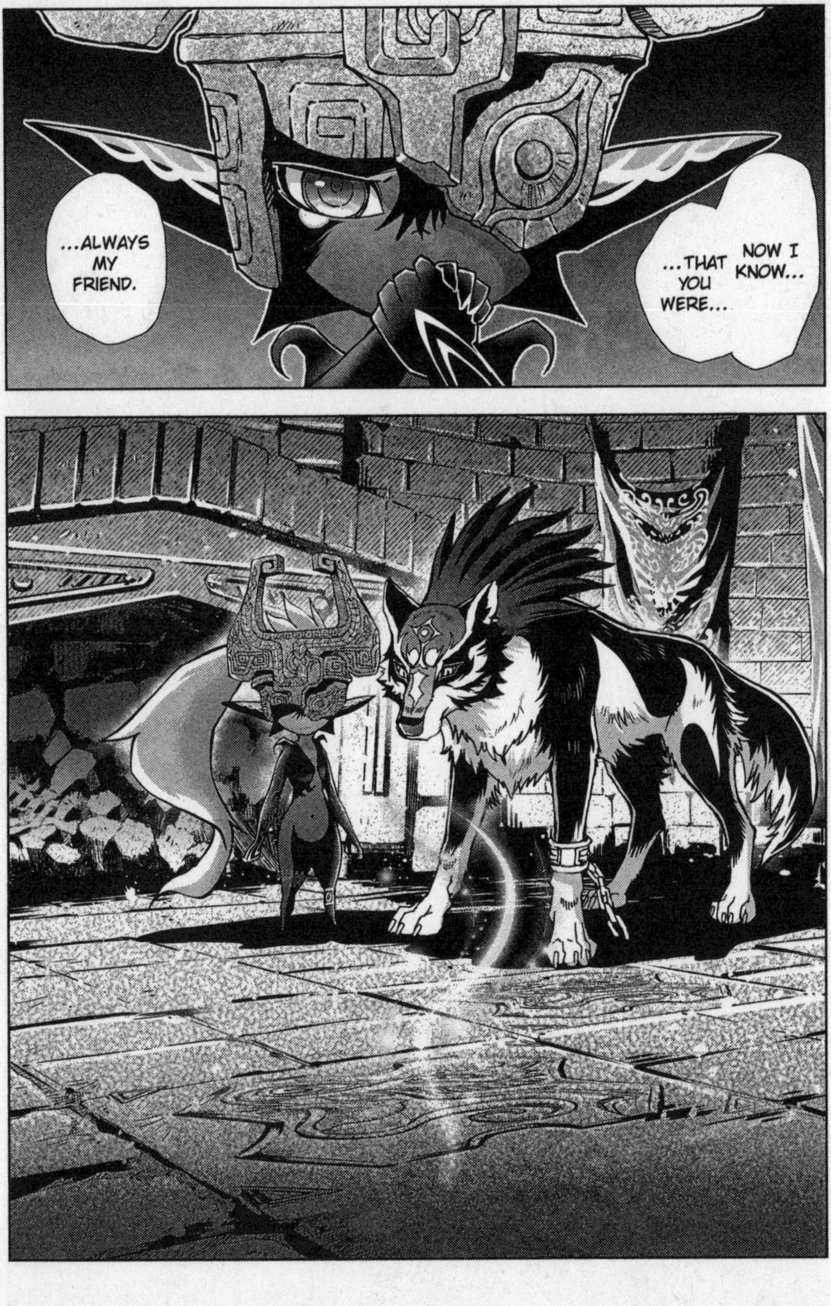
NOW I KNOW...
...THAT YOU WERE...
...ALWAYS MY FRIEND.

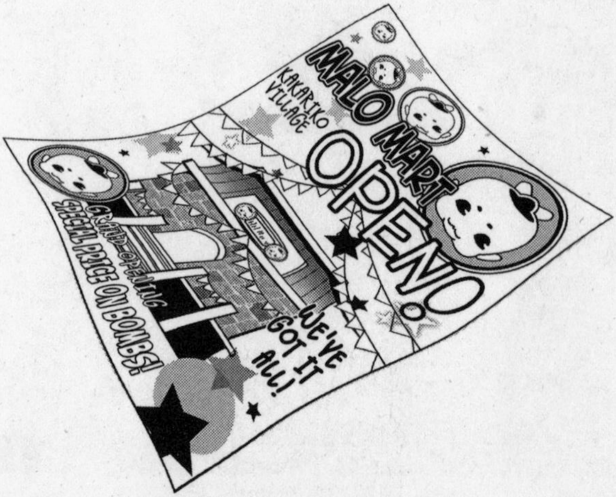
MALO MART OPEN!
KAKARIKO VILLAGE
WE'VE GOT IT ALL!
GRAND OPENING
SPECIAL PRICES ON BOMBS!

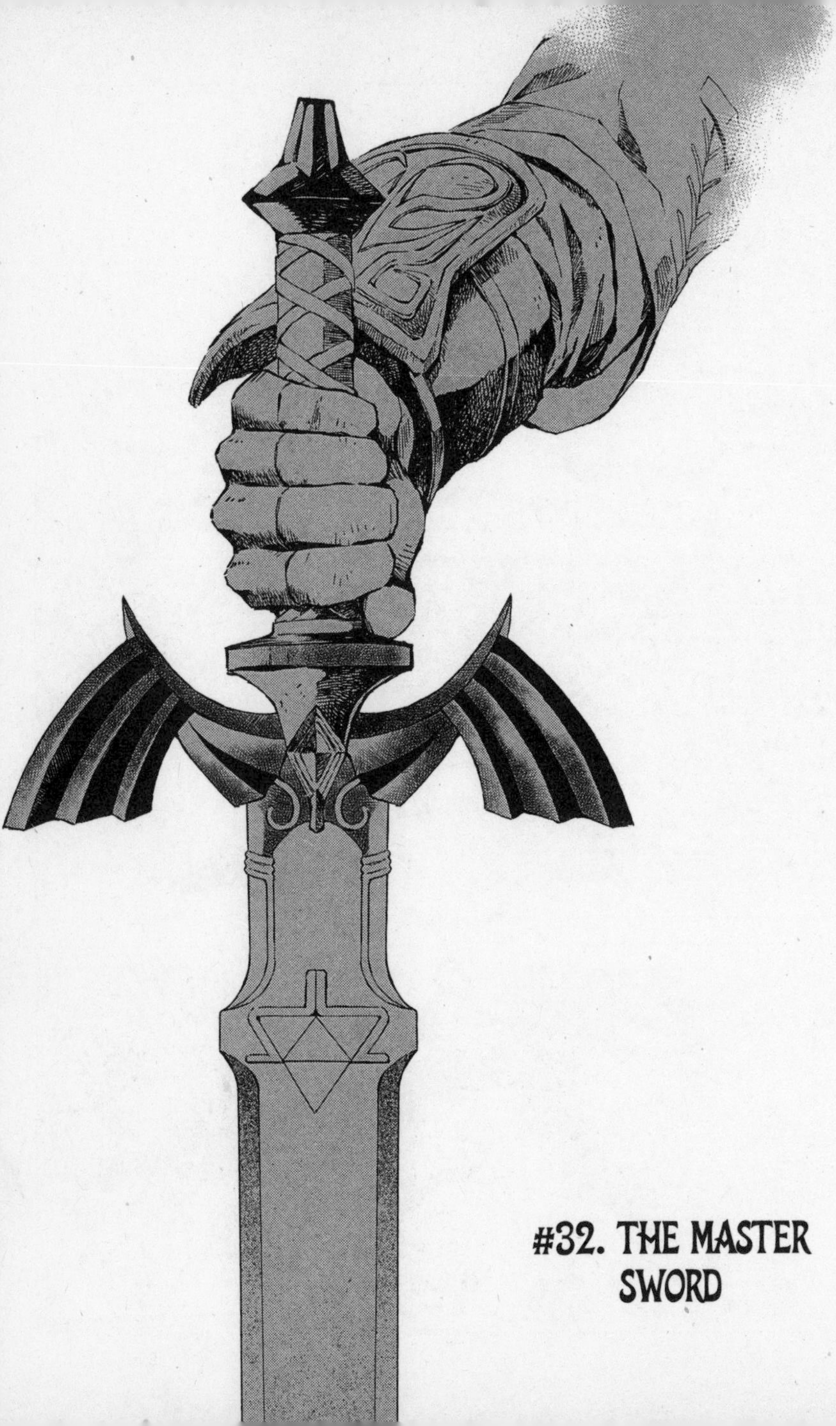

#32. THE MASTER SWORD

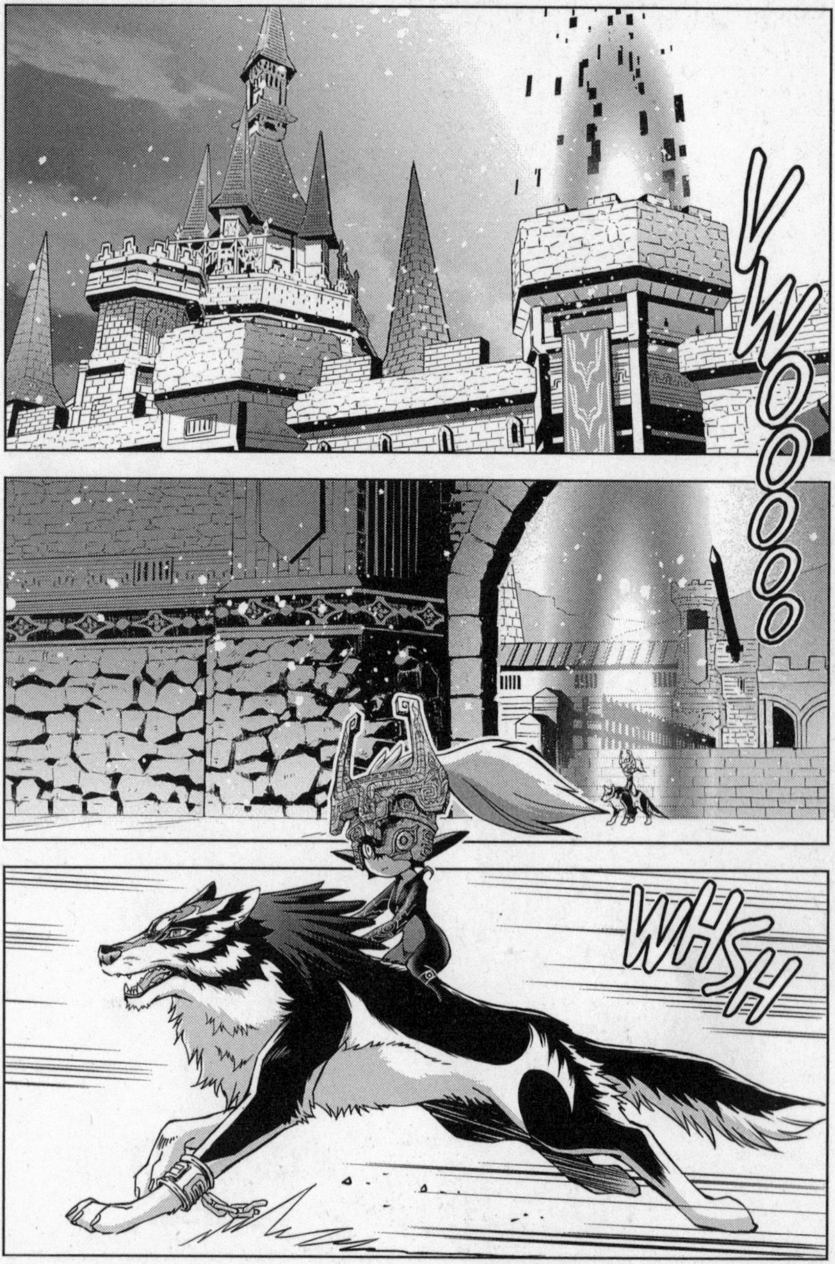
VWOOOOO
WHSH

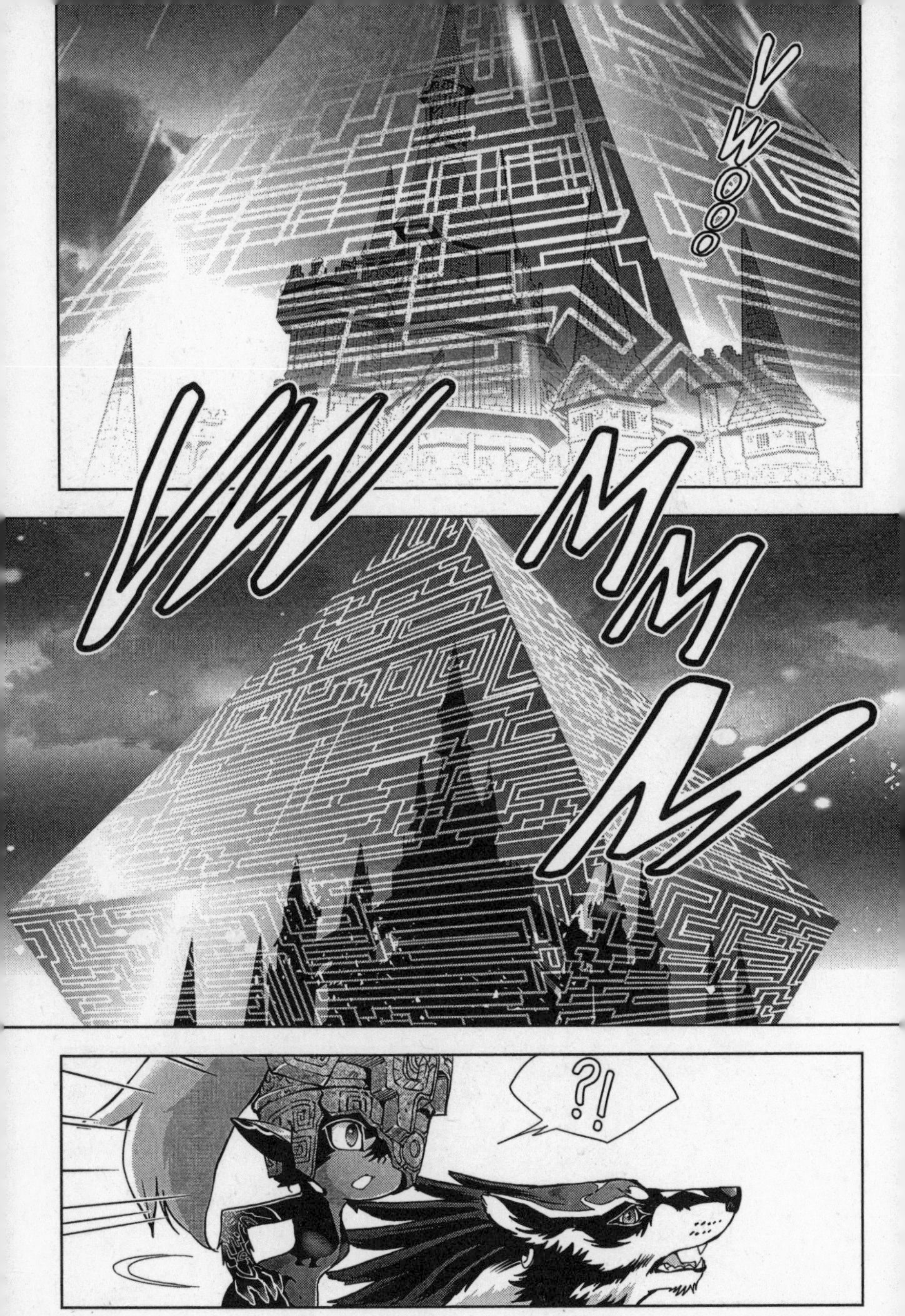
VWOOO
VWMMM
?!

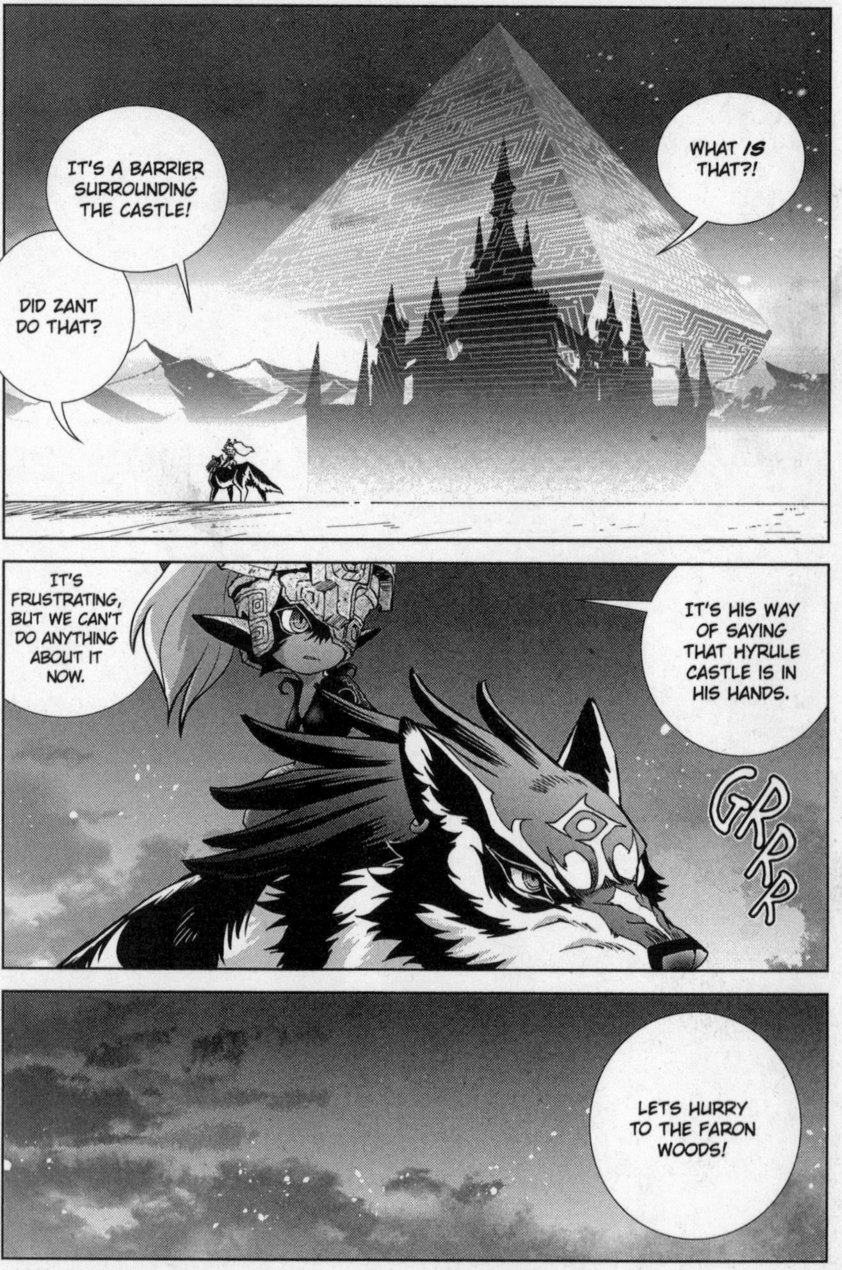
WHAT *IS* THAT?!
IT'S A BARRIER SURROUNDING THE CASTLE!
DID ZANT DO THAT?
IT'S HIS WAY OF SAYING THAT HYRULE CASTLE IS IN HIS HANDS.
GRRR
IT'S FRUSTRATING, BUT WE CAN'T DO ANYTHING ABOUT IT NOW.
LETS HURRY TO THE FARON WOODS!

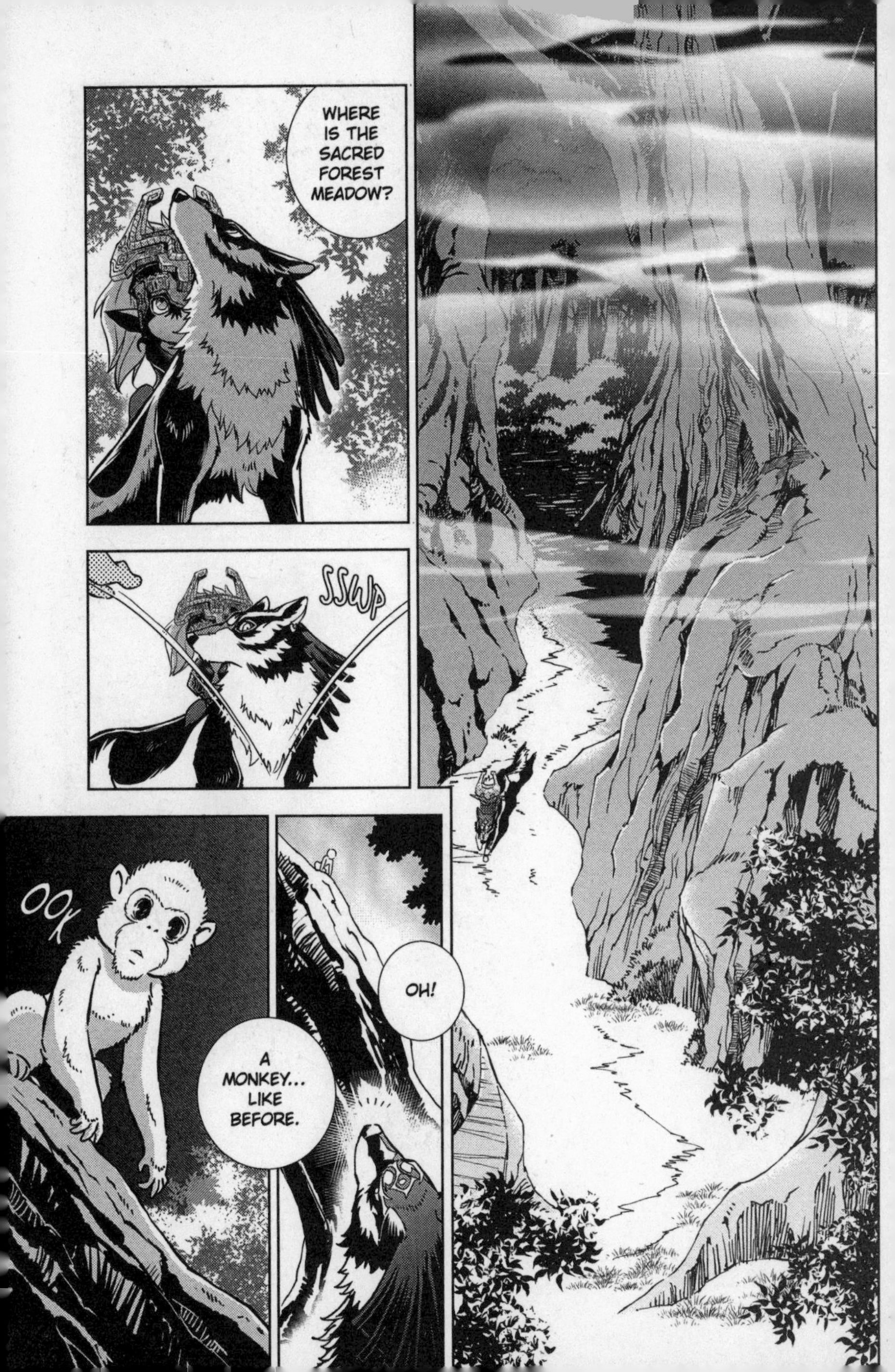
WHERE IS THE SACRED FOREST MEADOW?
SSWP
OH!
A MONKEY... LIKE BEFORE.
OOK

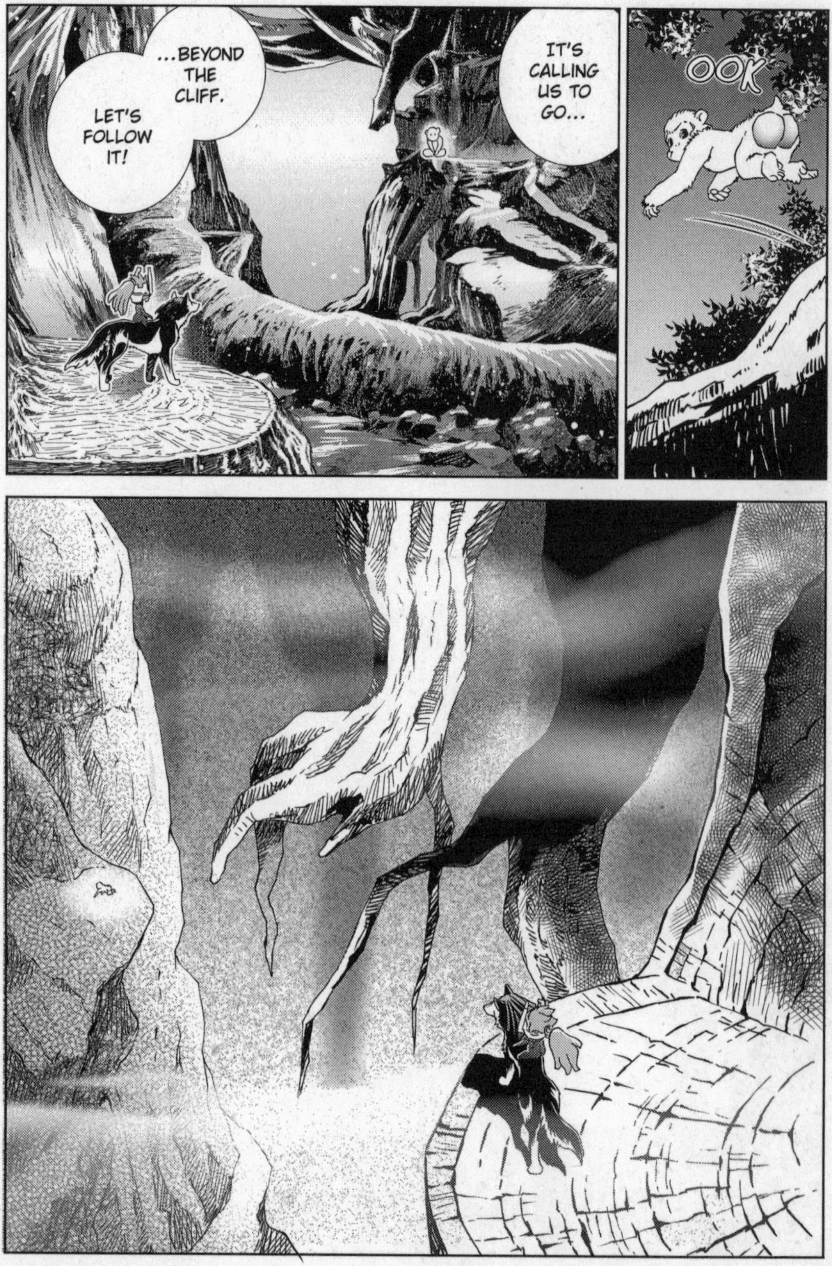
OOK
IT'S CALLING US TO GO...
...BEYOND THE CLIFF.
LET'S FOLLOW IT!

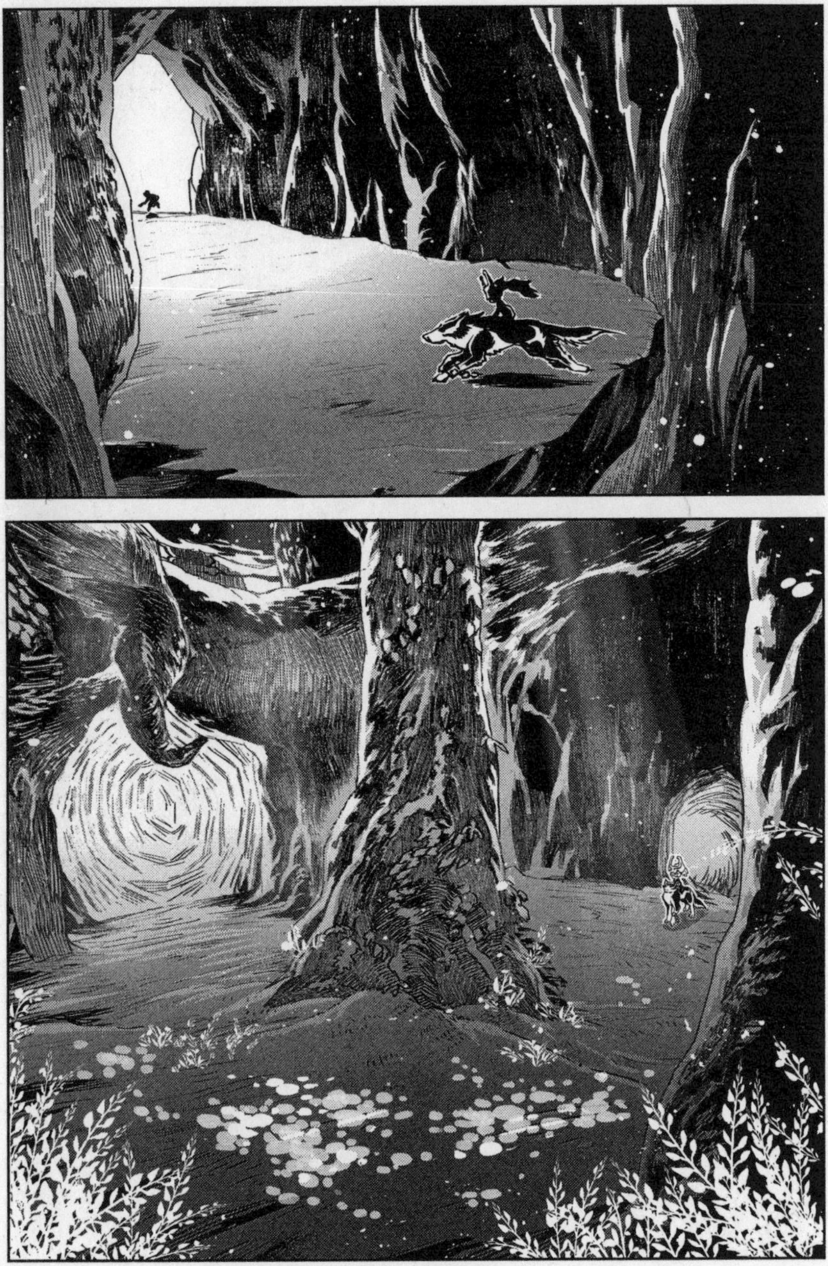

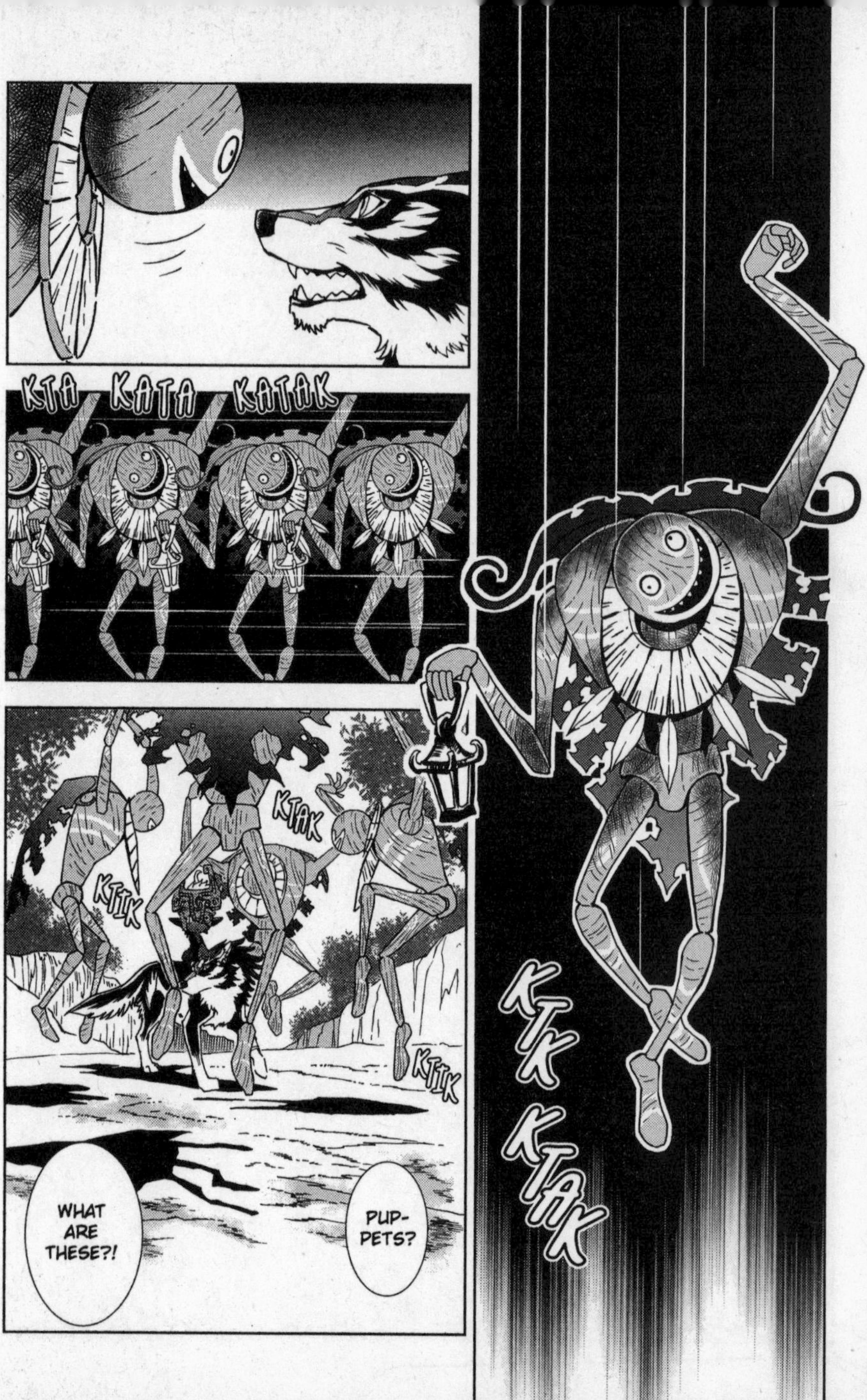
KTIK KTAK
KTA KATA KATAK
KTAK
KTIK
KTIK
PUP-PETS?
WHAT ARE THESE?!

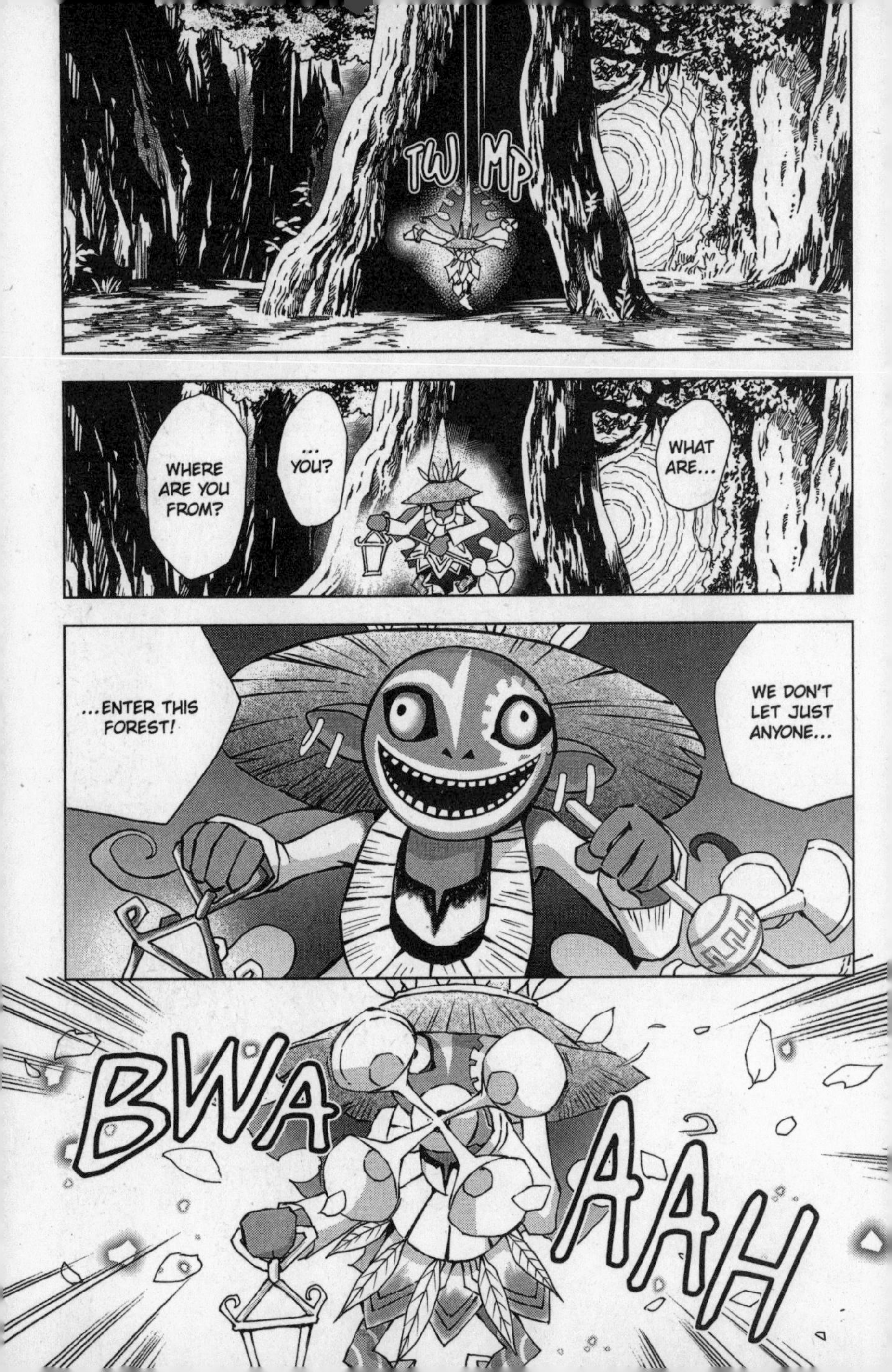
TW MP
WHAT ARE...
...YOU?
WHERE ARE YOU FROM?
WE DON'T LET JUST ANYONE...
...ENTER THIS FOREST!
BWAAAH

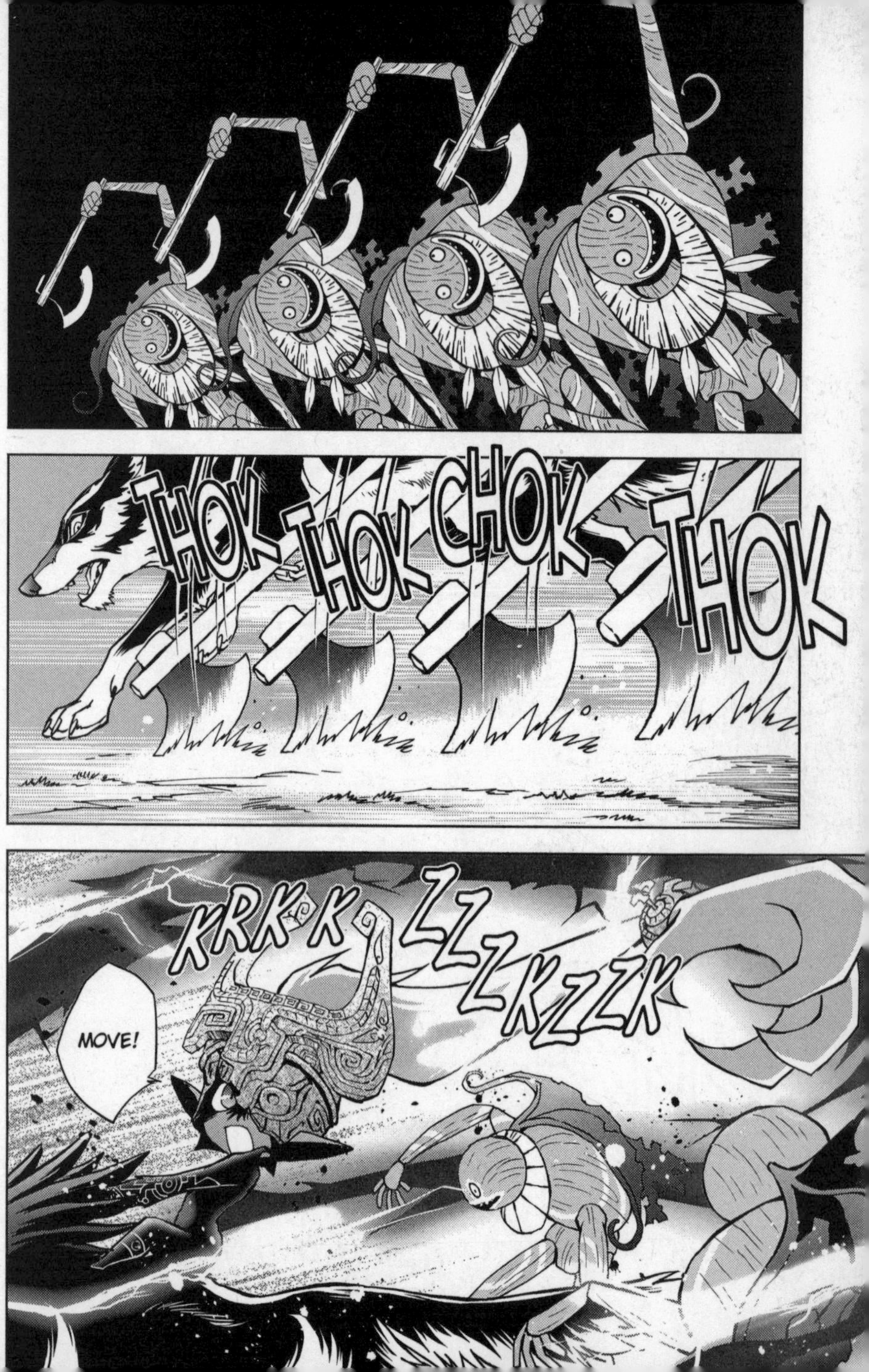
THOK
CHOK
THOK
THOK
KRKKK
ZZZKZZK
MOVE!

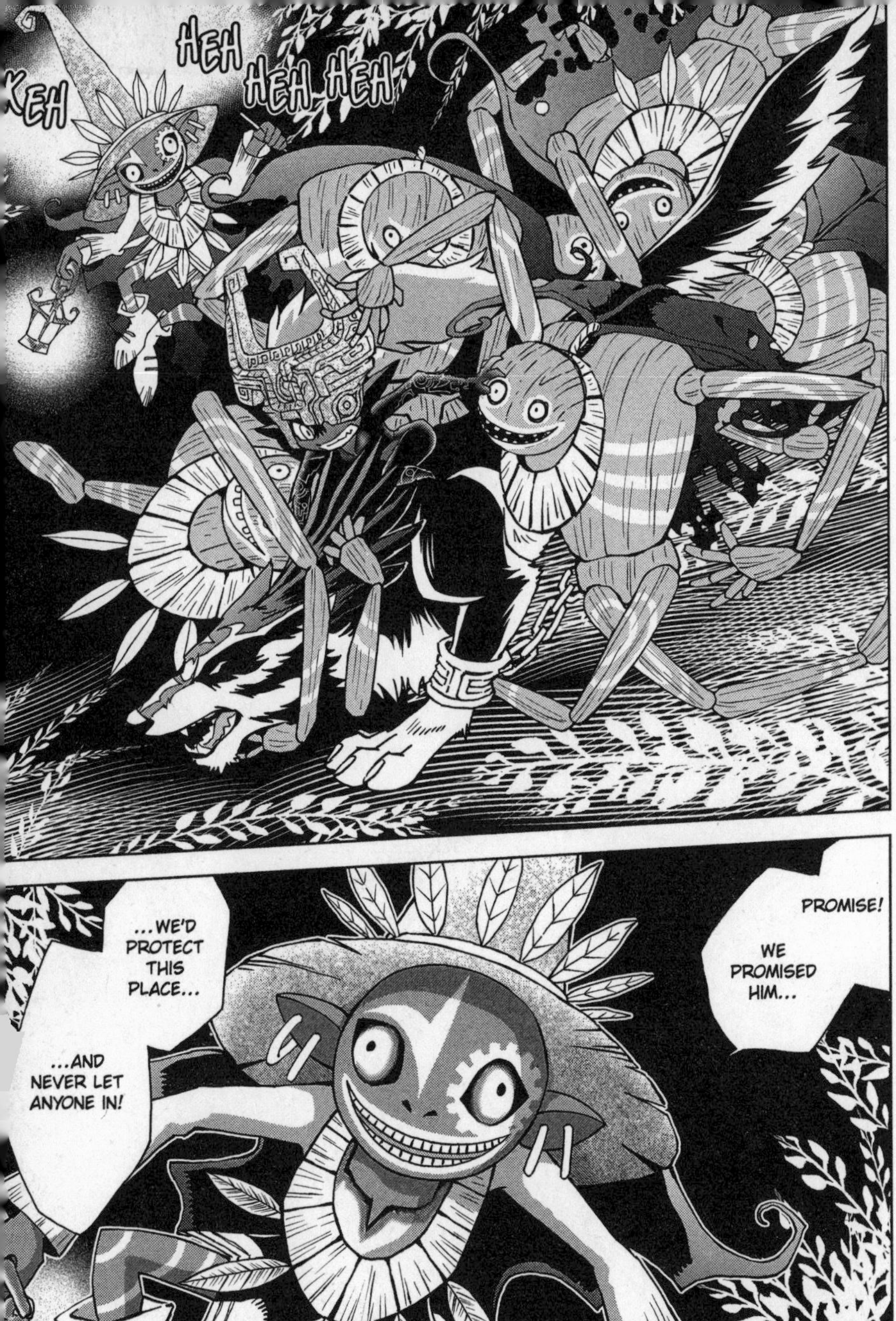
HEH HEH HEH
KEH
PROMISE!
WE PROMISED HIM...
...WE'D PROTECT THIS PLACE...
...AND NEVER LET ANYONE IN!

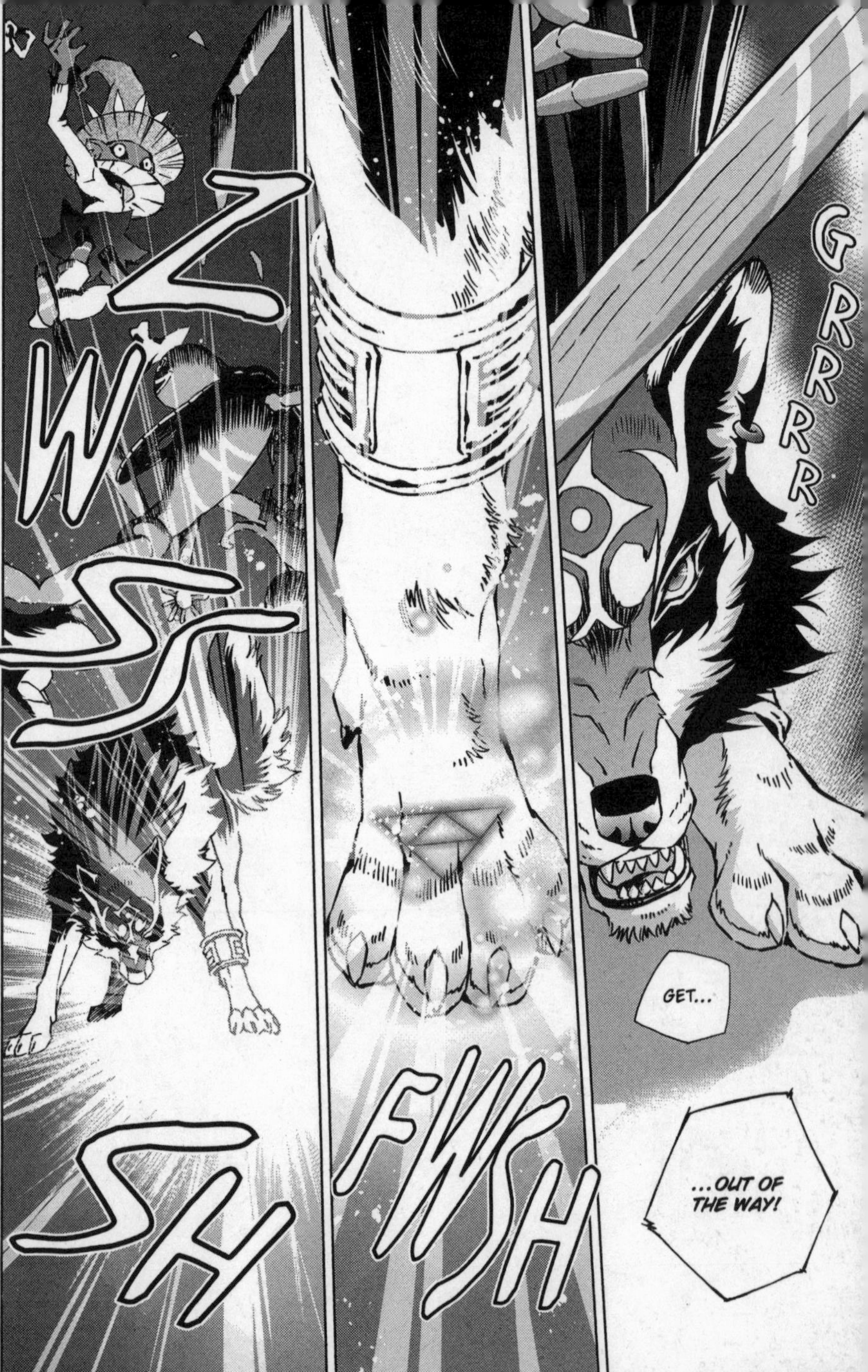
GRRRRR
GET...
...OUT OF THE WAY!
FWSH
WSSH

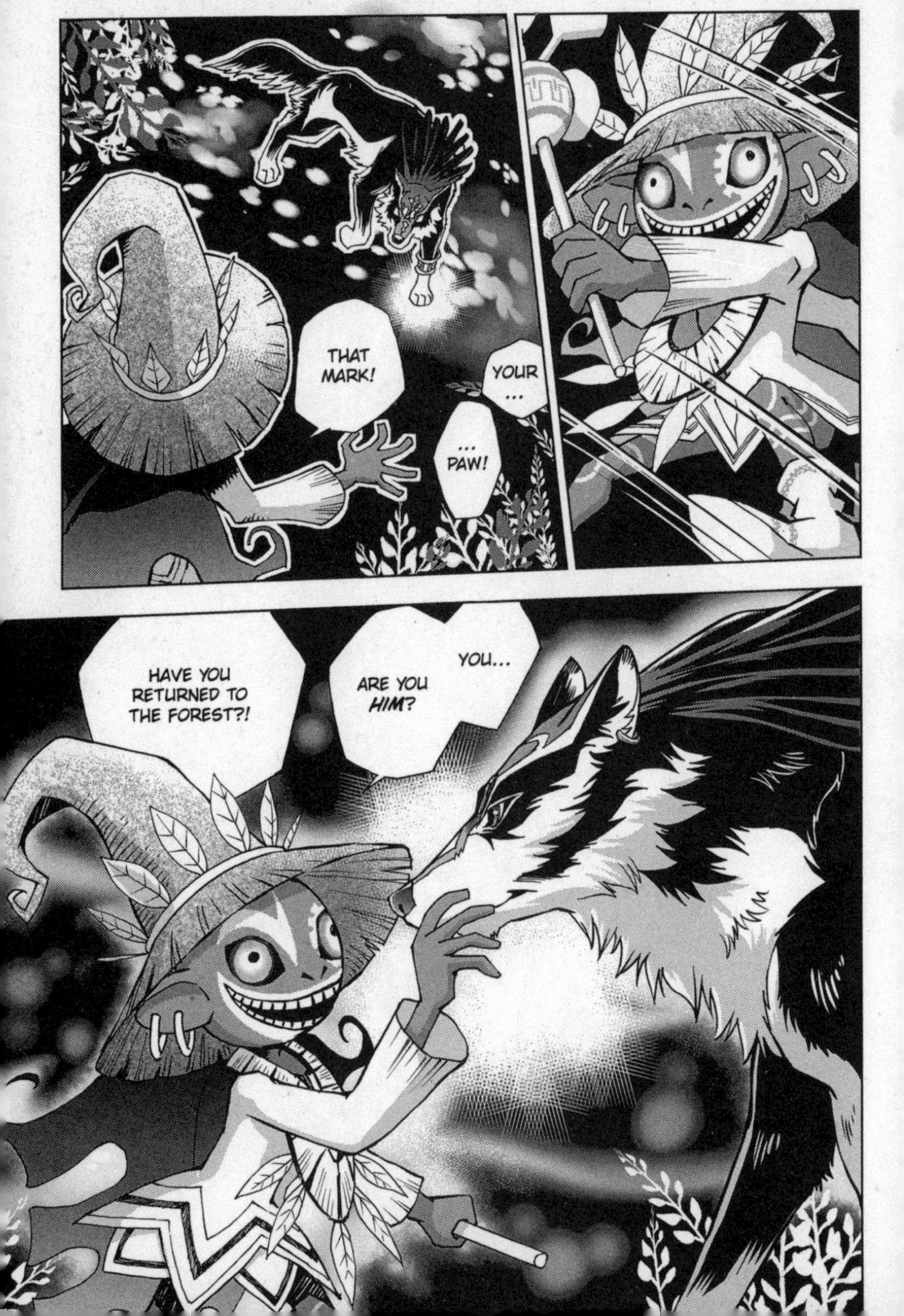
THAT MARK!
YOUR ...
... PAW!
YOU...
ARE YOU *HIM*?
HAVE YOU RETURNED TO THE FOREST?!

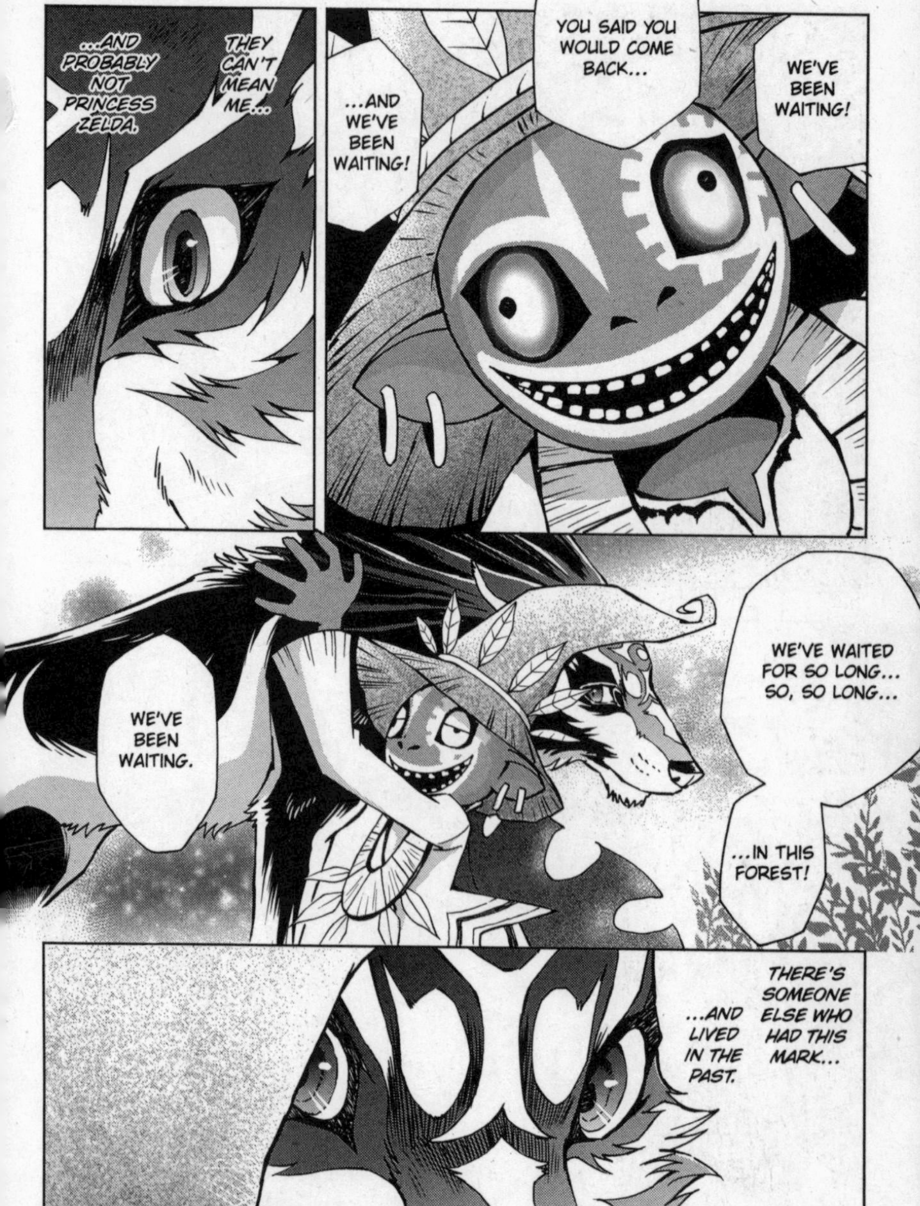

YOU SAID YOU WOULD COME BACK...
WE'VE BEEN WAITING!
...AND WE'VE BEEN WAITING!
THEY CAN'T MEAN ME...
...AND PROBABLY NOT PRINCESS ZELDA.
WE'VE WAITED FOR SO LONG... SO, SO LONG...
...IN THIS FOREST!
WE'VE BEEN WAITING.
THERE'S SOMEONE ELSE WHO HAD THIS MARK...
...AND LIVED IN THE PAST.

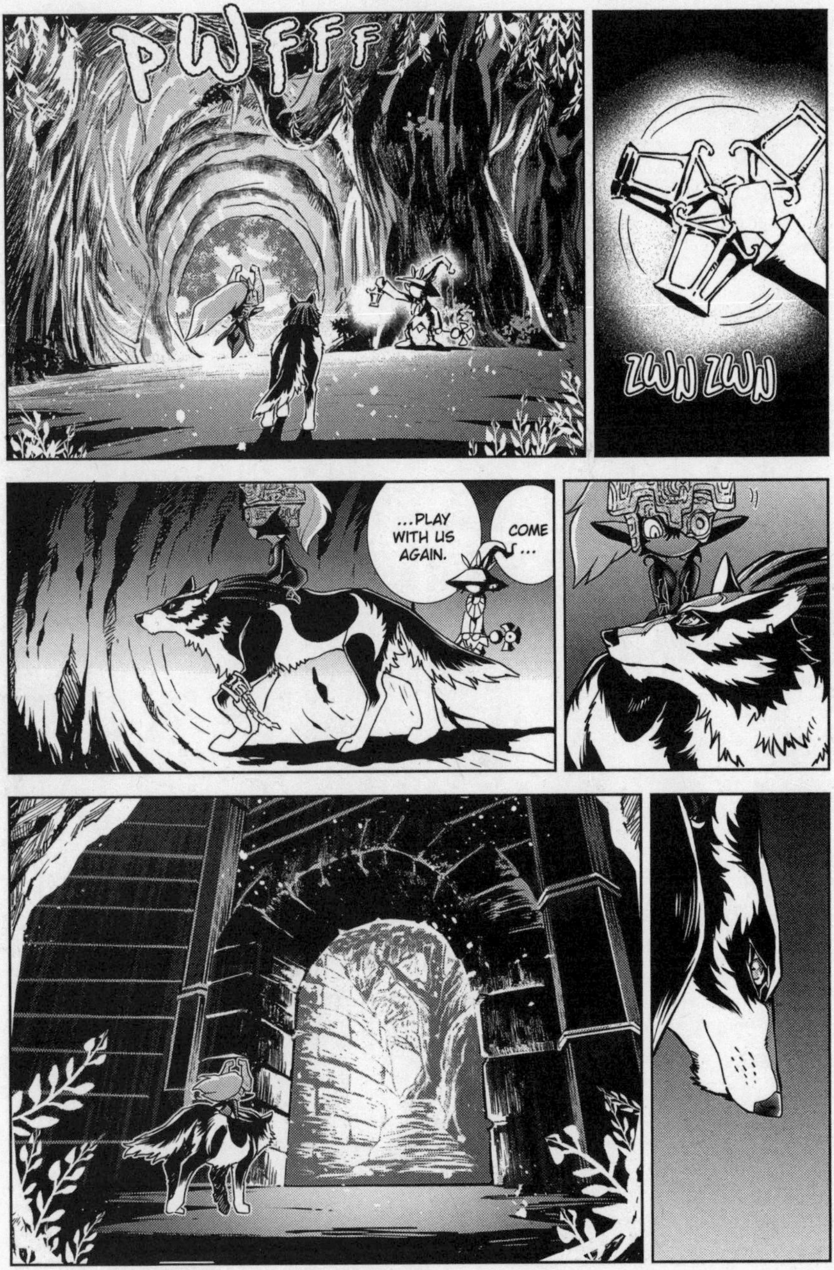
ZWN ZWN
PWFFF
COME ...
...PLAY WITH US AGAIN.

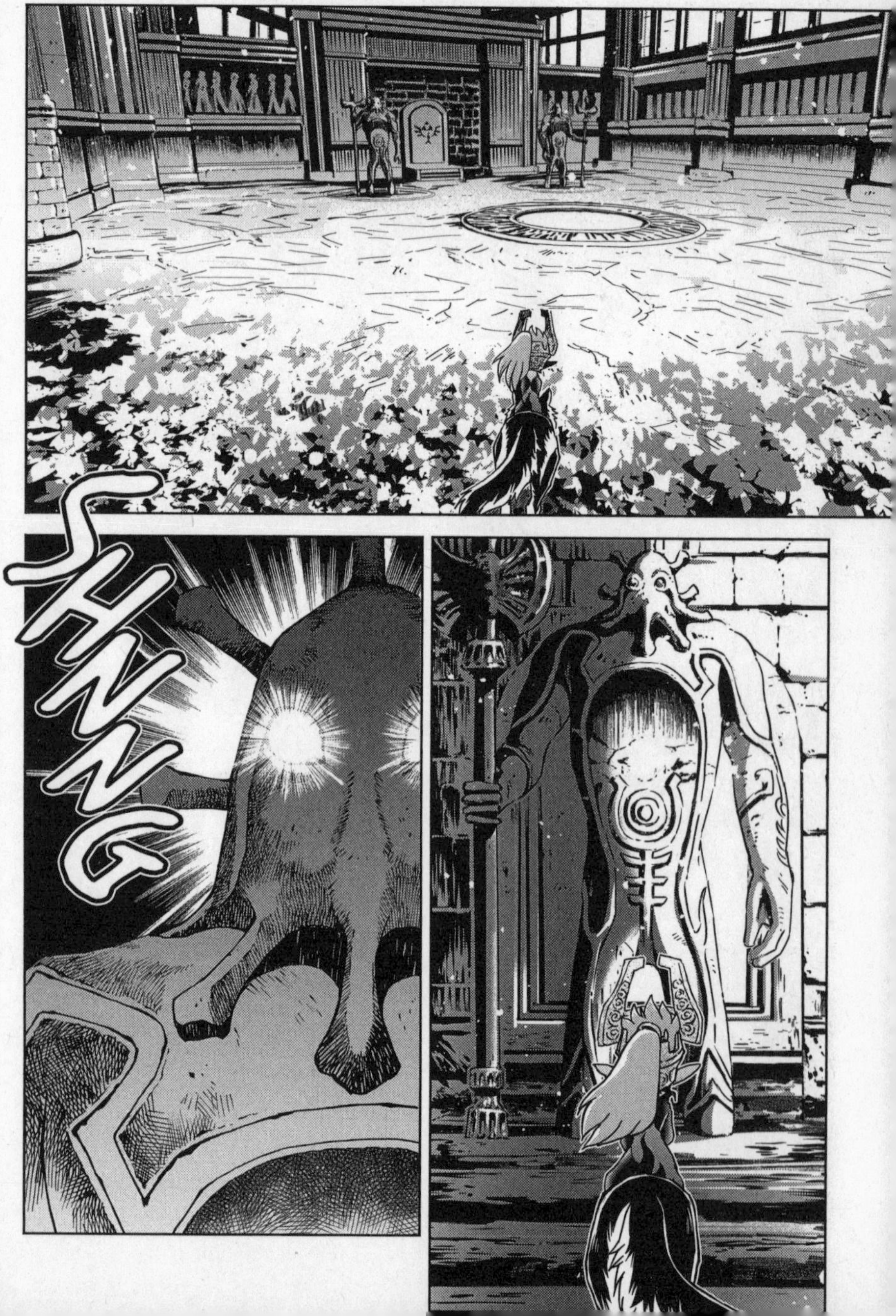
SHNNG

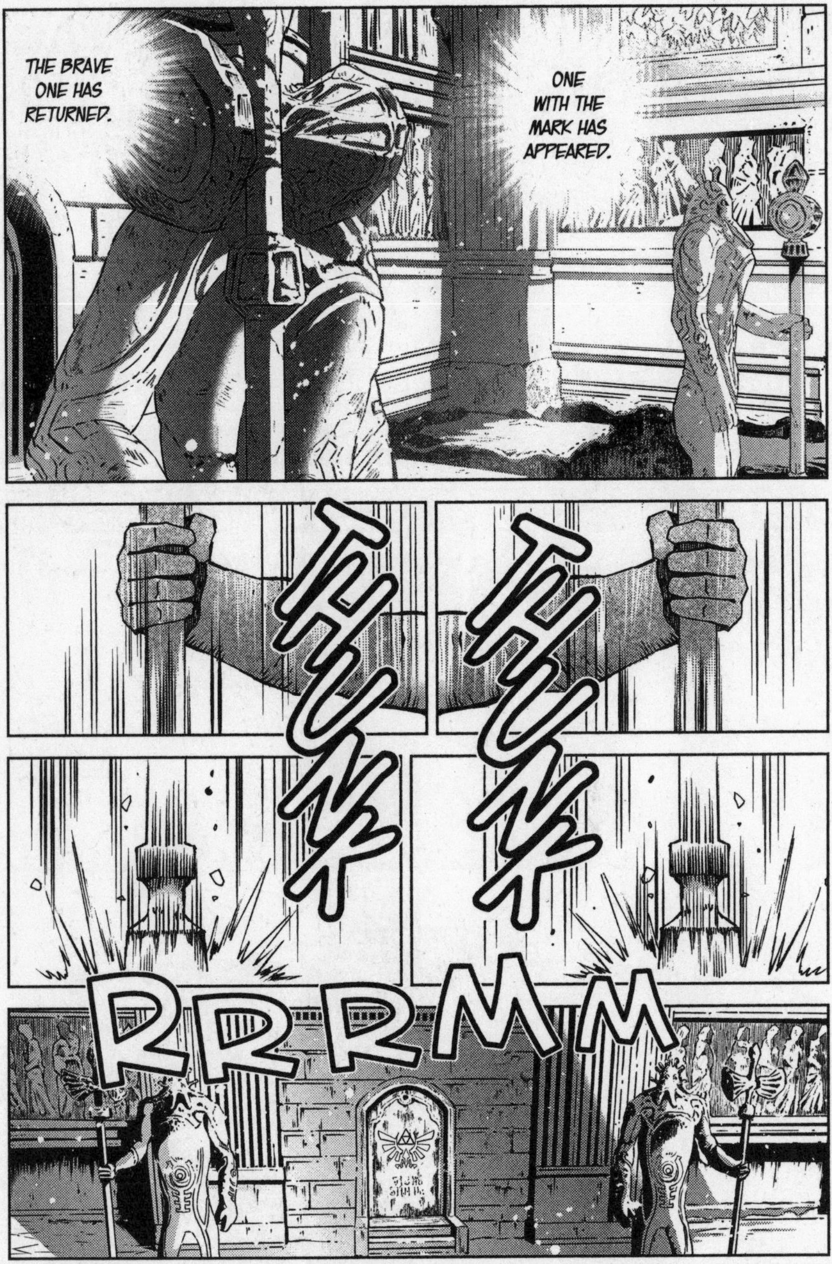
ONE WITH THE MARK HAS APPEARED.
THE BRAVE ONE HAS RETURNED.
THUNK
THUNK
RRRMM

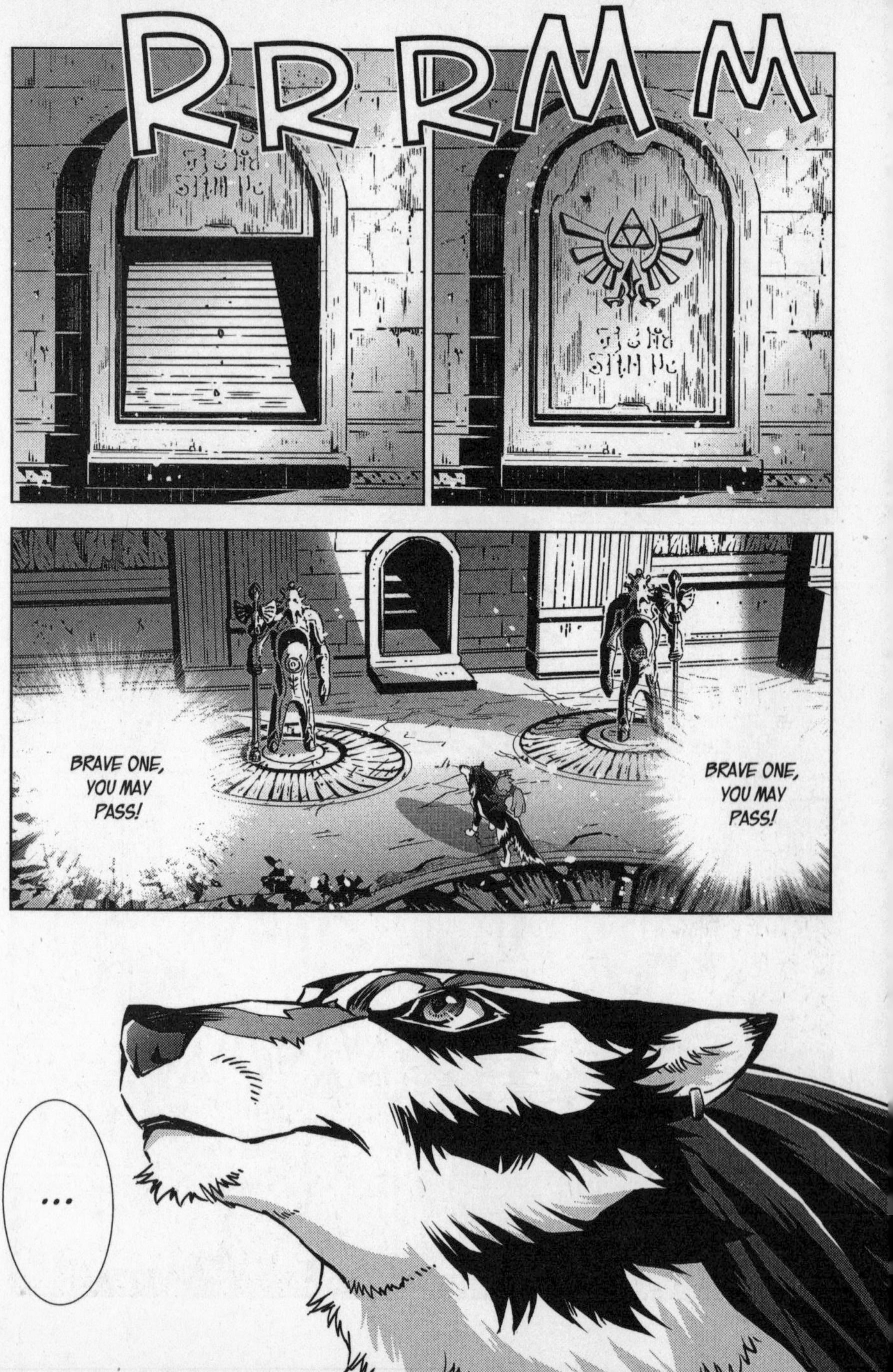
RRRMM
BRAVE ONE, YOU MAY PASS!
BRAVE ONE, YOU MAY PASS!
...

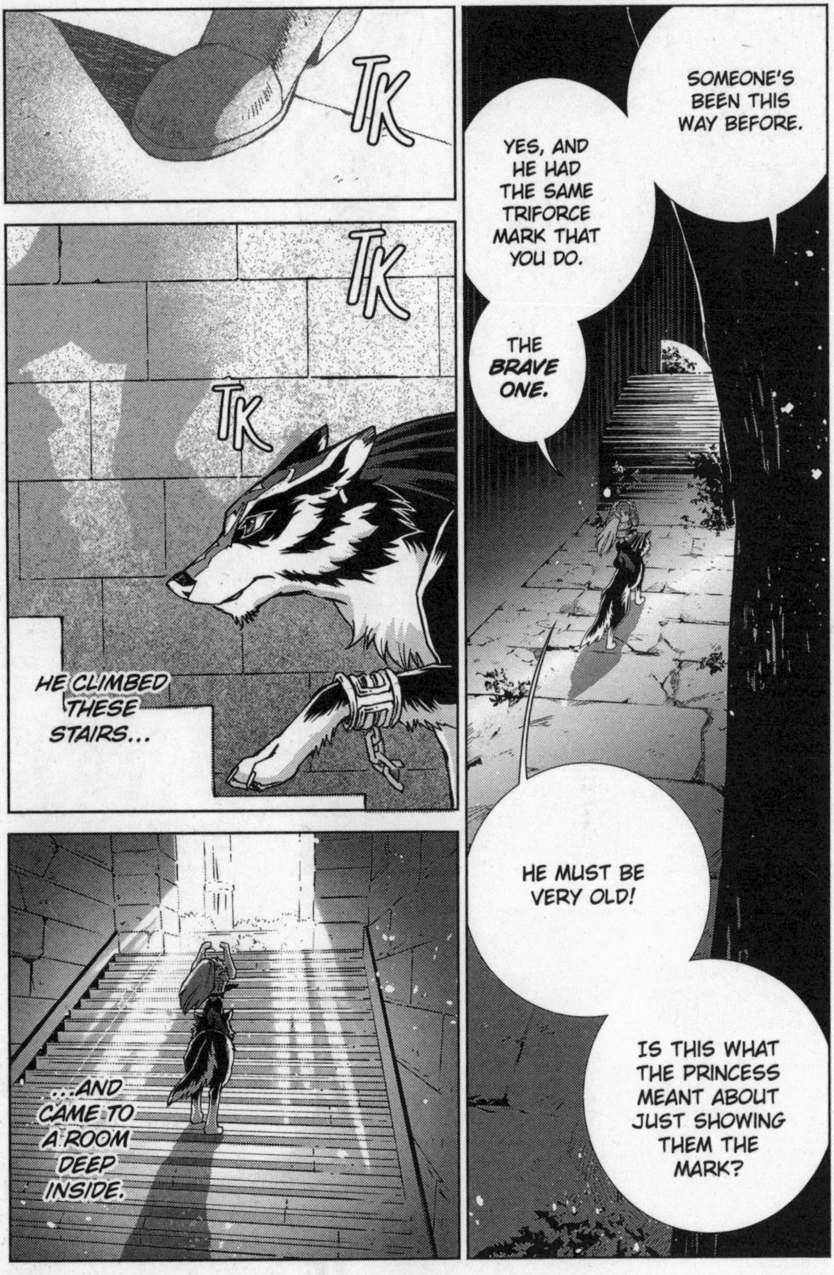
SOMEONE'S BEEN THIS WAY BEFORE.
YES, AND HE HAD THE SAME TRIFORCE MARK THAT YOU DO.
THE *BRAVE ONE.*
HE MUST BE VERY OLD!
IS THIS WHAT THE PRINCESS MEANT ABOUT JUST SHOWING THEM THE MARK?
TK
TK
TK
HE CLIMBED THESE STAIRS...
...AND CAME TO A ROOM DEEP INSIDE.

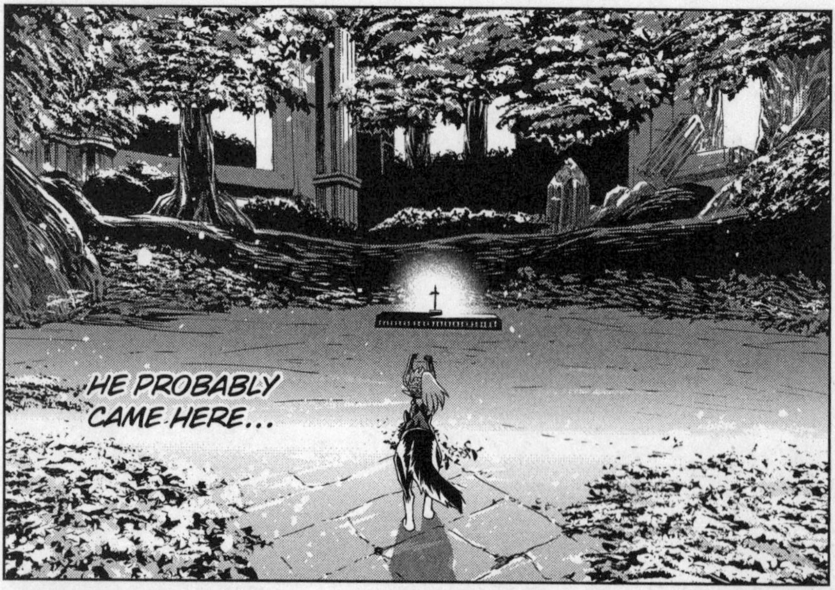
HE PROBABLY CAME HERE...
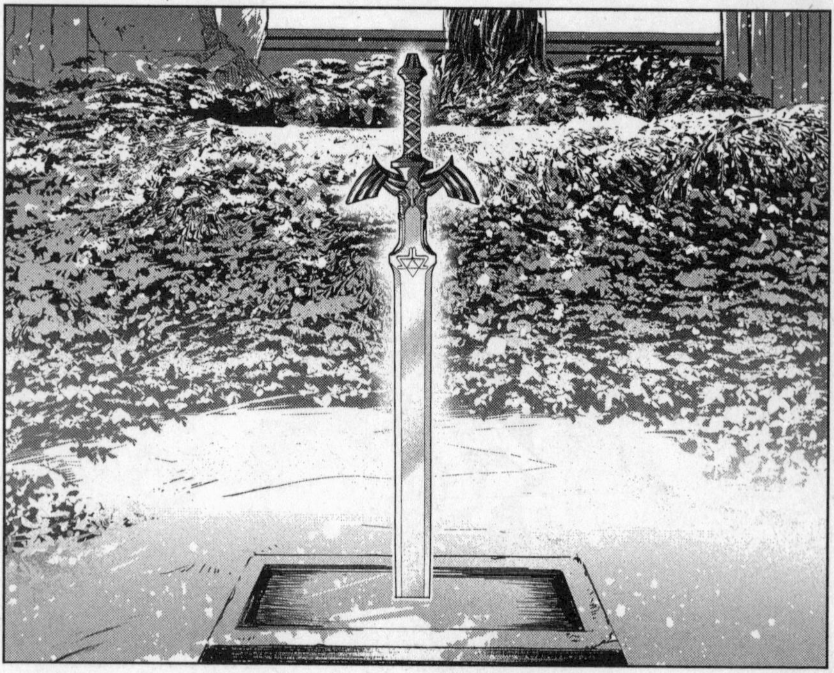

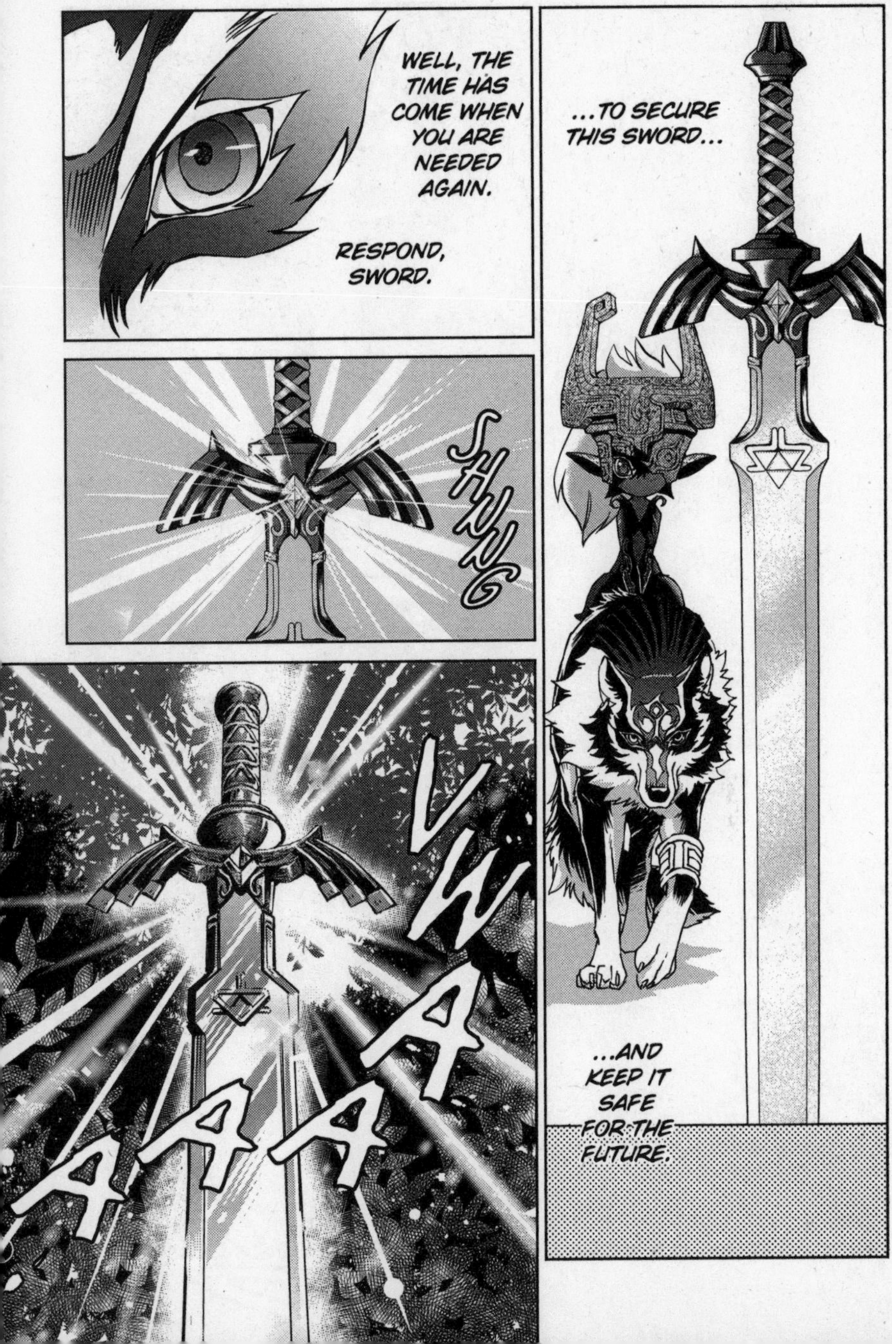
...TO SECURE THIS SWORD...
...AND KEEP IT SAFE FOR THE FUTURE.
WELL, THE TIME HAS COME WHEN YOU ARE NEEDED AGAIN.
RESPOND, SWORD.
SHING
VWAAAAA

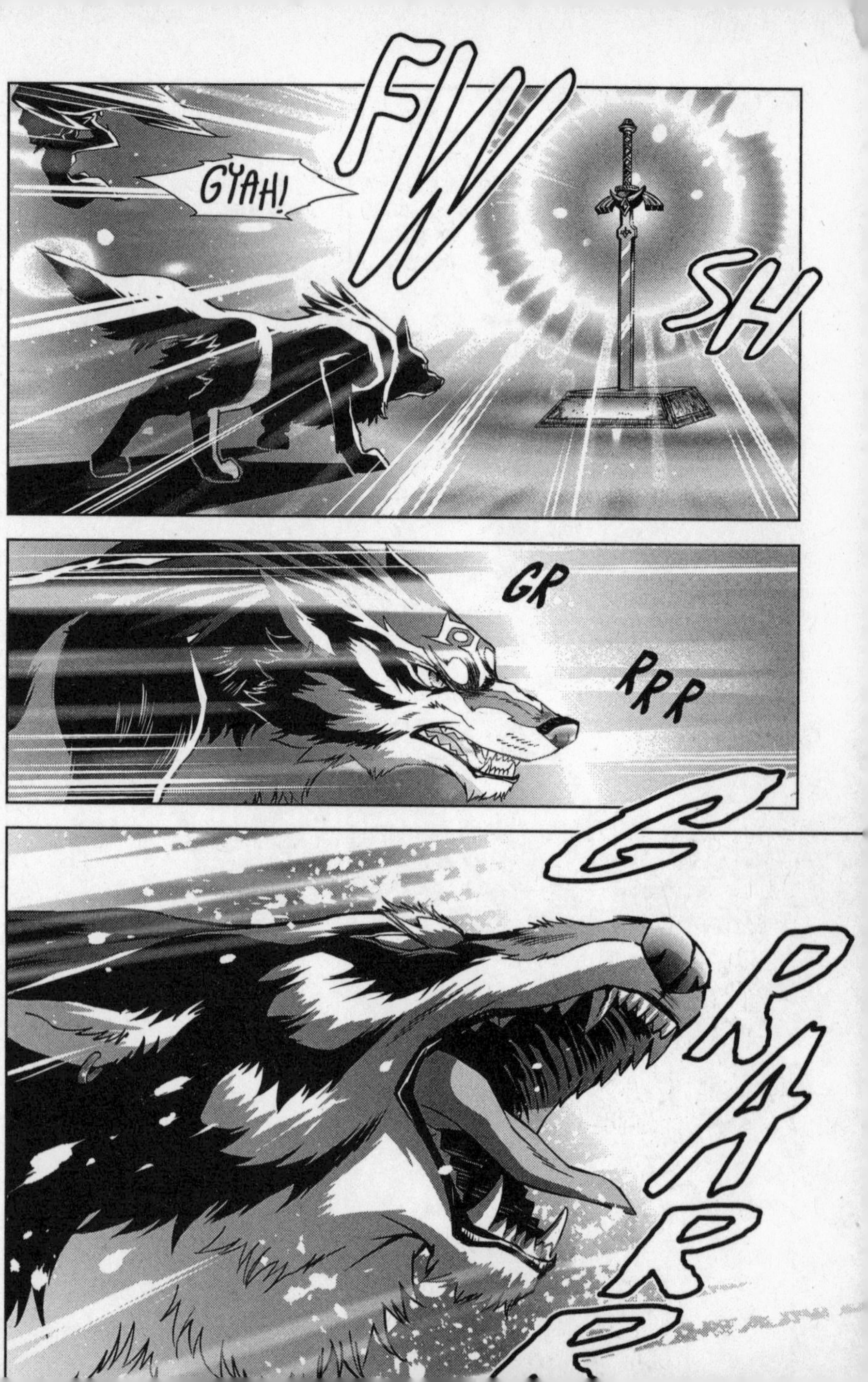
FWSH
GYAH!
GRRRR
GRNARR

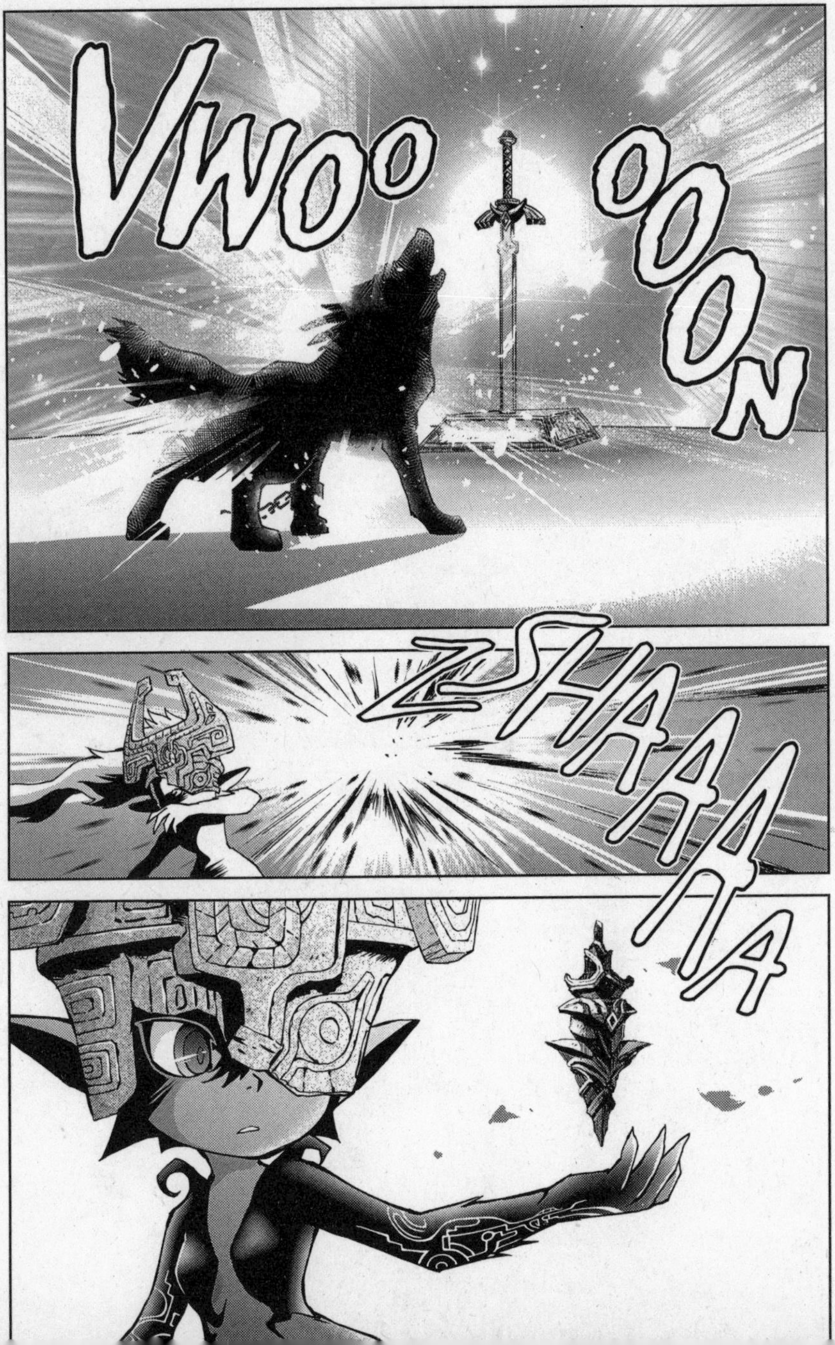
VWOOOOON
ZSHAAAAAA

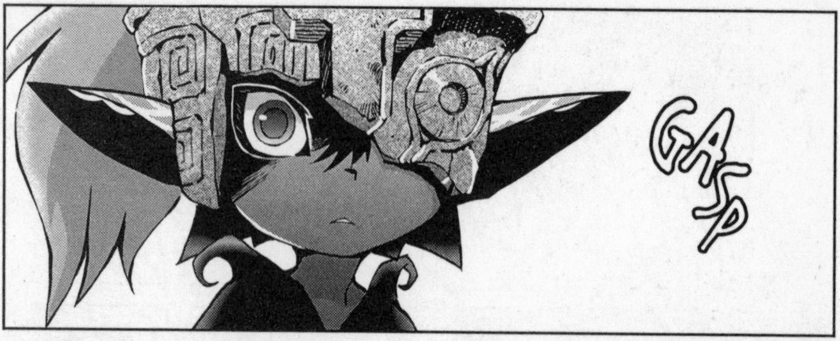
GASP
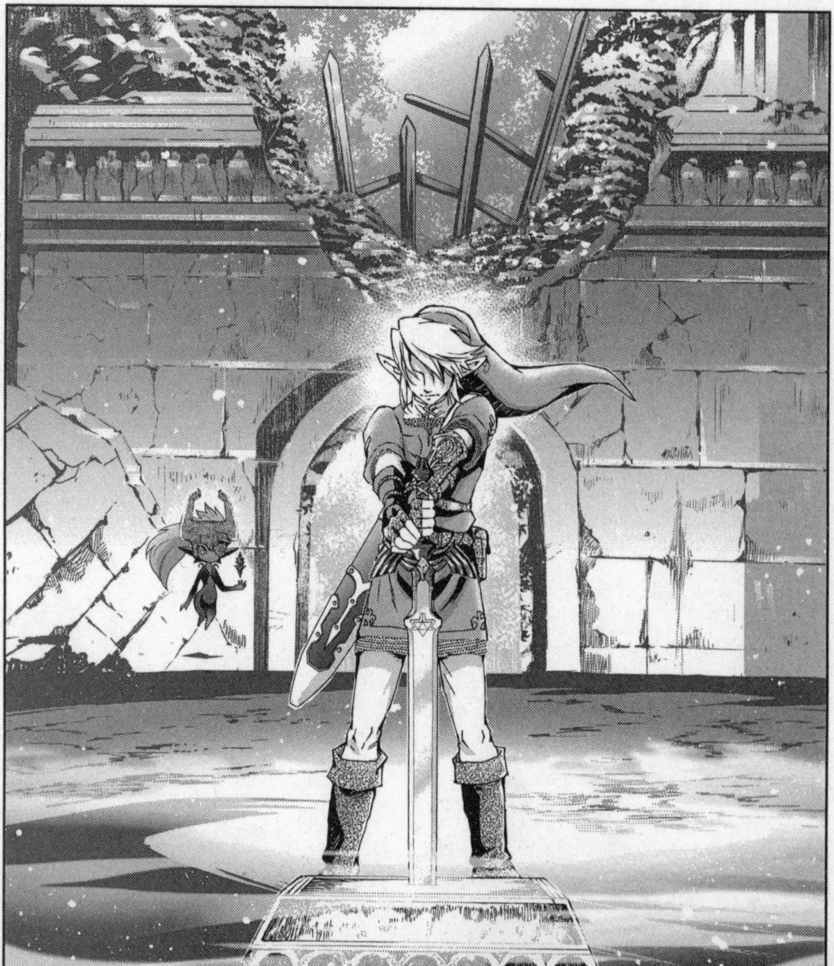

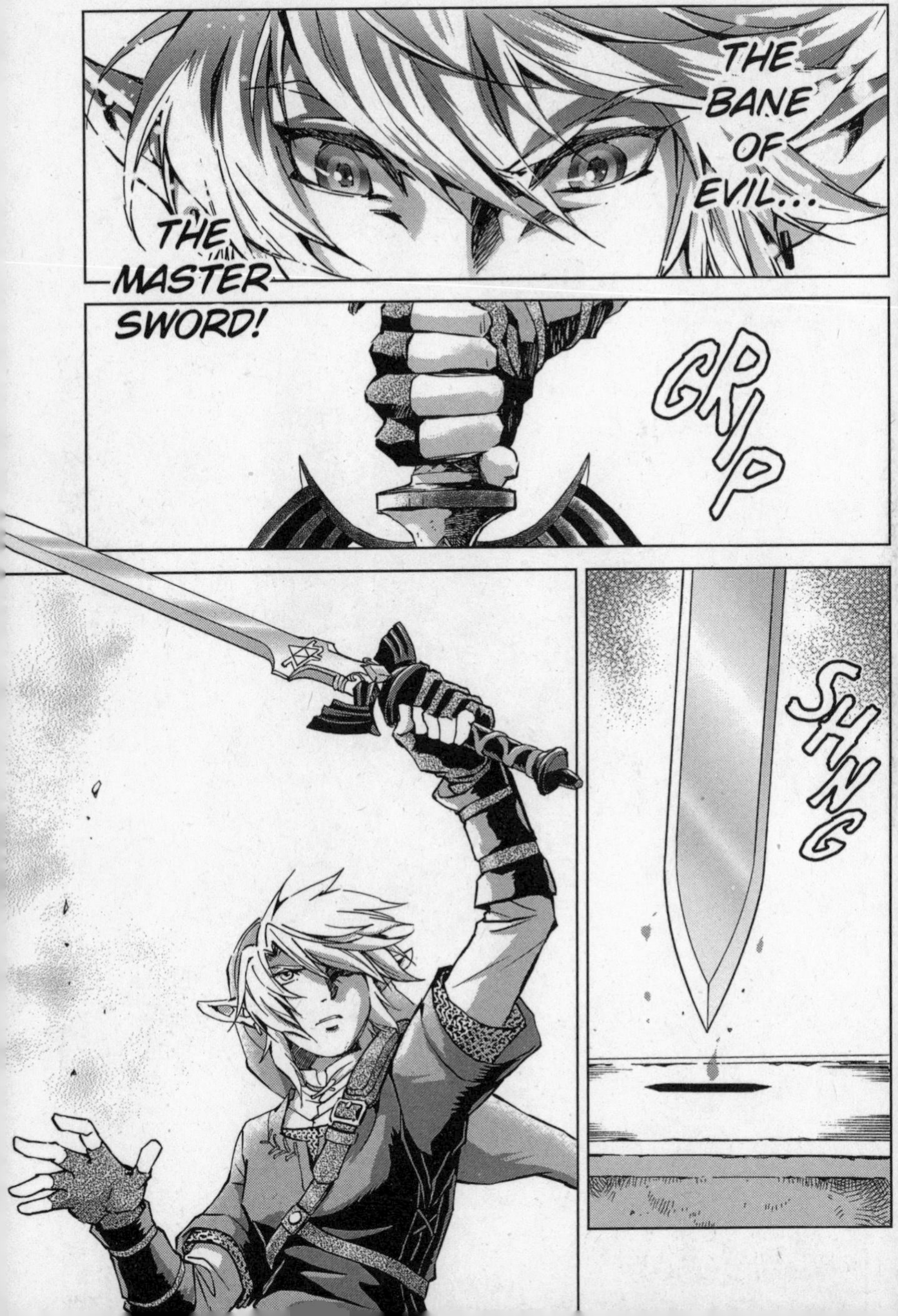
THE BANE OF EVIL...
THE MASTER SWORD!
GRIP
SHING

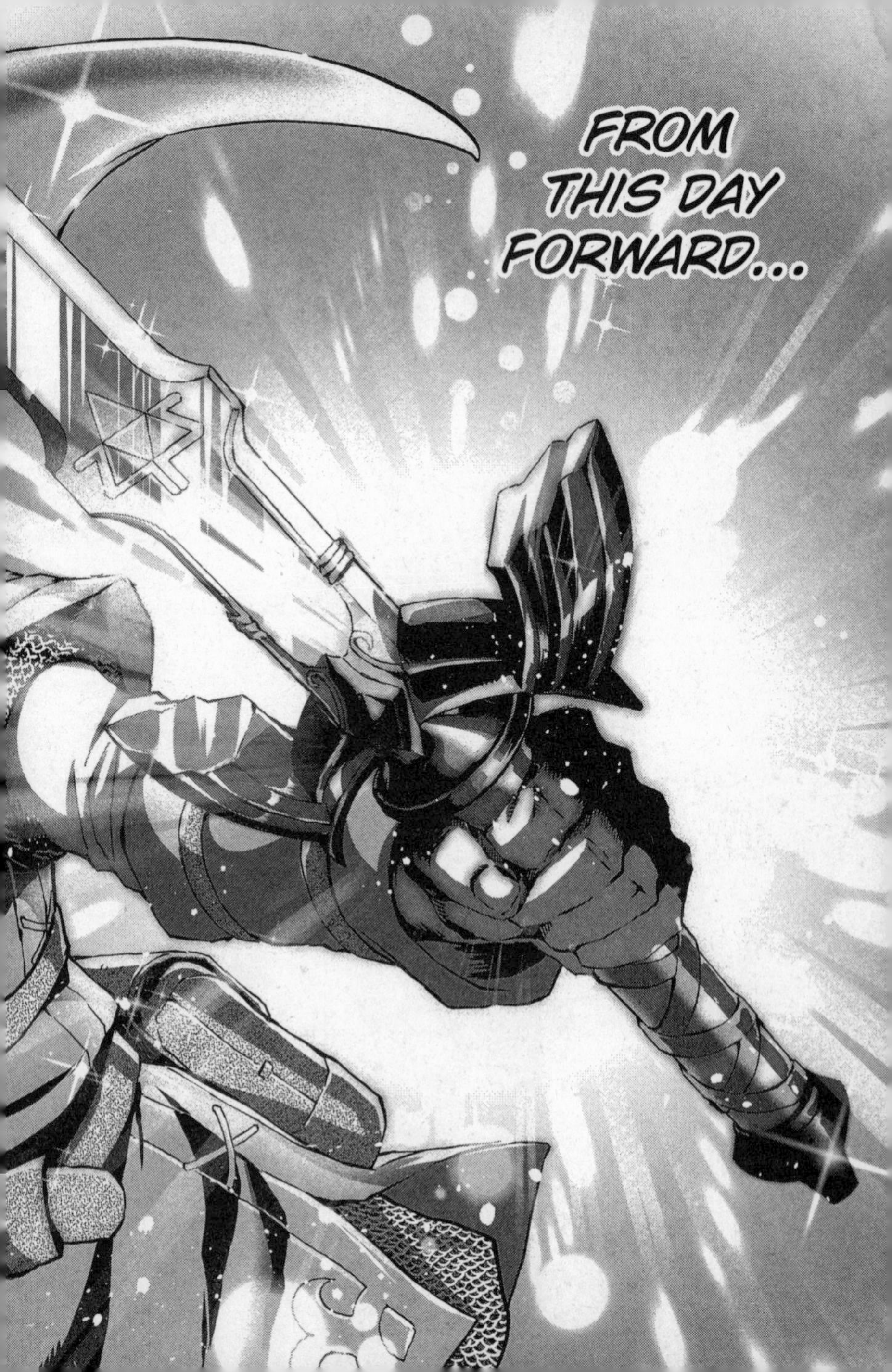
FROM THIS DAY FORWARD...

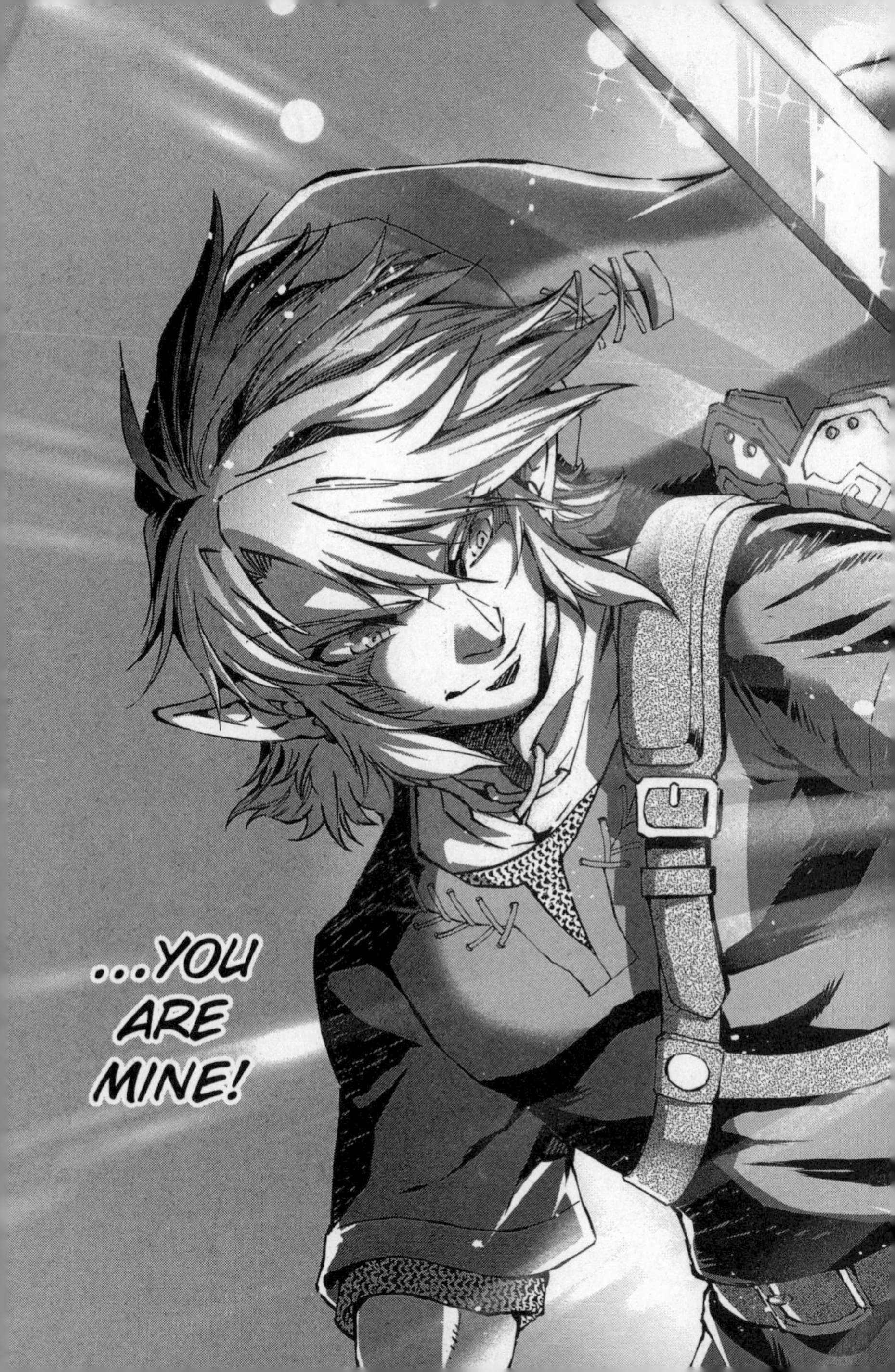
...YOU ARE MINE!

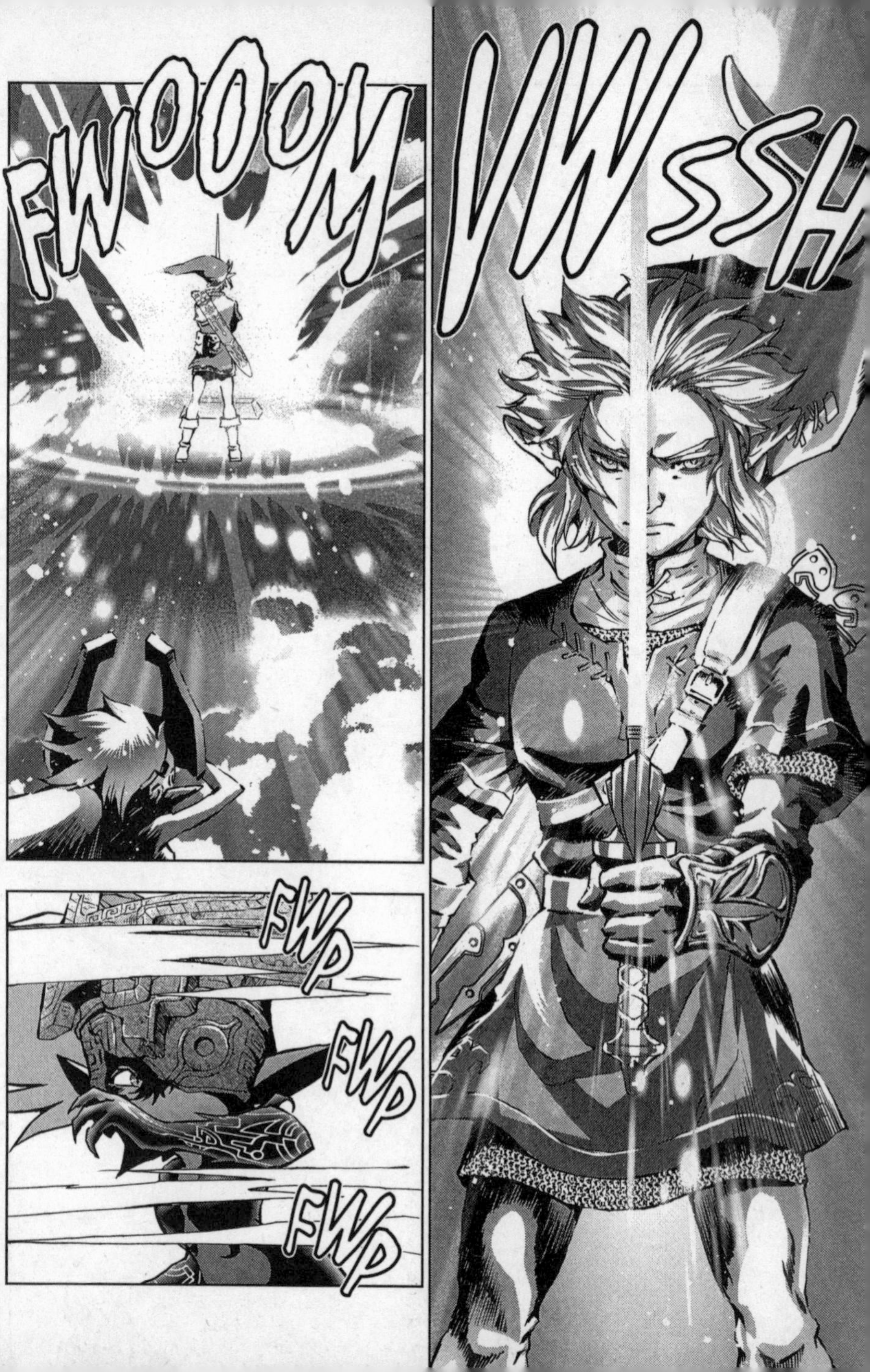
VWSSH
FWOOOM
FWP
FWP
FWP

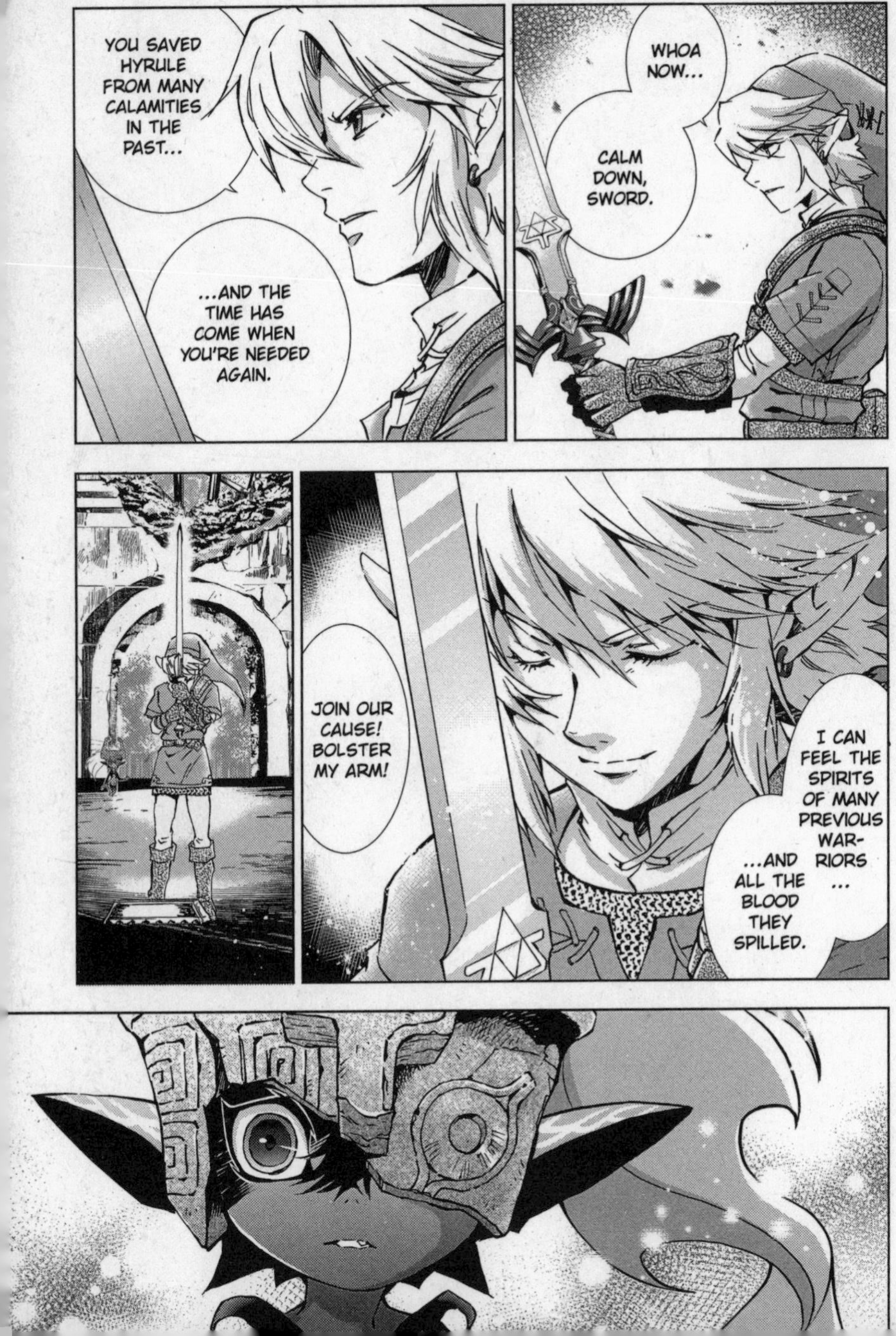
WHOA NOW...
CALM DOWN, SWORD.
YOU SAVED HYRULE FROM MANY CALAMITIES IN THE PAST...
...AND THE TIME HAS COME WHEN YOU'RE NEEDED AGAIN.
I CAN FEEL THE SPIRITS OF MANY PREVIOUS WAR-RIORS ...
...AND ALL THE BLOOD THEY SPILLED.
JOIN OUR CAUSE! BOLSTER MY ARM!

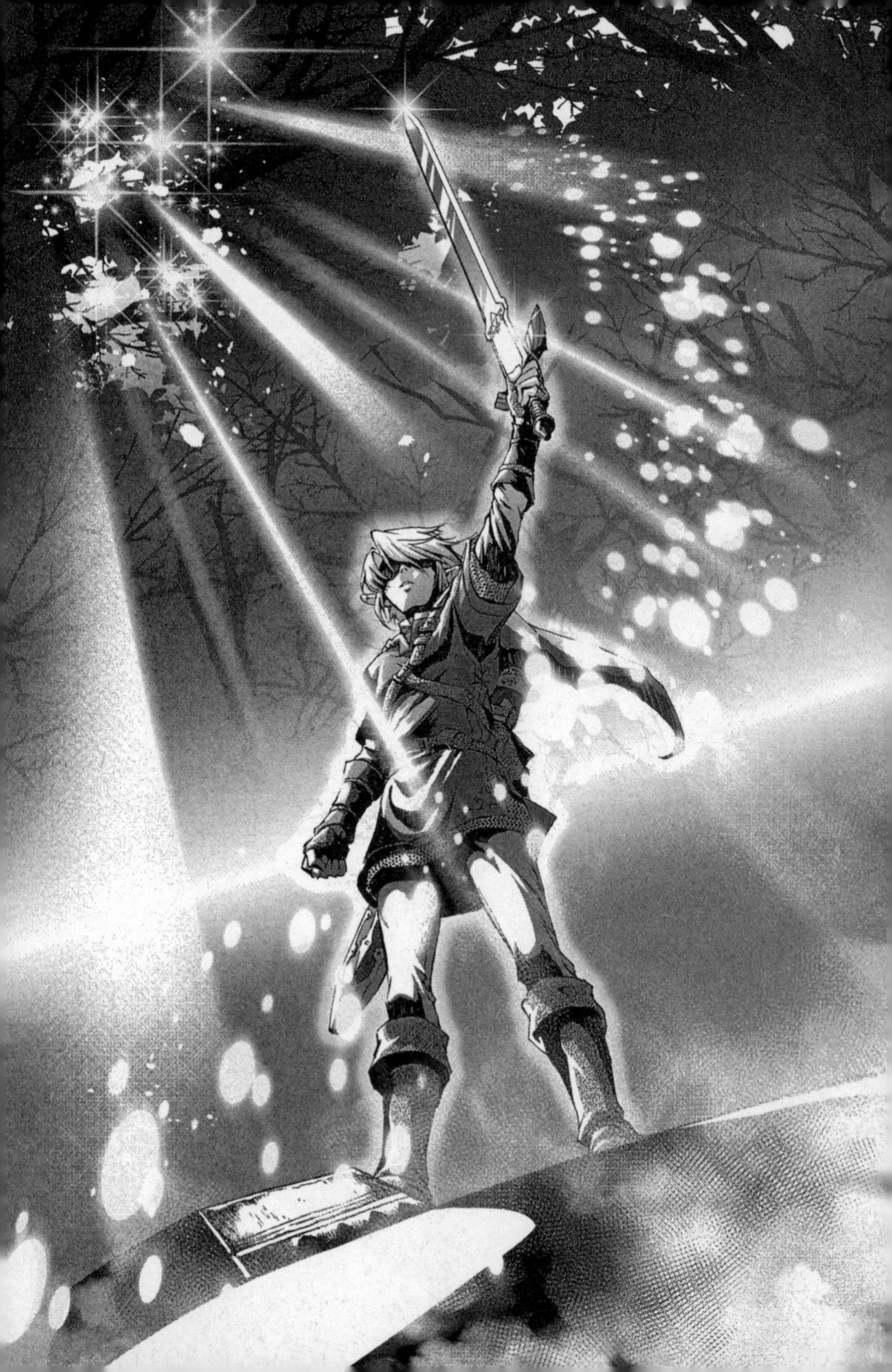

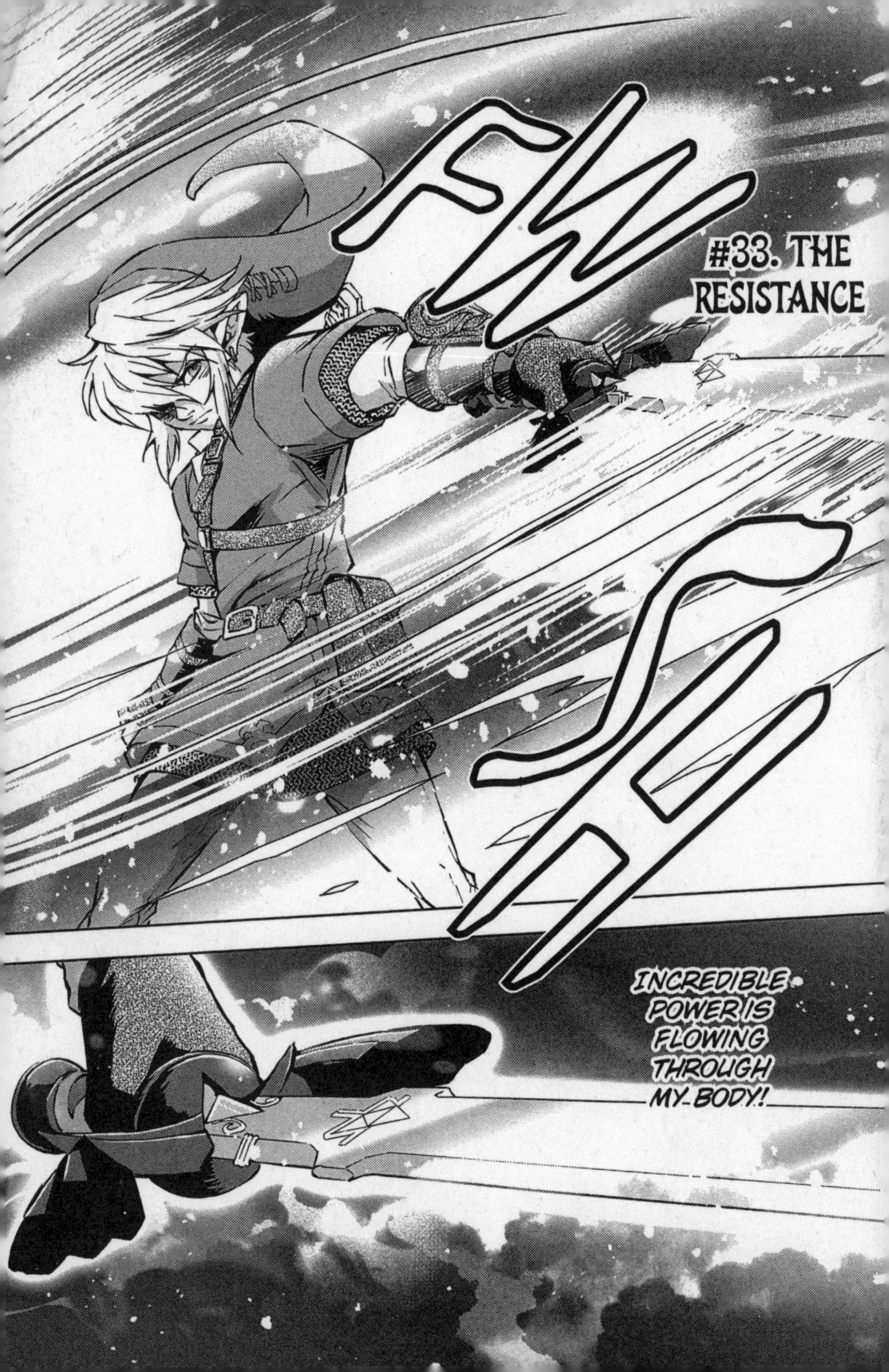
#33. THE RESISTANCE
FWSSH
INCREDIBLE POWER IS FLOWING THROUGH MY BODY!

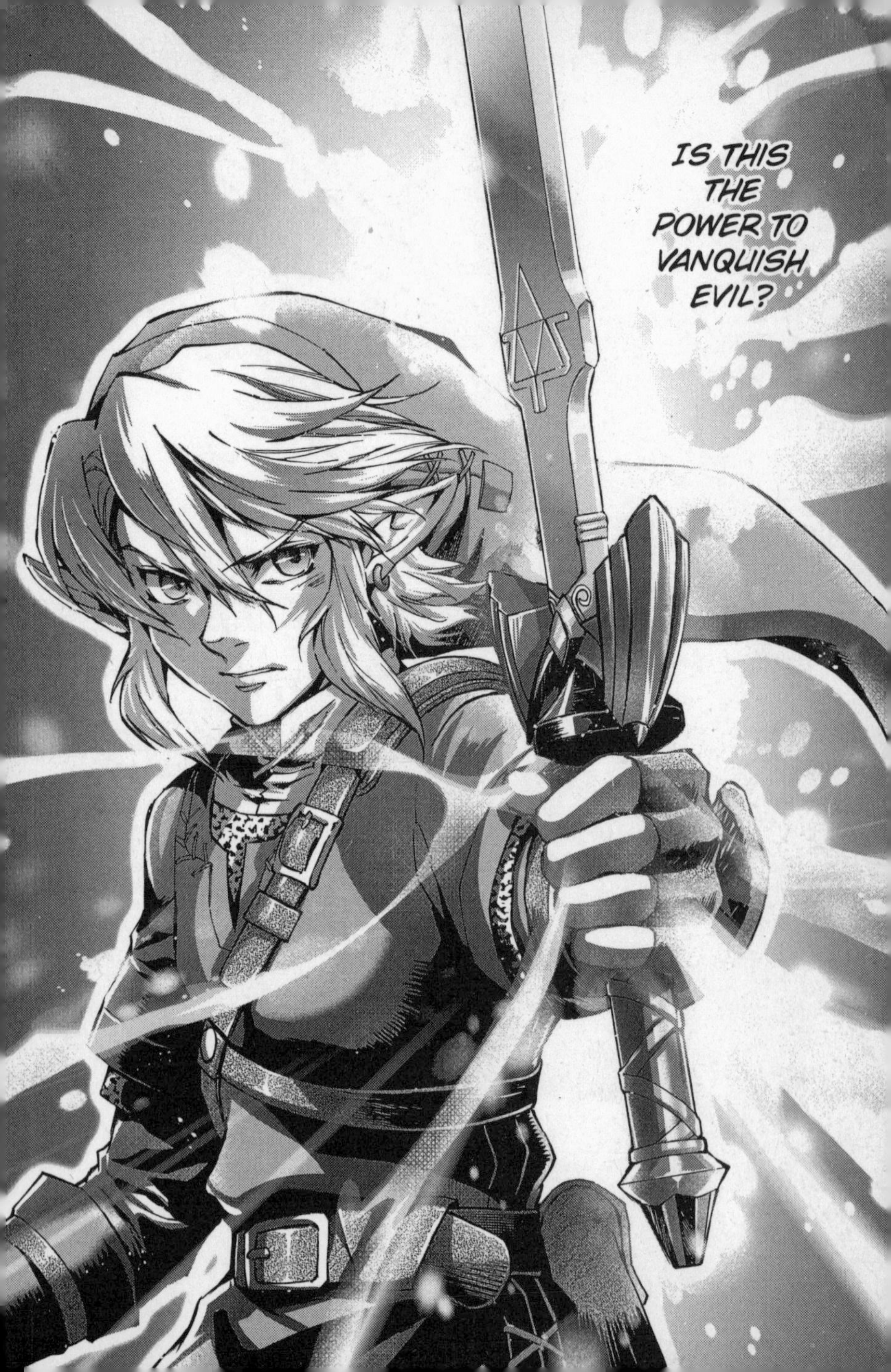
IS THIS THE POWER TO VANQUISH EVIL?

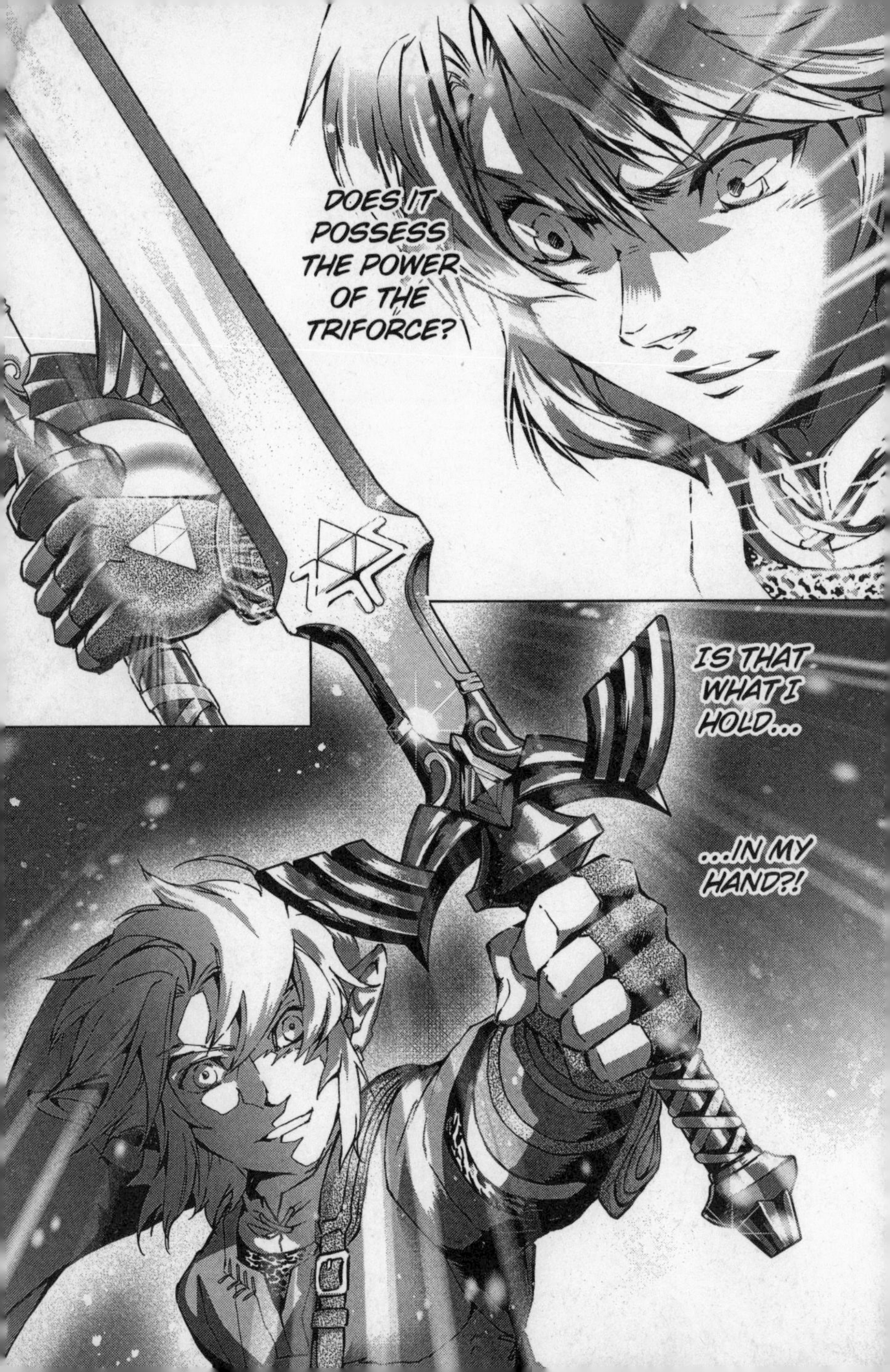
DOES IT POSSESS THE POWER OF THE TRIFORCE?
IS THAT WHAT I HOLD...
...IN MY HAND?!

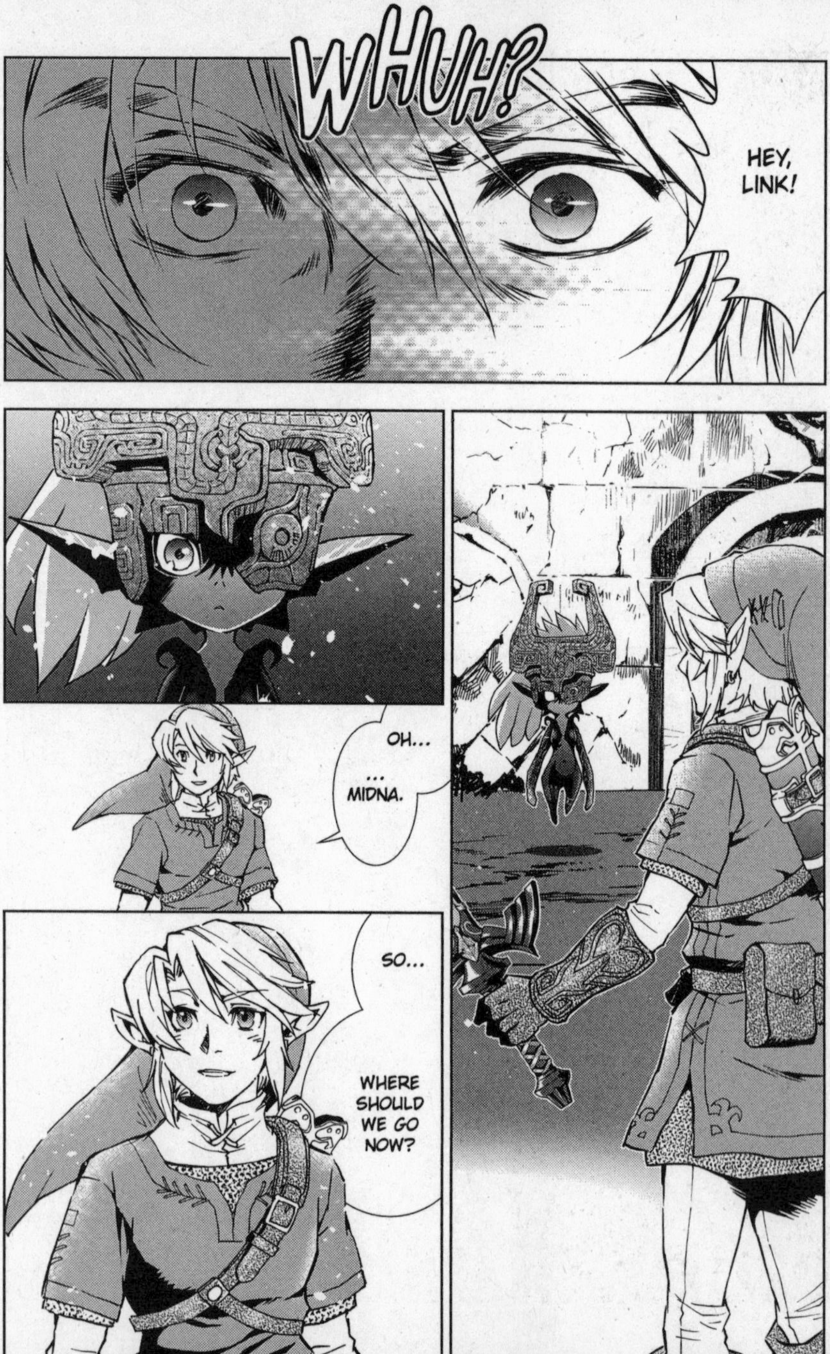
HEY, LINK!
WHUH?
OH...
... MIDNA.
SO...
WHERE SHOULD WE GO NOW?

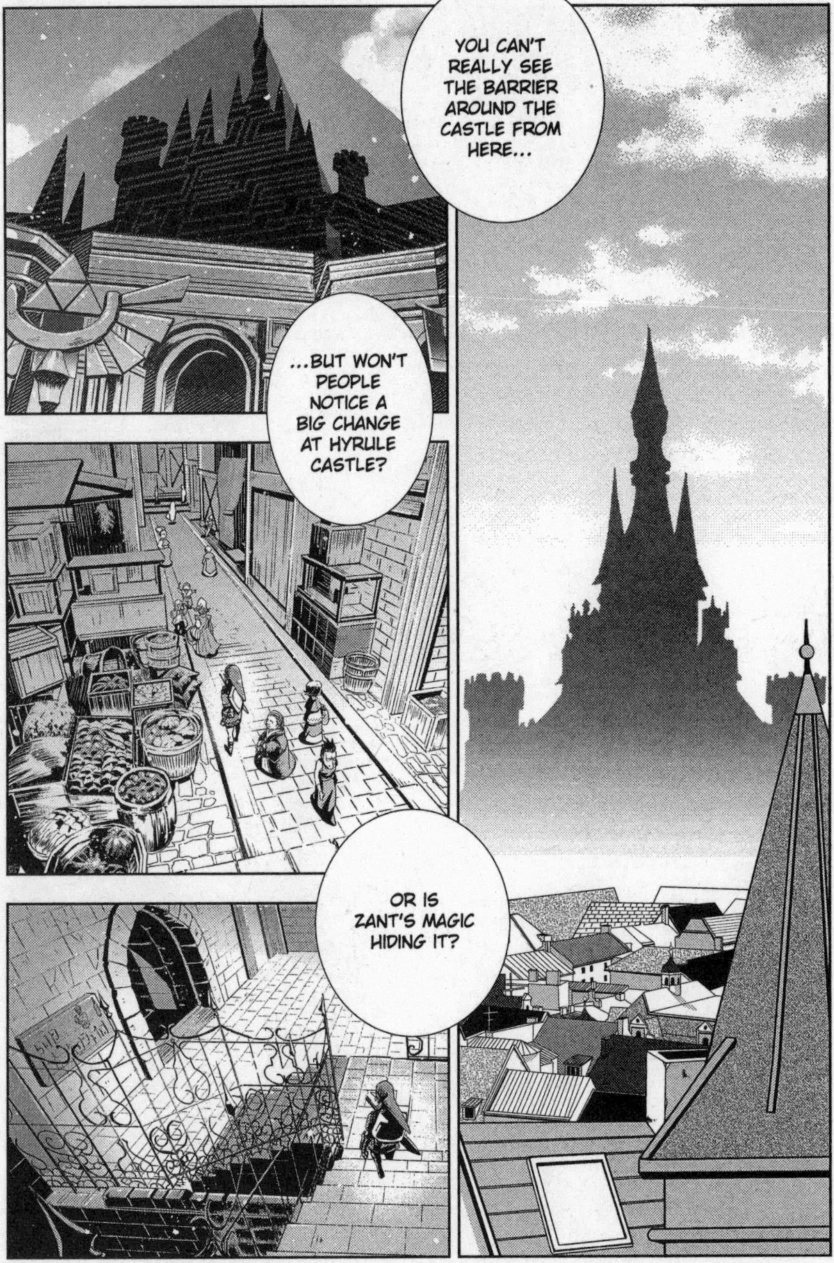
YOU CAN'T REALLY SEE THE BARRIER AROUND THE CASTLE FROM HERE...
...BUT WON'T PEOPLE NOTICE A BIG CHANGE AT HYRULE CASTLE?
OR IS ZANT'S MAGIC HIDING IT?

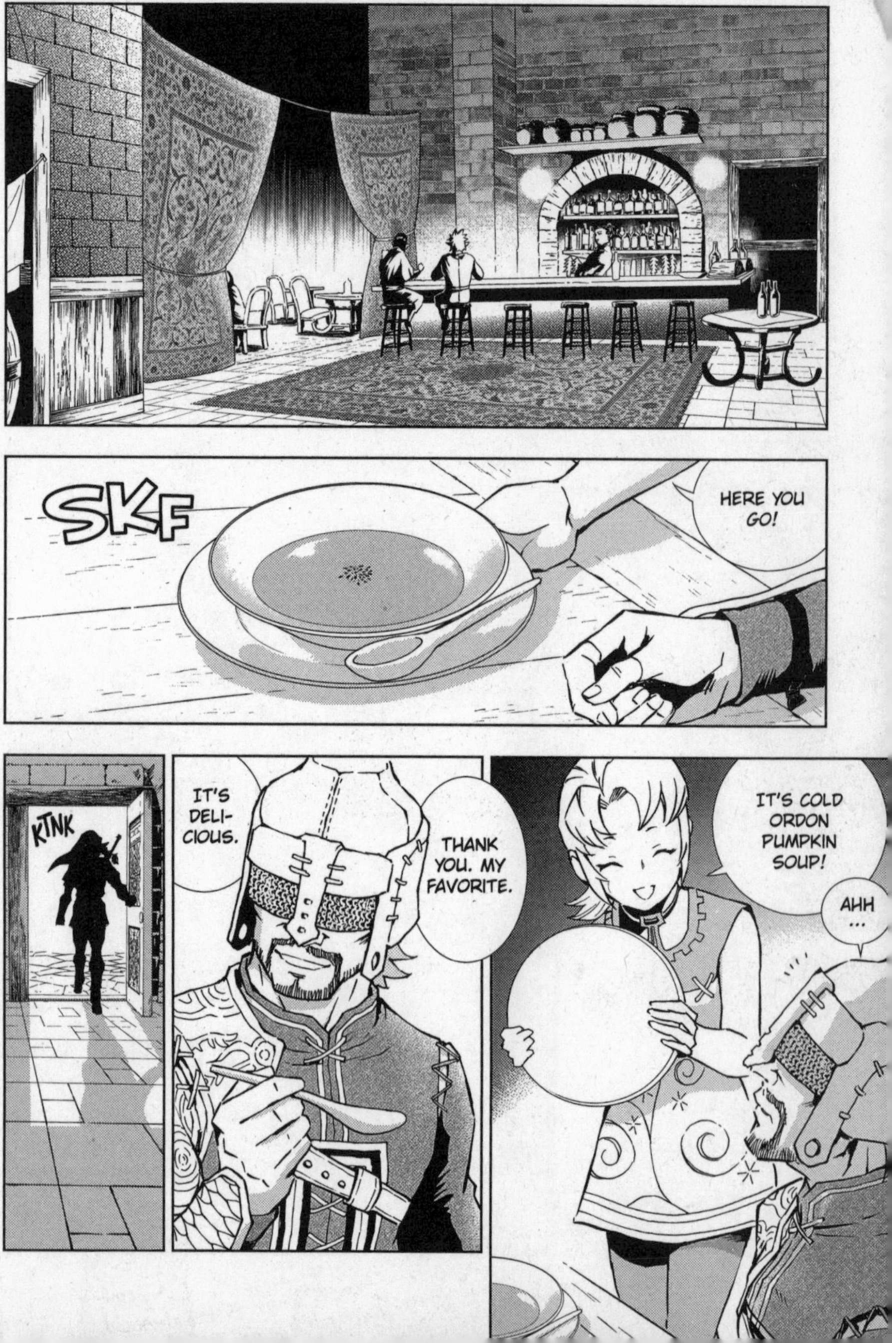
HERE YOU GO!
SKF
IT'S COLD ORDON PUMPKIN SOUP!
AHH ...
THANK YOU. MY FAVORITE.
IT'S DELICIOUS.
KTNK

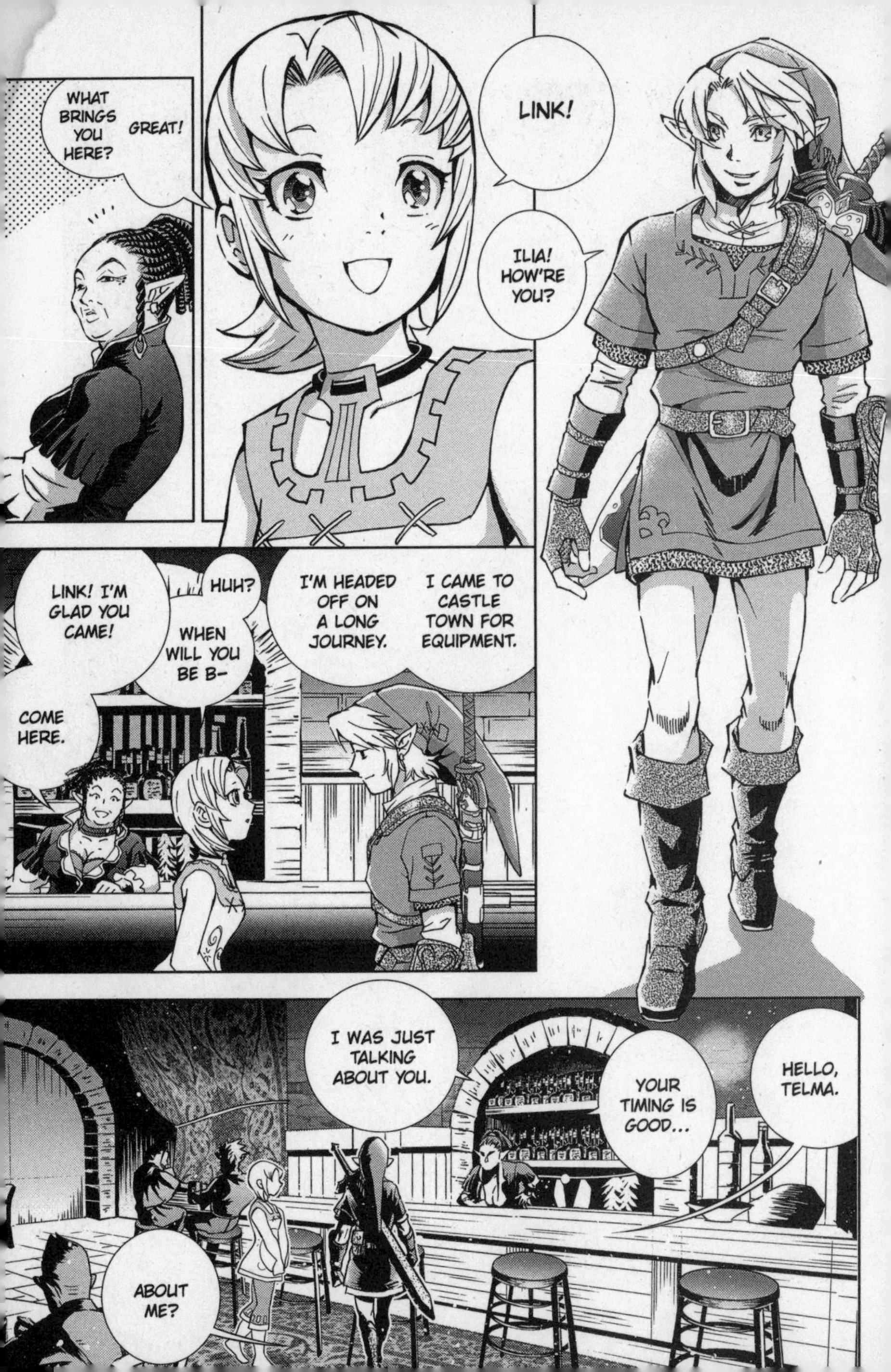
LINK!
ILIA! HOW'RE YOU?
GREAT!
WHAT BRINGS YOU HERE?
I CAME TO CASTLE TOWN FOR EQUIPMENT.
I'M HEADED OFF ON A LONG JOURNEY.
WHEN WILL YOU BE B–
LINK! I'M GLAD YOU CAME!
HUH?
COME HERE.
HELLO, TELMA.
YOUR TIMING IS GOOD...
I WAS JUST TALKING ABOUT YOU.
ABOUT ME?

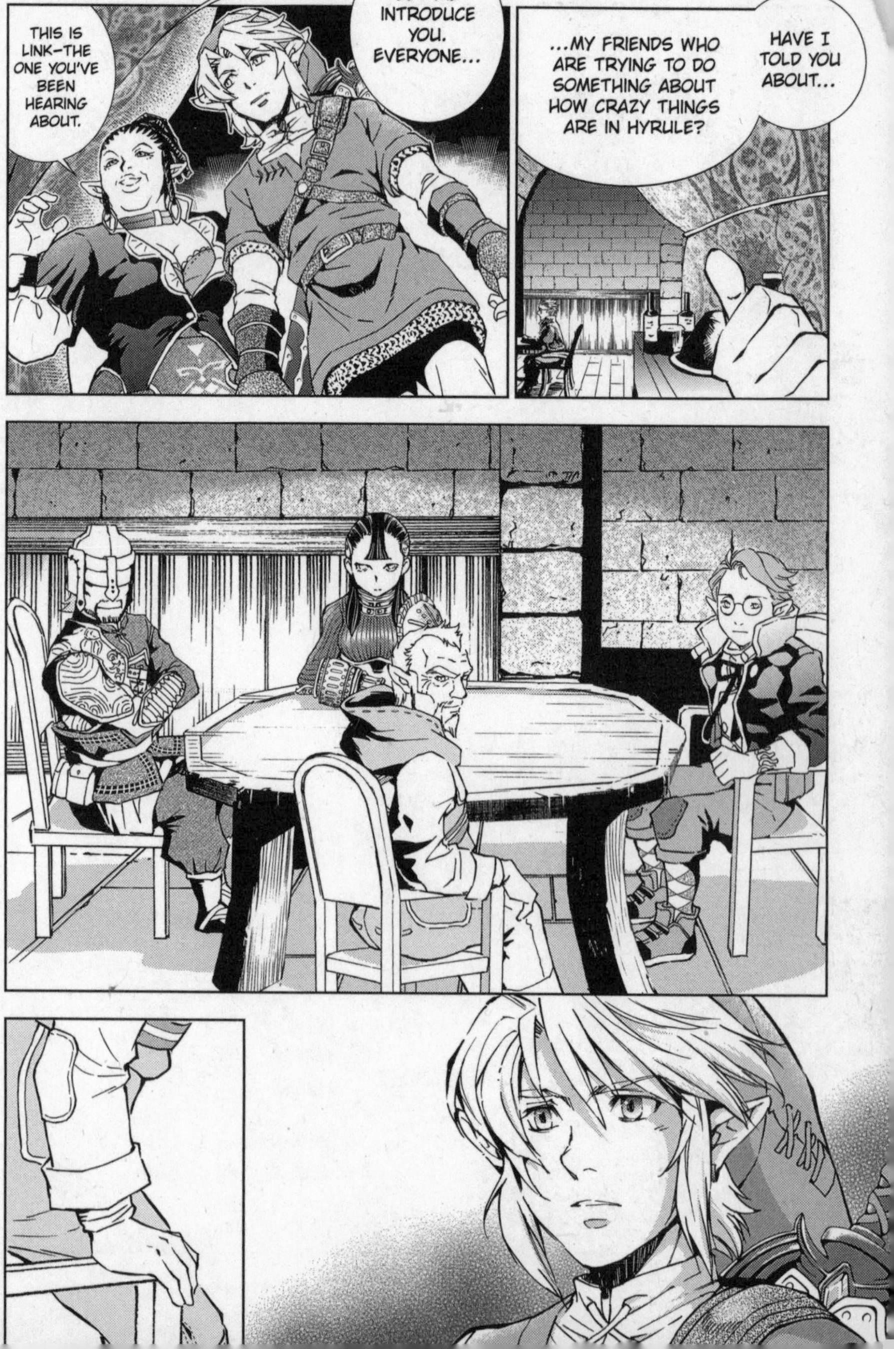
HAVE I TOLD YOU ABOUT...
...MY FRIENDS WHO ARE TRYING TO DO SOMETHING ABOUT HOW CRAZY THINGS ARE IN HYRULE?
LET ME INTRODUCE YOU. EVERYONE...
THIS IS LINK—THE ONE YOU'VE BEEN HEARING ABOUT.

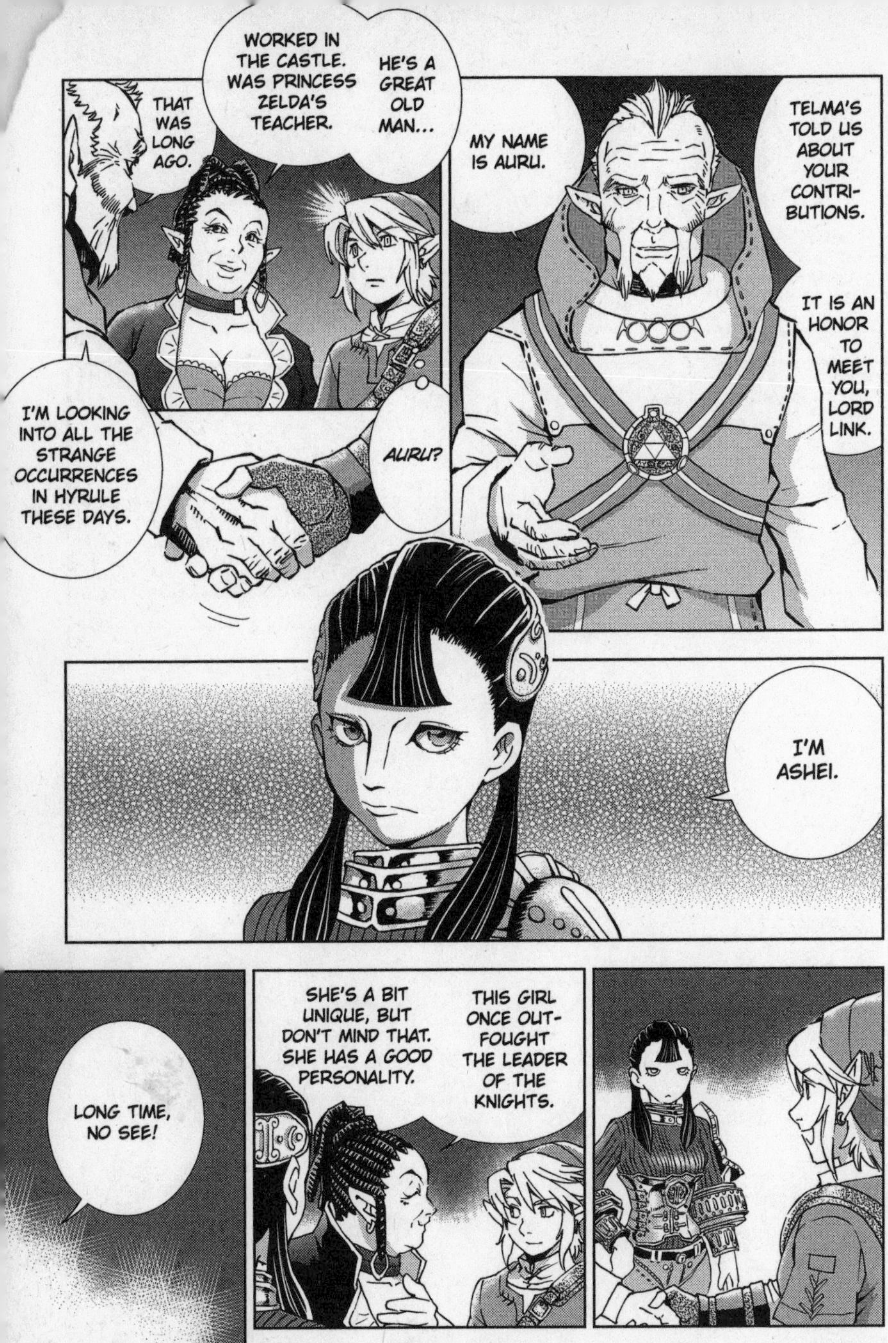
TELMA'S TOLD US ABOUT YOUR CONTRI-BUTIONS.
MY NAME IS AURU.
IT IS AN HONOR TO MEET YOU, LORD LINK.
HE'S A GREAT OLD MAN...
WORKED IN THE CASTLE. WAS PRINCESS ZELDA'S TEACHER.
THAT WAS LONG AGO.
AURU?
I'M LOOKING INTO ALL THE STRANGE OCCURRENCES IN HYRULE THESE DAYS.
I'M ASHEI.
THIS GIRL ONCE OUT-FOUGHT THE LEADER OF THE KNIGHTS.
SHE'S A BIT UNIQUE, BUT DON'T MIND THAT. SHE HAS A GOOD PERSONALITY.
LONG TIME, NO SEE!

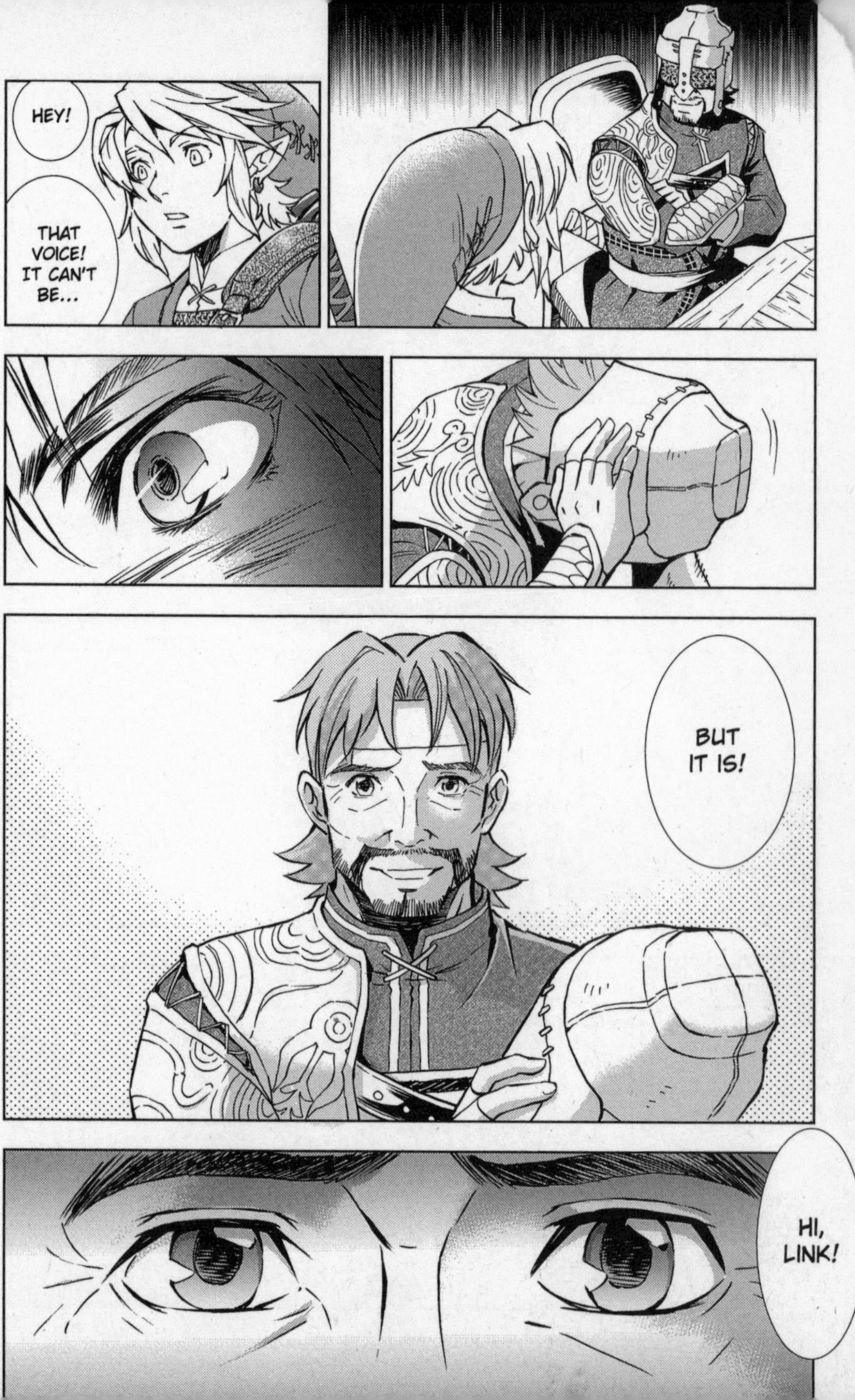
HEY!
THAT VOICE! IT CAN'T BE...
BUT IT IS!
HI, LINK!

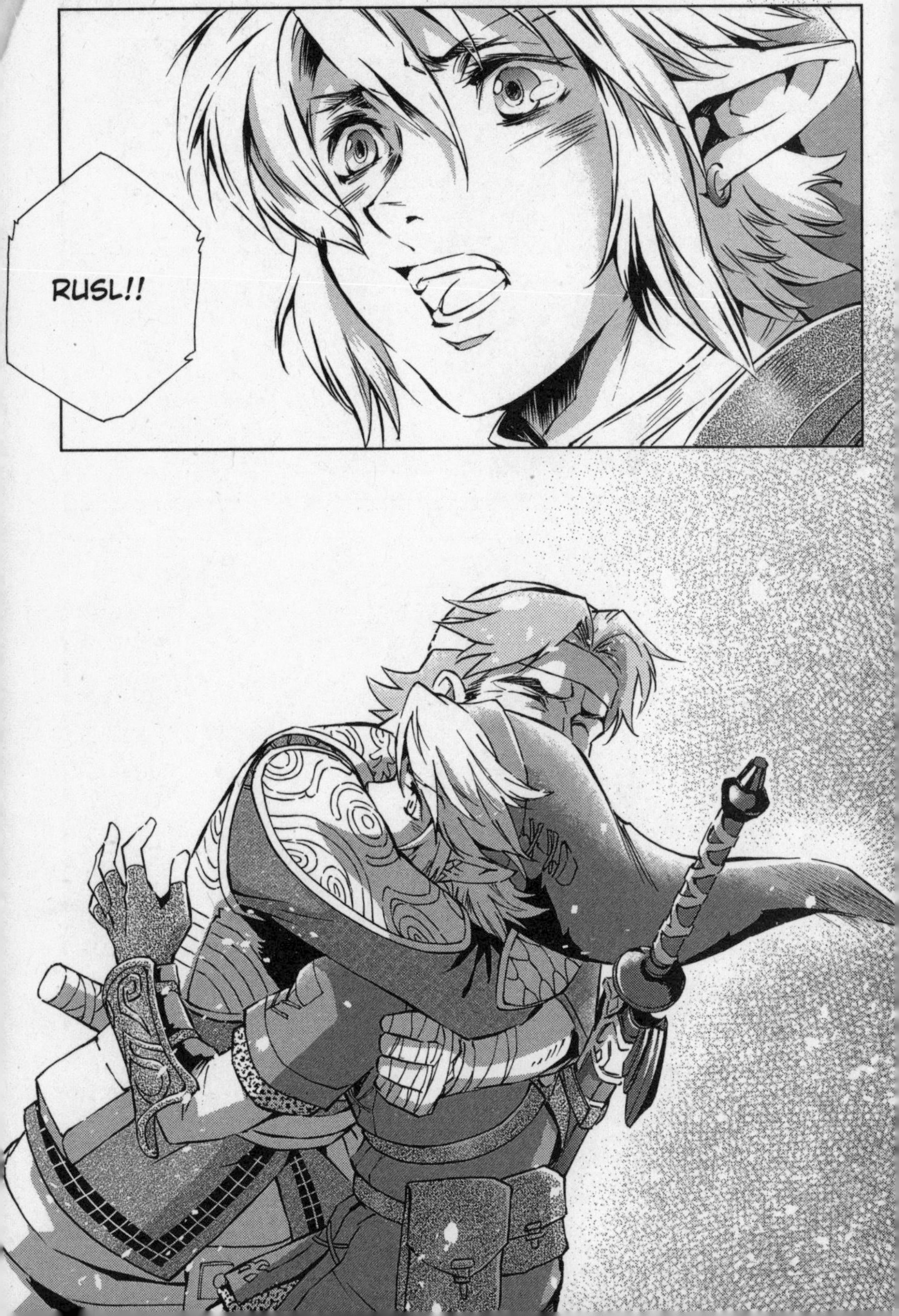
RUSL!!

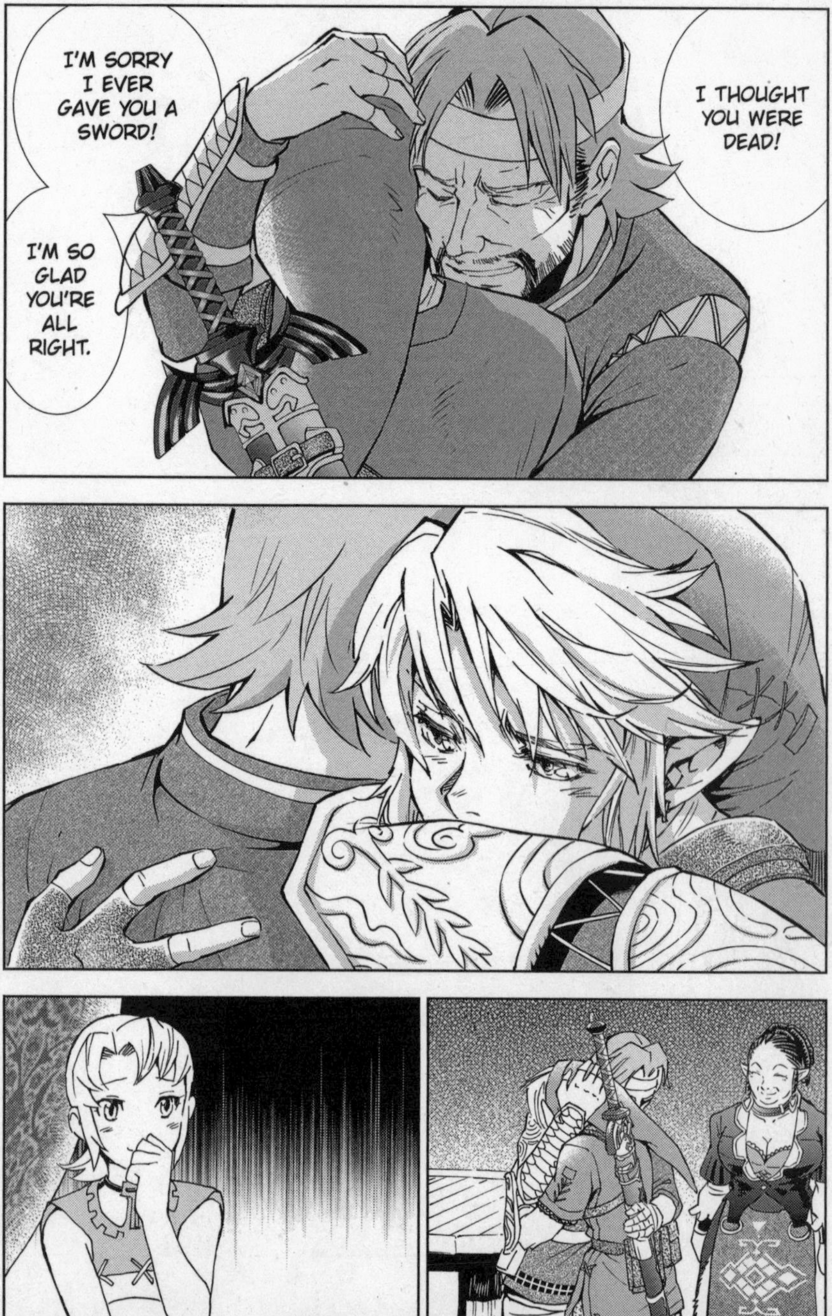
I THOUGHT YOU WERE DEAD!
I'M SORRY I EVER GAVE YOU A SWORD!
I'M SO GLAD YOU'RE ALL RIGHT.

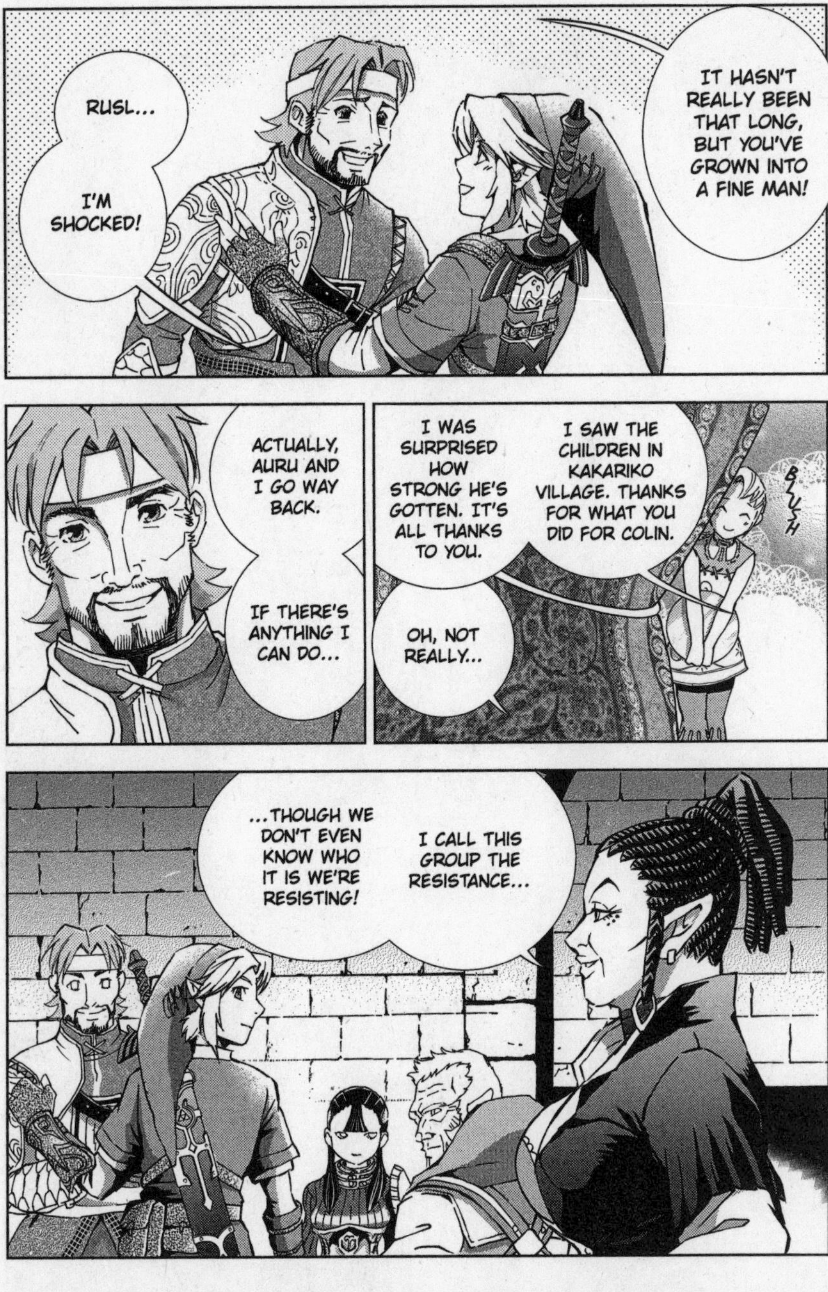
IT HASN'T REALLY BEEN THAT LONG, BUT YOU'VE GROWN INTO A FINE MAN!
RUSL...
I'M SHOCKED!
I SAW THE CHILDREN IN KAKARIKO VILLAGE. THANKS FOR WHAT YOU DID FOR COLIN.
I WAS SURPRISED HOW STRONG HE'S GOTTEN. IT'S ALL THANKS TO YOU.
BLUSH
OH, NOT REALLY...
ACTUALLY, AURU AND I GO WAY BACK.
IF THERE'S ANYTHING I CAN DO...
I CALL THIS GROUP THE RESISTANCE...
...THOUGH WE DON'T EVEN KNOW WHO IT IS WE'RE RESISTING!

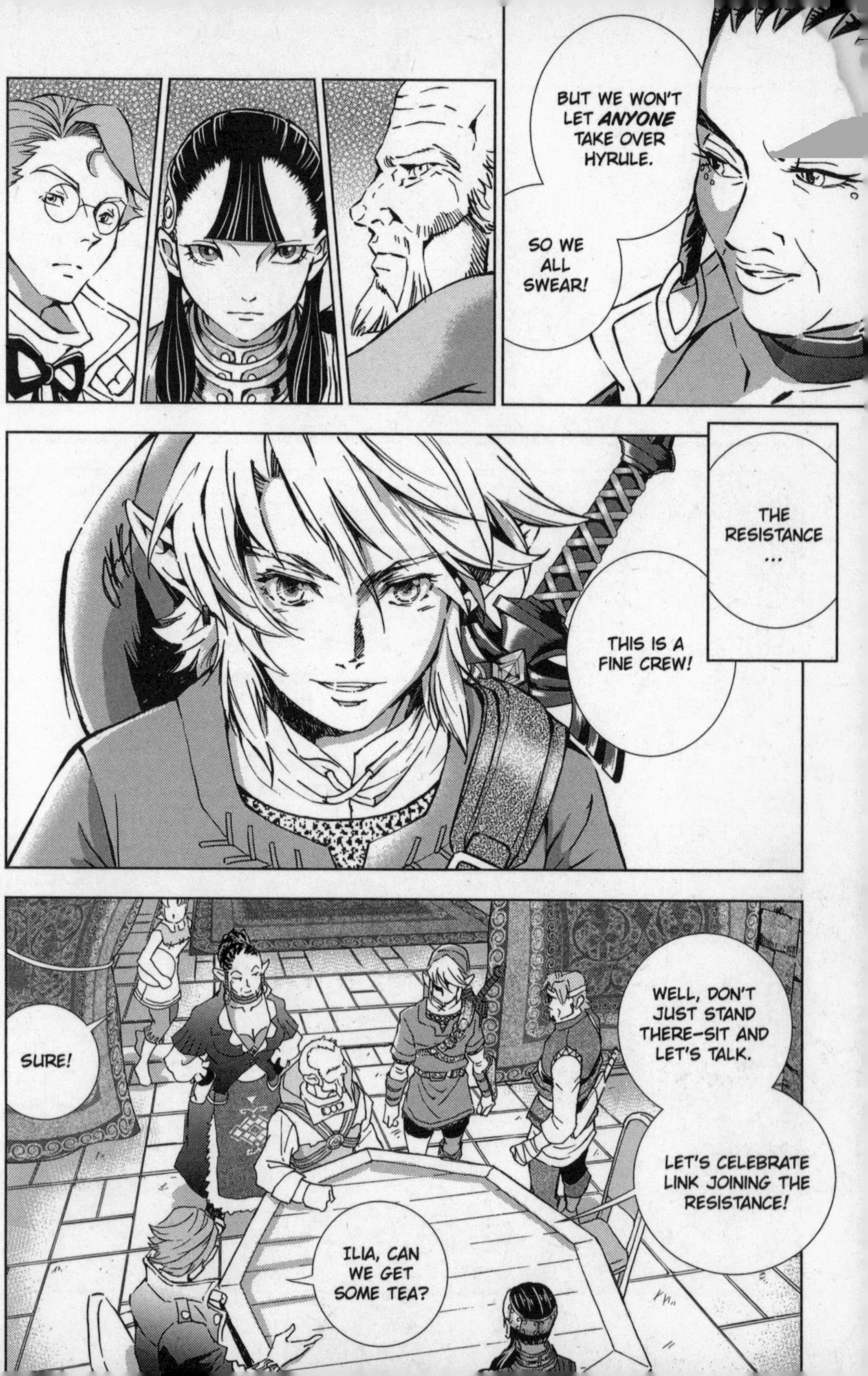
BUT WE WON'T LET ***ANYONE*** TAKE OVER HYRULE.
SO WE ALL SWEAR!
THE RESISTANCE ...
THIS IS A FINE CREW!
WELL, DON'T JUST STAND THERE–SIT AND LET'S TALK.
LET'S CELEBRATE LINK JOINING THE RESISTANCE!
ILIA, CAN WE GET SOME TEA?
SURE!

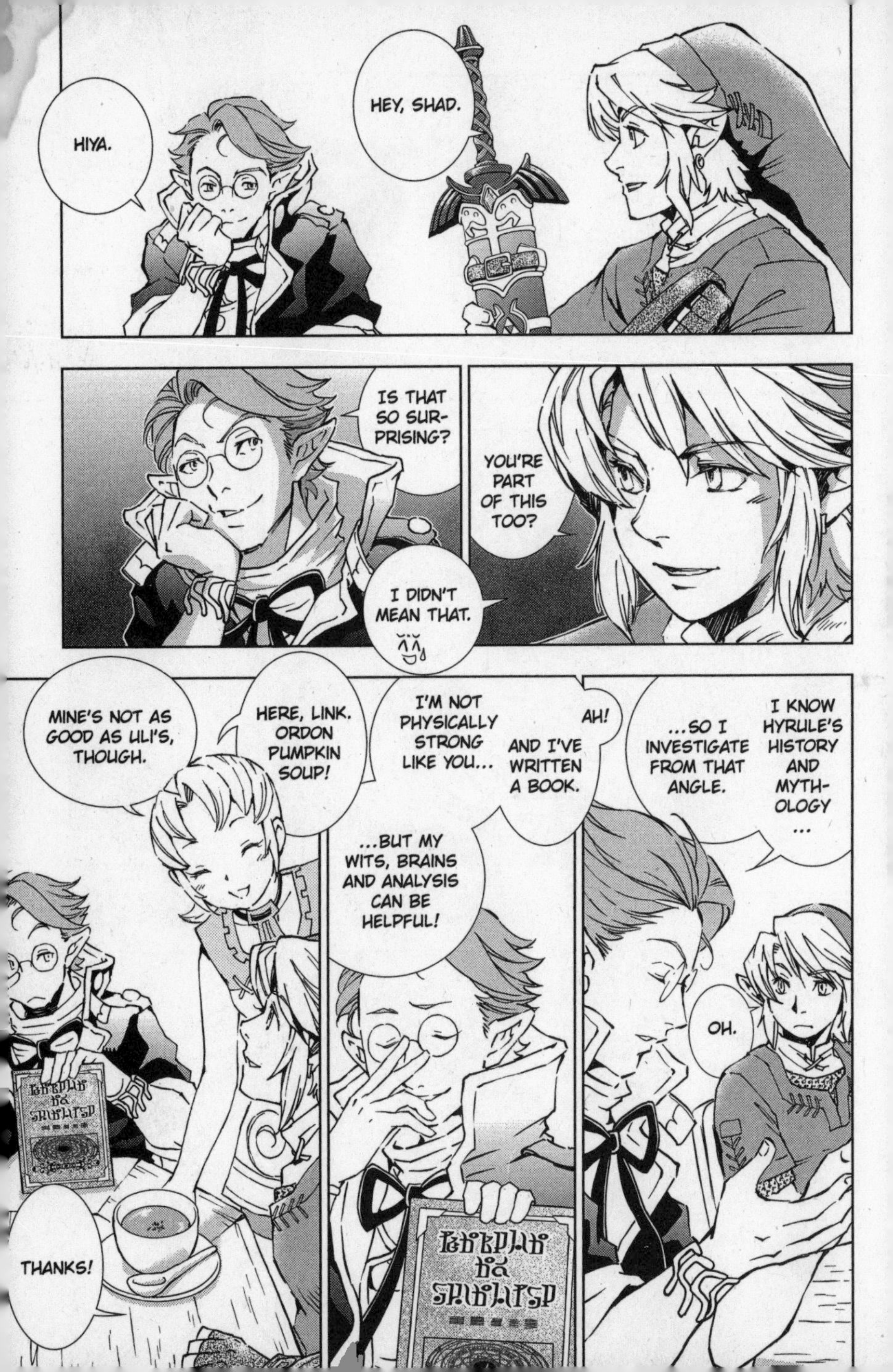
HEY, SHAD.
HIYA.
YOU'RE PART OF THIS TOO?
IS THAT SO SURPRISING?
I DIDN'T MEAN THAT.
I KNOW HYRULE'S HISTORY AND MYTHOLOGY ...
...SO I INVESTIGATE FROM THAT ANGLE.
OH.
AH! AND I'VE WRITTEN A BOOK.
I'M NOT PHYSICALLY STRONG LIKE YOU...
...BUT MY WITS, BRAINS AND ANALYSIS CAN BE HELPFUL!
HERE, LINK. ORDON PUMPKIN SOUP!
MINE'S NOT AS GOOD AS ULI'S, THOUGH.
THANKS!

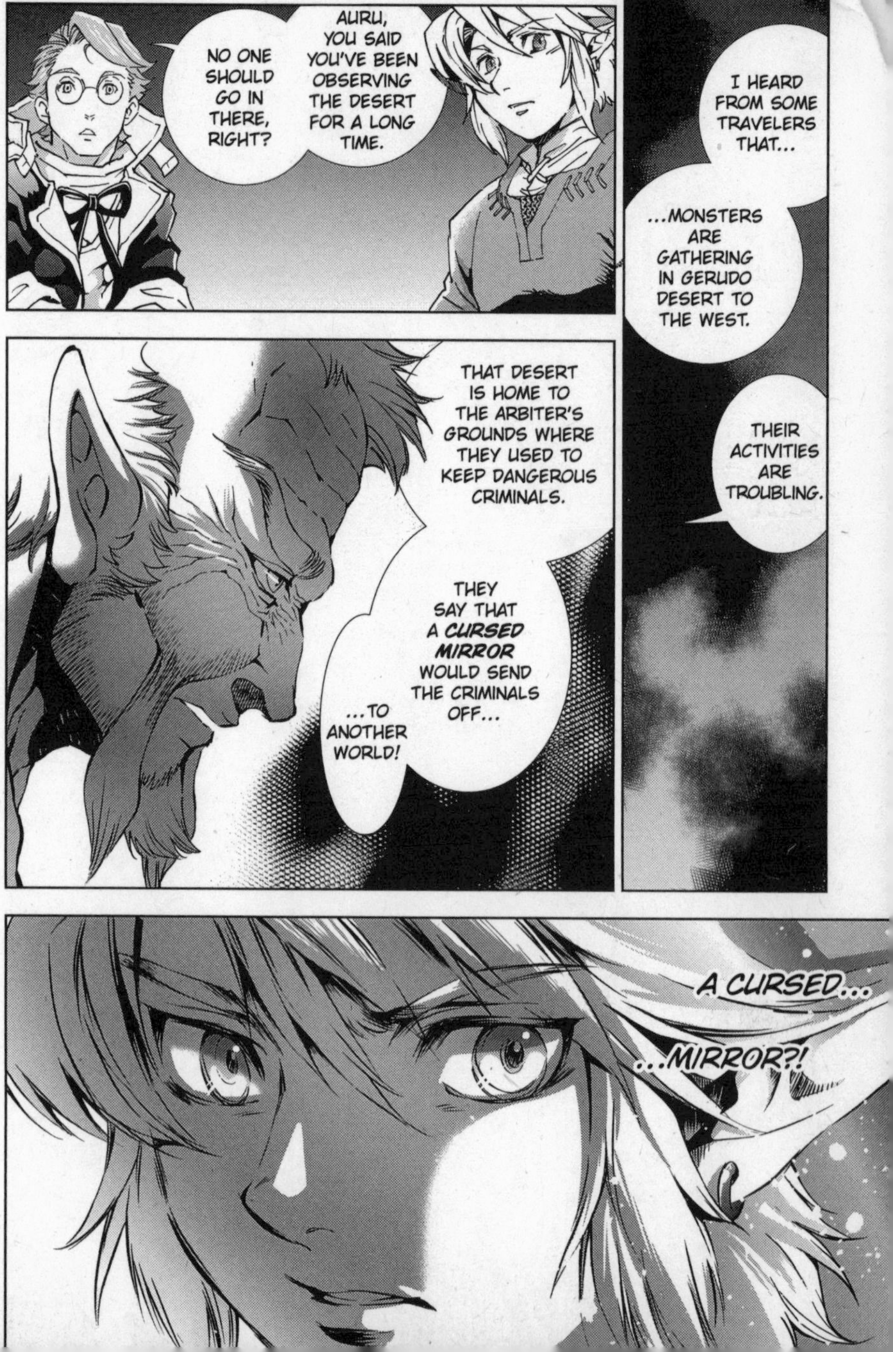
I HEARD FROM SOME TRAVELERS THAT...
...MONSTERS ARE GATHERING IN GERUDO DESERT TO THE WEST.
THEIR ACTIVITIES ARE TROUBLING.
AURU, YOU SAID YOU'VE BEEN OBSERVING THE DESERT FOR A LONG TIME.
NO ONE SHOULD GO IN THERE, RIGHT?
THAT DESERT IS HOME TO THE ARBITER'S GROUNDS WHERE THEY USED TO KEEP DANGEROUS CRIMINALS.
THEY SAY THAT A ***CURSED MIRROR*** WOULD SEND THE CRIMINALS OFF...
...TO ANOTHER WORLD!
A CURSED...
...MIRROR?!

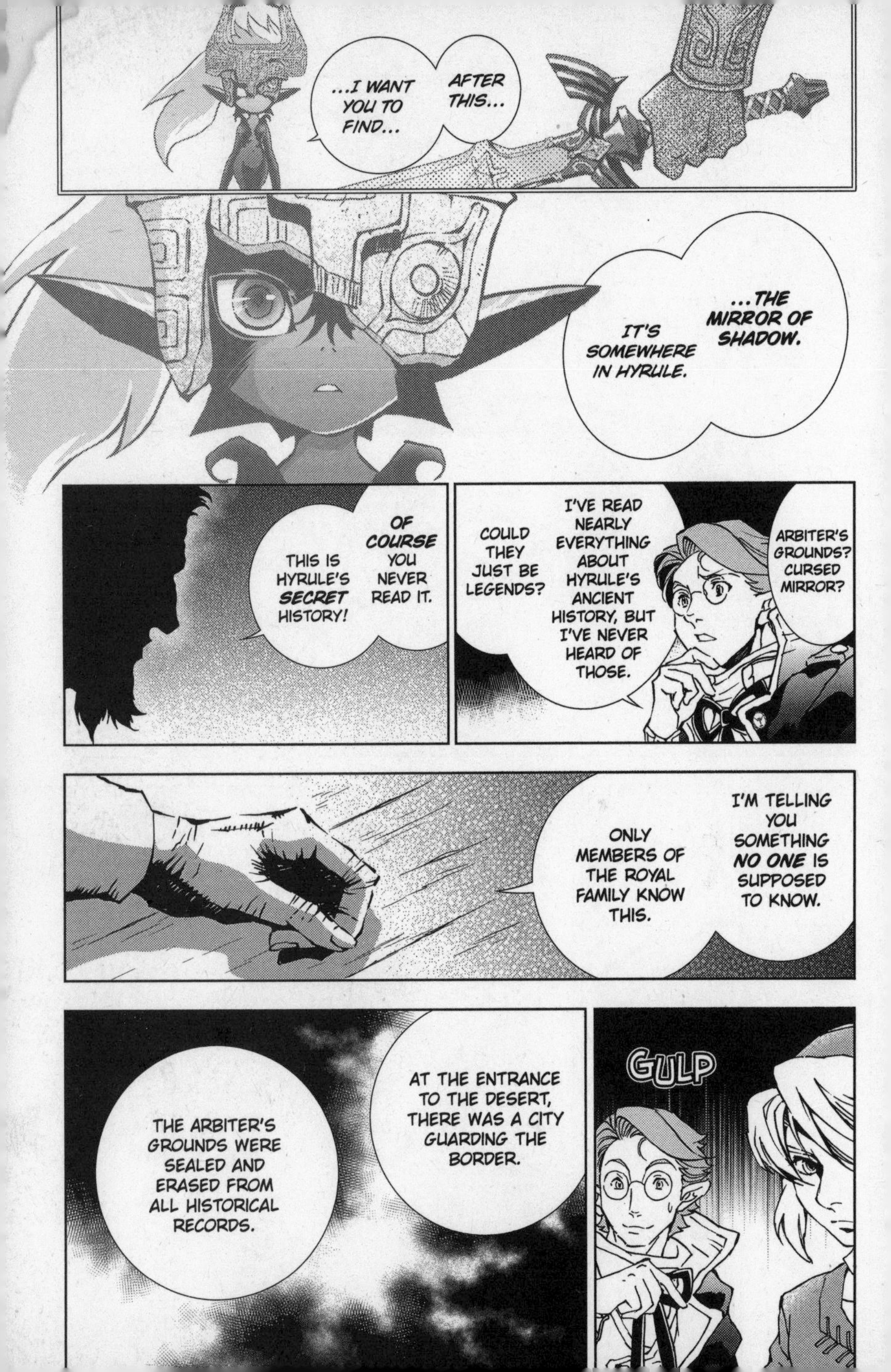
AFTER THIS...
...I WANT YOU TO FIND...
...THE MIRROR OF SHADOW.
IT'S SOMEWHERE IN HYRULE.
ARBITER'S GROUNDS? CURSED MIRROR?
I'VE READ NEARLY EVERYTHING ABOUT HYRULE'S ANCIENT HISTORY, BUT I'VE NEVER HEARD OF THOSE.
COULD THEY JUST BE LEGENDS?
OF COURSE YOU NEVER READ IT.
THIS IS HYRULE'S SECRET HISTORY!
I'M TELLING YOU SOMETHING NO ONE IS SUPPOSED TO KNOW.
ONLY MEMBERS OF THE ROYAL FAMILY KNOW THIS.
GULP
AT THE ENTRANCE TO THE DESERT, THERE WAS A CITY GUARDING THE BORDER.
THE ARBITER'S GROUNDS WERE SEALED AND ERASED FROM ALL HISTORICAL RECORDS.

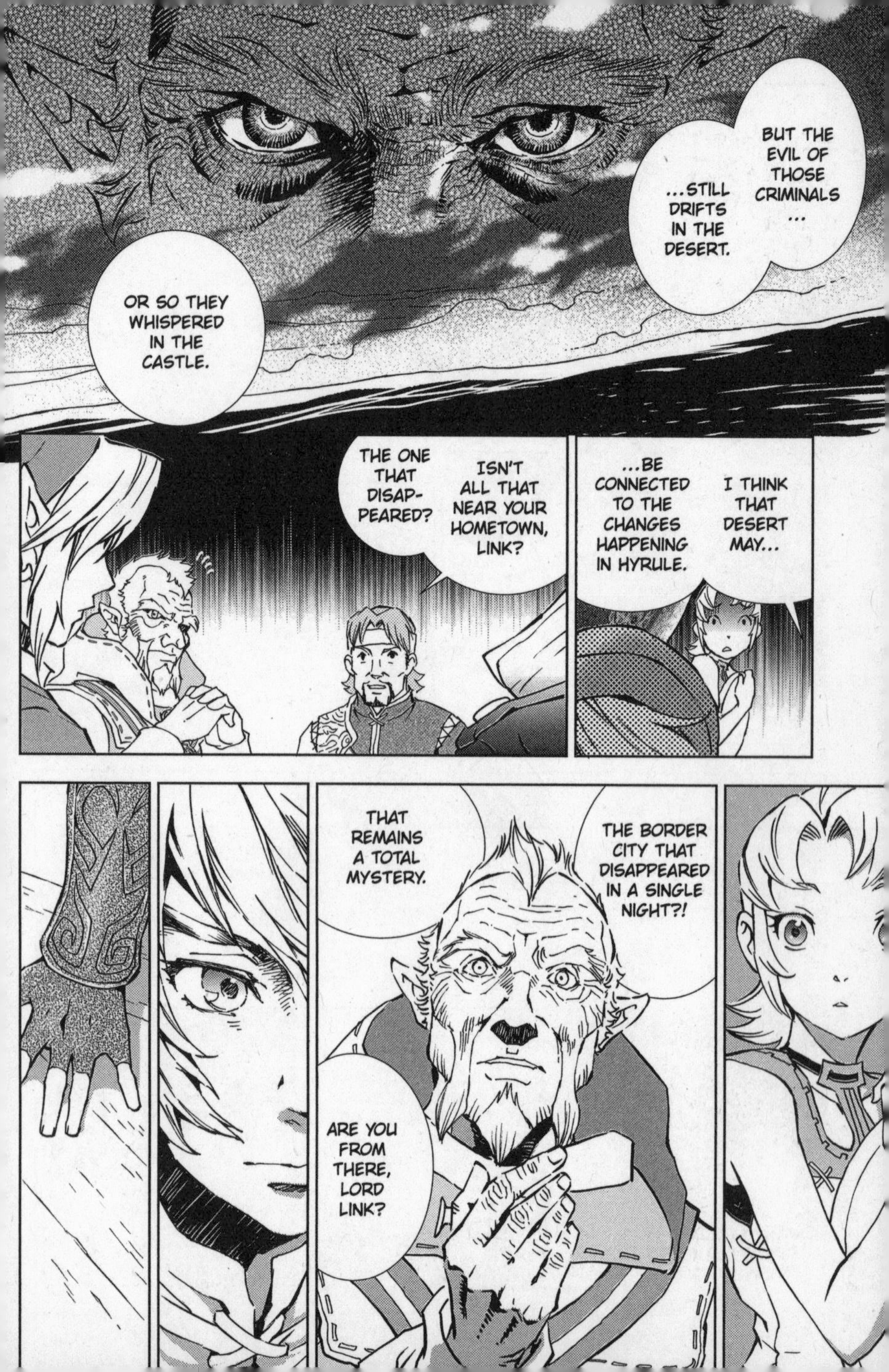
BUT THE EVIL OF THOSE CRIMINALS ...
...STILL DRIFTS IN THE DESERT.
OR SO THEY WHISPERED IN THE CASTLE.
I THINK THAT DESERT MAY...
...BE CONNECTED TO THE CHANGES HAPPENING IN HYRULE.
ISN'T ALL THAT NEAR YOUR HOMETOWN, LINK?
THE ONE THAT DISAP-PEARED?
THE BORDER CITY THAT DISAPPEARED IN A SINGLE NIGHT?!
THAT REMAINS A TOTAL MYSTERY.
ARE YOU FROM THERE, LORD LINK?

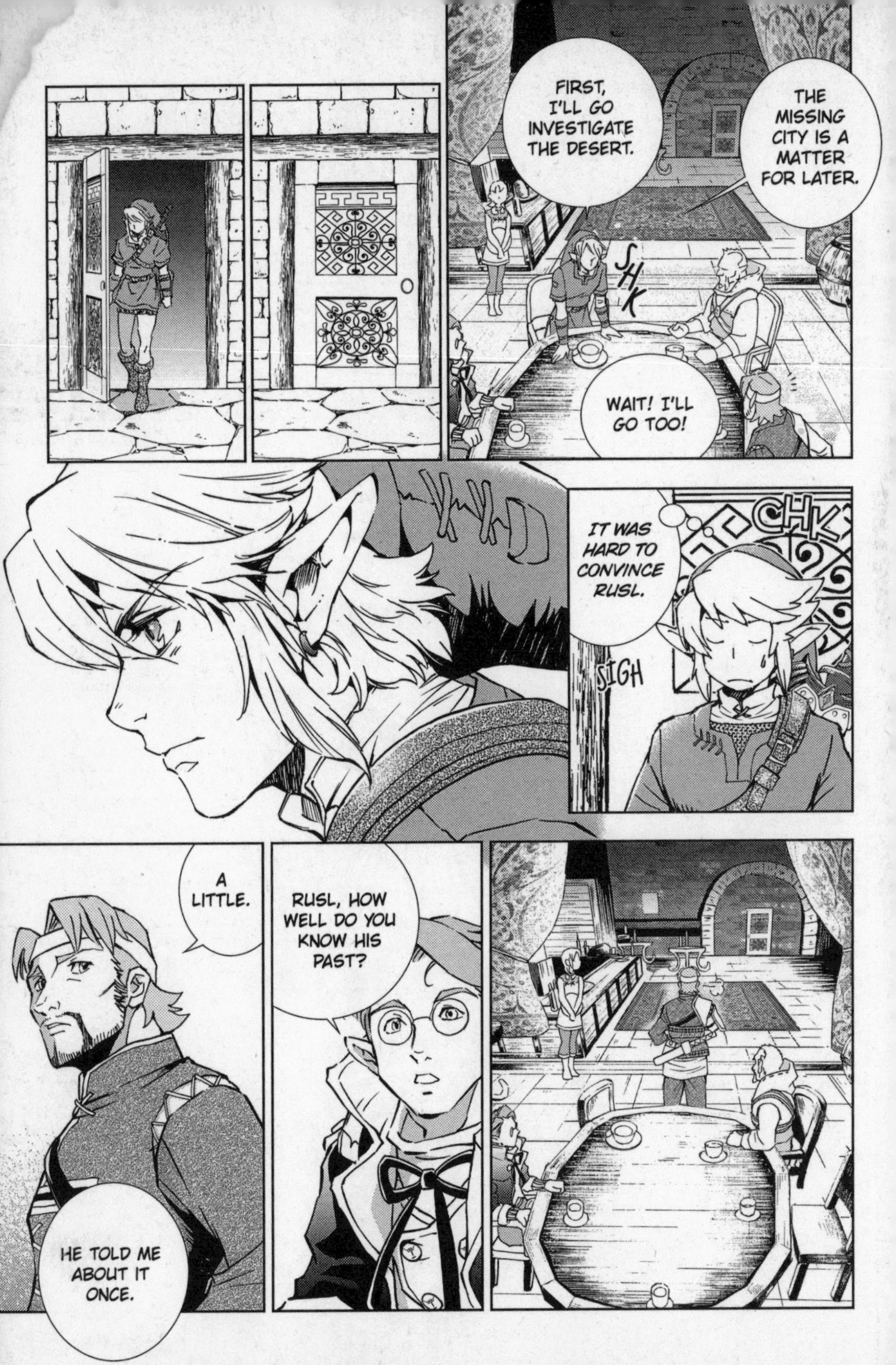
THE MISSING CITY IS A MATTER FOR LATER.
FIRST, I'LL GO INVESTIGATE THE DESERT.
SHK
WAIT! I'LL GO TOO!
CHK
IT WAS HARD TO CONVINCE RUSL.
SIGH
RUSL, HOW WELL DO YOU KNOW HIS PAST?
A LITTLE.
HE TOLD ME ABOUT IT ONCE.

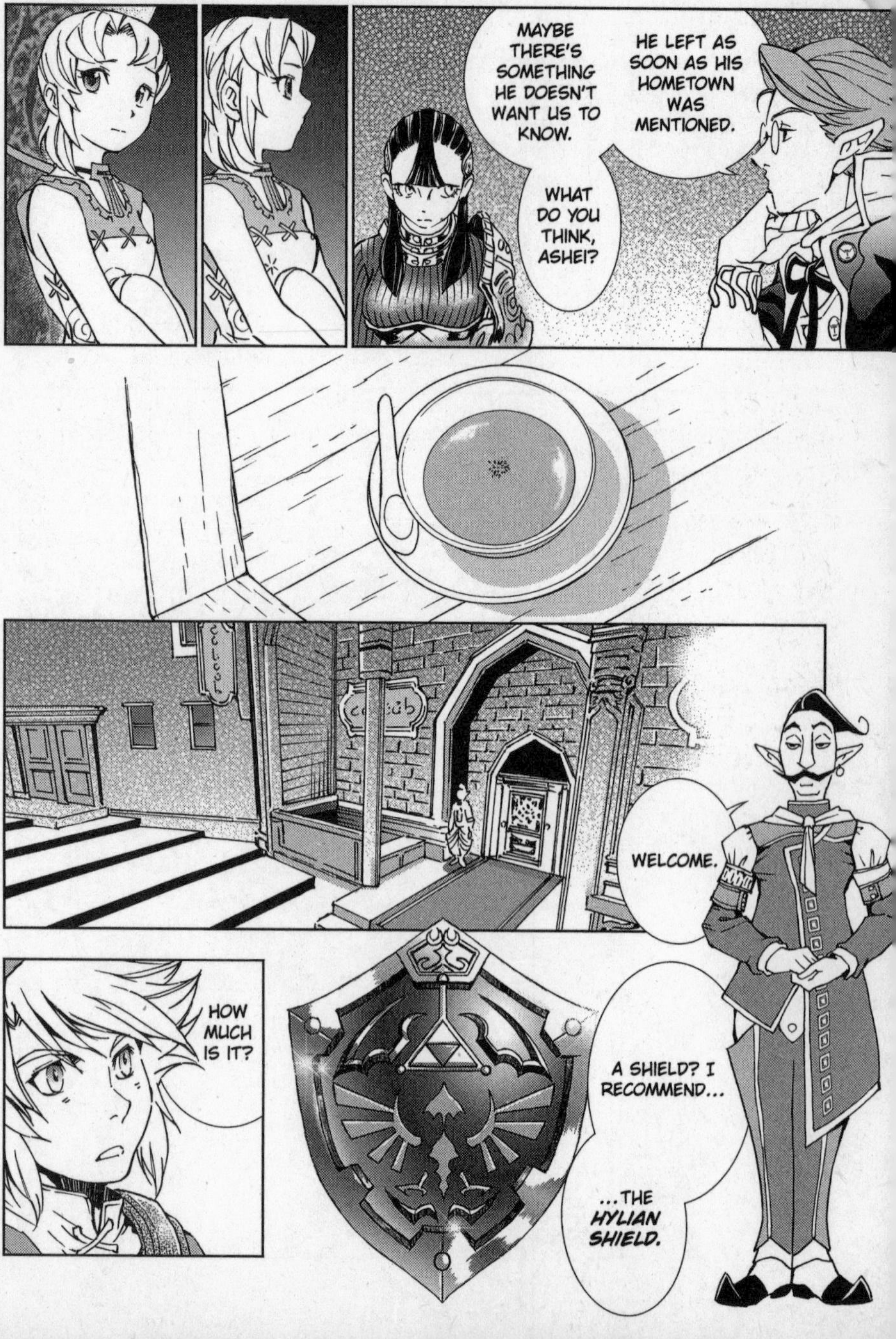

HE LEFT AS SOON AS HIS HOMETOWN WAS MENTIONED.
MAYBE THERE'S SOMETHING HE DOESN'T WANT US TO KNOW.
WHAT DO YOU THINK, ASHEI?
WELCOME.
A SHIELD? I RECOMMEND...
...THE HYLIAN SHIELD.
HOW MUCH IS IT?

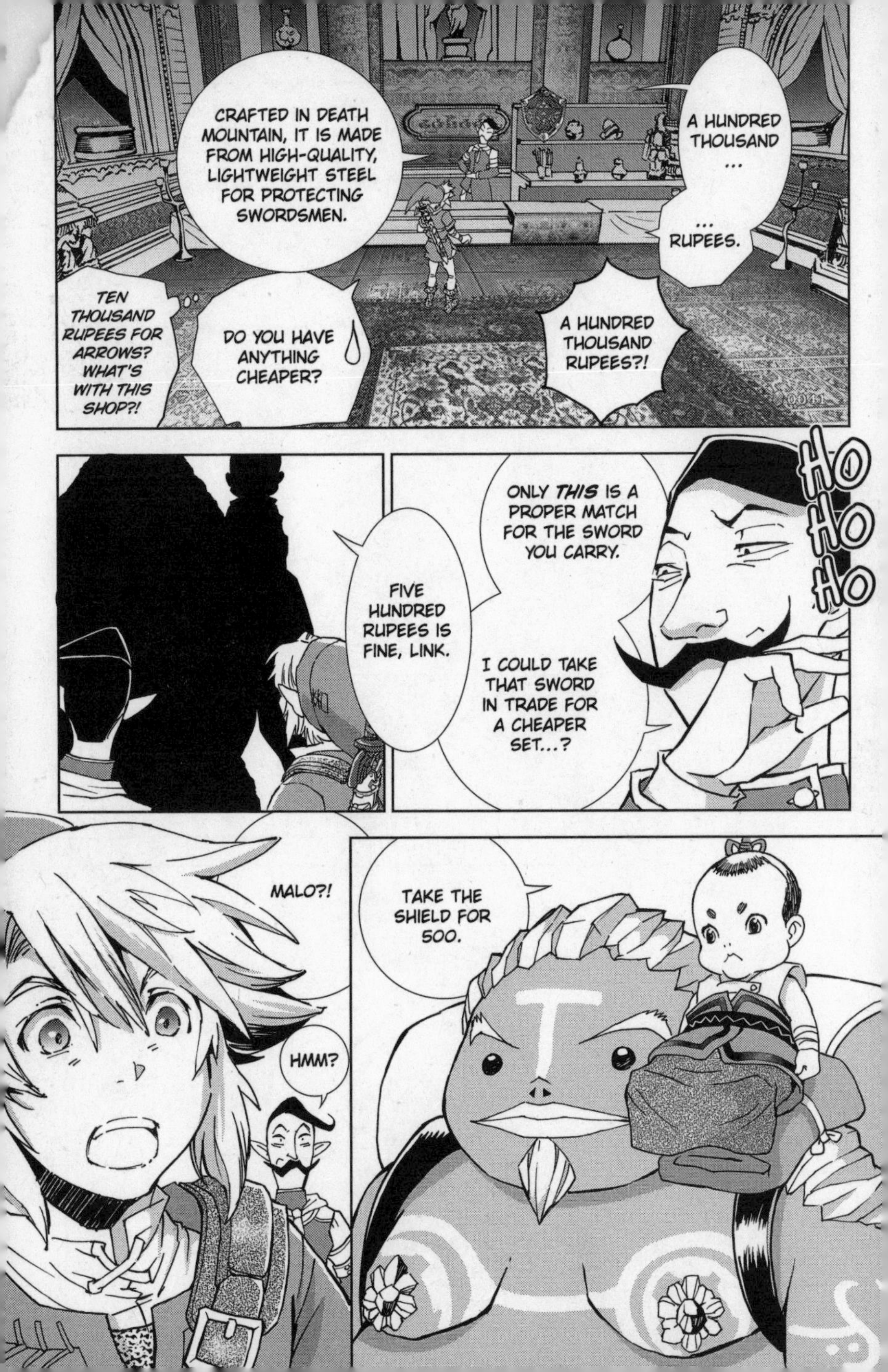
CRAFTED IN DEATH MOUNTAIN, IT IS MADE FROM HIGH-QUALITY, LIGHTWEIGHT STEEL FOR PROTECTING SWORDSMEN.
A HUNDRED THOUSAND ...
... RUPEES.
A HUNDRED THOUSAND RUPEES?!
DO YOU HAVE ANYTHING CHEAPER?
TEN THOUSAND RUPEES FOR ARROWS? WHAT'S WITH THIS SHOP?!
HO HO HO
ONLY THIS IS A PROPER MATCH FOR THE SWORD YOU CARRY.
I COULD TAKE THAT SWORD IN TRADE FOR A CHEAPER SET...?
FIVE HUNDRED RUPEES IS FINE, LINK.
TAKE THE SHIELD FOR 500.
MALO?!
HMM?

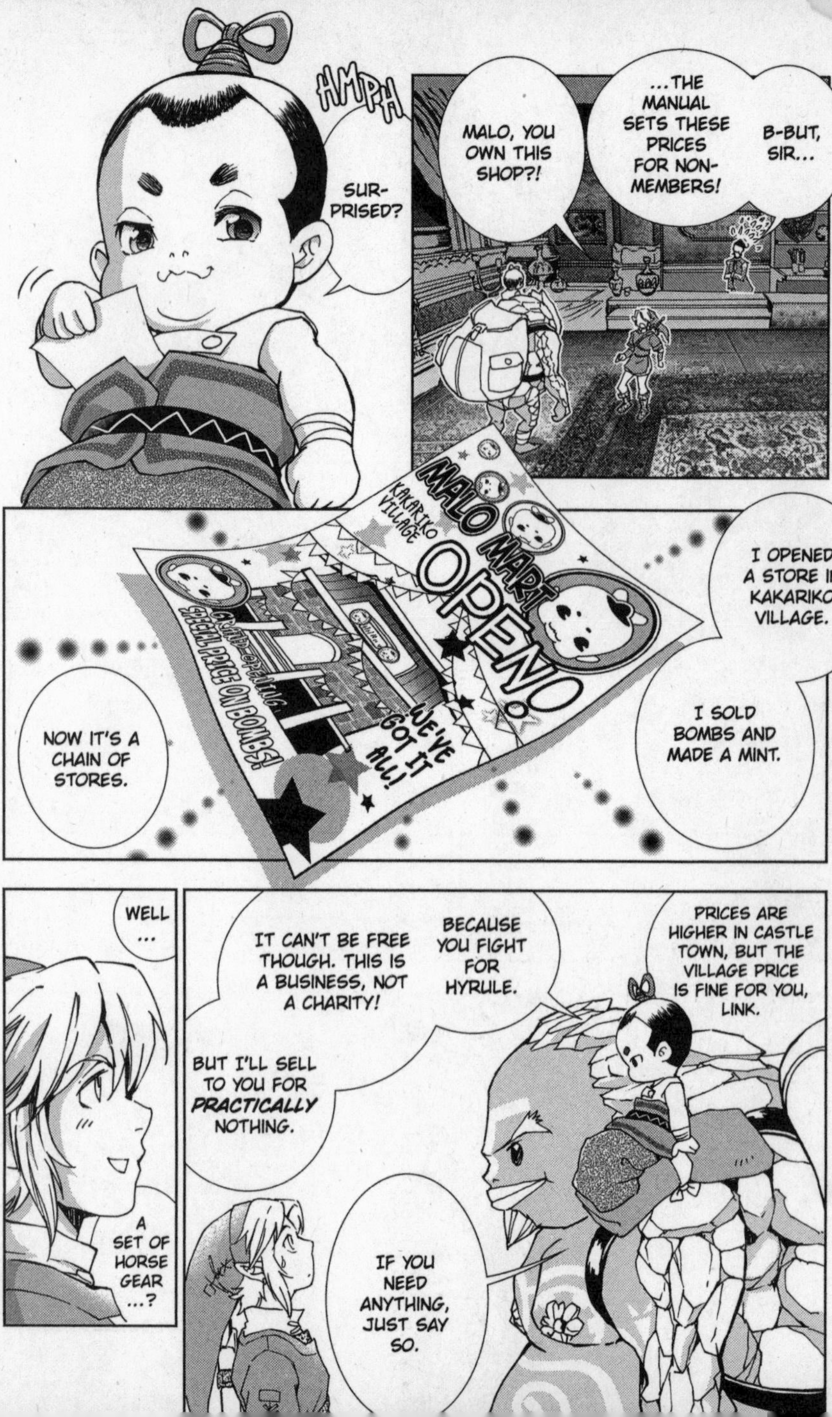
B-BUT, SIR...
...THE MANUAL SETS THESE PRICES FOR NON-MEMBERS!
MALO, YOU OWN THIS SHOP?!
HMPH
SUR-PRISED?
I OPENED A STORE IN KAKARIKO VILLAGE.
I SOLD BOMBS AND MADE A MINT.
MALO MART OPEN!
KAKARIKO VILLAGE
WE'VE GOT IT ALL!
GRAND OPENING
SPECIAL PRICE ON BOMBS!
NOW IT'S A CHAIN OF STORES.
PRICES ARE HIGHER IN CASTLE TOWN, BUT THE VILLAGE PRICE IS FINE FOR YOU, LINK.
BECAUSE YOU FIGHT FOR HYRULE.
IT CAN'T BE FREE THOUGH. THIS IS A BUSINESS, NOT A CHARITY!
BUT I'LL SELL TO YOU FOR *PRACTICALLY* NOTHING.
IF YOU NEED ANYTHING, JUST SAY SO.
WELL ...
A SET OF HORSE GEAR ...?

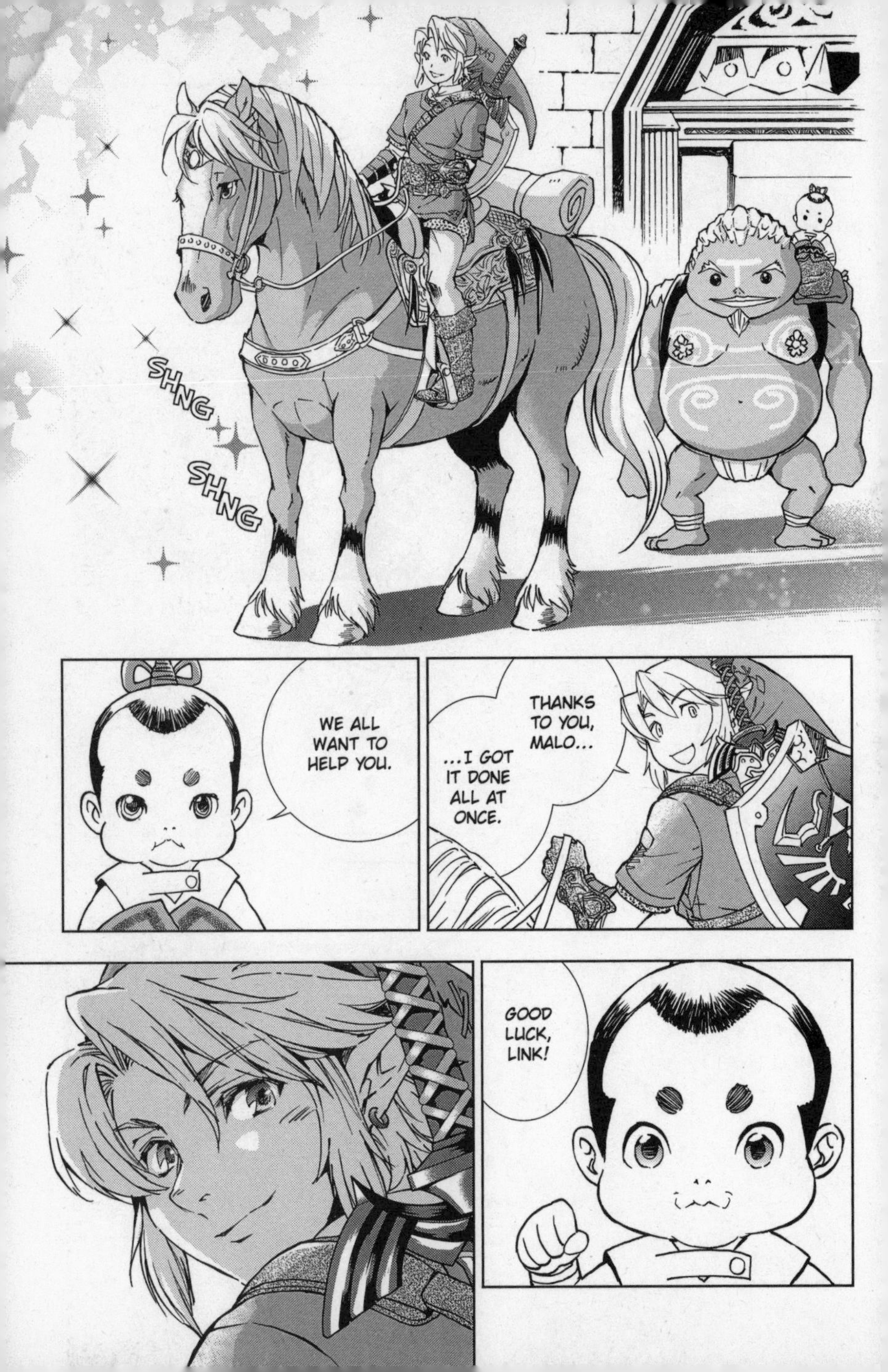
SHNG
SHNG
THANKS TO YOU, MALO...
...I GOT IT DONE ALL AT ONCE.
WE ALL WANT TO HELP YOU.
GOOD LUCK, LINK!

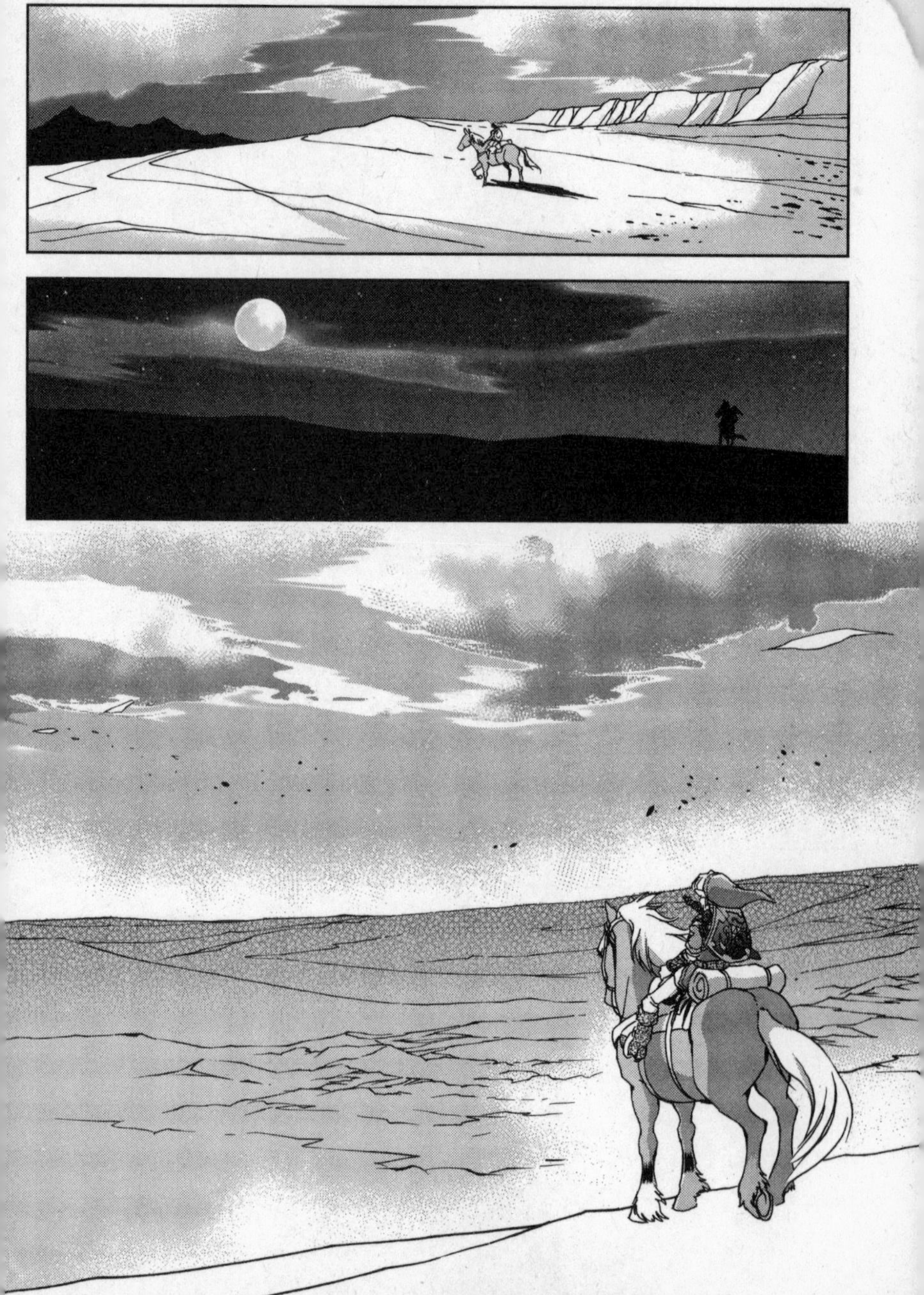

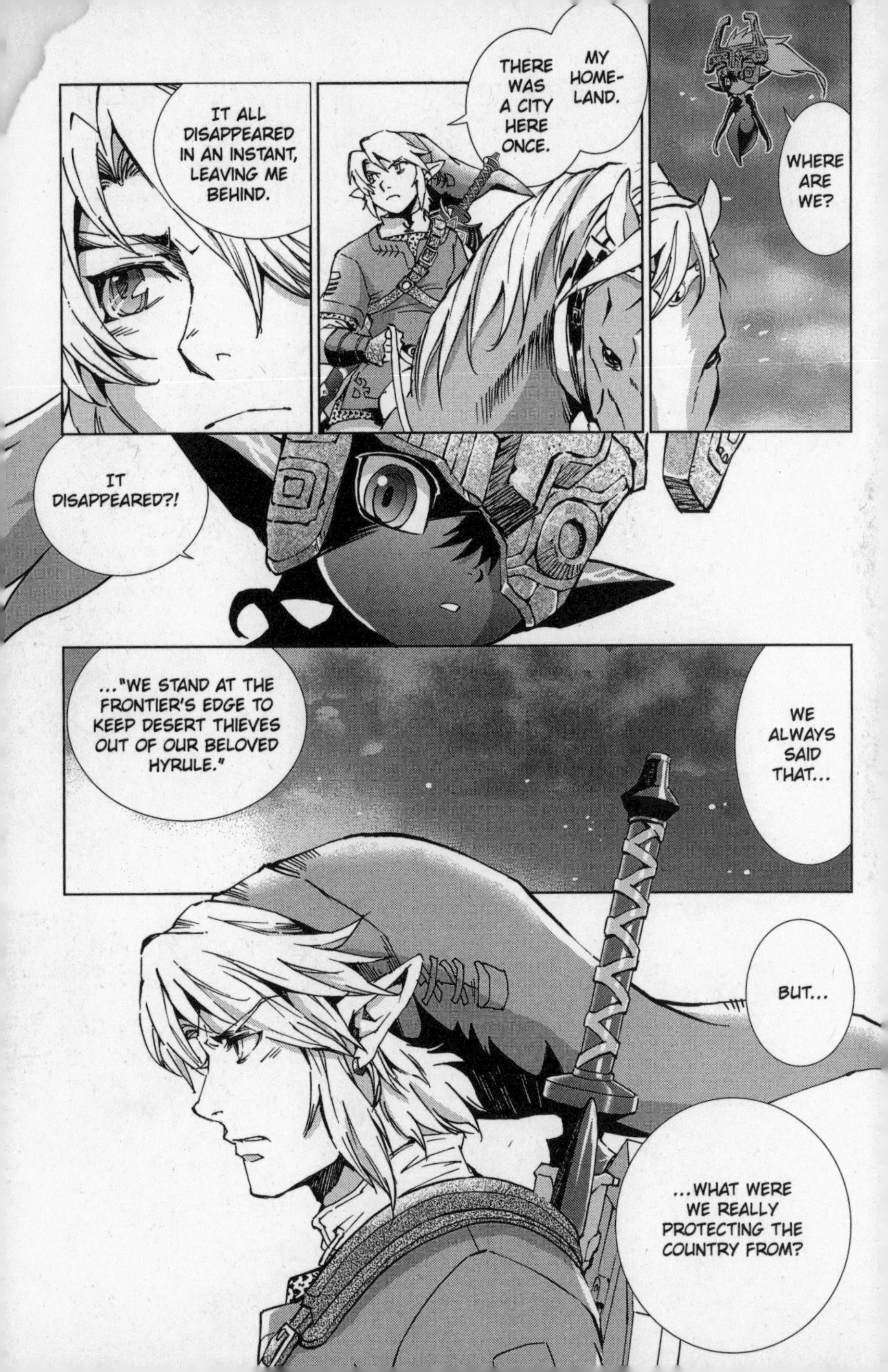
WHERE ARE WE?
THERE WAS A CITY HERE ONCE. MY HOMELAND.
IT ALL DISAPPEARED IN AN INSTANT, LEAVING ME BEHIND.
IT DISAPPEARED?!
WE ALWAYS SAID THAT...
..."WE STAND AT THE FRONTIER'S EDGE TO KEEP DESERT THIEVES OUT OF OUR BELOVED HYRULE."
BUT...
...WHAT WERE WE REALLY PROTECTING THE COUNTRY FROM?

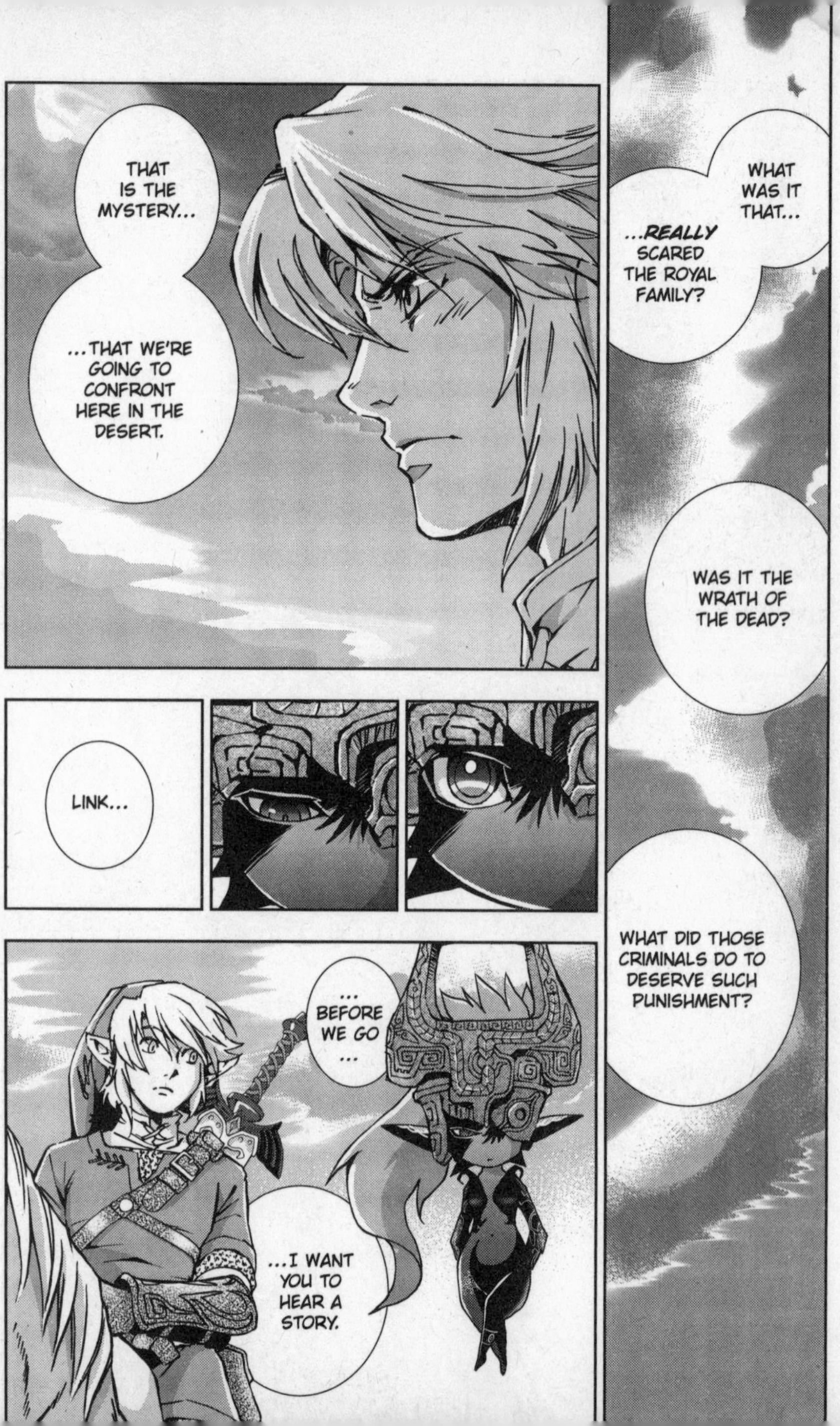
WHAT WAS IT THAT...
...REALLY SCARED THE ROYAL FAMILY?
WAS IT THE WRATH OF THE DEAD?
WHAT DID THOSE CRIMINALS DO TO DESERVE SUCH PUNISHMENT?
THAT IS THE MYSTERY...
...THAT WE'RE GOING TO CONFRONT HERE IN THE DESERT.
LINK...
... BEFORE WE GO ...
...I WANT YOU TO HEAR A STORY.

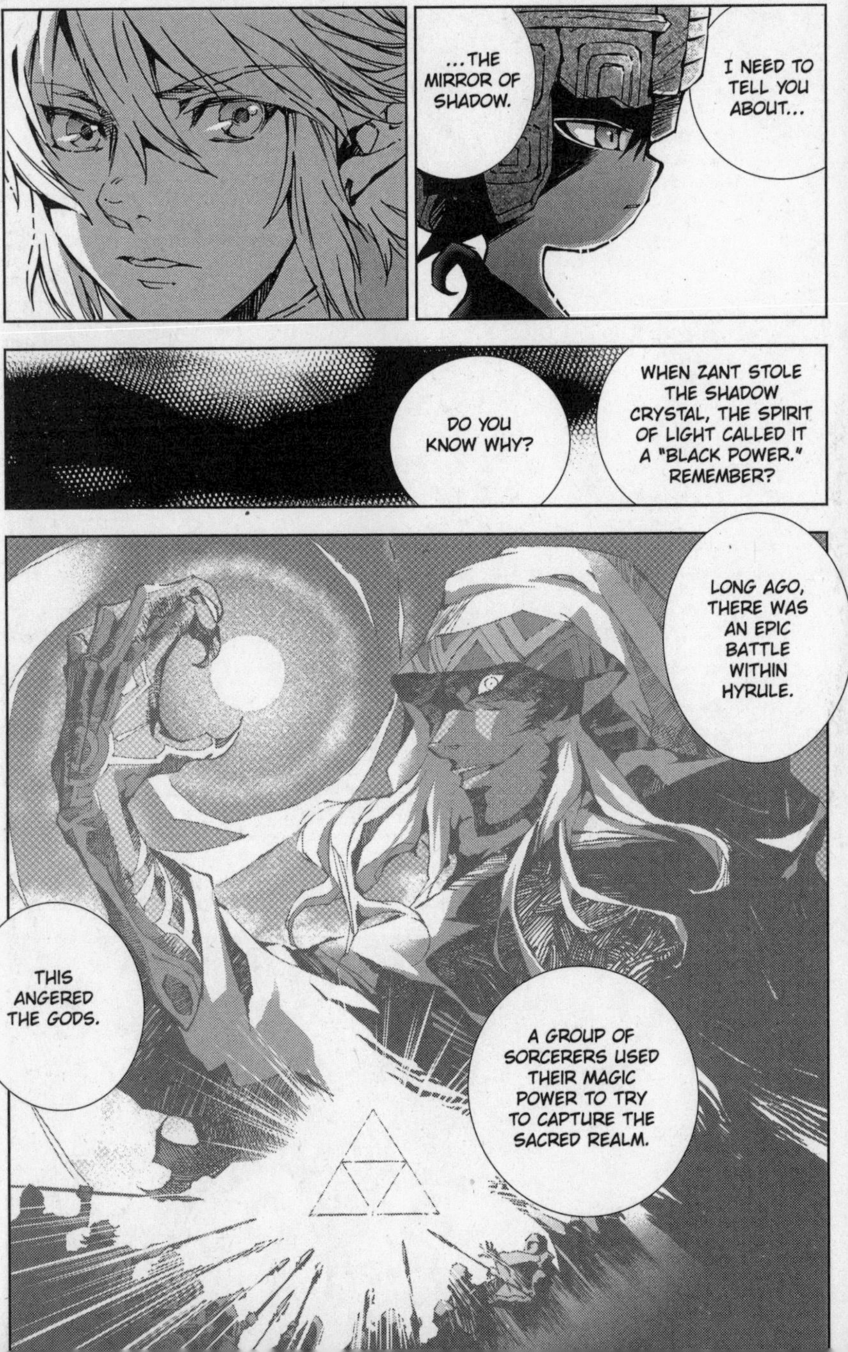
I NEED TO TELL YOU ABOUT...
...THE MIRROR OF SHADOW.
WHEN ZANT STOLE THE SHADOW CRYSTAL, THE SPIRIT OF LIGHT CALLED IT A "BLACK POWER." REMEMBER?
DO YOU KNOW WHY?
LONG AGO, THERE WAS AN EPIC BATTLE WITHIN HYRULE.
A GROUP OF SORCERERS USED THEIR MAGIC POWER TO TRY TO CAPTURE THE SACRED REALM.
THIS ANGERED THE GODS.

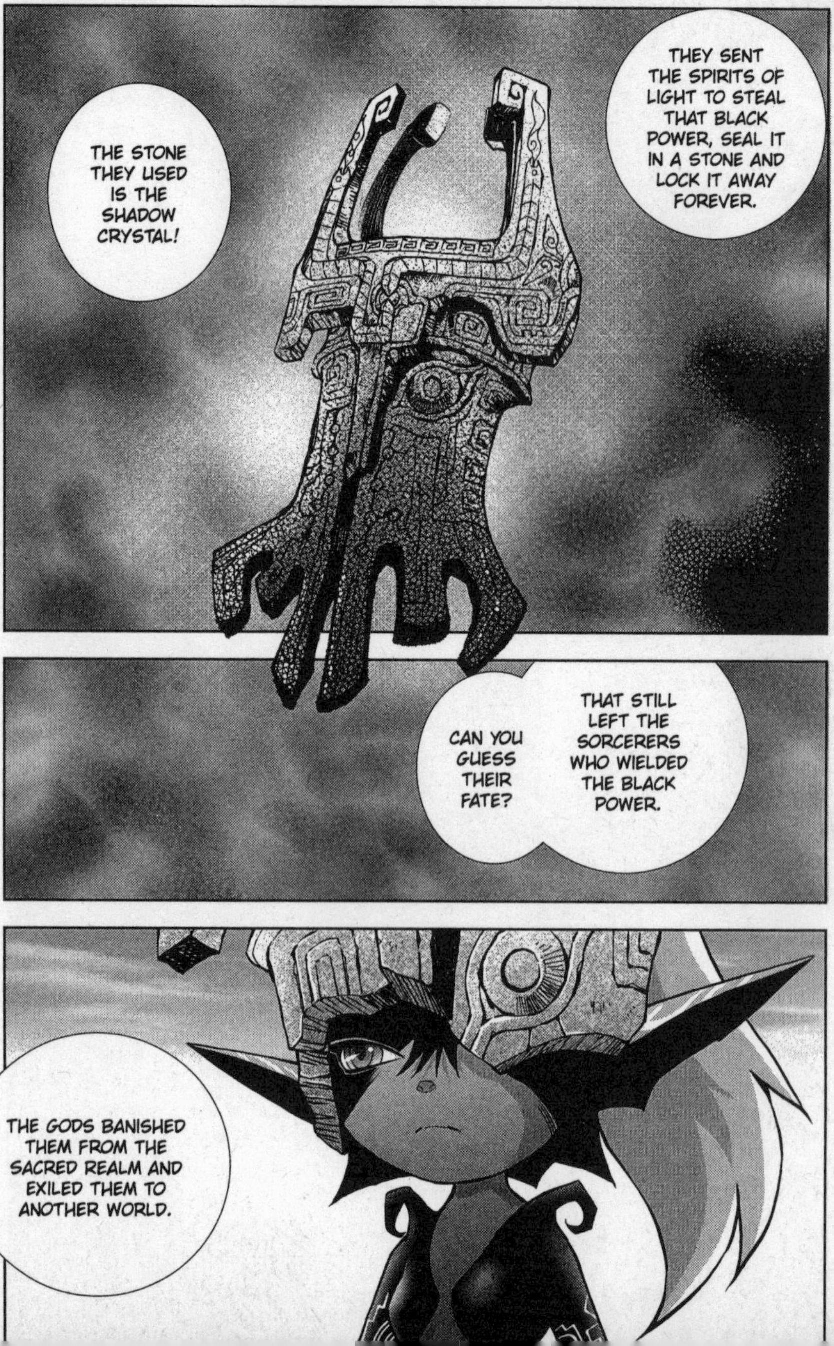
THEY SENT THE SPIRITS OF LIGHT TO STEAL THAT BLACK POWER, SEAL IT IN A STONE AND LOCK IT AWAY FOREVER.
THE STONE THEY USED IS THE SHADOW CRYSTAL!
THAT STILL LEFT THE SORCERERS WHO WIELDED THE BLACK POWER.
CAN YOU GUESS THEIR FATE?
THE GODS BANISHED THEM FROM THE SACRED REALM AND EXILED THEM TO ANOTHER WORLD.

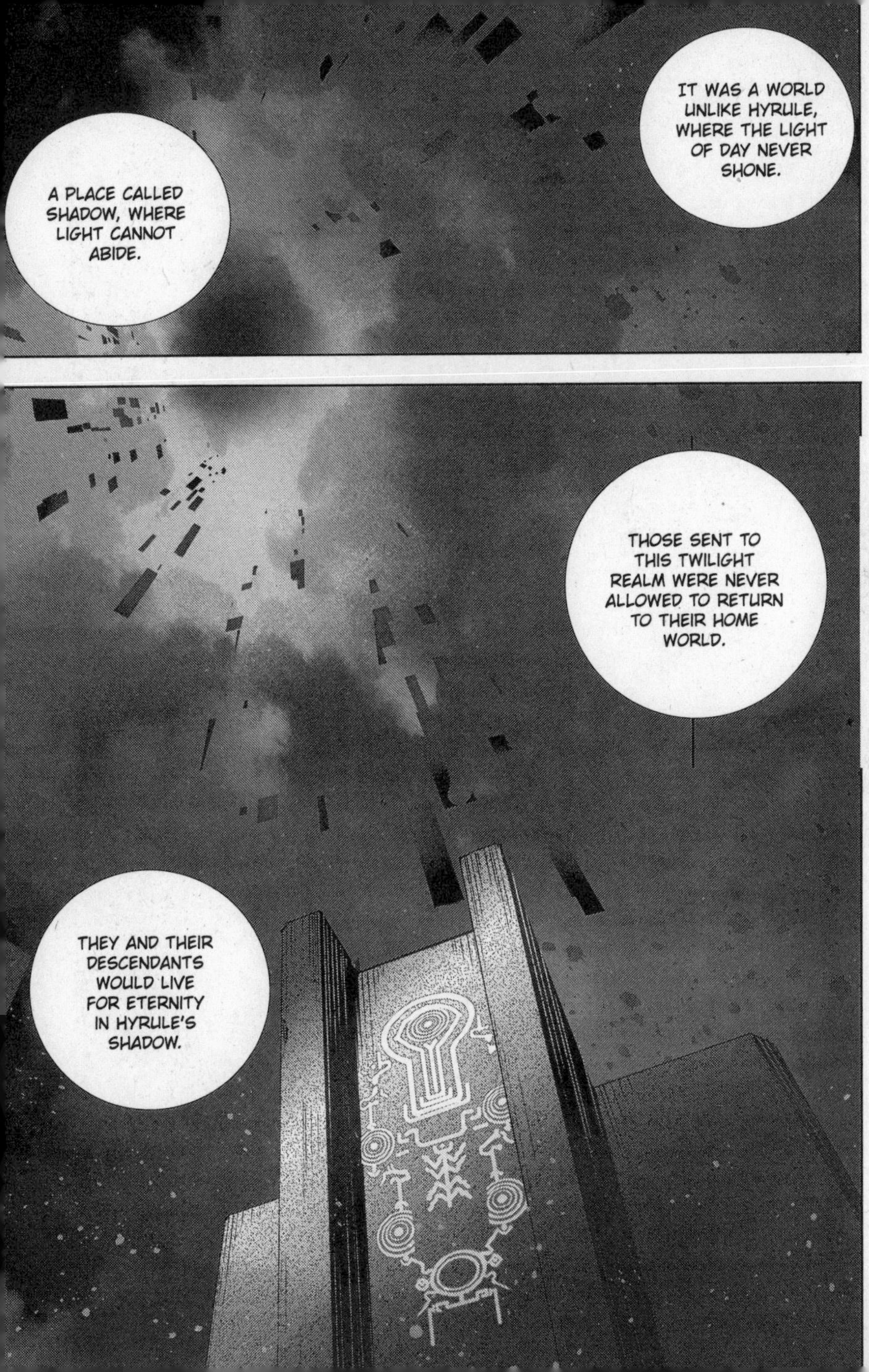
IT WAS A WORLD UNLIKE HYRULE, WHERE THE LIGHT OF DAY NEVER SHONE.
A PLACE CALLED SHADOW, WHERE LIGHT CANNOT ABIDE.
THOSE SENT TO THIS TWILIGHT REALM WERE NEVER ALLOWED TO RETURN TO THEIR HOME WORLD.
THEY AND THEIR DESCENDANTS WOULD LIVE FOR ETERNITY IN HYRULE'S SHADOW.

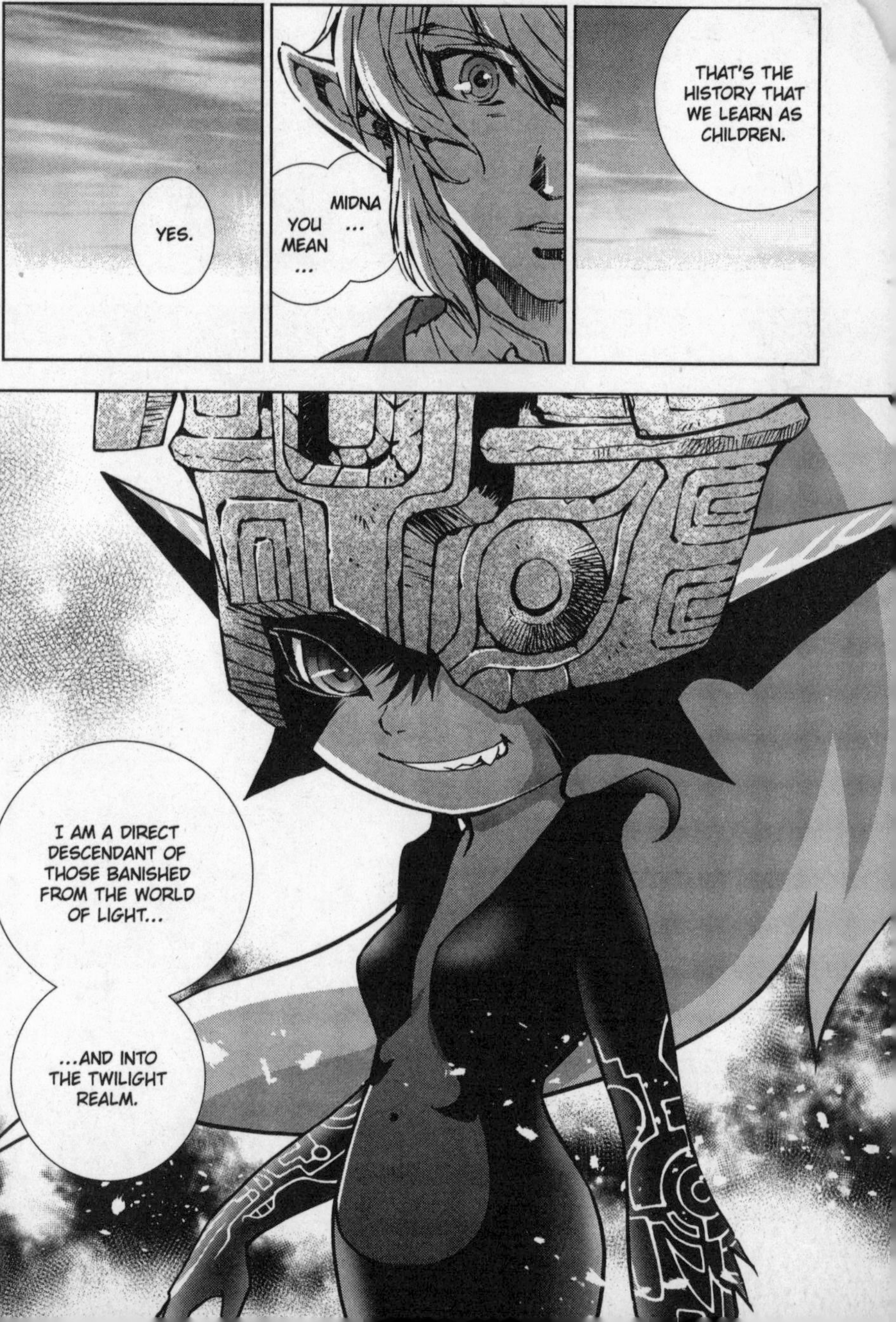
THAT'S THE HISTORY THAT WE LEARN AS CHILDREN.
MIDNA ... YOU MEAN ...
YES.
I AM A DIRECT DESCENDANT OF THOSE BANISHED FROM THE WORLD OF LIGHT...
...AND INTO THE TWILIGHT REALM.

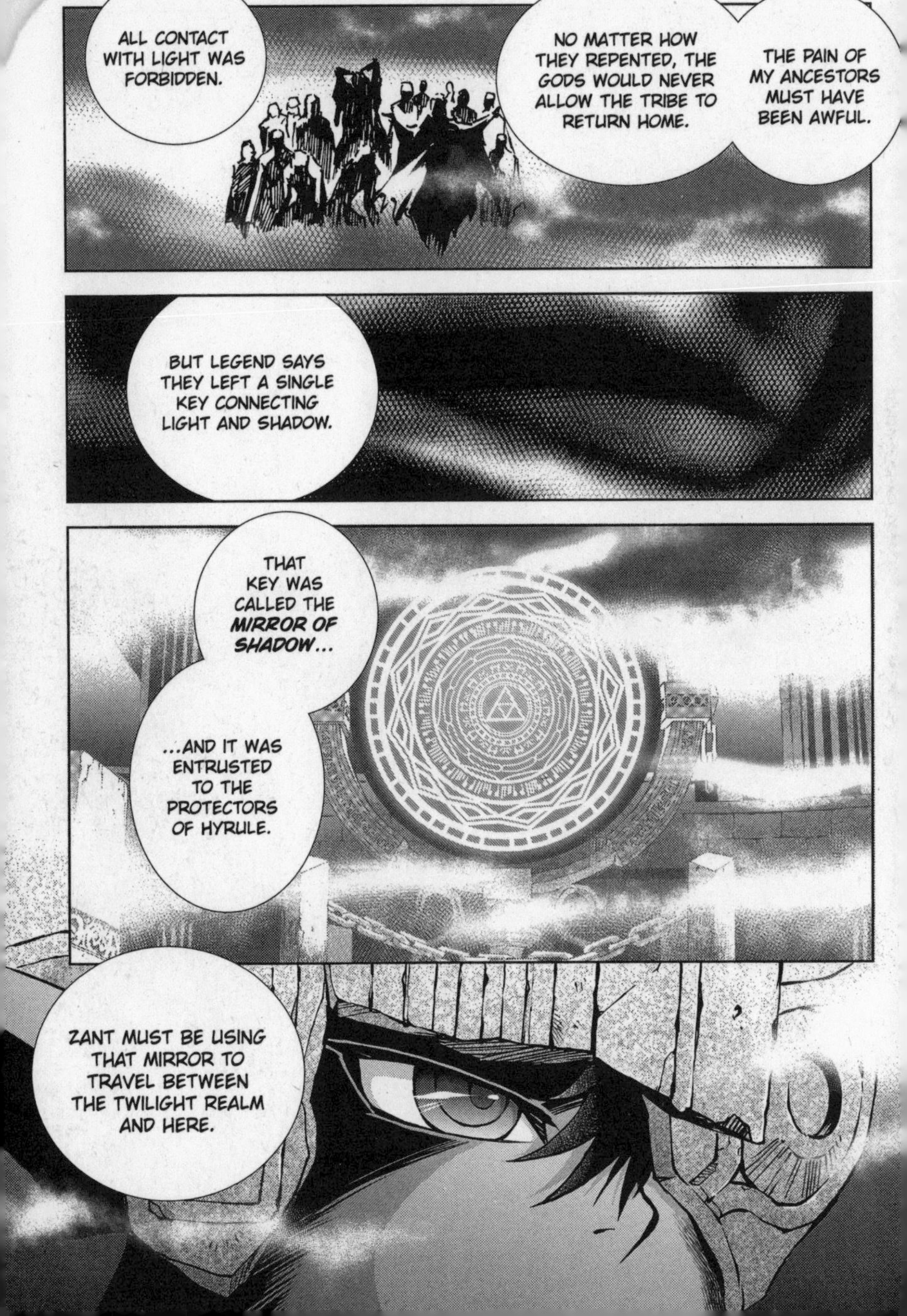
THE PAIN OF MY ANCESTORS MUST HAVE BEEN AWFUL.
NO MATTER HOW THEY REPENTED, THE GODS WOULD NEVER ALLOW THE TRIBE TO RETURN HOME.
ALL CONTACT WITH LIGHT WAS FORBIDDEN.
BUT LEGEND SAYS THEY LEFT A SINGLE KEY CONNECTING LIGHT AND SHADOW.
THAT KEY WAS CALLED THE *MIRROR OF SHADOW*...
...AND IT WAS ENTRUSTED TO THE PROTECTORS OF HYRULE.
ZANT MUST BE USING THAT MIRROR TO TRAVEL BETWEEN THE TWILIGHT REALM AND HERE.

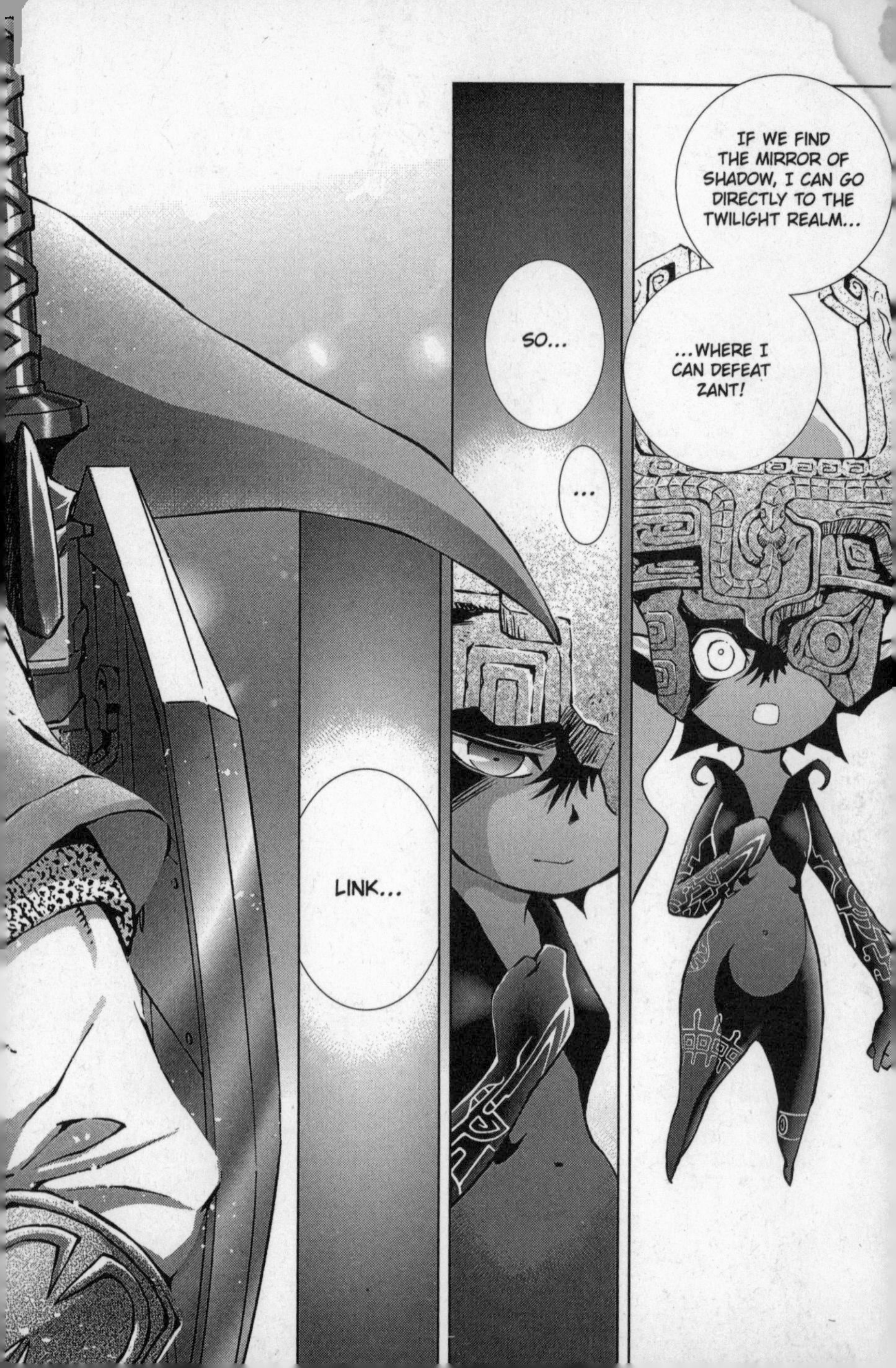
IF WE FIND THE MIRROR OF SHADOW, I CAN GO DIRECTLY TO THE TWILIGHT REALM...
...WHERE I CAN DEFEAT ZANT!
SO...
...
LINK...

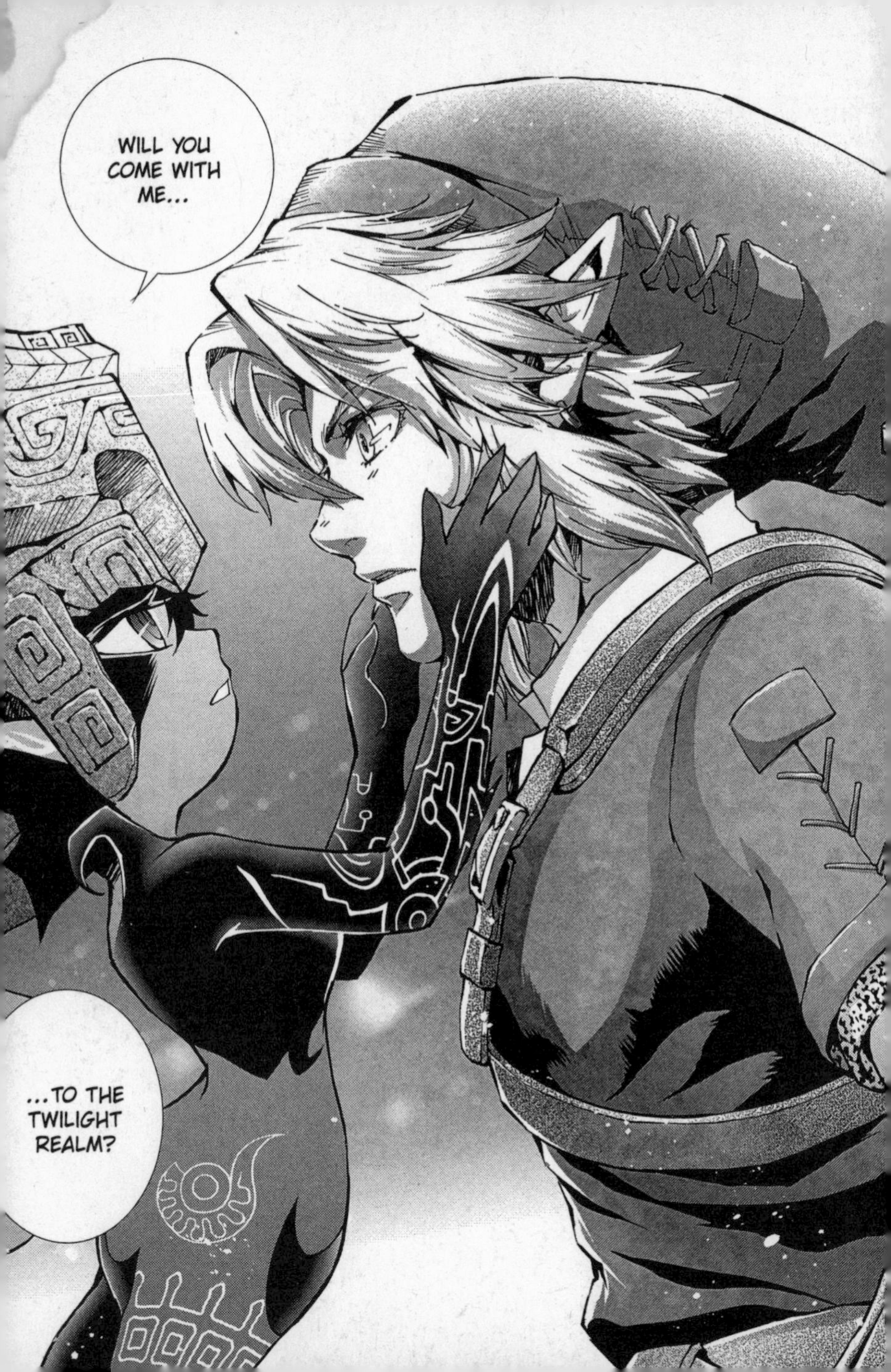
WILL YOU COME WITH ME...
...TO THE TWILIGHT REALM?

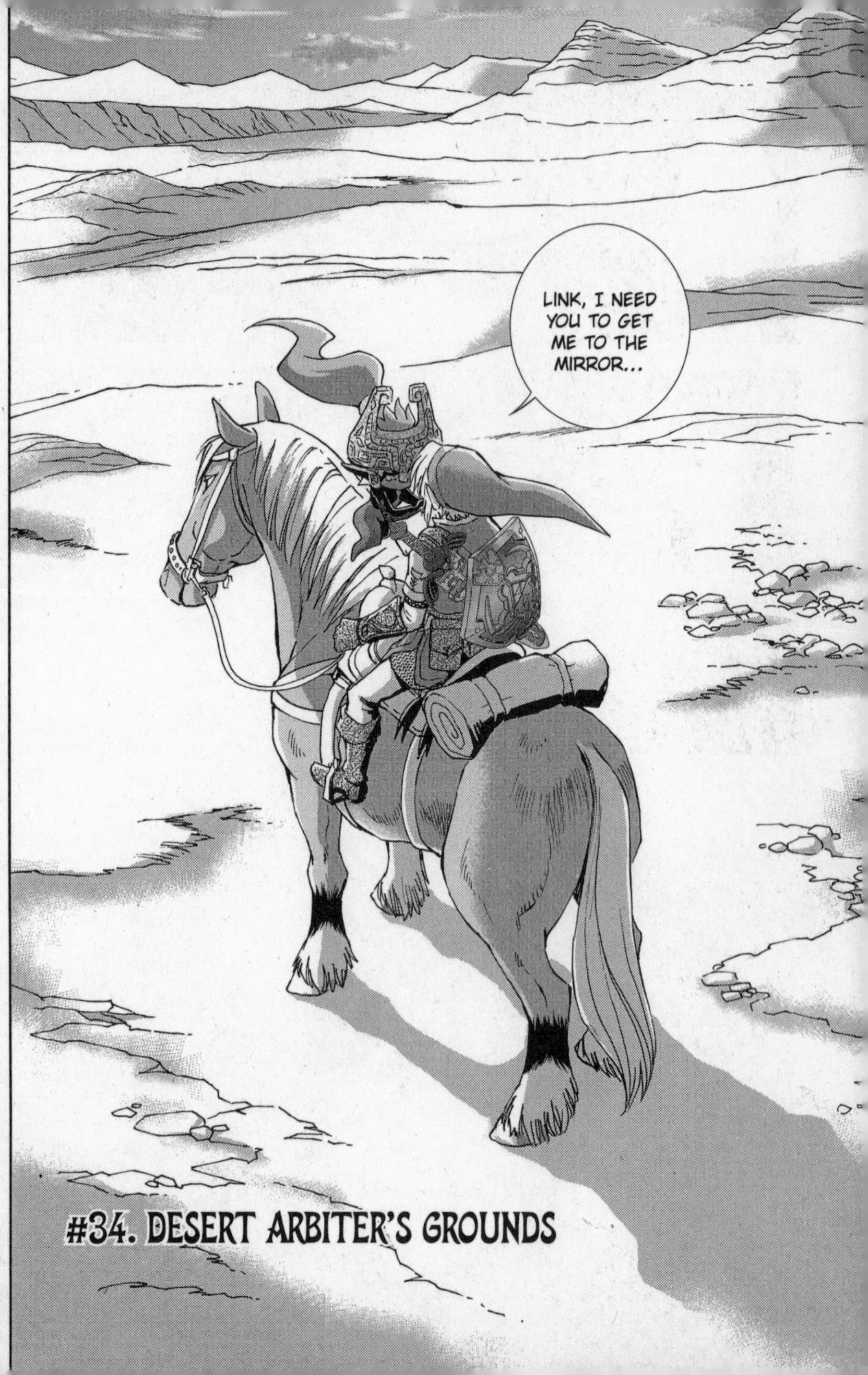
LINK, I NEED YOU TO GET ME TO THE MIRROR...

#34. DESERT ARBITER'S GROUNDS

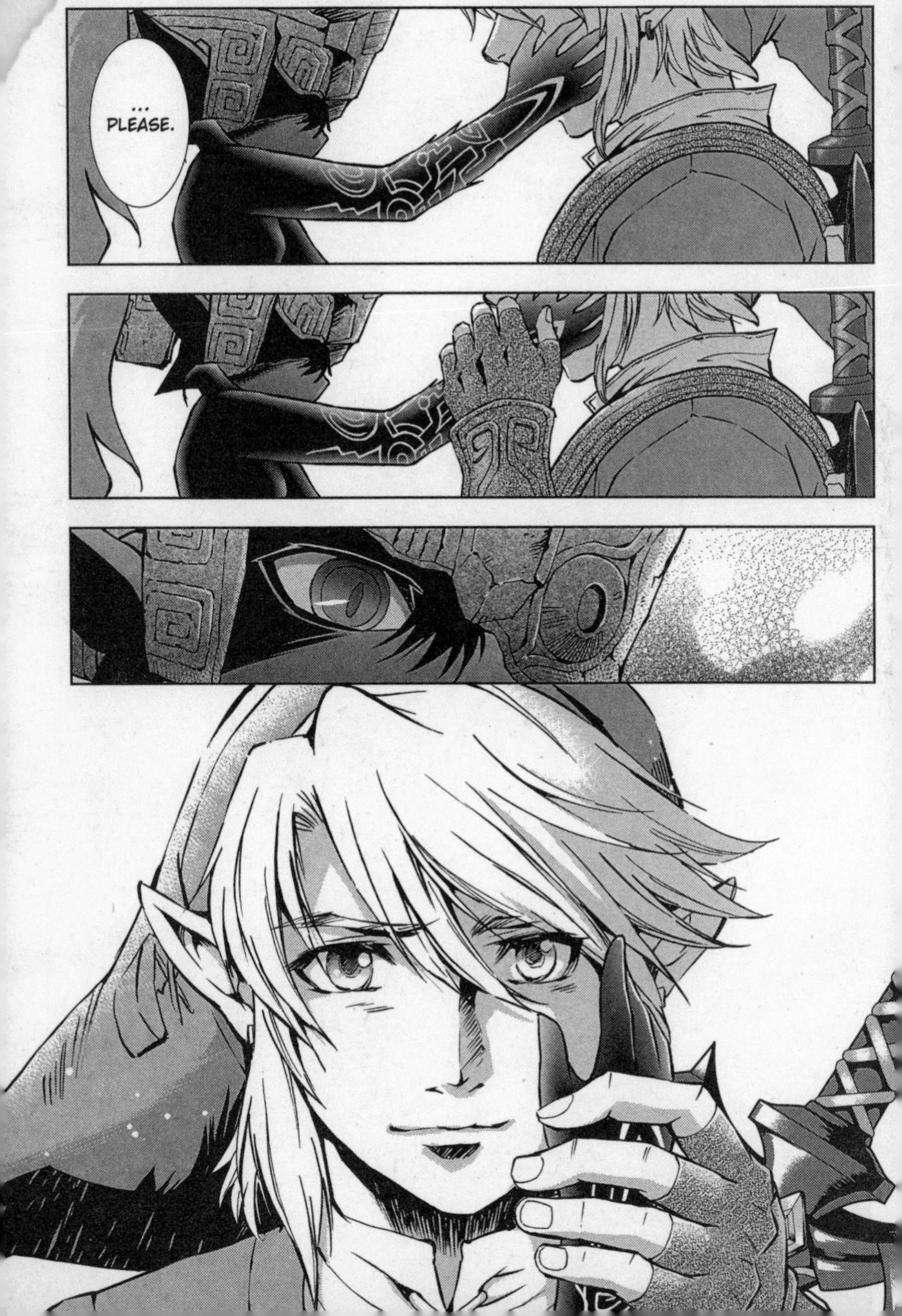
... PLEASE.

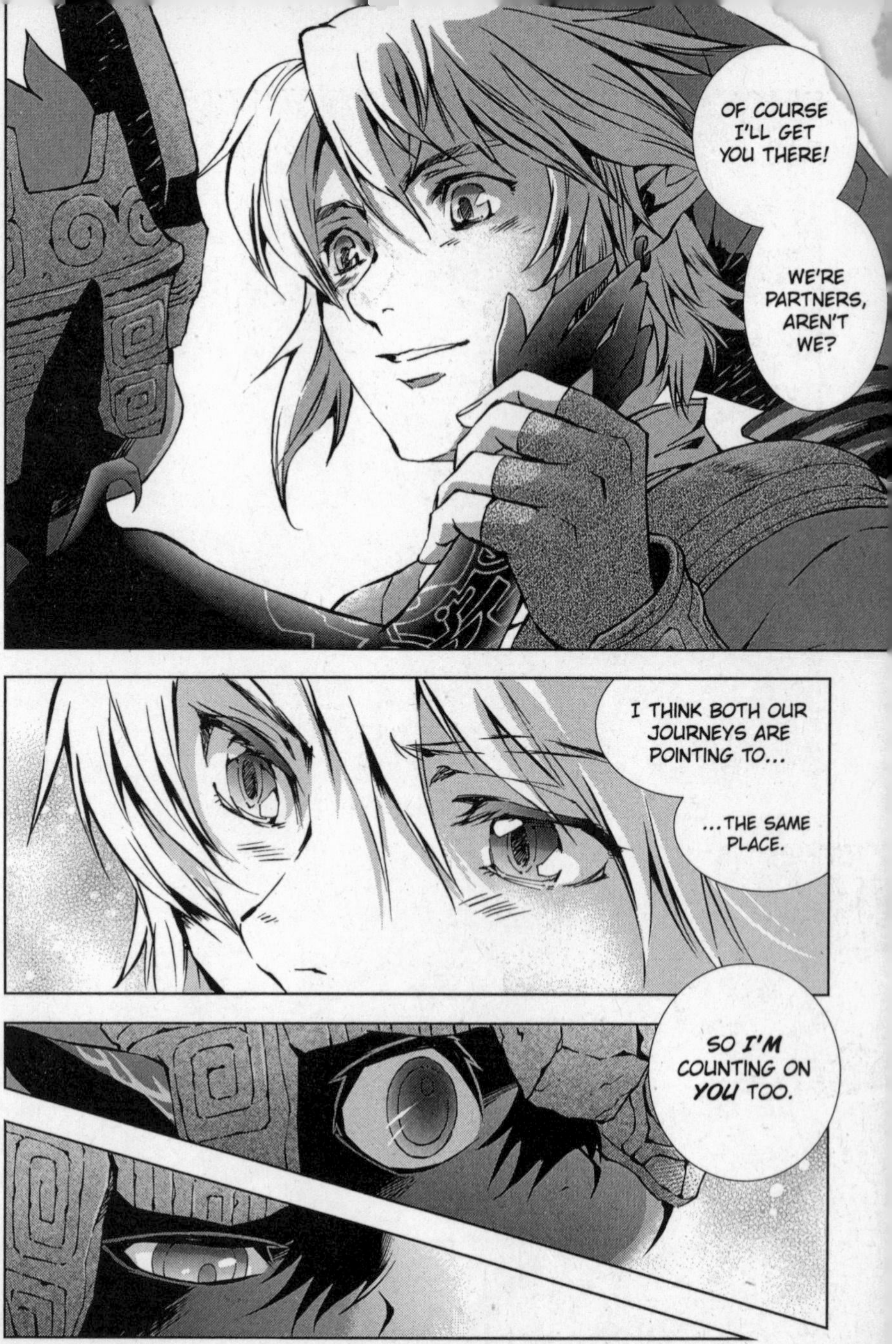
OF COURSE I'LL GET YOU THERE!
WE'RE PARTNERS, AREN'T WE?
I THINK BOTH OUR JOURNEYS ARE POINTING TO...
...THE SAME PLACE.
SO I'M COUNTING ON YOU TOO.

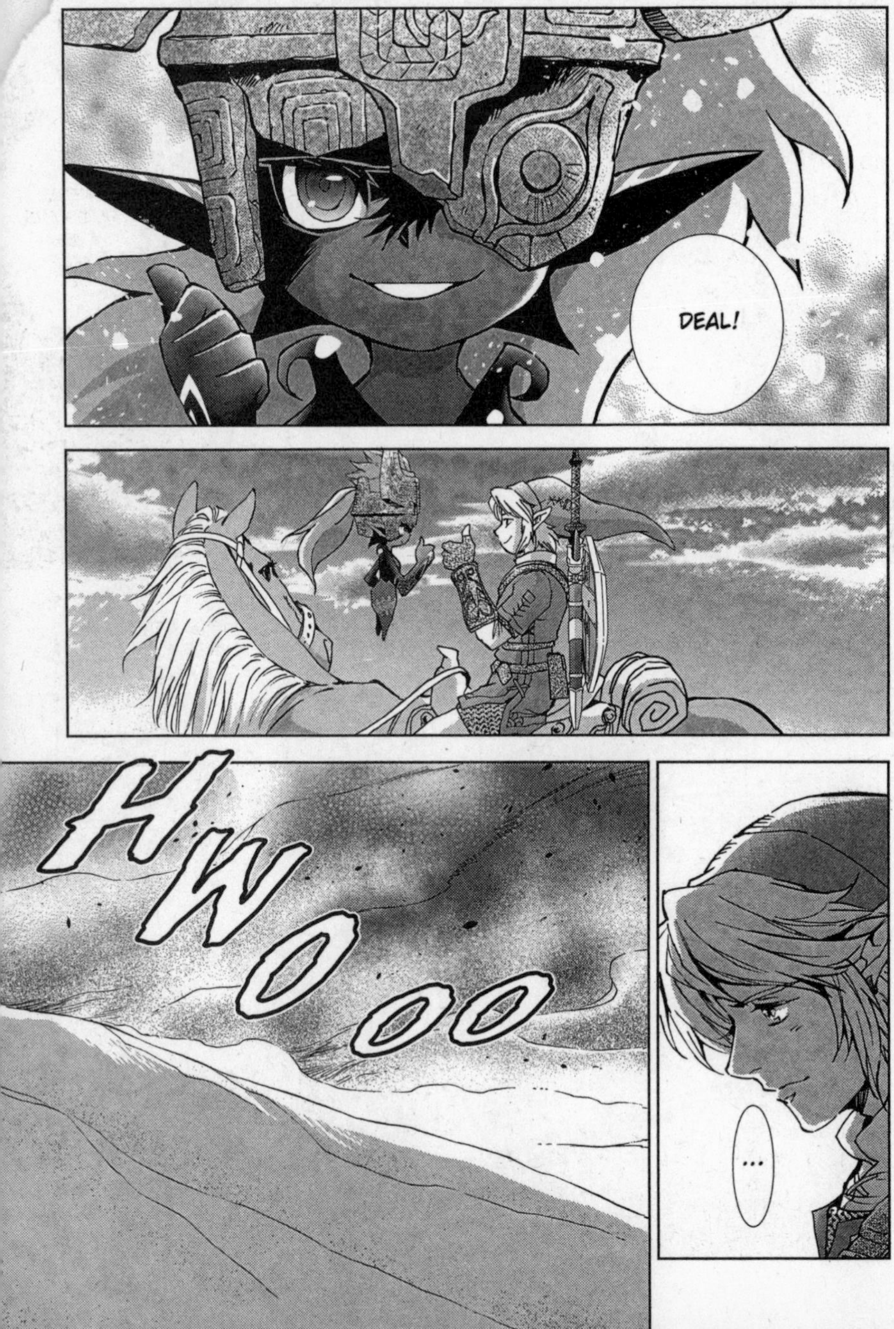
DEAL!
...
HWOOOO

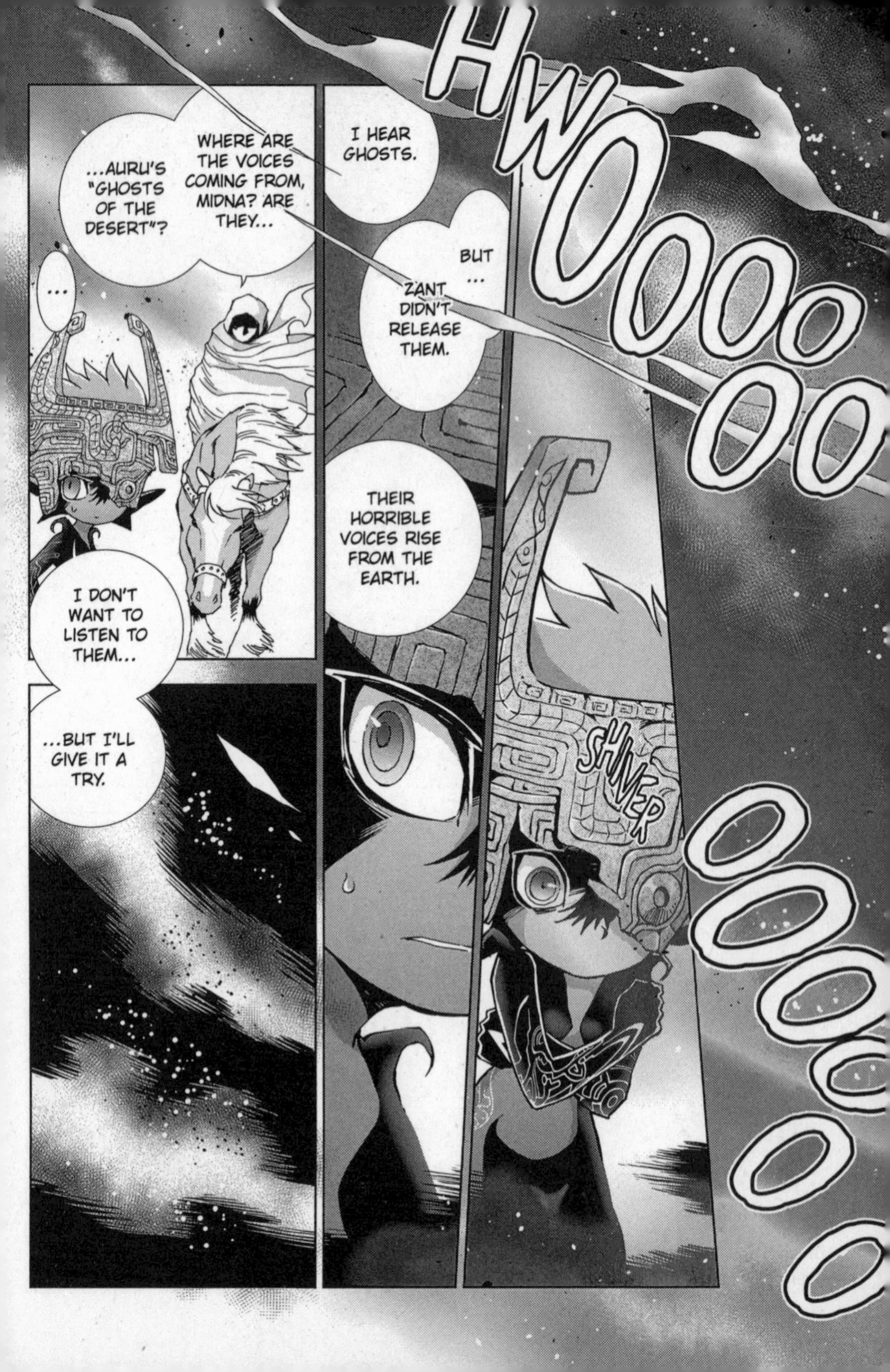
HWOOOOOOOO
SHIVER
OOOOOOOOO
I HEAR GHOSTS.
BUT ...
ZANT DIDN'T RELEASE THEM.
THEIR HORRIBLE VOICES RISE FROM THE EARTH.
WHERE ARE THE VOICES COMING FROM, MIDNA? ARE THEY...
...AURU'S "GHOSTS OF THE DESERT"?
...
I DON'T WANT TO LISTEN TO THEM...
...BUT I'LL GIVE IT A TRY.

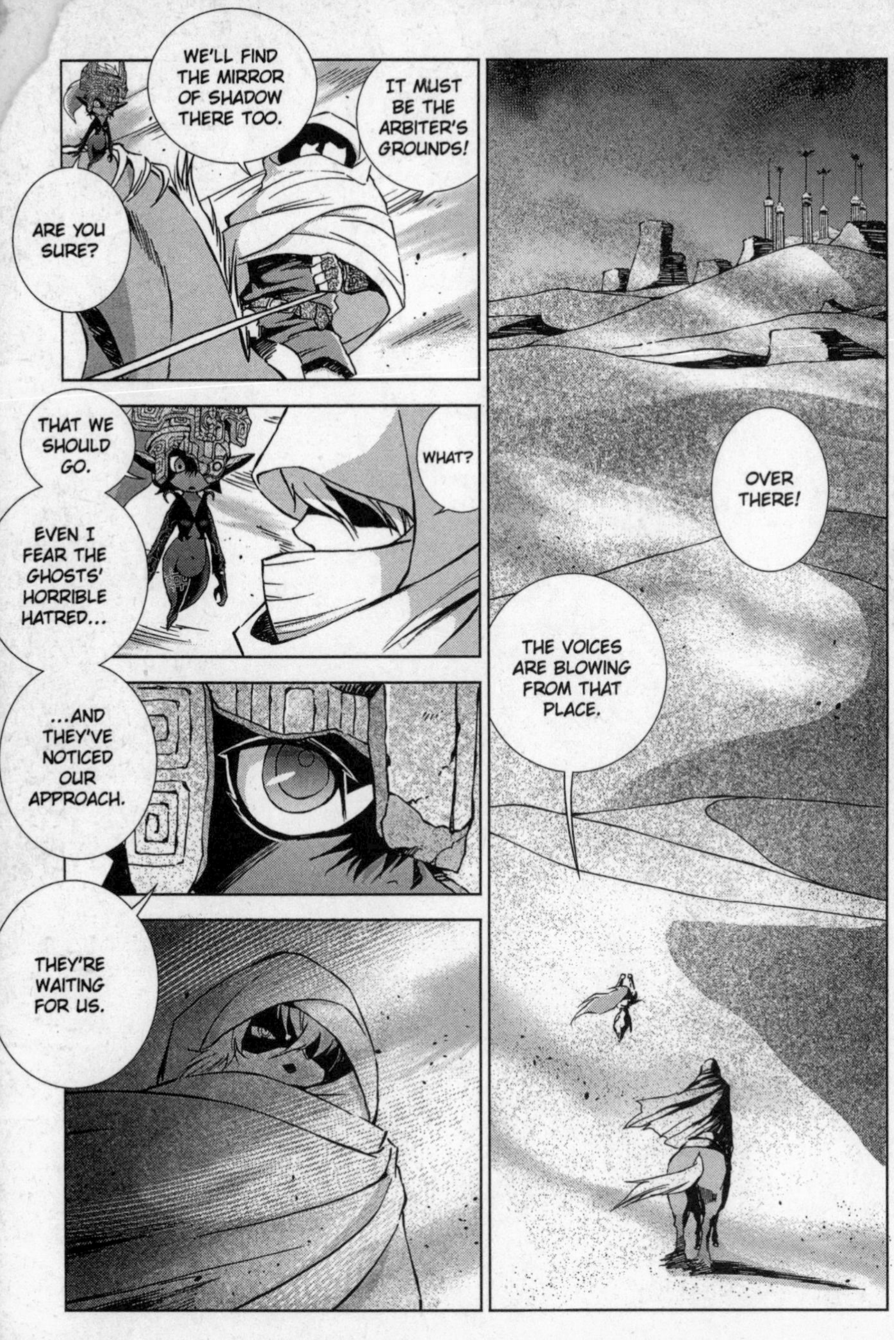
OVER THERE!
THE VOICES ARE BLOWING FROM THAT PLACE.
IT MUST BE THE ARBITER'S GROUNDS!
WE'LL FIND THE MIRROR OF SHADOW THERE TOO.
ARE YOU SURE?
WHAT?
THAT WE SHOULD GO.
EVEN I FEAR THE GHOSTS' HORRIBLE HATRED...
...AND THEY'VE NOTICED OUR APPROACH.
THEY'RE WAITING FOR US.

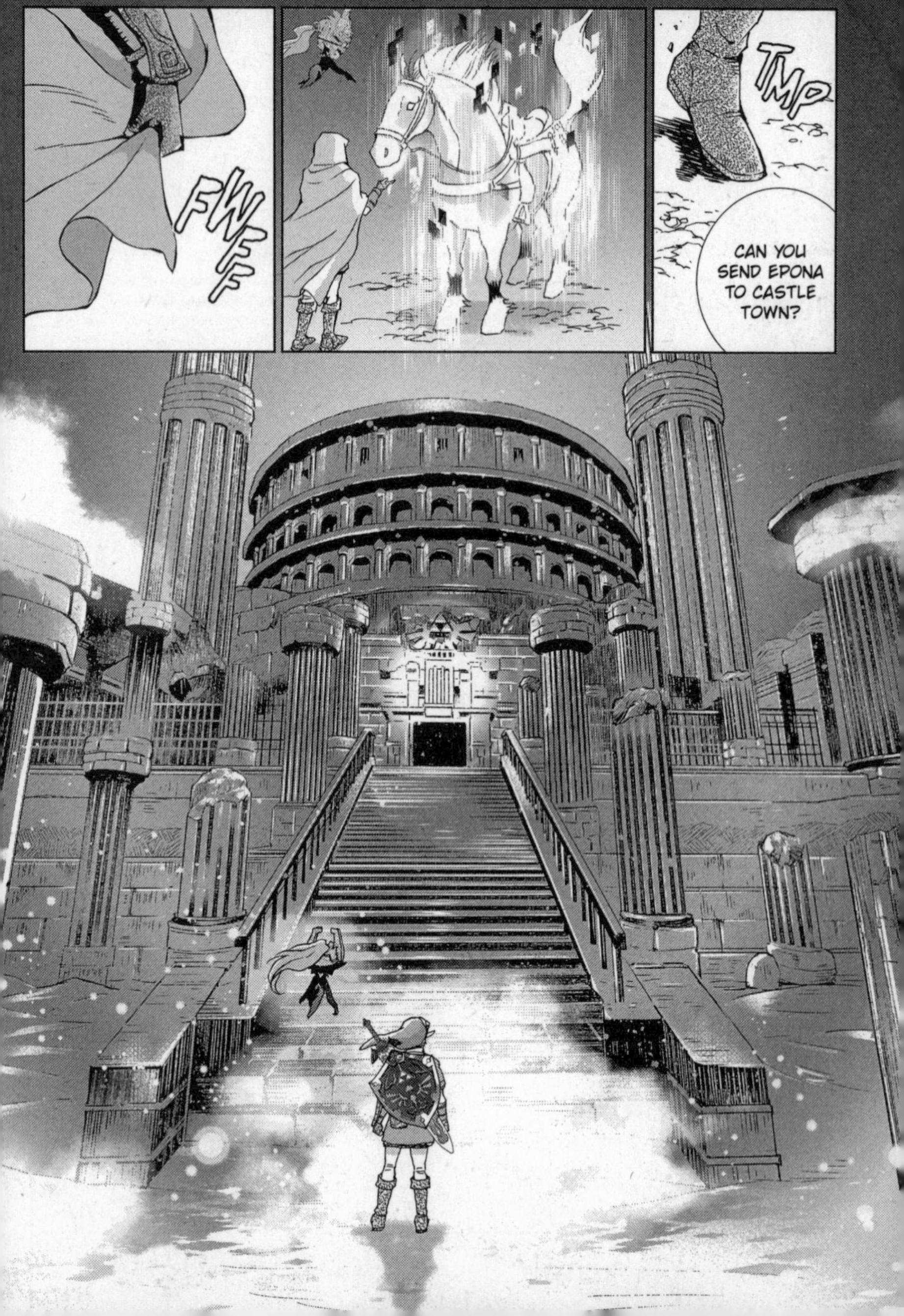
TMP
CAN YOU SEND EPONA TO CASTLE TOWN?
FWFF

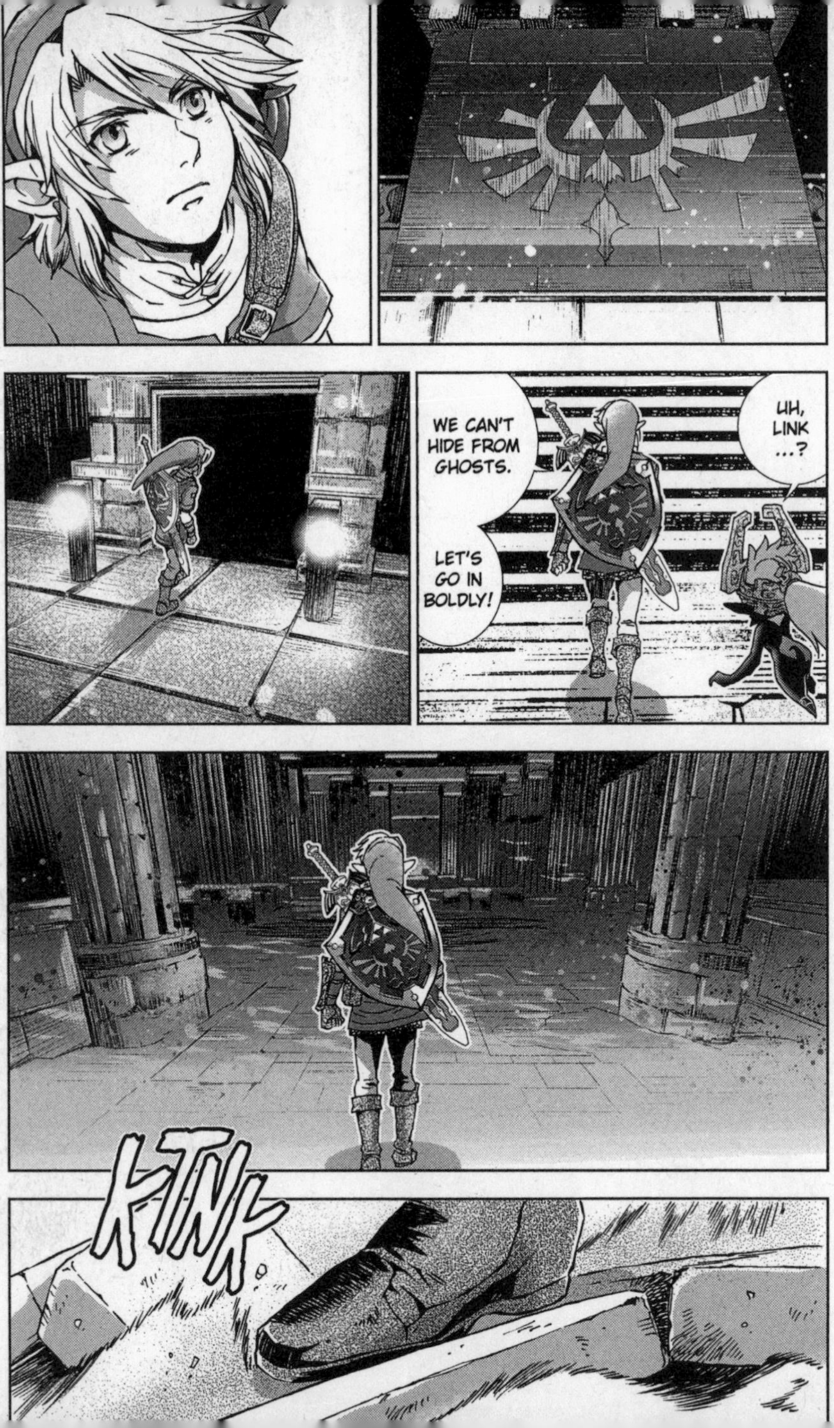
UH, LINK ...?
WE CAN'T HIDE FROM GHOSTS.
LET'S GO IN BOLDLY!
KTNK

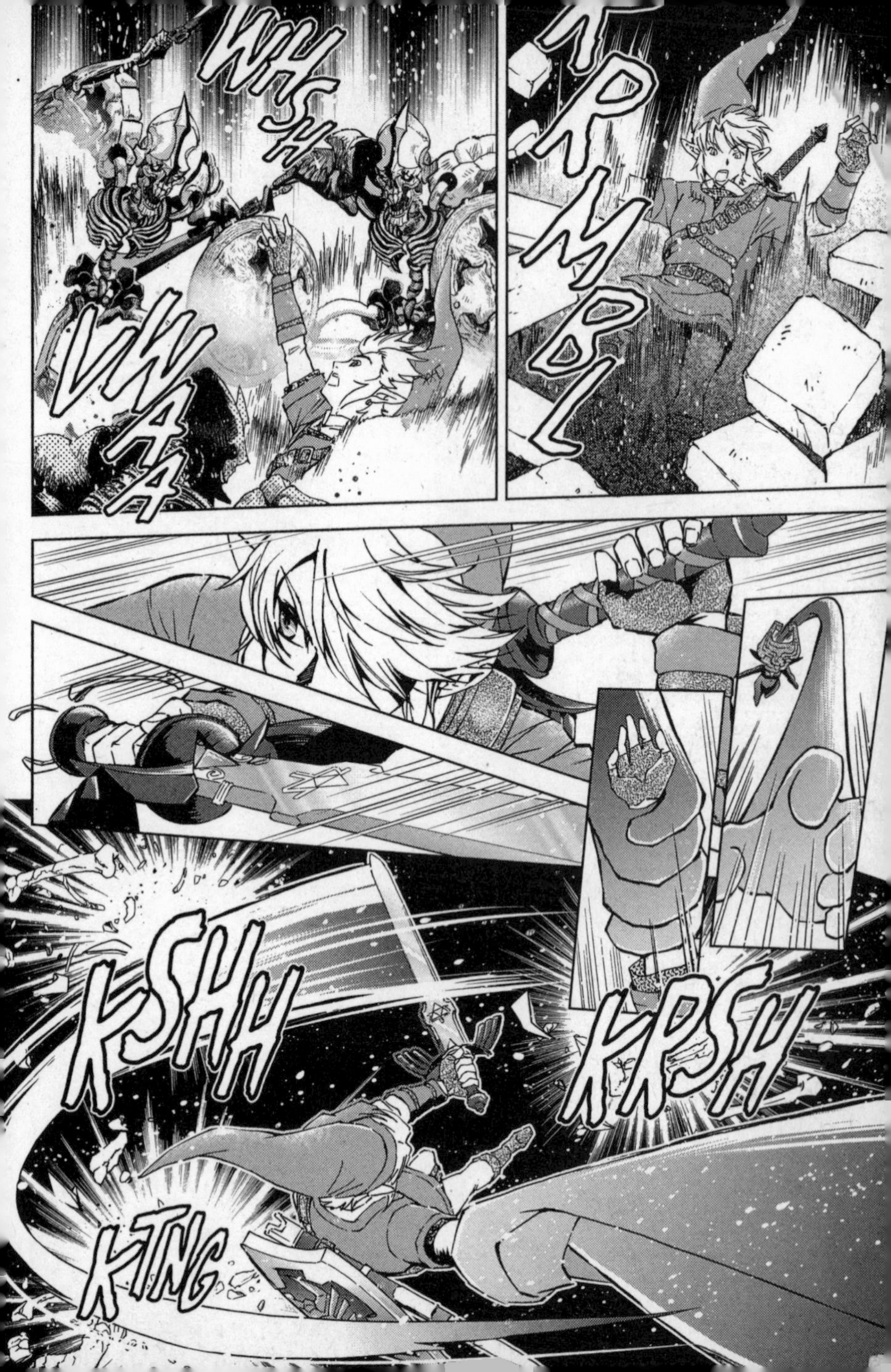
KRMBL
WHSH
VWAA
KRSH
KSHH
KTNG

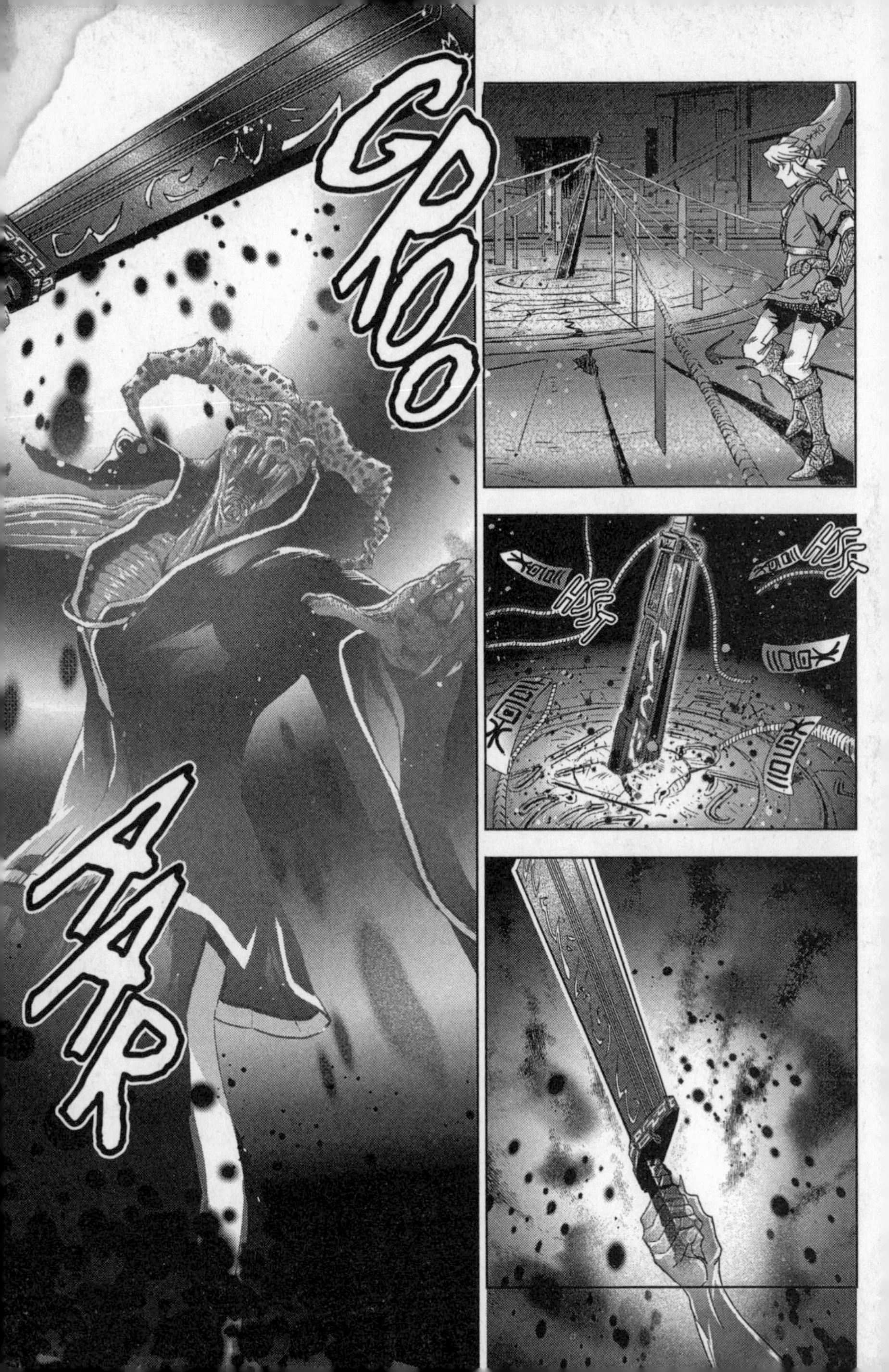
HSST
HSST
GROOO
AAAR

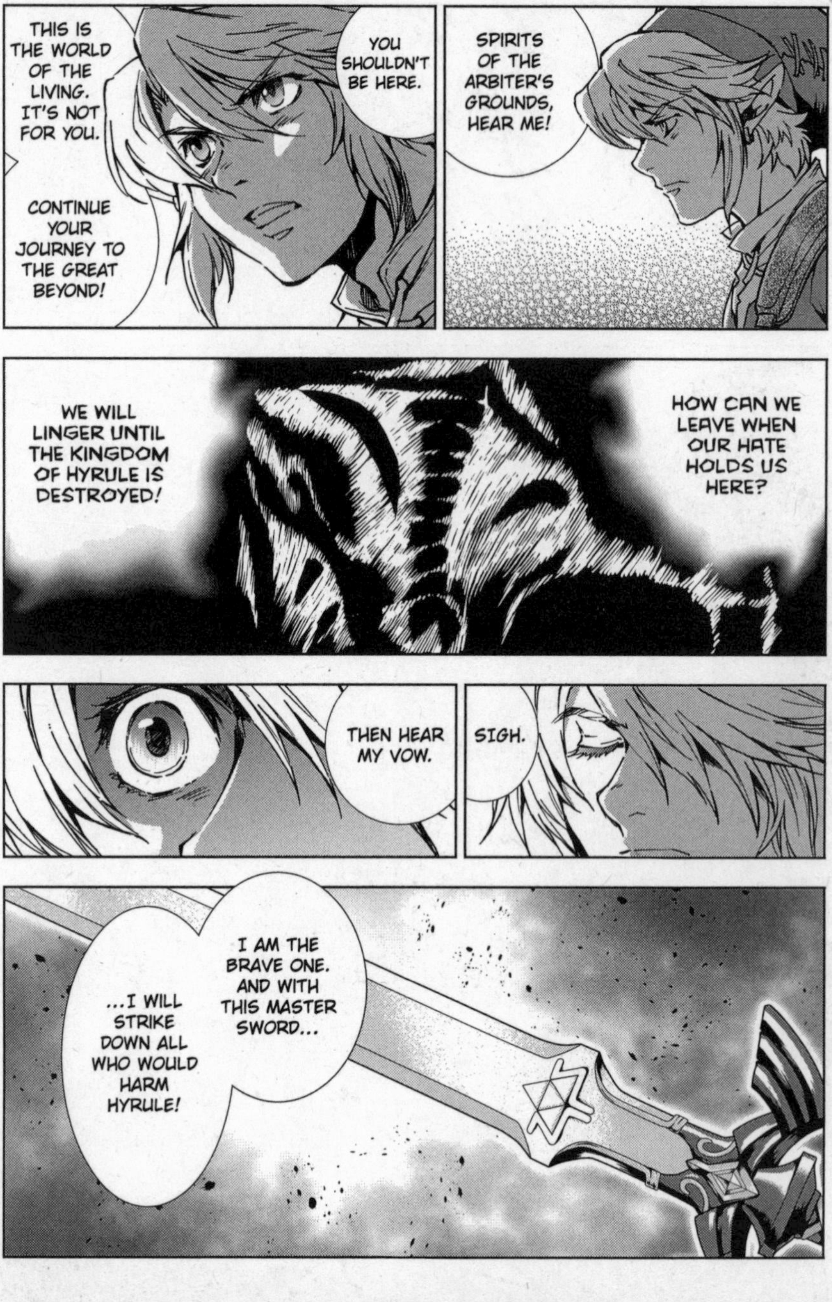
SPIRITS OF THE ARBITER'S GROUNDS, HEAR ME!
YOU SHOULDN'T BE HERE.
THIS IS THE WORLD OF THE LIVING. IT'S NOT FOR YOU.
CONTINUE YOUR JOURNEY TO THE GREAT BEYOND!
HOW CAN WE LEAVE WHEN OUR HATE HOLDS US HERE?
WE WILL LINGER UNTIL THE KINGDOM OF HYRULE IS DESTROYED!
SIGH.
THEN HEAR MY VOW.
I AM THE BRAVE ONE. AND WITH THIS MASTER SWORD...
...I WILL STRIKE DOWN ALL WHO WOULD HARM HYRULE!

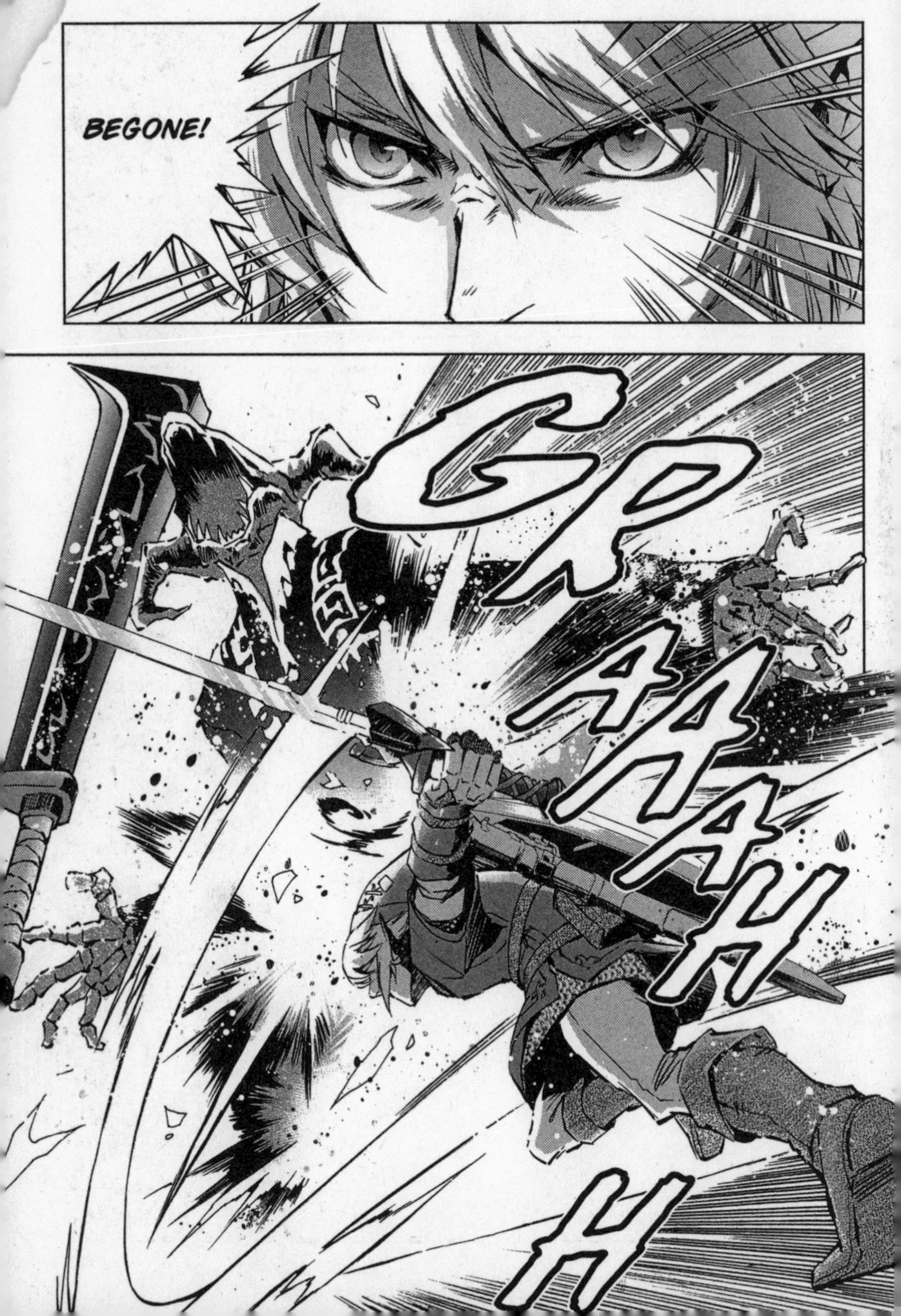
BEGONE!
GRAAAHH

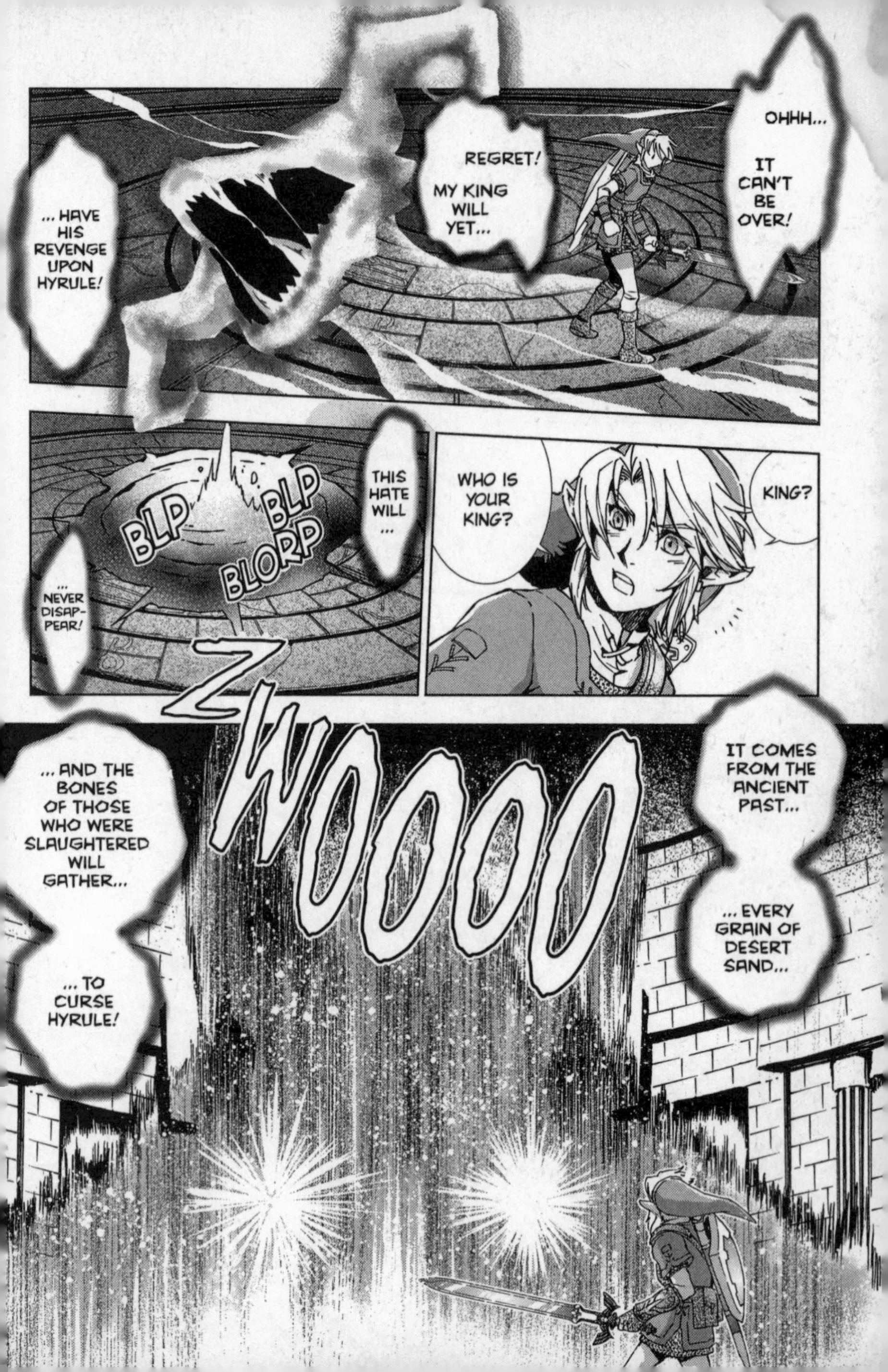
OHHH... IT CAN'T BE OVER!
REGRET! MY KING WILL YET...
... HAVE HIS REVENGE UPON HYRULE!
KING?
WHO IS YOUR KING?
THIS HATE WILL ...
BLP BLP BLORP
... NEVER DISAPPEAR!
ZWOOOO
IT COMES FROM THE ANCIENT PAST...
... EVERY GRAIN OF DESERT SAND...
... AND THE BONES OF THOSE WHO WERE SLAUGHTERED WILL GATHER...
... TO CURSE HYRULE!

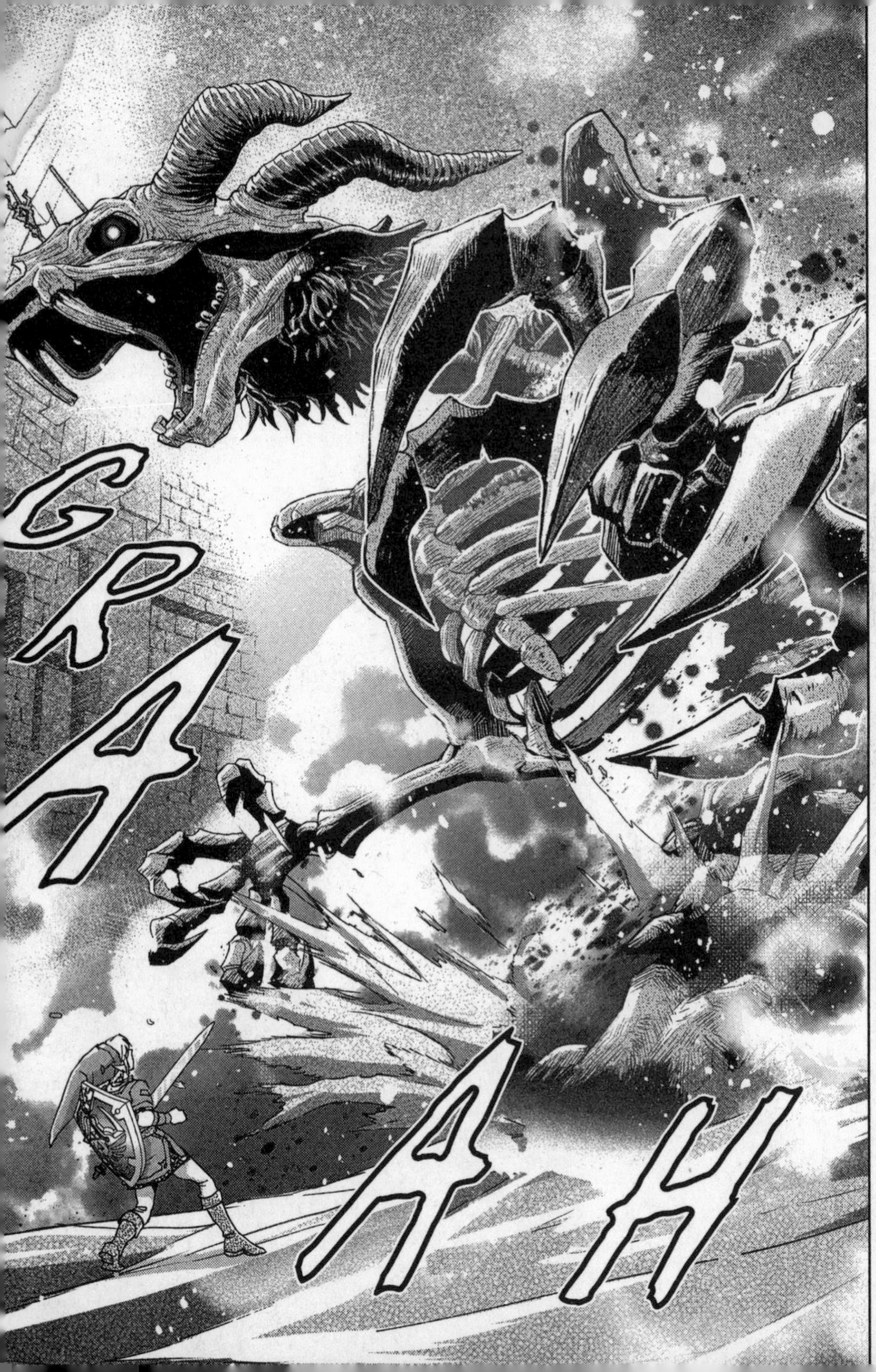
GRAAH

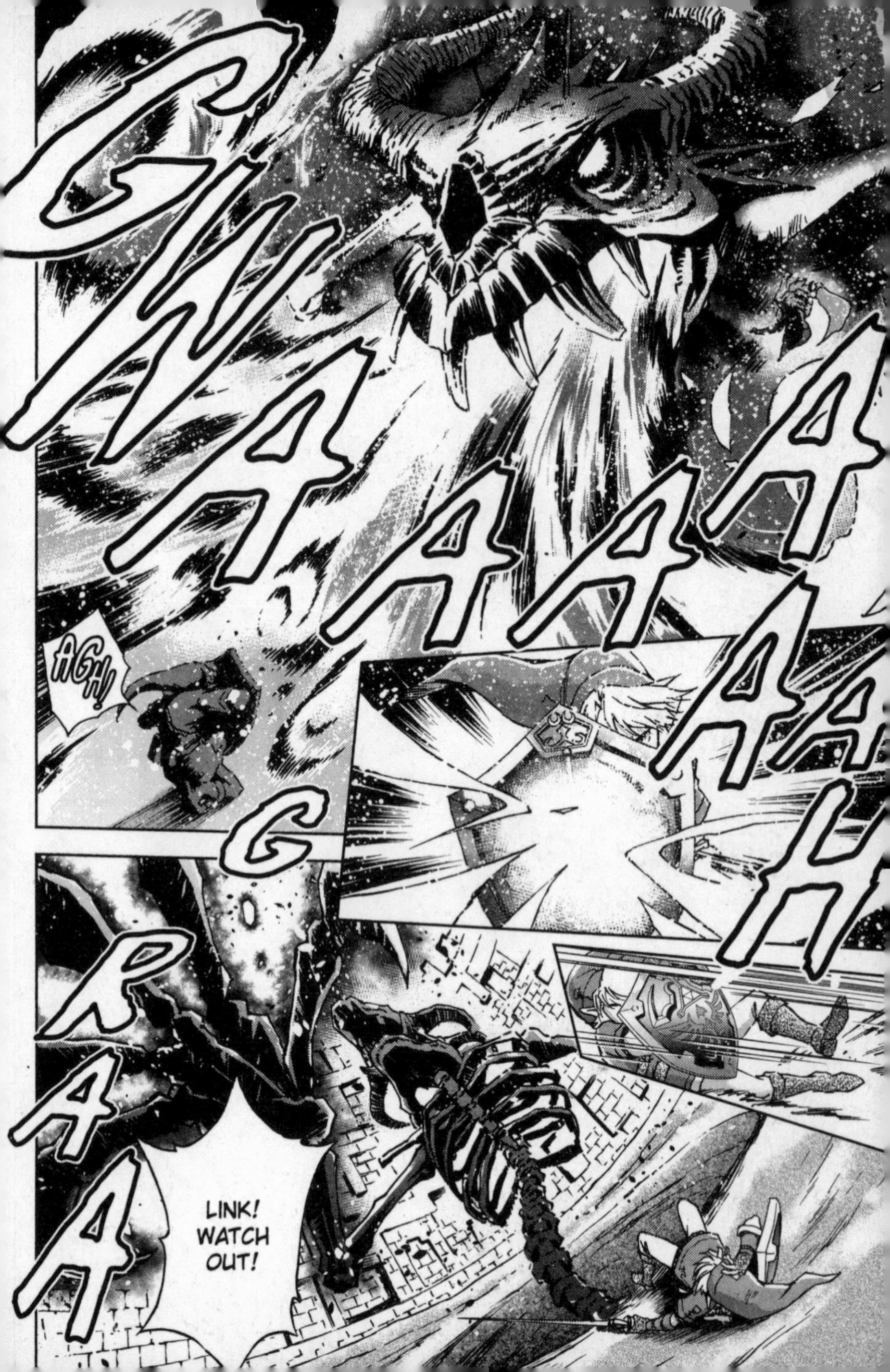
GWAAAAAAAAH
AGH!
GRAAA
LINK! WATCH OUT!

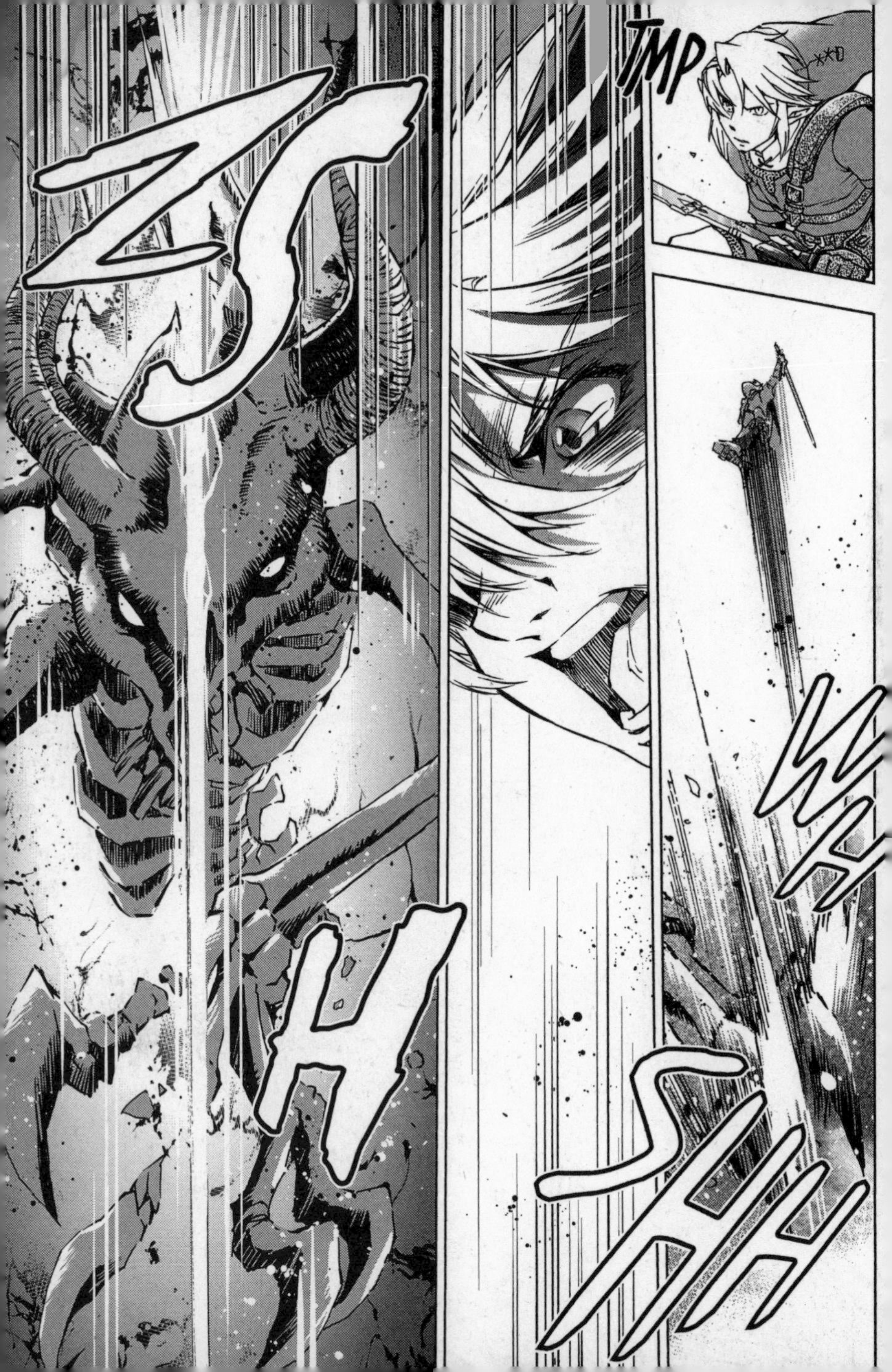
TMP
WHH
SHHH
ZSH

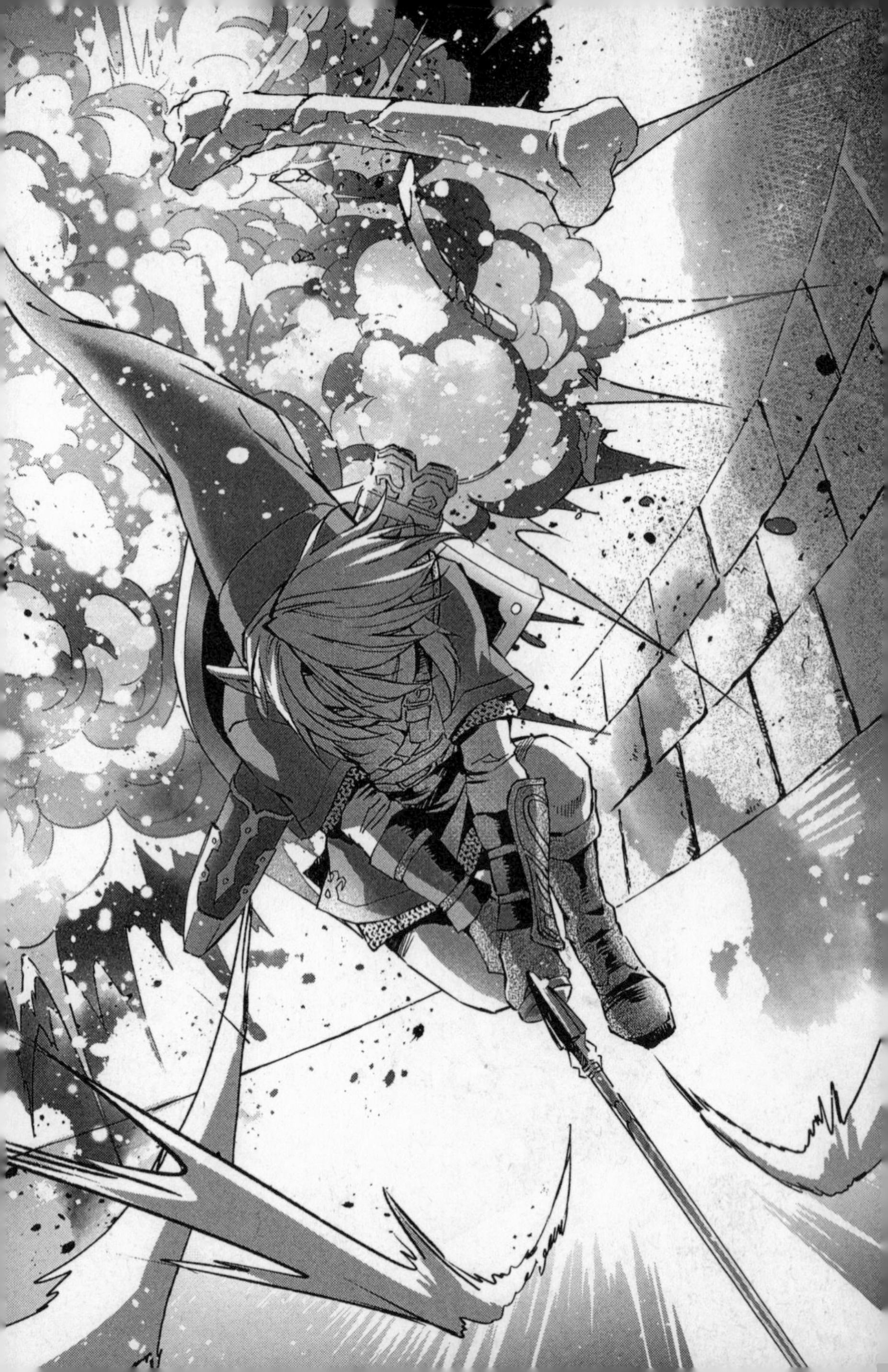

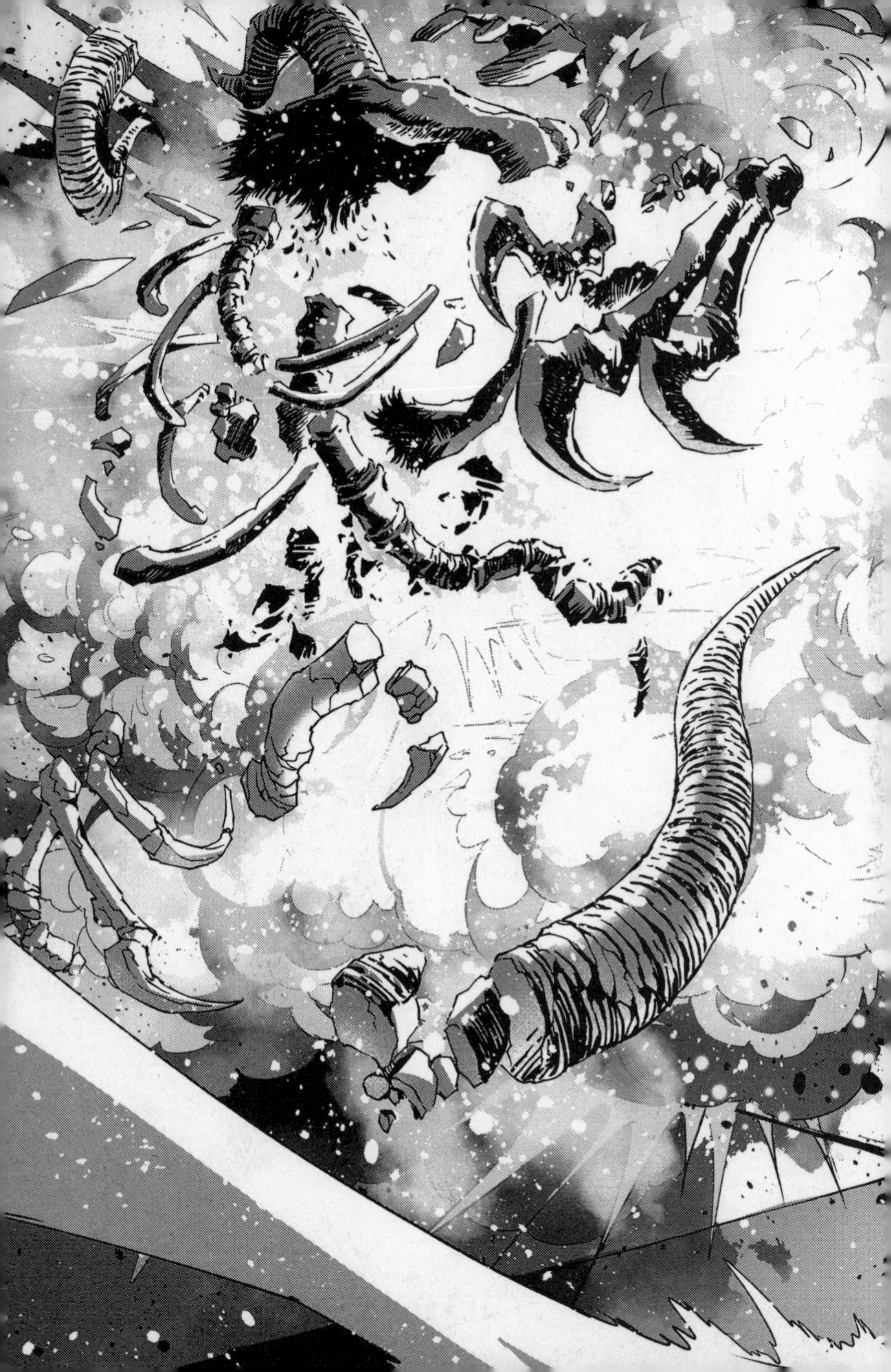

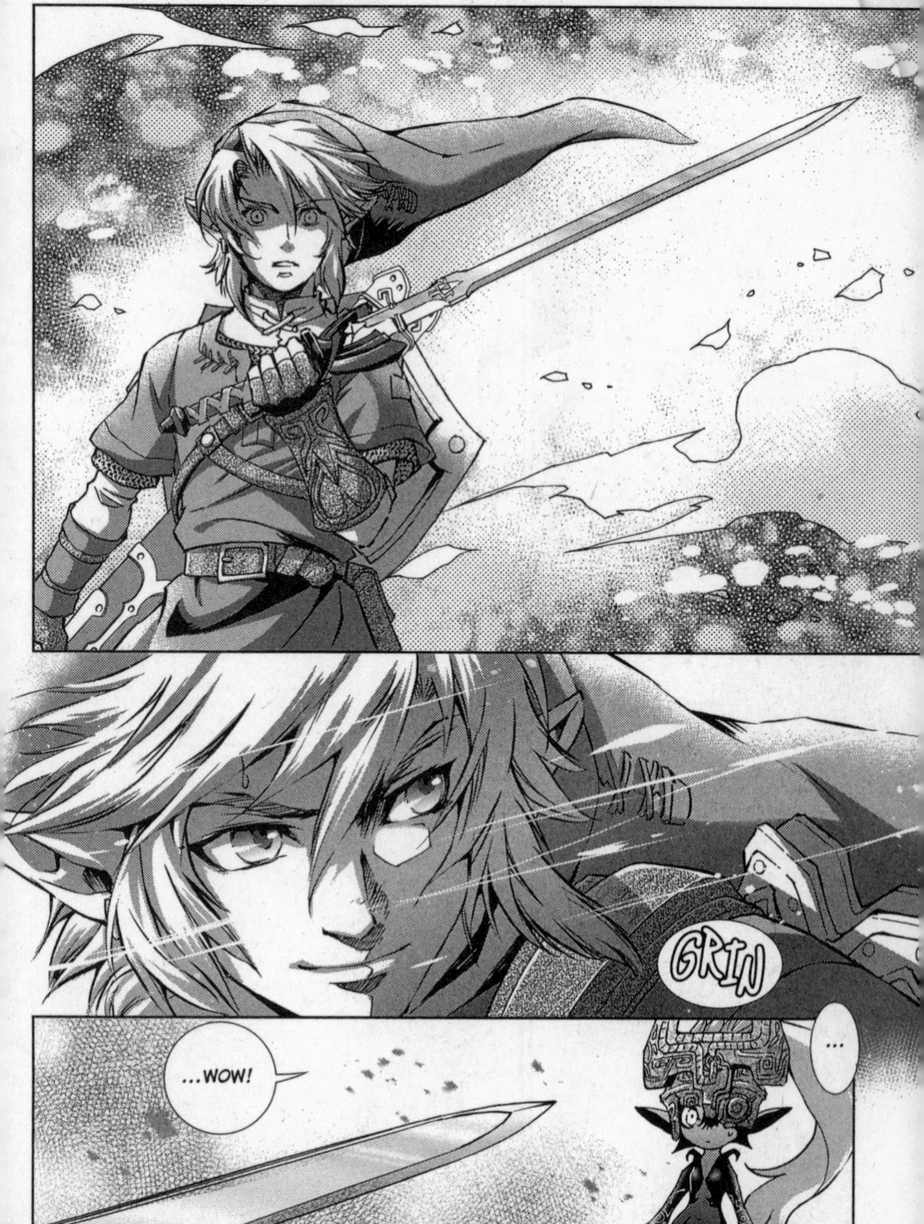
GRIN
...
...WOW!

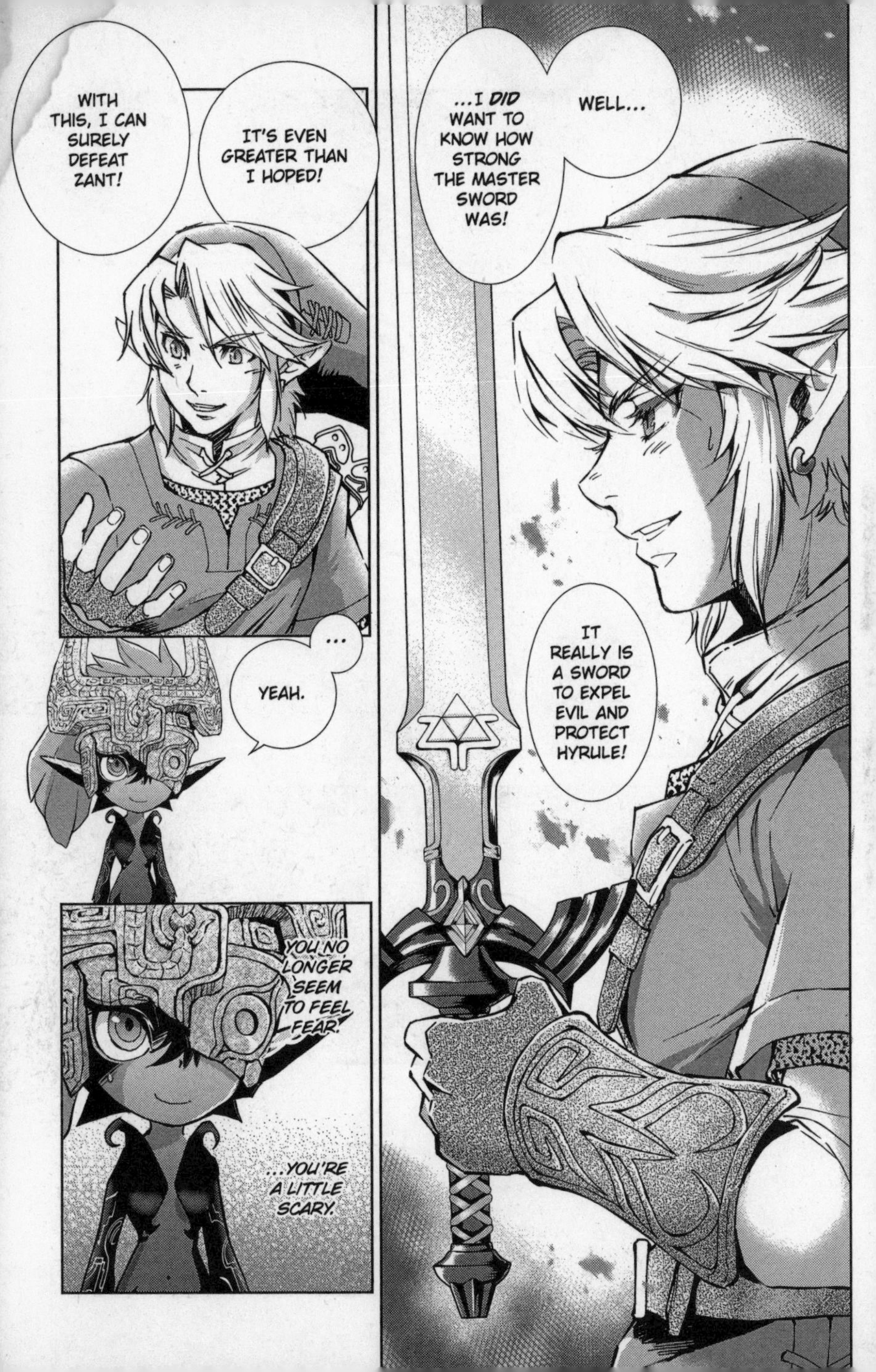
WELL...
...I DID WANT TO KNOW HOW STRONG THE MASTER SWORD WAS!
IT REALLY IS A SWORD TO EXPEL EVIL AND PROTECT HYRULE!
IT'S EVEN GREATER THAN I HOPED!
WITH THIS, I CAN SURELY DEFEAT ZANT!
...
YEAH.
YOU NO LONGER SEEM TO FEEL FEAR.
...YOU'RE A LITTLE SCARY.

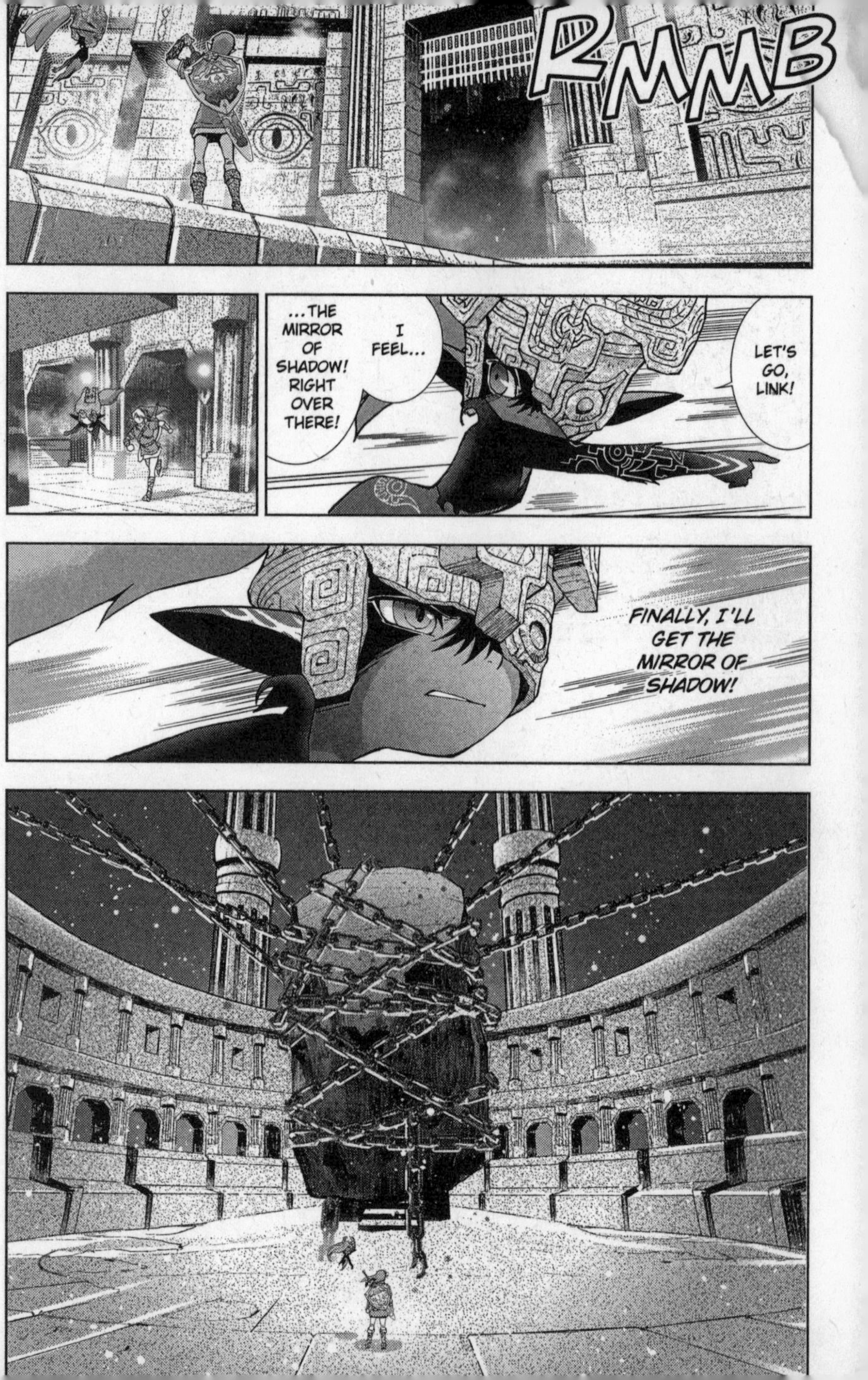
RMMB
LET'S GO, LINK!
I FEEL...
...THE MIRROR OF SHADOW! RIGHT OVER THERE!
FINALLY, I'LL GET THE MIRROR OF SHADOW!

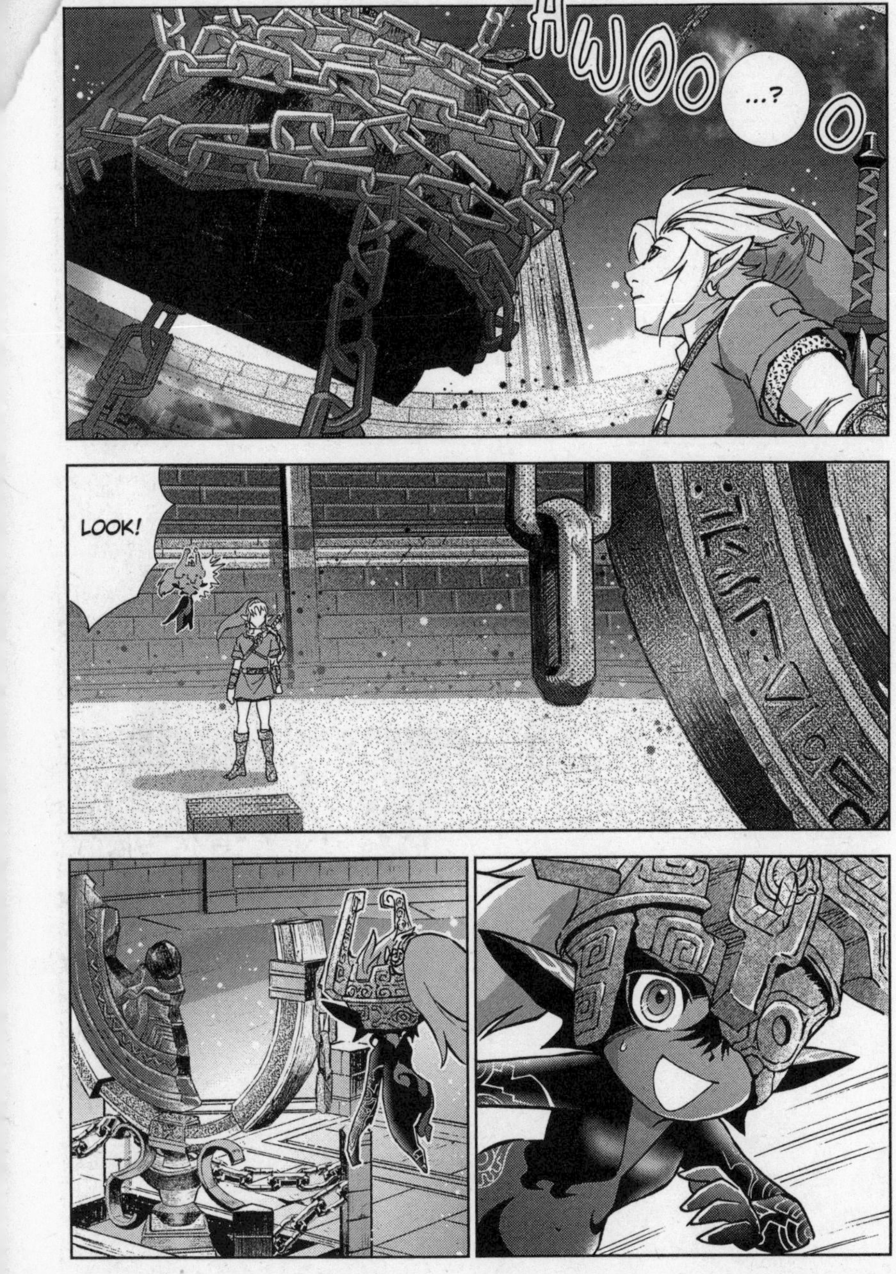
HWOOOOO
...?
LOOK!

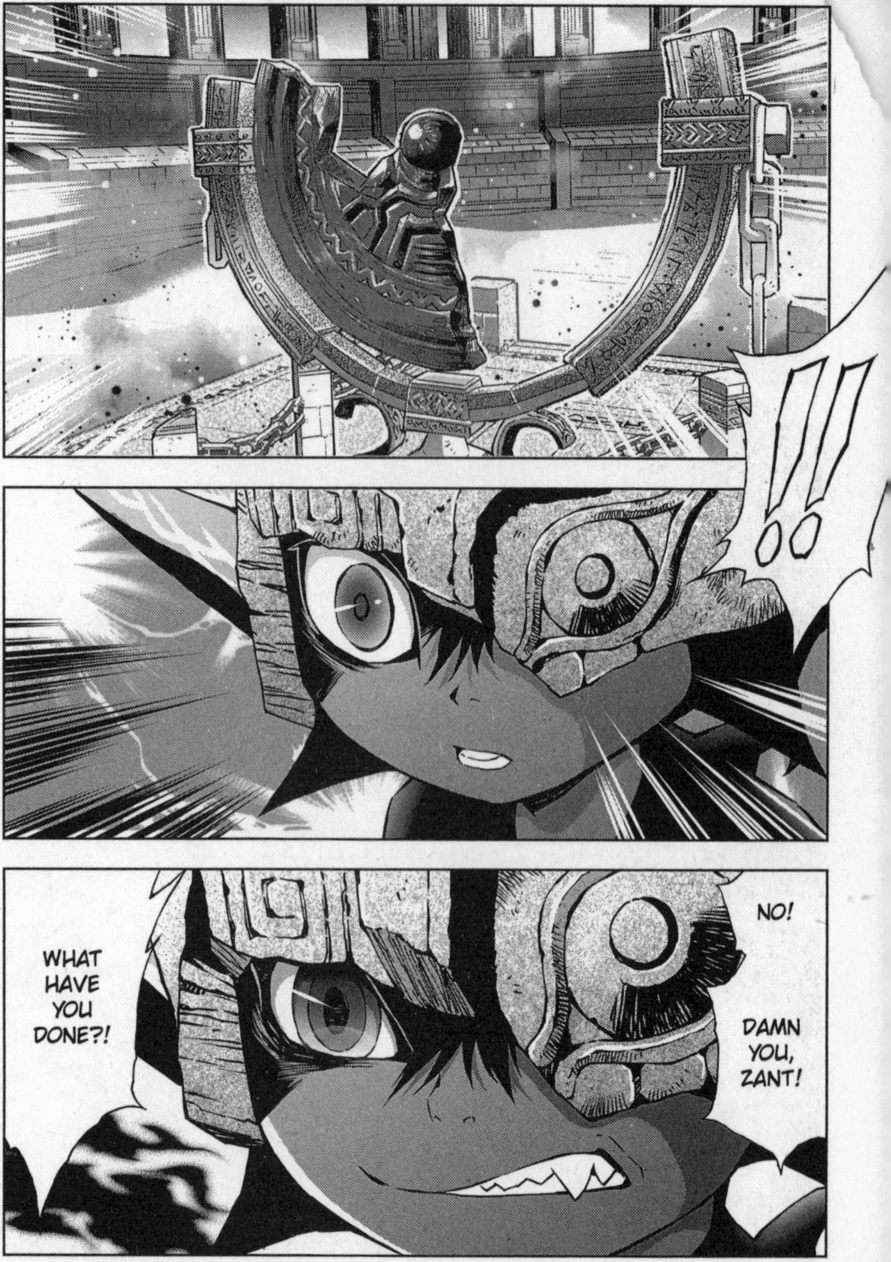
!!
NO!
DAMN YOU, ZANT!
WHAT HAVE YOU DONE?!

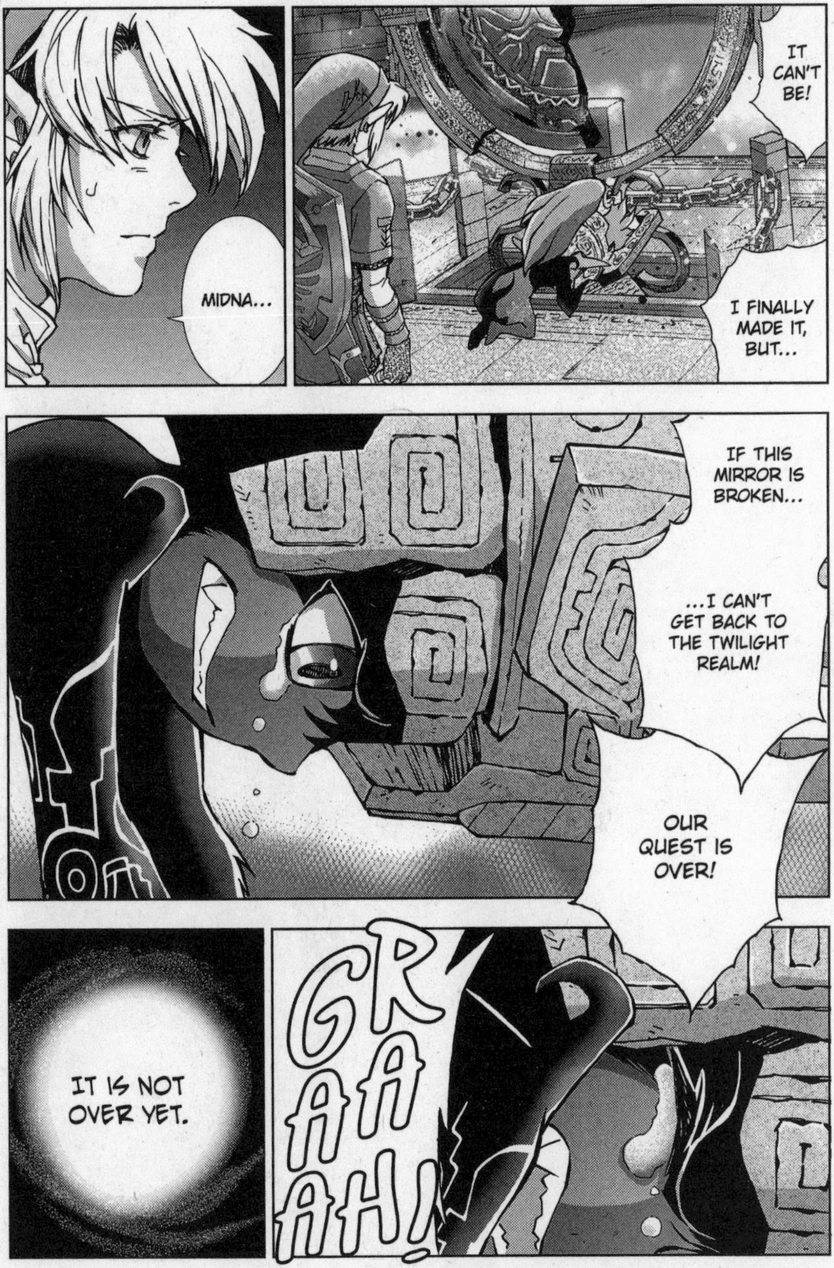
IT CAN'T BE!
I FINALLY MADE IT, BUT...
MIDNA...
IF THIS MIRROR IS BROKEN...
...I CAN'T GET BACK TO THE TWILIGHT REALM!
OUR QUEST IS OVER!
GRAAAH!
IT IS NOT OVER YET.

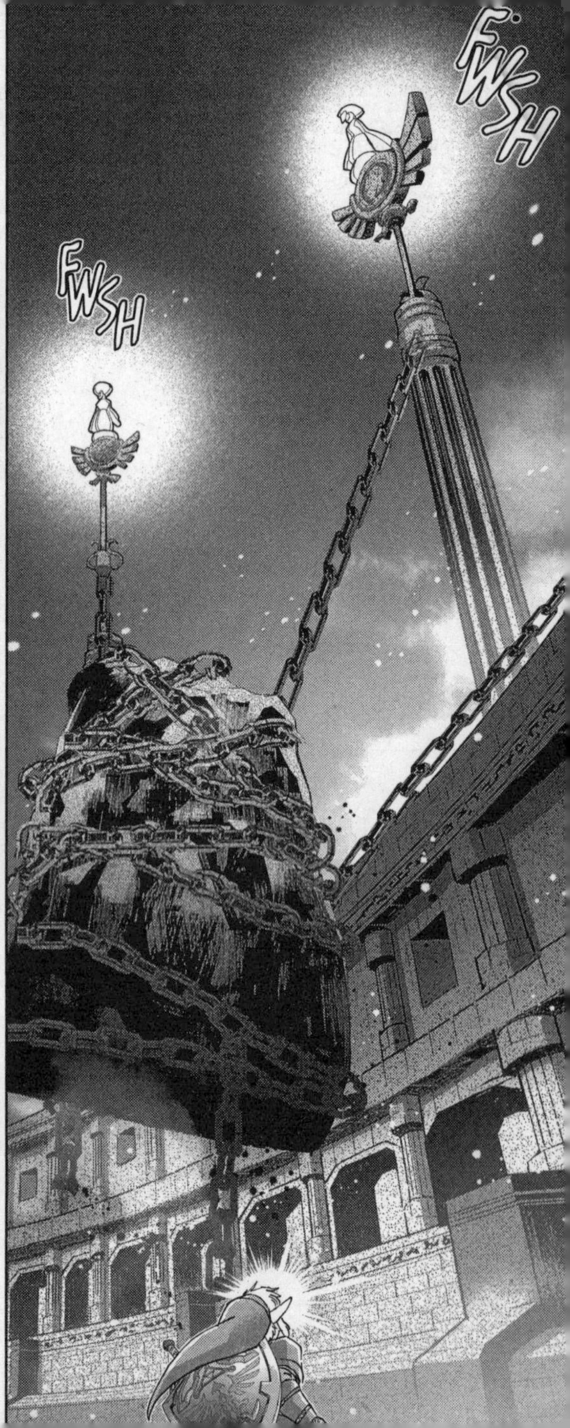
FWSH
FWSH

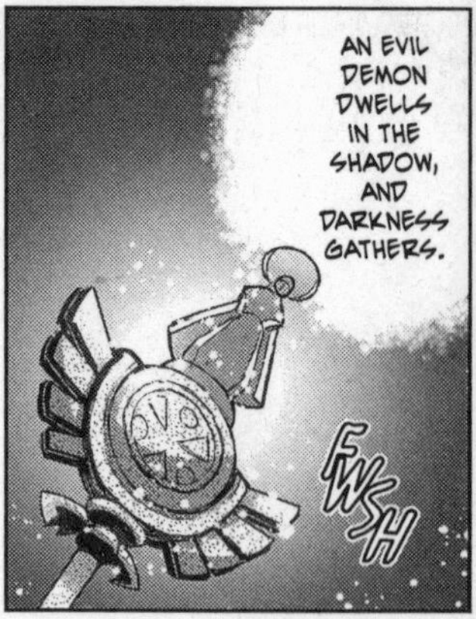
AN EVIL DEMON DWELLS IN THE SHADOW, AND DARKNESS GATHERS.
FWSH

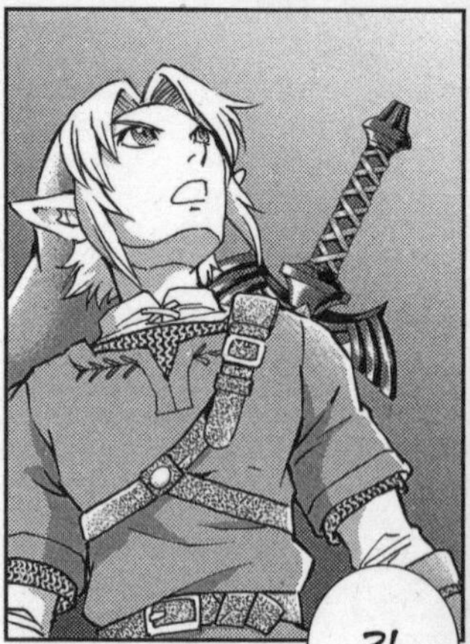
?!

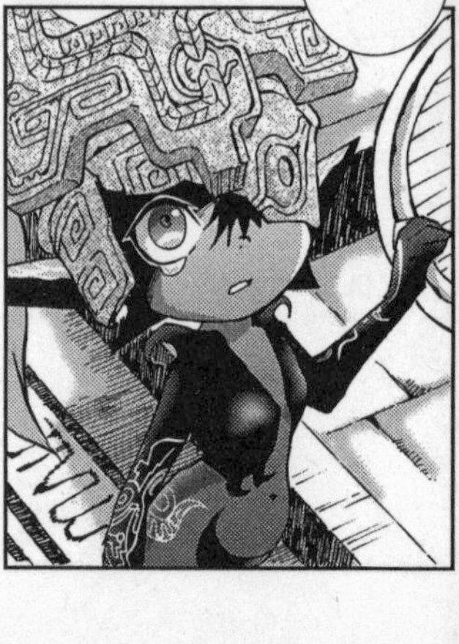

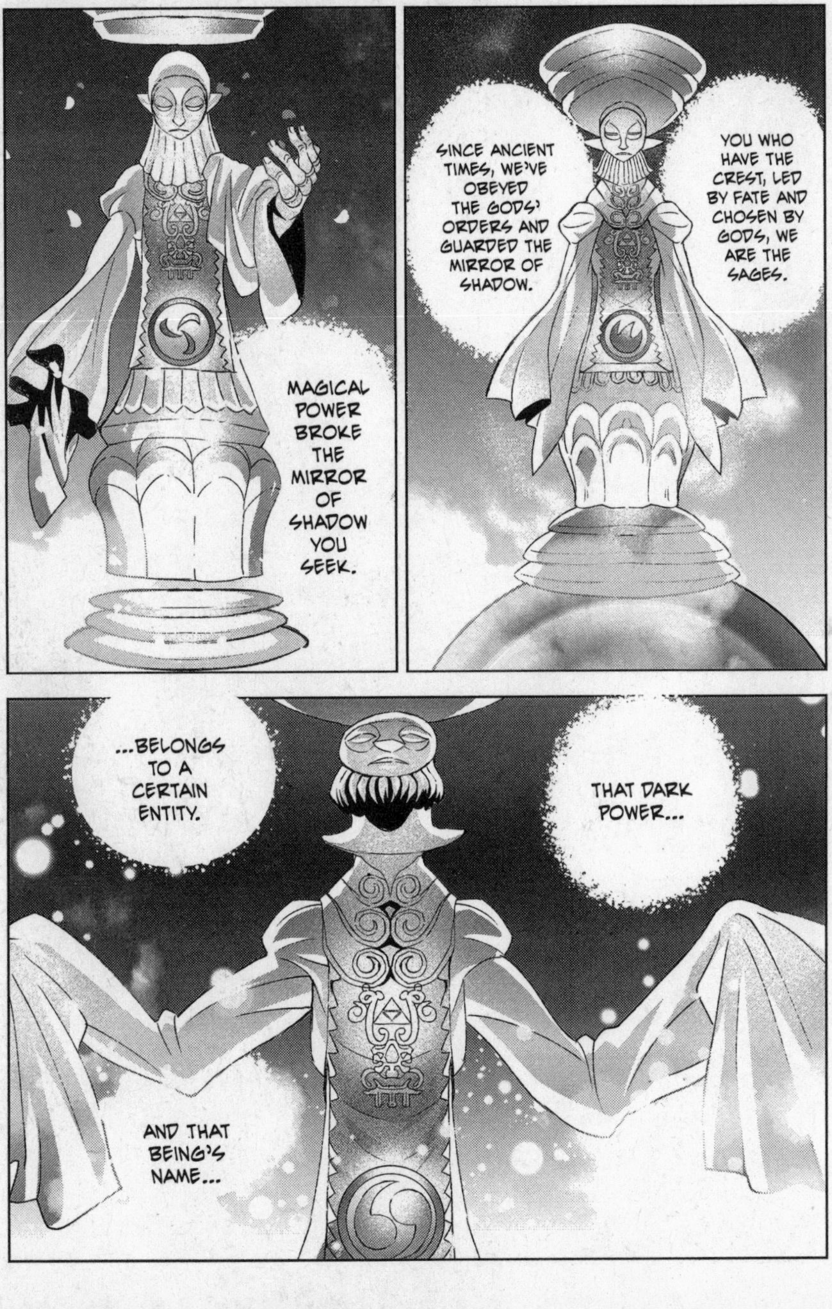
YOU WHO HAVE THE CREST, LED BY FATE AND CHOSEN BY GODS, WE ARE THE SAGES.
SINCE ANCIENT TIMES, WE'VE OBEYED THE GODS' ORDERS AND GUARDED THE MIRROR OF SHADOW.
MAGICAL POWER BROKE THE MIRROR OF SHADOW YOU SEEK.
THAT DARK POWER...
...BELONGS TO A CERTAIN ENTITY.
AND THAT BEING'S NAME...

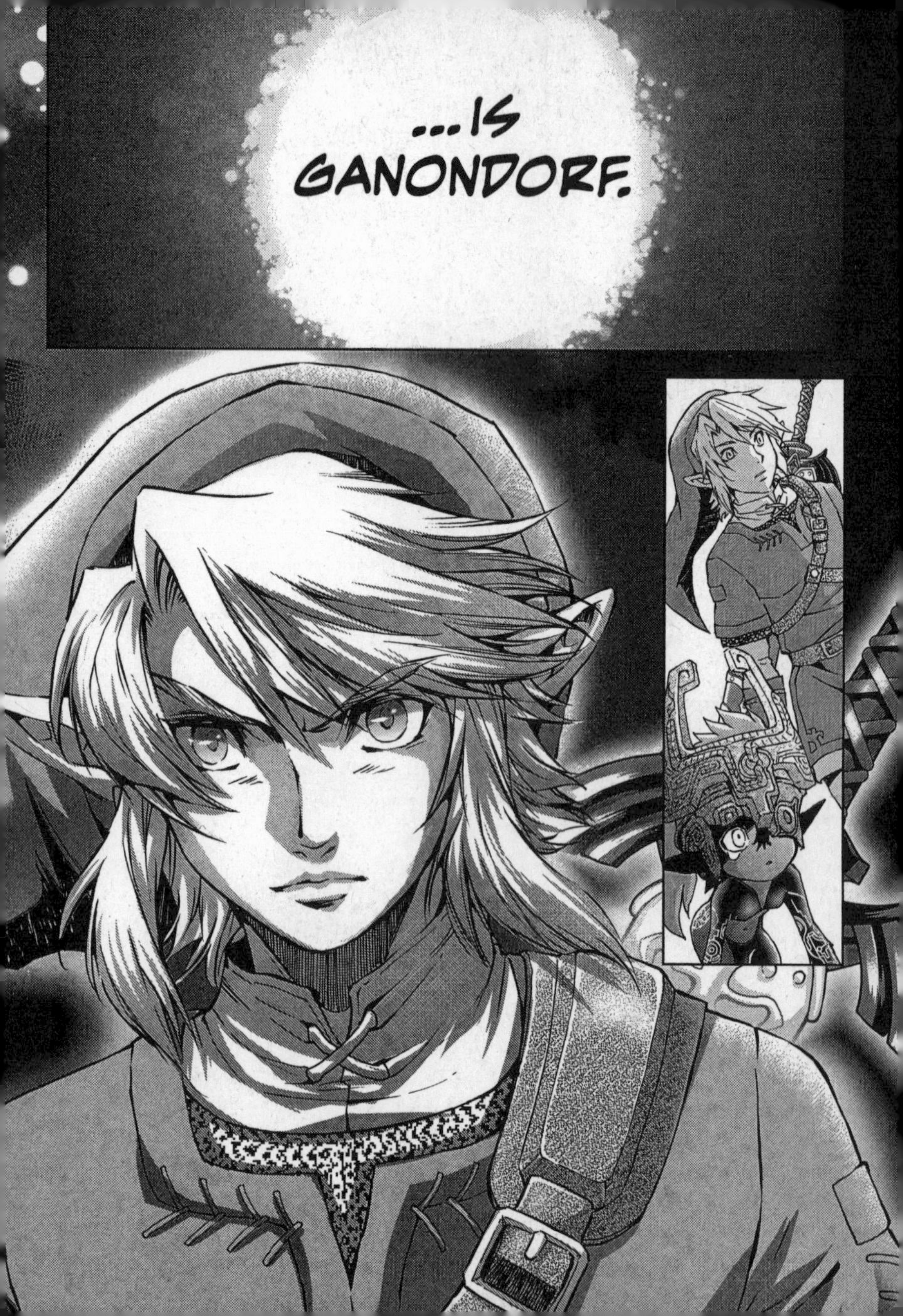
...IS GANONDORF.

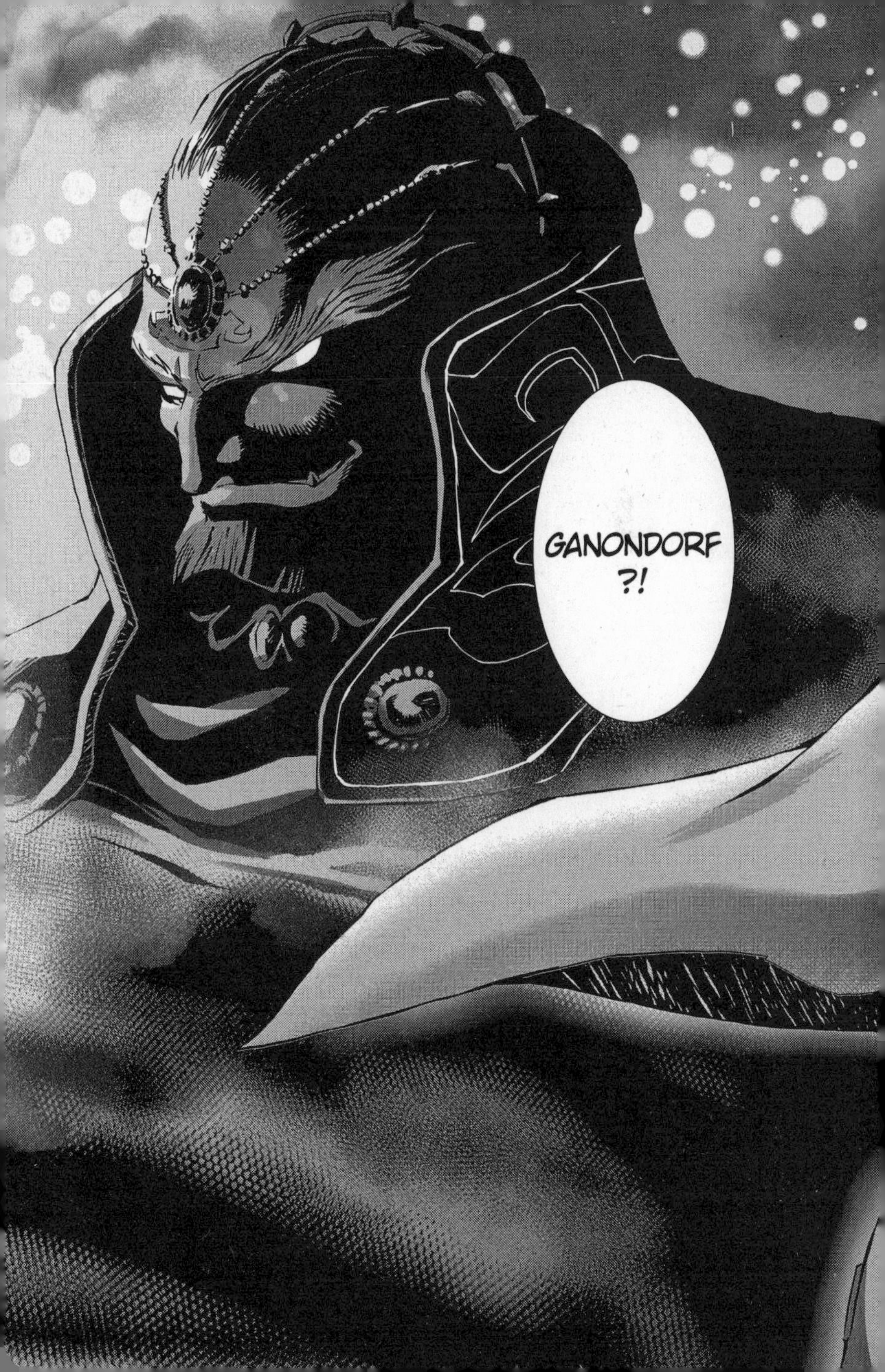
GANONDORF ?!

AUTHOR'S NOTE

Link has finally drawn the Master Sword.
It's a scene appropriate for the climax of
the middle stage of the story, so we've given
it all our strength. Link has had a hard
time, but it's also been a very long journey
to this point for those of us creating it. The
battles between Light and Shadow will
finally reach a turning point. Please join us
for the second half of the adventure!

Akira Himekawa is the collaboration of two
women, A. Honda and S. Nagano. Together they
have created ten manga adventures featuring Link
and the popular video game world of *The Legend
of Zelda*™. Their most recent work, *The Legend of
Zelda*™: *Twilight Princess*, is serialized digitally
on Shogakukan's MangaONE app in Japan.